BURNING LAKE

Maurice F Simpson

Burning Lake

This is a work of fiction. Names and characters are products of the author's imagination while places and incidents have been used fictitiously. Any resemblances to actual persons living or dead, locales, events or establishments are entirely coincidental.

Acknowledgements

I was inspired to write this, my first work of fiction, by my good friend and colleague Dr. Surendar Kilam who challenged me to tap into my experience as a family physician with a special interest in emergency medicine and my life long residency in Alberta, Canada, home of the famous oil sands resources and vibrant First Nations communities. Throughout the process I was fortunate to have friends and family to read and reread bits and pieces and praise, scoff or actually advise me on all manners of literary effort.

My son Kevin, a teacher of English specializing in English as a Second Language (esl) not only provided timely grammatical advice but also took the photographic art from Dr. Kilam and turned it into the cover art.

My daughter Shannon Watts not only unknowingly provided her name to the arch villain but willingly reviewed much of the legal stuff that snuck into the manuscript from time to time.

I am greatly indebted to Kathy Lee, my friend and mentor in editing, word processing and formatting. Without her contribution I could not have completed this work.

Finally, the grunt work of editing every word, sentence and punctuation mark fell to my wife Marlene who continues to astound me with her eagle eye. While no manuscript survives without the occasional miscue, my family and friends took my rough and imperfect fantasy, reduced almost all of those miscues, and presented the final product to the world on my behalf. Any remaining miscues are entirely on me.

About the Author

Maurice Simpson was born and grew up in the small city of Lethbridge, Alberta, population 15,000. Southern Alberta was the heart of the irrigation farming industry and Lethbridge was within an hour's drive of two of the largest aboriginal communities in Canada.

He graduated from the University of Alberta in 1960 with a Bachelor of Science in Pharmacy and in 1967 with an MD. By that time, Lethbridge had more than doubled in size to 37,000. In comparison, Fort McMurray had a population of 3,387. The story takes place in a mythical setting about 90 minutes southeast of Fort McMurray, circa 2015, by now a resource city of 125,032 including the immediate surrounding area.

Beginning a Family Practice in 1968 in Lethbridge, Maurice became involved almost immediately in emergency medicine and EMS activities and in the mid-eighties became the first Medical Director of EMS for the integrated Lethbridge Fire and EMS Service. With the coming of the regionalization of the Provincial Health Service, he found himself involved in the organization and direction of Continuing Care and was fortunate enough to be consulted by a Dene First Nations community where he saw first hand the incredible potential for community development in both public health and social development.

Now retired, he has dabbled in authorship, first with the publishing of a self-help book entitled "Being Your Own Best Doctor" and now, on a dare, a fictional account of the trials of a rural community struggling with multiple challenges including health, corruption, crime, a touch of romance and ethnic conflicts. Dr. Simpson and his wife Marlene enjoy a blended family of six children and ten grandchildren.

Part I

1

Things were going much too smoothly and I should have known it couldn't last. I had just finished checking a cute little 6 year old girl who had complained all night of a pain in her ear. Her mother was a technician in our medical records department and had some knowledge of medical jargon and in a couple of minutes, between the two of us we had the tearful little girl smiling and looking around while I filled her mother in on the latest wisdom on treating earaches.

Midweek, evening shift and a hot summer day…they are usually hot summer days…and I was humming along from one minor crisis to the next. I love this work…usually. Tonight put an end to usually.

Amirah, our team leader and general jewel of the house, took me aside with a worried look and I started to suspect that the fan was filling with that smelly stuff. Amirah is a joyful soul who guides the unit with smarts and inspiration. The daughter of a professor of surgery, she learned her nursing at Jeddah where she was enrolled in the BSN program and was one of the first women to graduate. Not satisfied with her progress she accepted a scholarship to the master's program at Canada's Queen's university.

Amirah has a nose for trouble long before it surfaces and I found myself downshifting rapidly from my coasting cloud to all alerts on red. In muted but urgent tones she relayed a message from my boss, Doctor Faraj Haik. I'm not sure he fully trusts me so he rarely calls me for sensitive stuff like "The Prince is coming in" or "the Minister of Transport was concerned by your comments that neighborhood roads disguised as donkey paths were contributing to trauma from too many crashes". He usually goes through Amirah for this stuff.

"What's up with Faraj? Are they cutting the budget again or just his salary?"

Amirah rolled her eyes like she usually does when I fail to show respect to my masters and whispered,

"There is a high level politician from Washington coming in with a hangover and a rash someplace that he doesn't want to talk about. He doesn't want to see a local about it." I guess he hadn't been briefed about my authority dysfunction. She said, "You must be discrete and not make waves on this one. This guy is with the State Department in Washington and I think he is pretty powerful".

Though power doesn't heal a headache or the clap I had been in this country long enough to know when to dive for cover. She led me to a private room where I encountered a sullen and evasive man who waited until Amirah left then said,

"Doc, this goes no further than this room."

I said, "I hope it doesn't. I hate when we get shut down because of epidemics of clap."

I guess that was the wrong thing to say because he started to stutter and stammer and didn't seem to quite understand my humor. People often don't.

He began a tale that started with an invite from an aide to my buddy at the transport ministry to attend a little party about three weeks ago after an evening of meetings. It ended with a blackout sometime through the night following too much of the forbidden fruit both animal and vegetable. Since then he has had a succession of headaches but the rash just appeared last night. The headaches were easy to explain. I always wonder how these visiting dignitaries get access to booze on a nightly basis when I have to limit my taste for single malt to infrequent visits to a buddy in a foreign compound. I suspect he had a ready supply of home brew, a source of fusel oil or amyl alcohol often found in screech and since he had no neurologic signs, no prior history of headache and was still moderately pissed, his headaches probably came from that stuff. Just to be sure I ordered a CT and we moved on to the rash.

Syphilis is not often encountered in an emergency ward in a Saudi hospital. While it is present it is more often encountered in expats from Africa than local Saudi females. So I was intrigued by the plight of my patient and after confirming the diagnosis and prescribing the requisite antibiotics I gently nudged him about his contact and contact reporting.

"None of your f#@n business Doc. Just get rid of this shit so I can get on with my business".

I tried to convince him that a good citizen would have some concern for the citizens of his host country but he clammed up and that was that.

Contact identification in a strict Muslim country where adultery is rewarded with whipping and other unpleasant indignities is difficult at the best of times. Add into the mix a party with booze and sex sponsored by a high level ministerial aid and you get my dilemma. No way was this guy going to fill in a contact form. Confidentiality and morality police are probably mutually exclusive.

I went on with the rest of the evening and put the incident out of my mind. A few days later I was summoned to Faraj's office, a rare occurrence. We get along pretty well but in matters political he is wary of my loose cannon tendencies.

"I have a problem." he began. "That Washington guy with the STD you saw a few nights ago complained to his host, the Minister of Transportation, about your attitude and professionalism. He has asked me to make enquires."

The culture of the Middle East particularly Saudi Arabia is a contrast of wealth and misery firmly entrenched in the society and difficult for a westerner like me to comprehend. I am constantly confronted with taboos in language, women's issues, investigative technique and even staff interaction. However, this was dangerously close to the last straw. My contract was coming up for renewal in six weeks and I still had four weeks of holidays. After going back and forth with Faraj about the ethics and propriety involving this issue I finally told him to stick his contract where it belonged and further informed him that I was gone as soon as I could legally leave.

Though the last three years have been financially rewarding and the people are warm and hospitable, I still struggled with the culture shock I continued to experience as I daily came face to face with some of the profound differences between Middle East cultures and my slightly red neck development in western Canada. Political correctness is not one of my virtues…or is it a vice? As a matter of fact, for the last while I had been thinking that it was about time that I chased a pot of gold at the end of some other rainbow. This little encounter with an abusive political hack just stiffened my resolve to move on so I made the big decision and I guess the next two weeks will be a flurry of packing and occasional tearful goodbyes.

I don't have much of a family left in Canada; just my parents who spend the spring, summer and fall in Alberta and winter some place in the southern USA. We seem to have gone our separate ways over the past few years.

I have, however, kept up a sporadic long distance communication with an attractive brunette with high ambition and a low sultry voice. I had met Carol a couple of years ago in a bar during a ski trip to Vale and we seemed to hit it off pretty good. She was heading back to some high level executive position in the health industry in Calgary and I was booked out the next day to return to my job in the desert. We traded email addresses and phone numbers and drifted off to our different hotels that night but in the next few months found ourselves in a long distance relationship that didn't seem to be going anywhere. Calgary was starting to look like a reasonable next step in my life. Time to move on.

2

Two weeks later I finished my last shift, gave all my friends a hug and a cuddle where it was safe and headed for my apartment to finish my packing. It had been a good three years with lots of excitement and like I said, good financial reward, but I had trouble staying committed to this place. My temperament just didn't fit the challenge and I felt if I stayed longer I would overstay my welcome or worse. I had managed to get rid of most of my stuff and shipped a few of my more valuable souvenirs home so all I had left I could carry in a backpack. I waved goodbye to my neighbours, grabbed a cab and headed for the mountains half way around the world for some skiing, hot tubbing and anything else that came up.

Riyadh to Calgary is about a full day and a half with a couple of stopovers and because my contract allowed me business class I settled in, in comfort. As I enjoyed the first sips of a surprisingly good scotch I recalled, with a little excitement, my long distance conversation with Carol a few days before.

"Hey...it's Paul. Wadda you mean Paul who?" I wasn't sure if she was playing it cool or teasing me or if she had moved on to a new chapter in her life and was now out of my league.

However, after some getting to know each other again we arranged to meet in Calgary and head to Lake Louise for a ski and soak. Little did I realize that I was leaving a culture where women were subservient and heading back to a culture where women were mom, boss, social manager, fashion hitler and even sometimes just plain fun.

She met me at the airport and we headed for Lake Louise and the hills. Now I'm in as good a shape as most macho dudes but jet lag and a well-stocked bar on the plane put me into never never land for a couple of days and we were kind of slow getting going. The rest of the time was somewhere between ok and OK and we headed back to Calgary; she to her senior bureaucrat job and me to the search for a new career and a new purpose in life.

Finding a new job back in my old world was not a problem. I was well trained, had lots of experienced and hadn't burned my bridges in spite of my tendency to piss off colleagues and administrators with my often annoying leaps to judgement.

I landed an ER job at the new hospital in Calgary (the one that replaced the old one that the government blew up for fun or money, I'm not sure which. It was a time of turmoil in the

world of health). My new job was an appointment to the staff of
the emergency department of the new hospital. This gig came
with all the full waiting rooms commonly encountered in the
urban ER departments and I was soon into the to and fro of
politics, making money, buying toys and hanging with my
fellow buds. Carol called three or four times and I called back a
couple of times. Both of us seemed to have our own ideas about
life liberty and the pursuit of a good life so nothing really
developed between us for the first half dozen months. However
fast forward two years and it seems she chased me 'till I caught
her or was it the other way around? We eventually found
ourselves in the middle of a destination wedding; you know,
one of those gigs where those who can't afford it meet you in
Mexico for the nuptials and the party. Life was good and work
was busy and busy and busy. Carol has this thing about running
things. If it's worth doing it's worth doing for money and
career.

Our lives continued to careen along more separately than
together; me on my treadmill and Carol on her ladder. I think I
had enough medical smarts to know it couldn't last and she had
enough ego to believe she could make it last forever if only I
was more ambitious. On top of that her father was a big shot
politician with lots of bucks, well connected and in control. I
think he lined me up with three jobs that paid twice what I was
making and all I had to do was sell my soul and serve his
daughter. Ah for the quiet and peace of the Saudi countryside!

One day I was sitting alone on a break in the docs' lounge nursing a coffee when one of my former Profs came in. I hadn't seen him in three or four years and we immediately started to get caught up. I guess I was feeling pretty blue and in no time he had me pouring out my soul and tasting all the bile of my despair. He hadn't changed a bit.

"What the hell is wrong with you Cross? I thought I taught you better than that. Medicine isn't what you do between paydays and trophy wives. It's a calling and you were damn well called. The sooner you realize that the sooner you can start to act like the pro I thought you were."

He got up and left and I was alone and feeling like I was stomped on in a corral by a pissed off steer.

Carol and I continued to drift along for a while, me with my doubts and Carol with her career and her visions for me and mine. Both of us seemed too caught up in a sea of apathy and neither of us found either the time or commitment to make any changes. Finally, after a particularly nasty fight about nothing we decided to indulge in some obligatory counseling. The thing about counseling is, as George Carlin used to say, "You gotta wanna!"

Neither of us seemed to "wanna".

* * *

I remember the night as clear as yesterday. I was wading through a waiting room full of misery both real and believed when the EMS guys rushed in with a sixteen year old kid with multiple stab wounds. We worked half the night keeping him alive but in the end his injuries were too severe. He died in the midst of his grieving family.

Halim was a second generation Lebanese kid whose mother worked at the hospital for the housekeeping contractor. I used to see him from time to time when he dropped by to visit his mother and probably to con her out of a few bucks. He was a quiet kid, a good student and often bugged me with questions about becoming a doctor and working in the third world. The night he was brought in he had stood up against some throwbacks to the caveman days who were bullying a girl waiting for the C train. They carved him up pretty good. I was desolate. All I could think of was the stench of evil invading the city and the seeming indifference of the Gen-Xers and untamed millennials who occupied it. I finished my shift, headed home to an empty house and a couple of single malts and sat out on the deck looking at the stars and wondered what the hell I was doing with my life.

Something kept nagging me about the last few years and my place in the world. As I looked ahead, all I could see was more of the same. Was this the beginning of the "burnout" that is so often described and predicted in our professional journals? I don't know if it was the scotch that was burning a hole in my gut or my despair that I was becoming that self-indulged useless piece of shit that I despised in a few of my more aggressive colleagues. At any rate, I didn't like the feeling and I felt that I was nearing a landmark tipping point.

About that time Carol breezed in from some meeting and chatted on about her latest triumph in her jungle. I countered or at least tried to counter with my experience and half way through my account she butted in and told me that we were going to a party the following night at some socialite's home and I needed to get some new clothes and don't be late. She hadn't listened to a word I said. Damn. Did I say I love women who wield control like a god given right?

The next day I called Doc Gilbert and told him I was ready to start practicing my profession. We met for lunch and after a long discussion he offered to put me in touch with some folks at Burning Lake. I later discovered that it's a small community on a lake near the Athabasca River in northern Alberta just south of the famed or infamous oil sands. During lunch I finally decided that Carol was history and within a short time the separation began. It was cool but civilized though she didn't really believe it would last. I didn't know what to believe.

Part II

3

Burning Lake is a small community a few klicks south east of Fort McMurray and near a First Nations reserve mostly populated by Dene. It is located on a secondary road in reasonable repair and the center of the oil sands is only about 90 minutes away on a good day. The community primary care clinic consists of a small medical office housing a clinical practice nurse with midwife training and a public health nurse. Recently they came up with funds to attract a physician to service the surrounding communities and reserves. So far no one has bit at their modest offer. Doc Gilbert was politically connected to the folks pushing for expansion and through him I was reeled in to jump off into the unknown. Remind me to put a lump of coal in his stocking this Christmas.

I pulled in to the village, such as it was, about an hour ago and I'm wondering how far it is to the nearest shrink. At least

Riyadh had people and places and doc stuff. But not to complain. Attached to the village grocery store is a lean-to with a smattering of spirits, the kind you drink. It wouldn't surprise me if there were some of the other kinds of spirits as well.

The offer came with a small cabin on the edge of town that used to be occupied by a Metis trapper who left to work for one of the big pipeline companies. The place was in reasonable shape and with a little TLC it looked like it could be made livable, warm and maybe even cozy. It hadn't been hard to locate and now, here I was, ready to start yet another chapter in my wanderings through life.

I unpacked my stuff and stowed it in the bedroom, looked over the four poster bed that had been left behind and imagined it with a bright duvet and a couple of pillows. By the south wall there was a new modern desk and file cabinet. The electrical outlets looked new and the place had even been hardwired for a phone. Out in the kitchen a relatively new fridge and stove with signs of modest use stood by a pantry with empty shelves and a couple of un-baited mouse traps. Looks like I will have a few companions over the next few months. The closet was cool and looked like it had been added uninsulated to the cabin as an afterthought but it made a great cold room for my groceries. Although there was a bar in this hamlet and also in the one down the road, it didn't seem like any other eating places could be found for a few miles. I guess I'll have to dust off my cookbook and put it to use.

The living room had a reasonable couch and chair with a couple of lamps and end tables and there was a stone fireplace on the east wall. Hanging on the wall was a *Calle* print *"In Search of Beaver"*. I shook my head and hoped it wasn't an omen. The trapper appeared to have been a man of taste and my spirits lifted a little. Someone had swept out the hearth and piled a few logs in the basket. Now I was ready to settle in. Mobile service was surprisingly good so my phone worked and I had internet service. All I need now is a wide screen TV with a decent sound system and I can start receiving visitors.

Shopping for groceries should be no challenge so the first thing on my list is stocking the cold room. Heading out the door I stopped at the sight of an old beat up dirty van that predated the modern SUV's by a few years pulling up in front of the cabin belching blue and sounding like the remnants of a demolition derby. A short pudgy woman somewhere between twenty and fifty years old climbed out, looked around through coke bottle lenses, spied me and said,

"You the doc?"

"Yep. What can I do for you?" She looked me up and down lit up her face with a broad and warm smile and said "Hi. I'm Louise. I look after the clinic, give the shots, pass out the pills and run the phone and radio. I guess I'm your nurse".

This was not my Amirah. I guess help comes in all shapes and sizes. I'm not sure who would be helping whom. "Hi

Louise. Happy to know you. I just got here and I'm heading to get some groceries. What's up?"

She stared at me for a few too many seconds then said,

"They told me they were sending some old fart up here to run the clinic. You don't look much like an old fart. Where's your wife?"

It's not often you run into people in the medical field who ignore the usual pecking order and set up their own pecking order. Louise looked like the head pecker in the territory. Again the broad warm disarming smile. "Nothing urgent Doc. A couple of people wandered in and wondered when you'd be coming over. Willie Buckskin is a little more short of breath and has a little chest pain but I gave him a pink lady and he gave me a big smile so I guess he will live a little longer. Alma came by with her girl who is six months gone and wonders when you want to check her. I told her to come back tomorrow after I had a chance to meet and greet."

None of the scenarios I'd encountered in the past seemed to help me process this stuff so I just smiled, said thanks and said I would drop in after I bought my groceries.

"There's no one at the store" she said. "Old lady Giroux is at the clinic waiting for you to come over so she can get her headache pills. Her son is headed for the city and she needs a new prescription. After she sees you she'll go back and open the store."

I guess if I want to buy some beer I'll have to go to work and clear out the waiting room. Louise pointed to the van and grunted,

"Hop in and I'll run you over."

"Thanks anyhow. I'll need the jeep to bring back my grub."

She gave me that big smile again, struggled back into the van, coaxed it to life and chugged off more or less in the direction of town.

Someone once told me that in every medical office there are two practices, the nurse's and the doc's. The lucky patients are the ones on the nurse's list. I could see where this was heading so I grabbed my jacket and keys, climbed into my jeep and followed the blue cloud down the road to my new life.

Two hours later, after giving old lady Giroux her prescription and my grocery list, I cleared out the last of the worried well and sat down for a coffee and an orientation to health care in the boonies. My groceries stood in the corner where Junior Giroux dumped them when he came over to pick up the prescription and the list of supplies he was to pick up for Louise. Looks like I'll get supper after all.

The road that runs through the hamlet and past the Reserve is a pockmarked paved secondary highway well chewed up by the trucks hauling equipment and workers to and from the camps. It doesn't seem to matter whether it is day or night, every few minutes another truck pounds its way past the settlement giving the sense that somewhere, sometime, the hotshot train is on an urgent mission to the area. Money, oil and frenetic activity have made this area something other than what the Creator intended or that is what it seemed like. Not surprisingly, the sleepy facade of the hamlet is often disturbed by the arrival of a victim from a highway crash needing patching or transfer to a real doctor and hospital for more urgent or complex care.

It takes only a short time to get the EMS helicopter from the big city to here when someone is really injured and there is a volunteer fire/EMS service that is more or less able to scoop and run with the patients not needing urgent air evacuation. Advanced paramedic training is a luxury that the volunteer guys usually don't have in most of these rural areas but I am often surprised at the level of expertise and experience lurking around the camps. I wonder how much help I'll get in this backwater town. While trauma from the highways or camps is a concern, I had been given to understand that most of my work would be care and maintenance of the communities. I could expect coughs, colds, sore orifices and a few pimples where pimples shouldn't be. I had no idea what the so called burden of illness might be but I imagined that I would soon find out.

4

Next morning I am up and anxious to try out the plumbing. My residence's former occupant was something of a mechanical enthusiast and he had installed, attached to the well, a pressure system that guaranteed high quality flow for an extended period of time. A propane tank supplied heat for a water tank and this was ingeniously supplemented by a solar system at the rear of the cabin that pre-heated the water flowing into the tank. My shower is long and invigorating but I probably should have taken a cold shower instead because I'm starting to feel drowsy and I want to sink back into my bed. Breakfast is a bowl of porridge, the real stuff not the sissy microwave stuff. I don't have a microwave anyhow. A couple of eggs and a slice of toast washed down with a couple of cups of black coffee do the trick to fill my tank and get me set for the day.

Arriving at the clinic early in the morning I'm surprised to see the old van parked in front of the door. I'm met by Louise who frowns at me then bestows her patented warm smile on me and grunts, "You're early." I've noticed that she often seems to grunt before breaking into normal English. She continues, "Things are quiet here so far but I expect they'll pick up later this morning when the reserves come in to pick up supplies. Every so often the residents get fresh cash either through treaty, oil sands pay outs or highways work. I think some of that showed up yesterday."

I busy myself with checking supplies, instruments, especially the coffee machine, and try to figure out the charting system. I am not sure why there is no super advanced electronic charting system like the big cities have. Maybe it is because Louise put the hex on the bureaucrats from health services and they never came back. Anyhow she shows me a simple system with the name and all the aliases on the folder. Some genius with an eye to the future had developed a system where the family tree for each patient was included and in many cases a snap shot of the patient grinning or scowling was attached to the inside of the folder. Documentation was terse and limited but quite adequate and informative. They should find the author and hire him or her for the big hospitals. Actually the author is sitting across from me staring at me through coke bottles. The more I see of Louise the more I am impressed.

"What do most of the people do with their time?" I mused. "Doesn't seem like much to do around here." No comment.

"What's the average age of the patients who come through here?" No comment but the trace of a smile.

"What's a busy day look like?" No comment but a little shrug of the shoulders. I was about to give up and shut up when Louise growled.

"New comer makes the coffee." Why the hell do I keep collecting these bossy women?

I got up, found the pot. It was sparkling clean and smelled fresh but I remember it being half filled yesterday so I knew it was used with regularity. They don't post rules around here. They make subtle hints. I wonder what happens when the hints aren't picked up. I don't think I want to find out. Two cups later Louise finally got her tongue going and is now filling me in on the life and dreams of Burning Lake. I get a complete history of the hundred or so residents of the hamlet, the 250 or so residents of the nearby reserve and the politics and family dynamics that pervade the days and weeks of the settlement. I guess she wanted to know if I could make coffee before she trusted me further. As she took a breath and started a new chapter, the door opened and a thin mousey looking slip of a girl in hospital scrubs slid through the door, gave me a look, smiled slightly at Louise and headed for my coffee.

"This is Marla, our public health nurse. Be good to her. She controls the vaccines, anti-snake venom, STD antibiotics and keeps the babies from crying when you're checking them with your cold hands."

Marla's hand shake is cool and not overly firm in keeping with her mousey persona.

"Hi Marla. I'm Paul or Hey or Doc or anything else you want to call me"

She blushes and smiles her shy smile and says,

"Nice to meet you Dr. Cross." Marla doesn't mutter.

The morning and afternoon flew by but the routine was relaxed, human, friendly and polite…except when a middle aged Metis lady with the improbable name of Mary Cameron burst through the door cursing and shouting, just about knocking me over and plopping herself in a chair .

"When are you bunch of jerks going to get me into that fancy pain thing for my wrist? I've been waiting three weeks for a message and today I tried to take a pot off the stove and spilled everything on the friggin, (she actually said friggin) floor. Who the hell are you?" Her eyes drilled me to the wall. Louise came to my rescue.

"Mary, this is Dr. Cross. He is going to work here for a while. Maybe he can help."

I had about five people waiting patiently in chairs and I wasn't sure I should let her bully me into letting her jump the queue. Yet she seemed to be on a short string with a long bite so I asked the patients if they thought it was ok if I saw Mary first. They said sure but much to my surprise she sat down at the end of the line and crossed her legs.

"You guys were here first. I got all day and my old man won't be home till later so I'll just sit here and visit."

I'm not sure who was going to get the lithium, her or me. Louise smiled her broad smile at me and Marla showed a little grin and I wondered if it was a setup. The rest of the afternoon passed by uneventfully and I eventually diagnosed Mary's old fractured scaphoid bone in her wrist. I didn't need an x-ray or fancy MRI. She made the diagnosis herself when she described how three months ago she tripped over a dog coming out of the bar and landed on the palm of her hand, felt a pain in her wrist which never went away. My examination seemed to confirm it and I arranged for an orthopod in the city to take her on and maybe fuse it or something. She promised me an apple pie.

The art of practicing medicine in a small rural community depends more on the expectations of the community than on any standards of care or physician know how. That is probably why it is easier to start a program than to downsize it after it gets going. It soon became apparent to me that we were all going to grow up together in this gig and all I had to do was keep my head on straight and try not to piss off too many locals. I had a good team in harmony with the townsfolk and it was my job to keep it that way.

5

Today I'm starting my second month in Burning Lake and I am struck by my new found sense of peace. Like most communities the people showing up are kids, pregnant women, a smattering of males young to middle aged and a significant number of elderly. While the number of diabetics seem to be concerning and booze problems are common, the misuse of pain pills and prevalence of recreation drugs seems about the same as what I saw in the big city. Because the population is low, I think that anybody using or abusing is easily identified and discouraged by community censorship. That doesn't mean that some bad actors don't live in the area but by and large I so far am not aware of any real evil bad guys. The two local reserves have a police force of three and the Royal Canadian Mounted Police stationed within the rather large municipal district patrol regularly.

My first visitor is not a patient but the newly elected chief of the Prairie Dene. The nearby reserve has just gone through a bitter election and the old chief and council was narrowly edged out by a group of young progressive people and their chief seems to have some issues on his mind. David Wah-Shee had just been elected Chief a few months before in a close battle with former Chief Sam Beaulieu and I was meeting him for the first time.

"Doc, you've been here for just a few weeks but already the people are wondering why you haven't paid any attention to what's goin' on." Talk about bursting my bubble.

"Hey, Chief, what the heck are you talking about?" He sat back, looked around as if to make sure we were alone in my small one room office and lowered his voice.

"Haven't you seen any locals in here looking for Oxy or treated any one speeding on ice?" That got my attention. I hadn't heard those terms since I left the big city ER. I was just getting comfortable with the slow rural pace and now this guy comes along and sends up some flags.

"Our reserve police just pulled over a couple of kids last night and found a pharmacy in their trunk. The school reported four fights in the lunch room and a sudden increase in empty desks just in the last two weeks. Hasn't anyone clued you in?"

Unless someone is passed out or talking to the spirits in loud voices most clinics don't usually see that stuff. The kids get high then it wears off. But I'm really surprised there has been no chatter. I pass that thought on to the chief and again he looks around and lowers his voice.

"The cops have been seeing an upswing in B&E's, assaults and car thefts in the last three or four weeks and there is chatter about a satellite gang from down south in Hobbema spreading that shit up here. I need your help."

This guy was wired into the shady world of the surrounding settlements which didn't surprise me. His brother was the police chief on the reserve. I knew I had to believe him. I told him I would keep my ears open and as far as possible would keep him in the loop. Reporting individual health contacts to the local fuzz is frowned on by the privacy cops but if there is evidence of a criminal code offense that changes things.

Illegal drug use in Saudi is not that big a problem. I think it has to do with the whippings and beheadings so I was a little rusty with the problem. My three years back in the big city seemed to be filled with heart attacks and trauma. My hospital was a long way from the inner city.

"Hey Doc. I guess I was a little hard on you. I didn't mean to come on so strong but this stuff worries me. We may have some big unemployment here but the ones that are working are making big bucks and the market is brisk."

We chatted for a while until the rest of the staff showed up and he promised to keep me informed and left. Our little clinic sees a dozen or so people in the morning and I'm looking at three or four walk-ins and don't know any of them so putting the chief's problem on hold I start my rounds.

Three patients in I'm talking to a twenty some male built like a tank and looking and smelling like a bunch of days in a swamp. In fact he had just come out of the bush where he was working fighting fires. I think I will be especially polite to this dude. However he is quiet and polite and complains about back pain. A guy fighting fires and having back pain without any reason triggers a few alerts and after checking him over and finding little I asked him what he thought it was and what I should do about it. Unlike most smart asses who say "You're the doc" and sit back and prepare for twenty questions, Gabriel, that was his name, unraveled a tale going back about four years when he got dragged by a pick-up during a disagreement with four or five tough guys from another reserve. He had a couple of crushed vertebrae and a busted hip and since that time has been living with pretty ugly pain. In spite of this he was able to hold a job fighting brush fires. He had tried most of the usual pills and poisons to keep him going but so far as I could tell, has avoided any narcotics. What to do? This guy had legitimate pain and a commendable work record. Do I introduce him to the powerful stuff and put him at risk of joining the club of young men hooked on hard stuff? He solved the dilemma for me by saying,

"Don't give me any of that Oxy shit or Percs. I just spent four months in rehab getting off them and I'm not going down that path again." He continued, "I work out in the bush and so far the guys I work with are clean. The camps are full of dealers but out in the bush we don't have much chance to connect. That suits me fine."

I sit there wondering what to offer and ask him how he manages in the bush. Evidently in rehab he was in a program that involved muscle strengthening and mobilization and sweat lodge sessions where life and stuff were tossed around. I began to wonder if I could get myself into one of those. Luckily for me he wasn't a seeker and just wanted reassurance that nothing more serious was happening. After he left I called Marla in and, recalling the Chief's concern, I brought the matter up.

"Marla, does a public health nurse deal with pain problems out here?"

"Sure. We do all sorts of palliative care. Most dying people want to stay with their family and we do what we can." She missed my point. This guy wasn't dying.

"Marla, what do we offer to people in pain who are not dying?" She looked at me with her shy smile and I think she was trying to process this doc who didn't seem to know anything about simple treatment.

"Don't you just prescribe some T 3s or Percocet?"

T 3s refer to Tylenol with Codeine and are a standard default pain killer for short term pain relief in a simple self-limited condition like tooth ache or bruised ribs. There's lots of those complaints in most communities. Wondering where this conversation was going I asked,

"But do we have any programs or anything for chronic pain?"

"Doctor Cross," she said. "This is Burning Lake. We're lucky to have a program for pregnant women." I wondered how Gabriel had found his way to rehab so she filled me in on the long and tortuous process filled with days living on the street, both in Fort McMurray and Edmonton and two or three arrests for possession of OxyContin. He finally was rescued by a plugged in social worker working out of remand and a sympathetic judge who agreed to go along with the recommendations of the social worker.

"We don't have those resources out here" she offered reluctantly. "There's lots of talk and promise and task forces and stake holder group meetings and budget excuses but nothing seems to get done." The light when on in my head. This may be the boonies but my people have been around and know what to expect from their organization.

"You are a public health nurse. Who is your boss and what does your boss think?"

Again the polite shy smile. "My boss is the public health manager at Fort Mac and her boss is the Medical Officer of Health for the area and his boss is the Chief Medical Officer of Health for the province. They seem to spend their time talking about infections and vaccination programs and women's cancers. They should pay attention to highway accidents but seem to let the Transportation people look after that. I'm not sure who looks after chronic pain on the reserves. No one told us."

"Couldn't you guys do that here?"

"No. But you could".

I should have kept my mouth shut. I'm not a militant or activist or whatever is the current word. She went back to her babies and I went back to aches, pains and coughs and colds. But there was a little itch starting in the back of my mind and I knew that sooner or later I would have to scratch it.

I remember a seminar I sat through a few years ago talking about diabetes and the impact it had on society. We were being bored to death with charts and power point displays run by a succession of young health professional enthusiasts. They all painted the same image. If the people were taught they would learn and change. In the midst of the propaganda session a lady in the audience stood up and interrupted.

"I have a comment and a question if you will allow me to talk."

She seemed to be in her late fifties or early sixties and looked like she had been dragged in to the meeting through a thrift shop clothes bank and ran into a hurricane. Her hair was a frizz ball of steel wool and her face resembled a fried newspaper but there was no mistaking the authority in her voice as she began to talk.

"I have worked in communities all over the north for the last thirty years and I have seen programs come and go but I have never seen one stay that was parachuted in from on high. Most people in this country already know more or less the stuff you are talking about today. What you and most bureaucrats never seem to learn is that the people will act when they finally decide to. When one mom joins with another couple of moms and they decide to do something about a problem the problem usually starts to get fixed. When you people finally start investing in community organization instead of community preaching you will start to see some results!"

She sat down and the room was silent. There were a few whispers and a couple of nervous coughs and then the enthusiasts continued with their power point explanations. I sat there with a discordant chorus of thoughts bouncing around in my skull not quite able to decode what I had just heard. Was she a wing nut or some loose cannon from Hicksville? Did she really have a message? Were all these pros missing the point? Was she a commie or even worse, a left wing liberal?

The seminar left me with no more useful information than what I had before I registered but the unexpected segue provided by the doc from the north stuck in my mind. Maybe that is what Marla was getting at today.

6

There is an early warning of winter edging in outside and a few flakes of snow are starting to fall as they dance on the light breeze now blowing in from the west. Right now the weather is pleasant but there is no mistaking the chance that the wind will shift to the northwest and soon climb to fifty klicks and the snow will increase. Louise tells me the forecast is for 20 cm. of snow before the sun returns in a couple of days. That's a pretty good dump for this time of year. Riyadh, why did I leave you?

Last week I took a break and drove up to Fort Mac for a look around and hung around the hospital ER for a couple of hours talking with the docs. I had never met any of them before but when they learned I was just down the road from them and so was really one of them they took me under their wing and soon we were swapping war stories with all the expected embellishments. They were interested in my experience in Saudi and one young doc had just signed a contract and was heading for my old haunts. He was eager to find out what he was in for but rather than poison his ambition with my own cynicism I gently steered him to my situation and tried to find out what I might run into over the next few months. I heard the usual concerns of too much work and too little help. The main concern was the carnage playing itself out every weekend on the main highway to the city. Crashes with serious injury and death kept these docs busy and sometimes they wondered if a war zone could be worse. Never having worked in a war zone I couldn't comment. As far as I could see, the most pressing concern was trauma and the thriving drug trade. Besides the usual brisk traffic of Oxy and Percs, Crystal Meth was becoming a problem and a new disaster was just over the horizon.

Some evil genius in the third world developed street versions of fentanyl, a potent narcotic several times the potency of heroin. Fentanyl is the main ingredient of the pain patch used by palliative care docs and veterinarians doing surgery on animals. This stuff was starting to show up all over the province especially on the reserves and several deaths had already been reported. So far we were lucky at Burning Lake and hadn't run into any problems. Money flowed pretty freely in the city and though the camps had pretty strict policies regarding drug use, the city was seeing more problems than a few years ago.

Because of the young average age, the large population of
single males or those acting like they are single and the six
figure incomes that boggle the mind, the trade in crack cocaine,
crystal meth and a variety of other street pharmaceuticals is
brisk and the city is struggling with the effects of the drug use.
Some estimates put the rates anywhere from two to ten times
the rate usually seen in cities of approximately the same size. I
started to appreciate what my friend the chief was getting at and
I sensed trouble on the horizon.

* * *

Right now I'm taking a break from the small procession of
community and reserve residents and thinking about my recent
conversation with Chief Wah-Shee and my visit to Fort Mac. It
seems to me that the inhabitants throughout most of the area
around Burning Lake are either quite young or getting on in
age. The young men and women usually head for jobs or school
in the bigger centers. Most of my clients are children in grade
school, young mothers or mothers to be who have either
returned or stayed behind while their friends sought their
fortunes farther afield. At the other end of the scale are the old
folks of the area and the First Nation elders. Maybe that is why
we haven't seen the drug problems that assail our city
neighbours.

I am pulled out of my reverie by Louise who had a little two year old infant in her arms and a young woman, presumably the infant's mother peering anxiously over her shoulder.

"Isn't she cute?" I guess she was referring to the infant because the mother was rather plain looking and slightly disheveled. "This is Tina" meaning the baby. I still wasn't introduced to the mother. Louise was showing a dimension I hadn't seen in her before. She looked like she could curl up with the little one and play all afternoon, oblivious to the small crowd sitting patiently in their chairs waiting their turn.

"Tina just got here last week. She was born in High Level but her father was from Fort Chip so they moved there. They lived the last two years in Fort Chip but the family split up and Tina and her mom moved back here to live with her sister on the reserve." She then looked at Tina's mom and introduced us.

"Cassidy, this is Dr. Cross. He's OK." I guess I needed the endorsement or the conversation would have ended there.

Cassidy looked me up and down, took her sleeping baby from Louise who gave her up reluctantly and started to cry. Cassidy, not Louise. I got them seated and sent Louise back to her patients; I'm not sure whose list Cassidy and her baby are on.

Through her tears and not a little anger she told of the last two years at Fort Chip and her life with an abusive alcoholic who beat her frequently and left her often to spend weeks in the bush hunting, trapping and mostly drinking. Finally after getting up nerve and getting some money from her sister she caught a ride here and moved in a couple of days ago. I still didn't have a clue what she was trying to tell me. At the risk of setting off another tirade laced with sobbing and not a little swearing I asked her gently why she came over to the clinic today. Baby Tina started to squirm and whimper and I thought I was about to do the same so I reached over and as gentle as possible said "May I?" and took the baby and laid her on my lap where she stuck her thumb in her mouth and went back to sleep. Wow! I didn't know I had that kind of power over a kid.

Cassidy told me she came over because for the last few months baby Tina would get real hot and then her eyes would roll up and she would start to twitch. After a few seconds she would stop and stare glassy eyed and go to sleep. She said that was the reason she got out of Fort Chip because she heard that the ground was bad because of the mining in the area. She had heard that the stuff in the ground made kids blind and gave them convulsions. I had spent the last five years either in Saudi Arabia or Calgary where I paid little attention to anything except my shift and my off shift pursuit of fun and games. That there was a pending political environmental storm gathering on the horizon hardly made it into my consciousness. I'd scanned the headlines and briefly dismissed them as so much tree hugging hysteria. Now here, I was confronted with a potential problem and had no real knowledge and only a smattering of information heavily weighted with bias, both from media and my own ignorance. When you don't know what's immediately below the surface common sense tells you not to dive in headfirst without checking what's in the water below.

For once I listened to common sense. Remembering my basic training I took to examining Tina. By this time she had wakened up and was still lying in my lap no doubt wondering who the new guy on the block was. The problem soon revealed itself when I saw the thickened ear drum with the thick smelly pus filling the ear canal. Her eyes were crusted and the quick look I got at her throat showed two huge tonsils that, at the moment looked pretty normal for a two year old. She did, however have a bunch of swollen glands in her neck. Nothing else showed up in her chest or belly and the rest of her looked ok. Other than the chronically infected ear I couldn't find anything else wrong.

Theorizing that Tina got recurrent ear infections and through the resulting fever she had a few infantile febrile seizures I felt reasonably confident in reassuring Cassidy that Tina would be ok after we cleared up her ear. I also made a note to pursue the seizure disorder in the near future. I guessed Tina would stay on Louise's list and she could arrange to look into her general living conditions on the reserve and keep track of her growth and development. I'm sure Louise agreed. We had some medicine on hand to start her treatment and I arranged to see her in two weeks, sooner of course if she got sicker.

In the last few weeks this was the second time someone came in and linked the mining activity in the area to some health problem. Not wanting to be prematurely branded as an alarmist tree hugger I stored my misgivings in the nether recesses of my mind and moved on.

The wind and snow was picking up outside and most of my waiting room area was clear but one young fellow was still there waiting patiently for a call. He looked about mid twenty, was well groomed and sat quietly reading something on his mobile phone. Thinking he was just passing through and remembering the crappy weather outside I called him over and asked him if I could help him.

Carl Reimer is a young guy from eastern Canada and works for an oil sands company in a joint venture with a large Asian company. He is in the area at a nearby camp monitoring the progress of a remote resource development company who is looking to set up a "matting" capability on the nearby reserve. That surprised me because matting is usually reserved for muskeg areas where heavy equipment must be moved over unstable land. To my knowledge no companies were currently operating on any nearby reserve land and though muskeg is a prominent feature no industry has moved into the area. The larger lake in the area is mostly a remote tourist fishing site located on the reserve. I couldn't understand why a matting capacity was being considered but being new to the area there was really no reason for me to know anything at all.

Carl stopped by this afternoon on the way back to the camp because he wanted to see a doc and the inbound blizzard put the big city out of bounds. His story was weird.

"Doc is this visit confidential? I mean I can pay cash so it doesn't go on the books."

That put me on my guard. "All my stuff is confidential and if you need to have no record of your visit you'll have to give me a good reason for cooking the books. Did you pick up something that needs immediate attention? If so, I want to let you know that contact info is a must. I already went through this half way around the globe and almost literally lost my head. I don't want to take a chance on that again."

He looked at me as if I was from another world and wondered what the hell I was talking about. Then the light came on.

"Hell no doc. I don't have the clap or anything else. I need someone to check my swelling hand. It started after I got it caught on a ladder at work a couple of days ago. I reported it to the safety guy but he didn't give me anything to fill out and I didn't think anything about it until I left the camp last night to inspect a couple of sites and my hand kept swelling."

I looked at the hand and noted a good deal of swelling over his left palm extending to his wrist. It didn't take a genius to see that he had a closed wound infection of the hand involving all his tendons. He must be pretty tough because these things hurt like hell. They usually have to be treated surgically and quickly.

I'm no surgeon and this is no hospital. We are about 90 miles
from the city and there is a blizzard outside. I called the district
RCMP and asked them about road conditions, told them my
dilemma and they said not to worry, they could get a four wheel
drive vehicle with chains here in about twenty minutes and get
my guy to hospital.

That being arranged I took a closer look at my patient and
asked him to go over the whole story again.

"Doc there is nothing to tell. I caught my hand on the sharp
edge of a ladder and felt a sharp pain for a few seconds. There
wasn't even much bleeding. The usual safety guy wasn't there
but the company guy that usually helps out with this stuff
looked at it and said not to worry. It didn't look like much. A
few hours later it started to swell and overnight the swelling got
worse and my hand feels kind of numb. When I started to sweat
like a pig I thought I better stop in here 'cause I had heard there
was often a doc here."

Why couldn't it have been a few days ago when the weather
was mild and it was mid-week? Anyhow I had some stuff to do
before he headed out. He wasn't sure of the last time he got a
tetanus shot so I got Marla to give him one and then I got him
packaged and ready for the trip. I started an IV in his other arm
and loaded him with a cocktail of antibiotics. Usually we wait
to see what bugs are growing but I thought it best this time to
use best guess and load him up. I phoned the hospital and
luckily got right through to the surgeon on call and told him

what we had. So much for confidentiality and cooking the books.

"Carl, why is it so important to keep this confidential?"

"I don't want to get anyone in trouble. I've heard that some of the companies sometimes cover up accidents so their record will look good and I didn't want to get anyone fired."

"Is the cover up practice common?" I asked and he hesitated and said that he'd heard of some creative reporting practices used by some of the companies but was sure his company was ok. We were interrupted by the arrival of a big two ton four wheel drive truck driven by a couple of guys from the nearby reserve. I guess they owed the cops a favour and they kind of like helping us out once in a while. The wind was dying down and the snow had stopped so I was reassured that Carl would be delivered safely. I asked him to drop in next time he was in the neighbourhood. Mission accomplished, I headed for my hidey-hole and fireplace for a well-earned sip of something and supper. For a recycled bachelor I'm getting to be a pretty good cook.

Part III

7

"Chief Wah-Shee, it's good to see you again. Are you holding up in the role of politician OK?" Today the chief is at the clinic looking like he had just lost an argument with both his wife and young daughters; a little confused, a little defiant but mostly pissed off. We have had a few talks since our first dust up and things seemed to be going good. I'm wondering what I did to get his back up. But I soon realized it wasn't me.

"Those slimy, two timing crooked thieves! You'd think they were rich white folk." The Chief wasn't always politically correct. Besides he knew we shared a common bond when talking about graft and corruption.

"What's gotten you all riled up?" I asked

"That no good ex-Chief really did it this time. That damn crooked family of his got together with Midnight Sun and made a deal to let them survey the whole south half of the reserve and set up a camp for one of those Asian energy companies. We thought they were doing a consultation for reserve road expansion and upgrade and today I found out the deal is for discovery and extraction of bitumen. I wasn't worried at first because everyone knows there are no significant deposits of bitumen on the Reserve but later on in the agreement hidden in one obscure phrase are the words *and any other mineral resources.* Those crooks may have signed away our rights to stuff we don't even know about".

Bitumen is the oily sand that is making the whole country rich and crazy at the same time. The First Nations have a lot of discretion who gets on the land and who doesn't but somehow the former reserve council let themselves get screwed into signing a contract that gave the gold to the gold diggers. In this case the gold was not only black, gooey and smelly. It might be any number of things.

"We've had the lawyers look it over and it all looks legal as hell. I don't know how they did it."

"Chief, I'm only a doc and I have trouble keeping my own books straight. Why talk to me about it?"

"I dunno." he mused. "I heard that there was a young lady accountant coming through here every once in a while to help you guys and a few of the junior energy service companies. I need to get some advice on how to tackle this thing and wondered if you could help to set up a meeting on the Q.T.?"

I'm not sure why the chief came to me. I haven't even met the accountant and didn't know squat about her. I'm trying to explain this to the chief when Louise came to my rescue.

"Isn't that the young genius working for Abrahms and Abrahms Financial in Fort Mac? She does forensic audits or something like that for a lot of these little companies that come through here. She came by once trying to see if we were interested and I told them that the government did all our stuff."

I guess there is a lot about running a business that I don't have a clue about. I let Louise take the lead.

"She's coming through next week and usually drops in for a coffee."

That's the first I've heard of it. I wonder where I was when she was through last. I said out loud mostly to myself,

"Remember I'm going away for a couple of weeks at the end of this week. You guys will be on your own unless I get that locum to agree to come."

The Chief and Louise chatted on and I guess they agreed to broker a meet but I'm still not sure what business it is of ours. I thought again about my patient with the infected hand. I remembered his association with the service company doing a prelim survey for matting and then I dismissed it from my mind. I guess he did ok because I got a thanks by email from him a few days ago. It never occurred to me to wonder if he could shed any light on the chief's stuff.

* * *

I'm talking to Health Services to see if they found that locum doctor for me. I guess they have some guy that just got his license and was looking to make some bucks. He evidently did his training in Pakistan and finally got through the B.S. lineup that most foreign graduates are obliged to suffer. Last I heard he hadn't committed. I hope I hear soon because I need a little fun in the sun and I have week in Vegas booked. A couple of other guys from Calgary are coming with me and it should be fun. We've all seen "Hangover" and know what not to do. I'll probably survive ok.

The Chief and Louise finished their chat and he left looking just as pissed as when he came in. I hope it works out for him. He seems like a nice guy and a pretty straight shooter but I don't think I'd like to cross him. Scalping is frowned upon and he wouldn't get much from my thinning dome anyhow but I wouldn't want to chance it. Besides, I remembered his brother is the police chief on the reserve and after my time in sand land I'm nervous about any cops giving me the look. I'm beginning to get a buzz in the back of my mind. First of all I'm hearing about oxys, percs and crack cocaine, then I'm seeing domestic abuse and sick kids and hearing it's something in the ground, then I come across shoddy safety stuff and now I'm hearing about crooked contracts. I thought I was living in Canada but this sounds like stuff in one of those central Asian countries ending in 'stan. I'm looking forward to Vegas but in the meantime I have to get back to work.

Marla and I have been talking about the rising rate of diabetics in the community. Every week we seem to find another one. This is Dene land. A generation ago they came out of the bush where they lived by hunting, trapping and if they were near any lakes, fishing for the abundant lake Arctic Grayling, Whitefish and Northern Pike. They walked almost everywhere and in the winter most travelled by dogsled. Diabetes was almost unheard of. In the last thirty or forty years the Dene began moving south, settling on reserves and living off the treaty money and cash from the resource companies. Trucks, snow mobiles, store bought groceries and booze became a way of life and diabetes became a modern plague.

I had told Marla about the comments of the lady doc who tore a strip off the diabetic seminar delegates but she still hadn't bought into it. Public health nurses are heavily into teaching and instructing and showing and preaching and sometimes even scolding. Most of them do a good job of providing information but the health professions as a whole get failing grades for motivation. Here we were, right in the heart of aboriginal land looking at a modern disease in an ancient people and we had a great chance to do something original. I shamelessly taunted Marla to be bold and look at the problem from some new angles. We tossed the problem around over coffee a few times but neither of us got any further than tossing it around. Program development, after all was a government responsibility. We had our own duties to keep up with. Little did I know how wrong I was.

I spent the rest of the day seeing the usual parade of illness, real or imagined, and in between patients I busied myself cleaning up my desk and getting my notes up to date for the locum doc coming in to work the next two weeks. I didn't know anything about him and I didn't want him to think I was one of those lazy uninterested burned out docs occasionally found in these backwood settlements. I'm pretty careful about recording pertinent stuff in the charts but I usually avoid the psychobabble that has started to invade the record. Louise's system suited me fine. The new doc, Jordan Aziz, has been confirmed and I'm sure Louise and Marla would keep him in line.

8

Marla looked up from her desk where she was reading about the progress for an upcoming meeting she was attempting to organize over on the reserve at the tribal office. She had taken my challenge and contacted the tribal council and spoken to some of the more prominent women residents. Her boss had no idea she had taken matters into her own hands and she had a shiver of apprehension as she thought about what she was doing. The meeting would take place soon after the return of Doctor Cross and Marla hoped she hadn't got herself in over her head. Dr. Cross didn't seem intimidated by the bureaucrats of the system but Marla worried that he might be making matters worse. Burning Lake had just managed to get a few bucks to set up a prenatal clinic once every two weeks and that had taken two years to set up.

What she saw when she looked up was a very young looking East Indian man about five and a half feet tall and weighing less than the average bantam hockey player on the reserve. He was clean shaven, wearing a shirt and tie and stylish eyeglasses which he nervously adjusted every couple of minutes.

"Good morning. I am Dr. Aziz. I believe you are expecting me."

Could this Doogie Howser wannabe possibly be the replacement for Dr. Cross? Louise had not yet arrived and Marla wondered what to do next. Just then the door opened and Louise bounced in, looked at "Doogie" and gushed "You must be Dr. Aziz. I'm Louise." Marla stared at the two of them with open mouth, wondering where Louise had suddenly found her couth. She didn't even mumble or mutter and certainly didn't order him to make coffee.

Dr. Jordan Aziz was a first generation Pakistani Muslim who grew up in Karachi and graduated from the medical college of Aga Khan University. He had just completed certification in the Family Medicine emergency program and was eager to begin saving lives. Neither Marla nor Louise knew anything about him except that he was licensed and male. His appearance also made them suspicious. He was either a gentleman or a shy teenager or maybe both. The next two weeks are certainly going to be interesting.

A couple of old ladies from town came through the door and stepped carefully to the nearest chairs, letting themselves settle and stared at the two nurses and their newest staff member. This was certainly a new development. Louise was busying herself making coffee and asking Doogie if he would prefer milk or maybe hot chocolate and Marla was abandoning her usual shy demeanor and rolling her eyes in wonderment. However the day soon got into gear and the ladies were quickly seen, advised and dispatched. This new guy seemed to know what he was doing. In the back of her mind Louise was thinking, "I wonder if we can keep both docs."

* * *

Chief Wah-Shee and his brother, the chief of police were sitting in the tribal administration office going through a pile of documents when a young lady came through the door. She carried a backpack instead of the classic brief case and her age looked like the low twenties. Her off duty life must have been marathon running because she was average height, slightly built but her stylish pant suit couldn't hide the contours of well-built thighs. Moving with confidence tinged with proper respect she introduced herself as Amy Pham.

"I work for Abrahms and Abrahms in Fort Mac and I heard you might need a little help on some number crunching."

Chief number one stared at her for a bit longer than what might be considered polite then introduced chief number two.

"Thanks for making the trip. We've got a ticklish situation here and we are trying to figure out our next step. We need someone who can make sense of all these contracts and their impact on this reserve. Our legal people say they're bullet proof but we don't like where they will be taking us. Your involvement has got to be on the Q.T. Even my office staff doesn't know what you're here for. She thinks it's for something about my off reserve businesses." The chief operated a very successful hotshot business but his off reserve income was subject to income tax.

Working with junior oil companies, service companies and reserve administrations was not new to Amy. A graduate of the U. of Saskatchewan's school of accounting, she had been through the blender in First Nation politics for at least three years and her master's thesis gave her some impressive forensic audit creds.

Chief number two observed "I hope you have a thick skin. This damn agreement stinks to high heaven and if I could find any evidence I'd lock the crooks up and drop the key in the muskeg." It must be tough being a cop in a community where tribal and family loyalty counts more than rule of law.

Amy put a grin on her face and replied,

"Maybe I can help. Some of my friends say I look more native than Asian so maybe I can con them into thinking I'm one of them."

Any thought that this was a newbie school kid was quickly dispersed and the three put their heads together and started to wade through the mound of paper.

* * *

It's ten a.m. Vegas time and I'm in a corner of the dining room of my hotel nursing a Bloody Mary and staring at the largest eggs benedict I have ever seen. I must be getting old because the pain of the morning is starting to beat the pleasure of the night before. I'm not sure whether I should pile on more pleasure or order more aspirin. Last night was a night of barhopping along the Strip. What makes Vegas great is the overabundance of good live music in even the smallest bars. We sipped our way through jazz, blues, country and even some chic tunes.

This morning my buddies from Calgary haven't surfaced yet but I'm waiting for a couple of my friends from the world of ER to join me. Every year we get together and talk about the similarities and differences in our work environments. Marc and his girlfriend Corey work in LA at different hospitals. She is in an upscale area that caters to the often rich and sometime famous. Crises there consist of heart attacks, strokes, gall bladder attacks and complications of pregnancy. Marc is in an inner city hospital where he sorts out knifings, drive bys and ODs. Both have to deal with the crazy world of private insurance, meddling administrators and lawsuits. I wonder what they will think of my situation.

I've been reviewing my experiences the last several weeks and have made the observation that medicine is easy. It's the people you deal with that make it tough. I should have been a vet. I wonder how Aziz is making out. I hope Louise doesn't put the run on him. I'm sorry I couldn't be there to meet him but on paper he looked ok. My mind turned to the worries of Chief Wah-Shee. Here I'm sitting in sin city, the home of legitimate American criminal enterprise. Who says crime doesn't pay. What makes it pay is the holy trio of government, business and consumer. When gambling and booze were illegal you had shooting and final beds of sand in the desert. Now it's legal and the shooting and trips to the desert seem to have stopped. At least that is what I'm told.

Working at Burning Lake I get the feeling that I keep slipping from the first world to the third world and back again almost from minute to minute. There, I had good access to high tech in a reasonable time frame and my patients didn't have to pay for it. That was the good news. The bad news was that corruption took on a different form. Big oil companies, aboriginal communities, civil (and not so civil) servants and entitled citizens often combined to form conflicts that didn't always work for the best interests of society. Fortunately rule of law was first class though sometimes slow and tortuous.

Missing women, boom town drug problems and a maze of contradictions in aboriginal tribal administration kept the challenges of justice struggling to keep up. Chief Wah-Shee had my sympathies. I had no idea that his problems were soon to become my problems.

* * *

Amy Pham ended her meeting with the brother chiefs and after working out an arrangement to start her audit in a couple of days she headed back to Fort Mac to fill in her firm about her new clients. Little did she know that the receptionist in the office was the niece of the ex-chief and the daughter of the reserve's version of the godfather. As her car pulled away she didn't see the office help writing down her license number. As she headed down the highway she was already putting together a plan to attack this problem. As soon as she got back she would pull out her research that got her the master's degree and review it. The problem outlined by the chiefs was not actually original. It was a pattern used over and over again as crooked tribal administrators and councils ran their shops and screwed their citizens. Somewhere in the mix had to be some slime ball lawyer on the take from someone in the resource company. She was confident that she could tie this up in no time.

The old administration certainly had the right to enter into contracts with outside companies for a variety of purposes. However if it could be shown that an illegal inducement, read bribe, was involved then the contract could be annulled in court. At least that's what she was taught in her administrative law classes. She was convinced that there must have been some cash inducements to get this deal done. No self-respecting crook would let some company come on to the reserve free of charge. There had to be a money trail somewhere. As she cleared the boundary of the reserve she drove past a large house with attached two story double garage with a large shop attached. Parked in the drive way was a new 4 wheel drive dually two ton with crew cab. Those things are not cheap.

Amy could see that there was some wealth amid the poverty and wondered if that was the ex-chief's place or the new chief's hot shot truck. She had been at Fort Mac long enough to know that hot shot business was essential to the smooth operation of the industry. She provided accounting services to a couple. Though she never learned the origin of the term she knew it meant a guy in a truck that would deliver anything anywhere in the oil patch at a moment's notice. Blizzards, floods, holidays and distance didn't seem to bother these modern cowboys. She would have to find out who really owned the place when she got back in a couple of days.

* * *

Wilfred Natannah stood at his window and watched the woman drive past his place. He didn't especially like the way she slowed down and looked around before speeding off. Alerted by his daughter, he wondered if this woman was going to be a problem. Maybe it was something he should warn his half-brother the ex-chief about. This was no time for anyone to poke around through the reserve finances. It was time to start to bury some of the loose ends…literally if necessary.

For the past two years Midnight Sun had been negotiating with the Prairie Dene about surveying on reserve land. The board and CEO of the company were tough negotiators but straight arrows. However their chief legal counsel wasn't above some creative arrangements that would never fly if either the company or the reserve inhabitants got wind of his creativity. Meeting on the side with Wilfred, Jozeph Laszlo crafted an innocent looking agreement whereby Midnight Sun would survey the reserve for the purpose of using matting for an all season road network through the south half of the reserve. In fact a well disguised side agreement was crafted to locate and secure the rights to extract a variety of riches under contract to a large Asian controlled energy company. Finder's rights had already been paid to Wilfred and Jozeph under the heading of miscellaneous expenditures on the company's spread sheets. They were sure the money was well hidden and unless someone knew what they were looking for it was unlikely they would get caught. Now those nosey upstarts and the police chief looked like they might be bringing in someone who might know what to look for. Maybe it was time to become a little more creative.

9

octor Aziz was blending right in without any hiccups. He
was very different from Dr. Cross; much more polite and
formal. Louise got the impression that it would take a grizzly
charging through the office to get him off his game. No matter
who came through the place he was quiet, considerate and
polite and seemed to know his stuff. In fact Louise was
wondering how long it would be before the health services
branch would start to bellyache about his lab and x-ray
requests. Some of the stuff he ordered she'd never heard of.
Some of the stuff he asked for could only be gotten in four or
five days and only after being Ok'd by the clinic services boss
in Fort Mac. Anyhow he always provided a reason for his
requests in the same calm considerate manner he used in the
clinic with his patients.

Doc Cross, on the other hand was the king of "make do" after some unkind words about the various departmental dictators. Because there was no pharmacy within sixty or so miles he insisted that there be at least a two day supply of common medications on site to tide people over until their prescriptions could be couriered to the clinic. These were the times that "good enough" was just as good as "best practice". However, as he showed with the guy who came in with the hand infection he could make a quick decision and get action right away. That guy, what was his name, Carl something or other, came through a couple of weeks ago to see Doc. Cross and they seemed to hit it off pretty good. He's pretty lucky he came in when he did.

Dr. Aziz's second week was just about up and he would be leaving Sunday. Doc Cross would be back Monday. Just two more days to go for Aziz. Louise and Marla talked about a little party for him. He was definitely a keeper.

Looking up from her appointment book she saw through the window the spotless new Murano that belonged to the young accountant drive by. She was just here a couple of days ago and now she's back. Wonder what's up. Dr. Cross was right. It's probably none of the clinic's business. Best to keep it that way.

Amy Pham pulled into the parking lot at the tribal administration office, grabbed her backpack full of stuff and headed inside. She was all juiced up to get going and see if these guys were involved in any dirty dancing. Neither chief were in but they had given her a key to the lock box that held all the documents that had anything to do with the agreement. She breezed a hi to the receptionist and missed the glare she got in return. She knew that Chief Wah-Shee had told his assistant that Amy's visits had something to do with his hot shot business.

The day passed quickly and Amy was making progress. Knowing she was looking for large sums that were not easily explained if examined closely she focused on all such transactions for the last two years. She found a half dozen of these and headed to the copier to scan them to her email at Fort Mac. She wasn't going to take a chance taking anything out of the office. She was just about finished for the day when Ms. Natannah came in with a cup of tea and said,

"I thought you might need this for the road."

"Why, thanks so much, Dawn." That was her name. Her pretty name didn't quite match her usual sullen disposition but maybe she had things on her mind that bothered her. Who knows? The family dynamics and politics on the reserves are sometimes hard to figure. Most of the time the people are warm and open and full of humour and hospitality. Other times they clam up and go into a shell. Dawn Natannah seemed to drift in and out of those moods.

Amy finished her tea, gathered up her notes and headed for her car. It was getting late and the sun would be down in about an hour and she wanted to get off the highway and home with

as little darkness as possible. The highways were disasters
waiting to happen after dark and she didn't need any disasters.
The day had gone well and she was starting to get a feel for her
task. Although she had no concrete evidence she felt she had
made good progress.

Passing the big house on the way out she remembered she
still didn't know who it belonged to but that could wait until
Monday when she planned to come back. She turned on the
music and settled in for the ride home. Twenty minutes later her
world abruptly changed. She just started to feel drowsy and in
spite of opening the windows and turning up the music she
began to see shadows curling in and out of the ditch beside the
road. All of a sudden she saw a huge misshapen hulk charge out
in front of her. She spun the wheel to miss whatever it was,
went off the road and into a gully hitting a tree and rolling. The
last thing she recalled was a sharp pain in her left arm followed
by a blow to her head as the airbag exploded and mercifully
saved her from the engine that was heading through the firewall
into the front seat.

* * *

Sometime later Amy awoke strapped to a stretcher in an
ambulance heading down the highway in the darkness with
siren blaring and lights flashing. The van seemed to be spinning
and she felt like she was going to throw up. She had a sharp

pain in her left arm and every time they hit a bump she
screamed from the pain. An ambulance attendant was sitting on
a bench next to her and bent over and adjusted an I.V. that was
in her right arm. She had a mask on and something, probably
oxygen, was being piped into her. The van rounded a corner
and she passed out again. She next came to lying on a stretcher
in a small room and a little man who looked young enough to
be her little brother was fussing over her. Some woman with
thick glasses stood next to the little guy. She looked vaguely
familiar then as she came into focus Amy cried out,

"You're the nurse! What happened?"

The nurse muttered "You hit a tree and wrecked your car.
You also hit your head and we think you broke your arm."

All the while the little guy said nothing but checked her
neck and shoulders, shone a light in her eyes and quietly asked
her to squeeze his hands and wiggle her toes. Her chest felt like
a truck had run over it and it hurt to breath.

The young guy, presumably the doc told her,

"A trucker going by noticed where you went off the road,
radioed into the EMS guys and then went to find your wreck.
Luckily you were still strapped in. You had half the motor in
the front seat with you. We think you stuck your arm out ahead
to save yourself and broke a couple of bones in it. You'll be ok
but we're not too sure why you went off the road." He went on.
"We called the EMS from Fort Mac to come and get you. Our

guys are not paramedics and I think we should send you in a properly equipped unit for your own safety."

"In the meantime we want to get a few blood samples to see if that will help us figure out what happened."

Amy looked around and tried to focus.

"Where's my stuff? Did you get my backpack with my iPad?"

Louise lifted up the bag and said "It's all here. Don't worry. You will be ok in a few weeks. We called the hospital and told them to expect you in an hour or so."

Still feeling like she had gone twelve rounds with a gorilla Amy closed her eyes and drifted off.

Jordan mused. "This is very unusual. She has not been drinking and she really didn't hit her head very hard. I wonder why she is so drowsy."

He went to the lab cabinet and pulled out a few tubes and proceeded to pull some samples of blood from her arm.

"I want a blood alcohol and a full tox screen as well as electrolytes. Have them send the results to my office in Fort Mac. I'll let you know if anything turns up."

Louise collected the samples, identified and documented them and then, in keeping with clinic protocol placed duplicates of the samples in the lab fridge. Lab samples were occasionally lost between Burning Lake and the big city lab and the backup procedure was not new. She could not ever remember it being of much value but who knew?

About 90 minutes later the paramedic unit showed up and took Amy. Only one more day and Dr. Aziz was finished and could return to his job in ER. Louise went home to bake a cake for their little celebration tomorrow and the settlement slipped into sleep mode. In the meantime Amy rode drifting in and out of consciousness with the worst headache she had ever experienced in her life. Much as she tried she couldn't quite keep straight where she was or what she had been doing. She kept waking up from a nightmare featuring a huge form rising up in front of her causing her to swing the wheel.

* * *

I landed in Fort Mac Sunday night just a little worse for wear from the effects of Vegas and believing that what happens in Vegas stays in Vegas because no one else would give a damn.

Actually my batteries were charged and my talks with my buds from LA had reawakened my belief that people are the same everywhere. It's the rules they play with and the toys they use that make the difference. Since moving to Burning Lake I was beginning to feel like I might belong and that I wasn't just another wannabe do-gooder passing through. They have gangs in L.A. and tribes in Saudi Arabia but here the main dynamic is capitalism and government bureaucracy dancing often in discord with the society they both serve. When I put aside my cynicism and think back to my reasons for being a doc other than making money and learning interesting stuff I remember that you have to be part of the fabric before you can do what the fabric does. That's what makes dedicated pros different from the starry eyed do-gooders.

In his novel *Musashi,* Eiji Yoshikawa observed,

"There's nothing more frightening than a half-baked do-gooder who knows nothing of the world but takes it upon himself to tell the world what's good for it." Sixty five years ago a British novelist, *C.S. Lewis* wrote;

"…those who torment us for our own good will torment us without end for they do so with the approval of their own conscience."

I guess if I'm going to have any impact on the community I find myself in I had better get to work and discover some more about the little world around me.

10

Pouring another cup of Louise's coffee I sit down before the trickle of town inhabitants start through the door. Louise is sitting across from me with a pad of notes and gracing me with her patented warm broad smile. I still haven't found out how old she is and I'm scared to ask. I suspect she is just old enough to be my mother or maybe my oldest sister. She no longer mumbles when she speaks. She gets right into it and paints a picture of the last two weeks including her glowing comments about Dr. Jordan Aziz and his calm manner and thorough approach to his profession. I wonder if there is a hint or mild reproach there. Nothing unusual stands out; just the usual mix of chronic illness, 'flu, minor bruises from a couple of domestic disagreements and one or two car crash victims that were patched up and transferred.

Winter is really settling in and the mercury is hovering around -17 C. but mercifully there is little wind and the sky is clear. Once in a while the warm sun and hotel swimming pool that were my life a week ago flash into my consciousness but I shake off the image and return to my chores. Today I have a few follow-up visits to get out of the way before Marla and I hold a meeting with four or five patients struggling with the reality of diabetes. Marla figured, and I agreed, that if we could gather together a few patients trying to cope with the newest aboriginal plague we could pass on some hints about self-care and also learn more about the impact of diabetes on our own local community. What could we lose? My uncle, a long retired G.P. told me that he learned more about the views of patients sitting in MacDonalds with a bunch of old farts than he ever learned slaving away in his office or quaffing a free meal paid for by some big pharma company that was pushing the latest wonder drug that nobody could afford.

Thinking of Marla's initial reaction to my rant that teaching and preaching had little effect on health care, I was amused that this little mousey nurse was being transformed into a community activist. Look out Burning Lake. Sister Marla is coming and you'd better be ready!

Skirting the privacy rules she had identified five ladies ranging from late forties to mid-sixties, contacted them and using the ruse of offering a support group had invited them over to the clinic for a chat. This was to be her group of militants. It was no good me dumping guilt on an obese sedentary late middle aged female who was doomed to a premature heart attack or even worse, an amputation in the final years of life. My scolding was efficiently neutered by the human quick default to denial. However Marla, remembering my story about the old doc who confronted the well intentioned pros, was proceeding to see if she could stir up some community activism through these unsuspecting elders. Evidence was popping up on reserves all over the country about the effectiveness of organizations like MADD (Mothers Against Drunk Drivers). Why shouldn't the same strategy work for diabetes, or domestic abuse or for that matter, substance abuse? Maybe we were on to something. Nothing mobilizes a community as much as a bunch of women pissed off at something or other.

* * *

"Doc, that's a pretty good thing you guys are doing over there. Do you think you got a chance to make it work?"

Chief Wah-Shee is referring to Marla's diabetes project. He knows that a lot of his people have the curse but it is only one of the clouds on his horizon.

"I don't know if we can get anything going or not. We can give the nudges and provide some support but it is up to your people to build it."

Like a lot of leaders the chief gets a little edgy when something involving a lot of work and expense gets tossed back to him. He paused a bit and allowed a brief "We'll see." Something else seemed to be on his mind.

"We just got started on that audit and I lost my accountant."

"What happened? Did you fire her already?"

"Didn't they tell you? She was only here one day and she got hurt when she ran her car into a tree on the way back to Fort Mac. The EMT's tell me she was acting kind of weird when they picked her up. She was well strapped in and only bust her arm. The airbags did their job and she didn't bust up her head or nothing but the EMT's said she was acting weird all the way back to your place."

This was news to me.

"I hadn't heard. Was she pissed or something?" The chief looked at me and didn't smile. "She'd better not have been. It happened about twenty minutes after she left here. Your other doc saw her and sent her up the road to the hospital. I haven't heard from her since."

Louise hadn't mentioned the incident other than to say that Aziz sent someone up with a busted arm. I made a mental note to check things out when I got to the clinic. We chatted about a few other things that seemed to be on his mind and he brought me up to date on some of the politics and little intrigues that seemed to ebb and flow through the community from time to time.

I was getting to like and respect this chief. He was pretty well educated and seemed to actually care about his people. It helped that he was a successful businessman. His hotshot service must be making him more than a few bucks. Renée, his wife, had been to my clinic a couple of times with their two little girls. They were well dressed and looked like they had just stepped out of an ad for Oshkosh. I hoped that he would get a handle on his legal problem soon. These things tend to boil up and sweep anyone involved into yesterday's news.

As I leave his office I get the feeling I'm missing something that could be important. The story about the accountant keeps bugging me and as I head into the health clinic I motion to Louise to come in and shut the door. She looks at me with a bit of a frown and asks "What's up?"

"Tell me about that accountant with the busted arm." She looks at me as if to say "What's to tell" then sits down and asks, "Something wrong?"

"The chief told me she was acting more weird than she should have after that fender bender."

"I guess she was acting weird. She kept crying and saying a ghost jumped out of the ditch and scared her. We thought she might just be in shock but she hadn't lost any amount of blood and other than the pain from her arm she seemed ok. Dr. Aziz grabbed a few samples of blood from her for the usual tox stuff and gave her a shot for the pain, checked her out pretty thoroughly and sent her on."

"What did the blood work show?"

"Nothing special. One of the samples said tox screen indeterminate whatever that means."

"Do we still have some samples in the lab fridge?" a pause and a look, "Sure".

I learned a long time ago that sometimes you've got to ask the right questions of the right people to get the right answer. I told Louise to send the sample to a lab in Vancouver that specializes in possibly suspicious blood samples. I made sure she would know to send along a brief history of the victim who donated the sample. This was probably overkill and would come back as a dead end but the nagging in the back of my brain needed to be switched off. That done I turned my attention to the day's routine.

There is a small flat screen television hanging from the wall in the little waiting room and it is usually tuned to some kids program The reception is good and the programs seem to be a better way of distracting my little patients than the old method of letting them play with a bunch of dirty old plastic toys that they seem to want to throw at every one walking through the door. Today someone has tuned in the 24 hour news channel and there are scenes of burning cars surrounded by ambulances and fire trucks. I wasn't paying much attention until someone thumbed the mute to off and the sound of a news anchor describing a scene of carnage somewhere in the world made me look up. This was another of those suicide bombings that seem to happen daily. I'm glad we don't have to worry about that here but with our pipelines and big oil sands projects I'm sure we could be a target if the crazies ever run out of people across the pond to hate.

There is actually a fairly big population of Middle East people in this area of the province. Last stats I saw had the aboriginal population about the same as the south and south east Asian population but half of the aboriginals live in the rural communities. Most Asians live in the city. I'm not aware of any hot issue conflicts between the two groups but there are definitely undercurrents of racial mutterings on both sides of the fence. It's impossible to be politically correct and totally frank at the same time. However most of the citizens are careful and there seems to be harmony between ethnic groups unless some crazies act up somewhere else in the world. With the latest round of home grown terrorism down east there seems to be a growing amount of Islamophobia spreading through social media and there actually have been a few demonstrations outside one of the mosques in Fort Mac I hoped it would all settle down and blow over. We have enough trouble with drugs and trauma and the inevitable domestic abuse. We don't need any terrorist activity around here.

11

Jozeph Laszlo pushed his chair back and took a sip of his excellent Jean-Pierre Moueix Pomerol. It was a woody Bordeaux that finished off the Schnitzel served in the discreet little Czech bistro hidden away in downtown Edmonton. He looked forward to his trips to town and a chance to dine here where on any given night some influential politician or deputy minister could be found and occasionally buttonholed for a mutually beneficial discussion. On this occasion he was the guest of Wilfred Natannah.

"Have you put that matter of the accounting snoop to rest yet?" he asked quietly while staring intently into the nervously shifting eyes of his host.

"For the time being I hope. That little potion you were able to get to me put her into la la land pretty quickly but she survived the crash. However she hasn't been back to the reserve and as far as I know she is just getting back to work. We'll keep our eye on her. Dawn managed to get into the files and get rid of the paper trail so if she comes back there won't be anything to find." Wilfred was confident that they were in the clear and he wanted to show Midnight Sun's legal eagle that he, Wilfred could be depended upon to keep things under control.

Jozeph regarded Wilfred for a few minutes and both sipped their wine while considering their next move. Jozeph didn't like loose ends and he hadn't come this far by being reckless. Still, the scheme he had concocted was both clever and complex and it would take someone a lot smarter than him to unravel it…and there weren't many around smarter than him.

Wilfred broke the silence asking, "What the heck was in that stuff you gave me to spike her tea?"

"You don't have to know. Just make sure you get rid of the rest of the tea leaves before someone tries to use it."

"Don't worry. It's long gone and no one suspects a thing."

"I hope for both our sakes you're right." The lawyer turned his thoughts to another issue.

"We need some action on that reserve that will put the police chief out of his depth and discredit him so the band can beef up the force with some private security; our private security. Our Asian partners are getting anxious that there are too many people snooping around and may clue into our enterprise. The CEO of Midnight Sun has no idea what we are up to and we have to make sure it stays that way. Here's what I want you to do."

He spent the next half hour outlining his plan and then got up and slipped unobtrusively away. Wilfred watched him leave, wiped the beads of sweat that had started to collect on his forehead and proceeded to finish the bottle of Bordeaux. "Goddamn shyster. They're all the same…Asshole!!"

* * *

The Air Canada flight from Gandhi International Air Port in New Delhi lifted off and climbed, turning slowly to the North West heading for Frankfurt. Adam Mir settled back for the flight anxious to eventually get back home to Fort McMurray. He had spent the last three weeks visiting relatives in Kashmir and attending the wedding of his cousin whom he had never met before. Adam worked as a geological engineer at one of the big oil sands projects and loved to travel and indulge his passion of photography every chance he got. Still single and earning good money he thought nothing of grabbing his backpack and taking off to some distant part of the planet. In his carry-on he had a portfolio of his best photos he had taken along to show his uncle and family. These he artfully arranged with sections of maps depicting the area where the photos originated. He was proud of his work and planned to publish it in a format for coffee table gifts.

Sitting next to Adam was a stranger who made a couple of attempts to start a conversation. Adam was not overly shy but was sleepy and wanted to pass the time snoozing. However the stranger was polite but persistent and actually engaging. He seemed to be genuinely interested in Adam's profession and his work at Fort Mac As they swapped stories Adam was persuaded to talk about his photography passion and he grabbed the backpack to pull out the portfolio. A few topo maps and pamphlets on the oil sands fell out as he was taking the portfolio from its protective case. Thinking nothing of it he stuffed them back into the pack and closed it. They spent the next hour talking about his pictures. His new found friend agreed they would make a great book.

The trip passed uneventfully and eventually after some 24 hours later and one stop at Frankfurt where he changed planes Adam eventually landed at Vancouver. He grabbed his stuff and headed with the herd of passengers to the Canadian Customs for the final necessary indignities before heading to Fort Mac. The lineup was crowded and noisy but moved along efficiently. He was getting hungry and looked forward to a beer and sandwich before taking off for Edmonton and Fort McMurray. It was not unusual for Adam to have a beer once in a while. Though Adam's family in Kashmir were originally Muslims his mother was Canadian born to an Irish family and his father was Kashmiri by birth who travelled to Canada as a youngster. He had wanted Adam to follow in his footsteps and eventually take over his very successful communications company back in Edmonton. However Adam preferred rocks and chemicals and got his degree in Geological engineering.

The line moved along and finally the customs guy signaled him over and reached for his passport. Adam thought nothing of it when the guy looked it over a couple of times then consulted a list in front of him. However when the officer motioned for another customs officer to come over Adam felt the familiar tightening of his gut and scalp that always happened when he was subjected to the damn profiling that seemed to be more frequent at international airports.

"Sir, you will have to come with me" What the hell? He stepped out of the line and followed the custom cop to an office.

"What's the matter?" he asked the back of the guy who said nothing and turned into a passageway with a door at the end. Opening the door he motioned Adam inside and said "Wait here." This had never happened before. There must be a mistake. He hoped they would sort it out soon. He didn't want to miss his flight.

The door closed behind him and he looked around the room. It looked a little familiar and his photographer's eye surveyed the setting and it suddenly hit him. This looked similar to the room where the cops beat the poor guy to death a few years back. That had been in the news and there had been enquiries and court cases about the affair. Suddenly he was afraid.

* * *

"Mr. Mir. It has come to our attention that you are in possession of materials that may pose a risk to the security of Canada." Adam Mir was stunned.

"What do you mean?" he stammered. What the hell was this nightmare that was unfolding? He didn't have a clue what they were talking about.

"May I see what you are carrying in your backpack?"

Adam had no idea if they could demand that without a warrant but he didn't want to seem uncooperative. There was nothing in his backpack and it had never been out of his sight. He opened it up and laid the stuff out on the table; a change of clothes, the allowed toiletries, a couple of pocket books, and his collection of maps, pamphlets and his portfolio.

"Mr. Mir, why do you have these maps? What is the purpose of your visit? "

"What visit? I'm on my way home. What the hell is all this about?"

"Please watch your language Mr. Mir and answer our questions."

"What questions? You asked me what the purpose of my visit was. I'm not visiting anywhere. I'm a Canadian and I'm on my way home."

The cop sat there for a few seconds then replied,

"Perhaps you forgot I just asked why you had these things." He pointed to the maps, brochures and the portfolio.

"Those are my personal property. I took those pictures and I own those maps. I picked up the brochures at the Travel Information counter at the Fort Mac airport." Now he was getting angry. It was all he could do to stop himself from calling these assholes a bunch of racists.

"Will someone please tell me what is going on?"

"Mr. Mir we have received information from a confidential informant that you recently visited Kashmir and are suspected of providing information about a vital part of Canada's energy infrastructure to undisclosed sources in India. We have been asked to apprehend you pending investigation by the RCMP."

By this time Adam Mir was really pissed off but he wasn't stupid. He told them as firmly and as politely as he could muster, "I know my rights. I demand to have a lawyer present before I speak to anyone."

The cop said "That's your right but we don't have to find a lawyer for you."

Adam took out his cell phone and at their nod of acceptance thumbed the number of his company's office, got his boss on the line, told him his problem and asked them to contact a lawyer to get him the hell out this place. The cops said. "I hope you don't mind waiting. This could take all day." They got up and left the room, locking the door behind them. A few moments later a Border Services Officer entered and told him to follow. He was led to a room with a table, a bench and a toilet. The door had a small observation window in it and there was a mirror, presumably two way, on the wall. They didn't take his cell phone but his backpack and belongings were removed. Funny they didn't take his phone. Maybe the idiots thought he was going to contact Osama's friends and wanted to catch him in the act. He stretched out as best he could on the bench and settled in for the wait.

Several hours later, long after his flight had left, a border cop and a young man in a suit entered the room.

The young guy introduced himself.

"My name is John Burrows. I'm a lawyer with Kapur and Company Immigration Lawyers. I have spoken with these gentlemen and have provided assurance that you are who you say you are. The RCMP have examined your effects and have determined that you pose no security risk." He added "I have been asked by your company to assist you in completing your journey."

Adam's feeling of relief was only perceptibly greater than his anger at the system and the unjust racial profiling. But first he would get out of this rat hole before he said anything else.

Burrows escorted him through the rest of the customs stuff and they entered the terminal proper. He suggested they grab supper and Adam, by now starved and thirsty readily agreed.

Over drinks and a steak presumably paid for by his company, Burrows filled him in on what had happened,

"We were able to determine that you sat next to a guy on the plane who spoke with you, confirmed you had a bunch of pictures and when you landed in Frankfurt he called to Border Services here in Vancouver. We haven't found out who he was or why he did it. The Mounties have opened up a file and hopefully this will all get straightened out. In the meantime I suggest you get a room here at the Fairmont and we'll get you out first thing in the morning."

* * *

Walking into the terminal at Fort Mac, Adam Mir noticed a small crowd and a guy with a big video camera. Several persons rushed over to him shouting "Mr. Mir, are you a terrorist"… "Did the police hold you for terrorism in Vancouver?"… "Are you going to sue them?"

A young lady with a mike pushed up close to him and demanded "What do you have to say about these charges?"

He angrily pushed through the crowd and hurried to the door where he jumped into a waiting cab.

"Those bastards have really done it to me," he growled to himself as he gave directions to the driver.

"Hey, aren't you that guy that was arrested in Vancouver last night. I saw it on TV. How come you're here?" Adam couldn't resist it. He said in his best matter of fact voice,

"I came back to set up a training camp out in the bush." Noting the dark face and beard and recognizing the accent of someone from the Middle East he said, "Do you want the location so you can join up?"

They arrived at his house and he paid the cabbie making sure he didn't leave a tip and, grabbing his suitcase and backpack, he headed for his front door. Someone had sprayed a target with a line through it that said "No Terrorists here." A bag of what looked like manure of some kind stood open at the entrance.

A feeling of dread he had never experienced in his young life came over him and he dropped his stuff on the floor, sank into a chair and sobbed uncontrollably.

* * *

Three weeks later a tanker driven by Saafir Kahn accompanied by Kabir, his brother careened around the corner coming into Burning lake crashing into the little Baptist church that had been in the community for over seventy five years. The resulting fire soon obliterated the landmark leaving a scarred ruin and a shocked community. The leased truck was destroyed but transportation safety inspectors on site quickly discovered that the rented tractor had a blown left front tire. Luckily there was no one killed. RCMP, after becoming suspicious that the men may have been illegally in Canada, took the two young drivers into custody to await the long process of court and inevitable deportation.

Somehow the rumor got started that the truck was sabotaged, and a crowd quickly gathered around the RCMP holding jail on the edge of town. It was Saturday night and the bar was just emptying. Word spread quickly and soon there were shouts of:

"Lynch those terrorist assholes!"

"Go back to sandland where you belong"!

The RCMP constable on site was on his phone to the next detachment looking for backup and also had calls into the reserve cops for help.

Fights between the pissed up pissed off bar patrons and some of the Lebanese crew from Midnight Sun broke out and things got ugly fast. With the arrival of the nearby reserve cops and the RCMP from the next detachment on their way in, order was restored and the town settled down. Burning Lake had never seen anything like that before. The Lebanese were lucky that the Prairie Dene were usually peace loving, unlike their cousins the Dogrib and Yellowknife. However, those same Dene didn't mind taking on a bunch of terrorists. Racism seems to be a card that every group plays if the provocation is strong enough. Ironically, most of the Lebanese were Christian.

Gilbert Ahnassay, the reserve police chief and half-brother to Chief Wah-Shee was sitting in a cruiser talking to the RCMP constable, comparing notes and digging for information. It was 2 a.m. and Burning Lake was now quiet. Turning from his laptop Constable Porter revealed,

"I got a hit on those two guys driving the truck. They have been on an apprehend list for 6 months after it was determined that they had slipped over the border down south and disappeared into the woodwork. I wonder what the hell they've been doing since then." He went on. "Those class one licenses were issued based on forged papers but we don't know where they got the forgeries."

Gilbert was quiet for a few seconds then wondered out loud, "Why here? Why now?"

He began to worry that something bigger than him was going on. He had only been in his position for six months and this stuff was a hell of a lot more serious than traffic tickets and drunks. He even thought he could get a handle on the escalating drug trade but terrorism was way out of his league.

"You can bet the politicians and the media will be screaming for more security for both the town and the reserve. Those guys at Midnight Sun are going to go ballistic. There must be ten or twenty guys from Lebanon working on that crew and they are going to feel the heat. Shit! What the hell do I do now? "

Taking a promise from Cst. Porter to keep him up to date Gilbert headed for home to catch up on his sleep. Tomorrow and next week were not going to be fun! There is something going on and probably has been going on for several months. This place, he mused, is not the place it seemed this time last year. The Americans were producing more oil than they were using, the American press were calling this land a cesspool of pollution, the oil prices were starting to drop, layoffs were threatened and yet some companies were still exploring, digging and drilling.

As he turned into his driveway the thought occurred to him that some new players were starting to show up and he had to start thinking more about what could come rather than what had gone. In the meantime that was enough for one night and he headed for his pillow.

Back in Burning Lake a light was still burning in the little motel on the outskirts of town.

Two men were sitting and looking at some maps. Fresh from a completed contract in Indonesia, these two gulf war vets were planning their next campaign. Their Asian employers wanted action and were not willing to wait too long.

One of the men yawned and stretched and smiled a comment "That was a pretty good night's work. I think we got a good start. A few more weeks of stirring the pot and I think we'll have something to show for all the risks."

His companion agreed saying, "So far things have moved pretty easily. We just have to make sure they stay that way. We'd better turn in and get some shut eye if we are going to get back to Edmonton tomorrow at a decent time". The light winked out and Burning Lake slept without a clue that it had a big bull's eye painted on its back.

* * *

In the sometimes violent world of political conflict a relatively new term was taking on a more prominent place in the discussions of news anchors and political pundits. Ecoterrorism was not, in fact new. The term had been around for years but was often dismissed as a catch all phrase for the tree hugging nut cases who preached that all the ice would melt and New York and the eastern seaboard were heading to be Atlantis number two. Ohio and Kentucky would suddenly become ocean front properties. But in the first decade of the new millennium these nut cases had all of a sudden become more sophisticated, more militant and more dangerous. They were well financed and as amoral as the various ethnic factions that continued to blow each other up with increasing frequency. Factor in the availability of well-trained special forces people no longer needed to defend their country and a rising force of mercenaries was not hard to imagine. Burning Lake was just one playground where these so called nut cases were hoping to play. Huge mining projects, pipeline construction at a feverish pace and new roads and infrastructure in a quiet backwater corner of civilized Canada were targets of opportunities that were destined to be exploited. Global greed and naked capitalism gone rogue were the new dimensions of ecoterrorism. Little did Gilbert Ahnassay realize the maelstrom that was about to invade his life.

12

The first month of winter in the northern extremes of the provinces can be pretty ugly but today was cold and clear and there was no wind blowing. The town was quiet and only the regular buzz of traffic caused by the heavy trucks rumbling through from both directions alerts the folks that business as usual is once again the norm. Amy Pham drove slowly through the town and past the burned out site of the old Baptist church on her way to the reserve. She didn't call the chief beforehand because she wasn't sure what her status was. She had been in and out of hospital a couple of times getting her arm operated on. In addition she had seen a procession of shrinks and physios who tried to get her body and mind back to normal. She had never crashed a car before and hospitals were a new experience. In good shape from her constant diet of three mile runs almost every day before her crash, she was gradually getting back to

her former level of fitness. Her bosses at Abrahms and
Abrahms were very supportive and let her heal at her own rate.
In the last couple of weeks she had started to think about the
project at the reserve that had been cut short. Today she hoped
to see the chief and try again.

As she pulled in to the admin. building she noticed both the
chief's big Yukon as well as the reserve police cruiser. This
was going to be interesting she thought to herself. Dawn looked
up as Amy stepped through the door way into the office. The
two women looked at each other, Amy in some confusion and
Dawn in a poorly disguised look of fear and hostility.

"I'm here to see the chief."

Dawn glanced at the closed door to the chief's office and
said "He's busy."

"Maybe if you buzz him and tell him I'm here he'll let you
know when I can come back."

Amy could not figure out why the frosty reception but she
had just driven eighty or so miles and wasn't about to turn
around and leave just yet. Why the sullenness she wondered.

Dawn got up and knocked on the door, stuck her head
inside and said. "Someone to see you." She closed the door and
wordlessly sat down at her desk and began working at her
computer. A few minutes later the chief came out of the office,
saw her sitting there and exclaimed,

"Hey. Sorry. I didn't know it was you. Come on in and grab
a chair. Gilbert and I were just going over some stuff that can

wait. How have you been? Did you get fixed up OK after that nasty crash you had?"

Gilbert chimed in. "Sometimes those roads can be tricky especially if it is snowing but as I remember the roads were clear. Do you want to tell us what happened?"

Amy had already filed a report with the RCMP and settled with her insurance company and she wasn't sure this stuff was any business of the reserve chief. However she answered pleasantly.

"Everything is OK now. I must have fallen asleep on the road. That's never happened before and I sure hope it never does again."

Turning to Chief Wah-Shee she explained "I'm sorry I didn't get back to you sooner but things were a little hectic for a while. I'm back to work now and I wondered if you still want me to go ahead with the audit."

Chief Wah-Shee shuffled some papers on his desk and looked over to his half-brother and back to Amy and said,

"We were actually talking about the audit when you showed up. So much has happened around here in the last few weeks we thought we might put a hold on it. You probably heard about our little dust up a couple of weeks ago."

"Things have not been all that good between our people and the folks at Midnight Sun and we're not sure that we should stir the pot just now. That crew of Lebanese they have working for them keep pretty much to themselves but once in a while we get called to some dispute or fight or argument or some other B.S. between them and our people. I think we should hold off for a while. Sorry you had to drive all the way down here."

Amy was mystified by their reaction and, though she had intended to tell them of her preliminary findings of her analysis of the spread sheets she had emailed to her office, something made her hesitate. Reluctantly she stood up and said,

"Sorry to take your time. I hope we can do business sometime in the future."

Funny, this time Dawn didn't offer any tea. Odd. She shrugged and headed out. It was early afternoon and she was a little hungry so she headed through town and stopped at the bar for a sandwich. Oh what the hell, a beer might go well with the sandwich. As she sat there nursing her beer and chewing the BLT she listened to the music in the background and felt something, she wasn't sure what. It wasn't her fault she cracked up the car and now lost her contract. She didn't know whether to feel angry or hurt or both. She had never backed away from a challenge in her life and she wasn't about to now. But what could she do? Obviously she couldn't sit here and drink beer all afternoon. She still had eighty some miles to drive.

The bar was quiet with just a low hum of country music in the background when a man sauntered in and looked around. The bartender looked up and said "Hey doc. You here for your soup and sandwich special?"

Amy stared at the good looking guy who hadn't noticed her. He was relaxed, looked fit and was dressed casually. Unlike most of the dudes in the bush he was clean shaven and maybe even a little hot looking. She went back to her sandwich and reluctantly stopped staring before he caught her.

"Do you always stare at the customers when they come through the door?" she heard and with a start realized he was talking to her.

"I'm sorry. I didn't mean to stare. I didn't think you caught me".

"I didn't see you. I could feel your eyes across the room"

Amy blushed and reacted. "I bet you've used that pick up line a few times before."

He looked her over and asked "Do I know you?"

"You sure have a lot of old pickup lines." Why the hell did she say that?

He grinned and replied, "Sorry to tease you. It's just kind of unusual to see anyone in here this time of day. I usually hang out at the clinic down the street and I just came in for a bite between patients."

"Oh my god you're the doc. Last time I was here there was a cute little boy looking like Doogie Howser from Bollywood. In fact he looked after me when I crashed my car and bust my arm. I'm Amy Pham. I was just down here for a meet with the reserve guys."

"Hi Amy. We finally get to meet. I'm Paul Cross."

Without being invited, he pulled out a chair and sat down at her table. "Hope you don't mind if I join you. It beats sitting in the corner and staring at you."

It is not often I get to meet a classy lady in a small town pub. I'm always up for opportunity and this was too good an opportunity to pass up. She had sparkling green-gray eyes that looked like they had been encrusted with tiny grains of diamonds. Her smile after she quit blushing was captivating and friendly but behind it sat a trace of cloud that she seemed to be trying too hard to conceal.

"How did your meeting go? Chief Wah-Shee told me that he might get you involved in some reserve business. I hope I haven't betrayed a confidence but he brought up the matter a couple of months ago. In fact he asked me if I knew anyone who could help discreetly with some accounting problems he was running into. Louise, our nurse came to my rescue and mentioned your name."

She frowned and glanced around at the empty pub as if to make sure no one was listening then replied.

"I don't know what the hell is happening around here. The chief asked me to look into some irregularities he'd discovered in recent contracts. I just got started when I wrecked my car and was out of commission for a couple of months. You probably heard. Anyhow, I drove down here today without letting them know I was coming and you'd think I'd walked into the place with moose turds on my shoes."

She wasn't making much sense but I could see that she was troubled.

"What did he tell you?" I'm not much for being subtle.

"Oh he was very polite but a lot more distant than the first time I met him. He said he didn't want to stir the pot with Midnight Sun because of the tensions between their crew and his people. I didn't buy that but what could I say? I must admit I'm pretty pissed but I guess I should have called a lot earlier to see if he was still interested in our services. I was so upset that I didn't tell him that I had emailed a few documents to myself so I could examine them more closely. And then the reserve cop was there and I thought maybe I shouldn't mention it and now I'm here blabbing all this stuff to you and I just met you. I shouldn't of had that beer."

Sensing that I should be serious for a change I assured her, "Of course what you just said is confidential so you don't have to worry about me and Louise would gnaw her arm off before she mentioned anything that happened in the office."

Amy smiled and brightened with an embarrassed "Thanks doc. I don't usually sit around the bars looking for shoulders to cry on but your shoulders seemed to happen by at the right time"

Was she hitting on me? I should be so lucky.

"Oh I should let you know. After I heard that you had been brought to our place after your crash I pulled your file and sent away your blood tests for another look see. Chief Ahnassay said the EMT guys reported that you seemed to be a little more shook up than what is usual for a crash like that. I hope you don't mind. I guess I should have called you first but I didn't even know you and didn't want to upset you if nothing came of it."

Again that worried frown. "What do you mean blood tests. I thought nothing came of them. I didn't hear from anyone. The shrinks and their team at the hospital just told me I had a little post traumatic shock whatever the hell that is!"

I wished I had kept my mouth shut but it was her right to know. I told her that I didn't expect to find anything and that the shrinks were probably right.

It was getting late and I had to get back to work so I stood up and said, "Nice to finally meet you, Amy Pham. Drop by for coffee next time you come through." I wondered if she would take up my invitation or if she thought I might be hitting on her. I was…sort of.

* * *

I'm just seeing my last patient and looking forward to an evening by my fireplace, a single malt at my side and some Etta James floating out of my Bose. I have a bunch of reading to catch up on and never seem to get the chance. We usually get a good assortment of newspapers so I have the chance to see the world from every angle but lately all the angles are straight lines. The crazies over there are getting uglier and it seems to be spilling over here. Ever since that tanker took out the church we have been wondering if we could ever be targeted. I sure as hell hope not. I've never worked a war zone and I never want to.

Oh shit! Chief Wah-Shee and his brother come through the door with thunder clouds surrounding their faces. What now?

"Hey Chiefs" I greet them with my usual respect. "What's up?"

They head into my office herding me ahead, shut the door and sit down.

Chief Gilbert starts out. "Doc, you ever seen Muriel Jacobs in here with a bust up face?"

"C'mon guys. You know I can't talk about who I see or don't see. What's this all about?"

I didn't know what they are talking about. I don't think I even know a Muriel Jacobs.

Gilbert led with, "She just came in and complained that she was beat up by a couple of Pakis. She was hitching a ride from the reserve where those Midnight Sun guys are working and these two Pakis picked her up, stopped on the way in and jumped her. She fought, got a busted face and they dumped her. That was last week and she finally got up the nerve to come in. She looks a little bruised but not too bad. We need someone to check her out so we have evidence if we catch these guys. We thought maybe she came to you."

"If she comes in I can check her but you guys will have to get her to agree to let me release information. These women aren't always happy to do that."

A few weeks back two women went missing and their bodies were discovered in a shallow grave about forty miles south of here. They had been brutally beaten and sexually assaulted. Since that time the community was awash in rumors and speculation. They had been last seen walking along a roadway about a mile from the reserve settlement and then seemed to have disappeared without a trace until their bodies showed up after a fluke discovery. A trapper walking his line discovered the shallow grave that had been unearthed presumably by animals. Now with the abduction of this woman Jacobs the rumors will gain traction. The speculation putting a couple of east indians into the mix was undoubtedly what was troubling the young chiefs.

David Wah-Shee spoke up and added a little fuel to the fire.

"Those guys working for Midnight Sun are worried about trouble with the locals and are talking about bringing in a bunch of rent-a-cops to beef up security. We have our own deputies and I'm not happy about having strangers parading through our land providing muscle for a crew of workers. This thing is getting out of control. The Jacobs thing is the first break for us and I'm directing Gilbert to work it for all he can get." He went on. "I know you can't fudge the privacy rules but we need a better description of those Pakis from her. She is scared shitless

and won't talk to us. We just thought if you can see her and get
her to open up we can get a break. I don't want to go head to
head with Midnight Sun until we sort out the contract they
have."

What am I now, a father confessor? I don't do this stuff.

"David, I'm a doc. I can't be seen as an agent of anyone. If
they can't confide in me they won't talk to me. If I lean on
them to be more open with you then they will think I'm
working for you. You know how these rumors start." This
conversation was dragging me to places I didn't want to go so I
tried to change the subject.

"How are you getting along with your forensic audit? Are
you making any progress?"

The two chiefs looked at each other then back at me.

"What audit?" asked Gilbert the cop.

"C'mon Gilbert. I know you were looking to get an audit on
the Q.T.. Chief Wah-Shee filled me in almost the first day I was
here. He asked me and Louise if we knew anybody that could
help and she suggested that accountant from Abrahms and
Abrahms. That was the one that crashed her car on the way
home from your place." I looked David Wah-Shee in the eye
and asked, "Has she made any progress or is that none of my
business."

Time for true confessions. They want info and I want info
though I'm not sure why I want to be involved. Maybe the

chance meeting at the pub with the spectacular Ms. Pham had
something to do with it.

David Wah-Shee paused a beat then said, "OK, she was in
last week for a few minutes looking to take up where she left
off but with all this going on I didn't want to stir the pot so I
kind of blew her off. Maybe I screwed up. I got so many loose
ends flying in the wind that I can't pay attention to my
business. This damn politics is no fun."

"Let's see." I offered. "You beat the godfather and his gang
then got snookered in a deal with a big energy company then a
bunch of drugs start showing up on the reserve then a couple of
bodies turn up followed by a complaint that a couple of east
Indian workers had assaulted a local. In the meantime a couple
of illegal aliens trash our landmark church and a home grown
east Indian from the big city gets accused of bringing terrorism
to the patch. Is that all that's worrying you?"

Maybe I could get something out of this discussion after all.
I really would like to see the elusive Ms. Pham again. What a
devious devil. I continue.

"Chief, why don't you bring back the accountant, do your
audit and if anything concrete turns up go public. I'm sure you
will have the support of most of your people and then maybe
you can renegotiate with Midnight Sun and save the world from
terrorism and I can get along with the simple practice of
medicine. In the meantime I've got a half dozen patients

waiting for me and Louise is going to scalp me if I don't get back to work. Or am I being politically incorrect?"

"Keep talking like that, Doc, and I'll scalp you myself" he grinned. "And I don't give a shit about politically correct."

13

It's five o'clock in the afternoon and time to close up and go home. This has been a really busy week and all the politics and reserve dramas have been pushed into the background by our 'flu campaign and community diabetes project that Marla has birthed and mothered to a prominent place in the consciousness of the town. She's got speakers coming in and giving pep talks and even lined up some high powered facilitators to come in and train the trainers. If she keeps this up I'll be out of a job. In spite of the 'flu immunization push we still see too many cases and I've been kept busy running out to see some old folks who live in around the edge of town. Yeah, house calls are still in vogue around here. Actually they are pretty interesting. They even offer you a sandwich and coffee once in awhile.

I'm just about to head for the door when the phone rings. I hesitated for a moment and am just about to say screw it but my conscience gets the best of me and I grab the phone.

"Paul, you old fraud, what the hell are you doing? Where are you? Where the hell is Burning Lake?" I recognized the voice of my old class mate Jeremy Butler. He was the sharpest tack in our class and went on to be a pathologist specializing in clinical pharmacology and forensic toxicology. He now works in Vancouver for a place called Lifetime Labs.

"Jeremy, great to hear from you. Did you get that sample we sent you? Maybe I should explain."

"Yeah that would help. What the hell have you gotten yourself into? You really threw us a curve ball."

"What do you mean?" I suddenly feel a little tension building and wonder what now?

Jeremy launched into a story that was to change my life and put me through a wringer over the next several months.

"We ran that sample against our standard panel of substrates and turned up nothing. I figured you wouldn't have sent it unless you were suspicious of something. I've only been working here for five years but we have substrates that go back over thirty years. I ran the sample twice against the old stuff and got the same answer twice. You must have turned over a rock up there wherever there is. Where is Burning Lake anyhow? Do you have a big population of Czechs and Hungarians?"

Was he smoking something? "Huh?"

"That sample was Doriden or Glutethimide, something that was around before you were born. It was pulled from the market about thirty years ago and you can't even buy it anymore."

"What is it?"

"It's a high potency sedative that was pulled because of its tendency to become addictive. You could still get it in the early eighties but after that it was only available in some of the eastern European countries." He went on. "That sample was loaded with Doriden. Somebody must have slipped your patient a mickey but don't ask me where they got it."

I stammered a thanks and after a quick exchange of personal stuff we broke off.

I sat down in a cold sweat and tried to process what I had just heard. What the hell do I do with that information? The lovely Ms. Pham had just become a target of a criminal action. I wasn't about to spread this to the local cops and I needed more info before I could involve the Mounties. We have enough trouble here without opening this can of worms.

Tomorrow looked like a light day and Louise could probably hold the fort here so I made a quick decision searched my address book and made a call.

"Abrahms and Abrahms. How may I direct your call?"

"This is Dr. Paul Cross in Burning Lake. I'm trying to reach Ms. Amy Pham. Is she available for a couple of moments?"

"One moment sir and I will connect you to her extension." That was easy. What the hell do I say when she answers? I resolve to play it cool and try not to act like the asshole I sometimes come across as when I'm nervous. Why did I leave Riyadh?

"Amy Pham here. Can I help you?"

"Ms. Pham this is Dr. Paul Cross here," So far so good. "I would like to talk to you."

"So talk Dr. Paul Cross. I'm all ears." Now what? Good thing she couldn't see my ears. They were hot and I'm sure bright red.

"Ms. Pham, something has come up." Whoops. That didn't come out right. I hope she has a sense of humor! "I just got a report on that blood sample. It doesn't point to anything that is a risk to you but I need to talk to you about it and I would just as not soon discuss it over the phone. Are you in your office tomorrow? I could be there sometime in the mid-morning."

"Doctor Cross, you're scaring the hell out of me."

"I'm sorry Amy. Can I call you Amy?" Mr. Cool. "I don't mean to scare you and this isn't anything to do with your health." Wow, now she will really think I'm hitting on her.

"You can call me anything you want but I'm calling you Doctor Cross until you tell me what the hell you're babbling about!"

Was I babbling? "I know this is alarming and confusing but the information I have has nothing to do with your continued good health. I'd rather not say anything more until I can discuss it more fully with you."

"Doctor Cross do you always make ninety mile house calls?" Now she was teasing me.

"Only once in a while." and only when I have trouble with tongue tie. "Let's leave it at that and I'll fill you in if you let me come tomorrow." Shit! What did I just say?

She laughed but I don't know at what and she offered. "Ten a.m., my office and don't be late or you won't get coffee." She hung up.

* * *

Doriden or Glutethimide, its generic name, is a sleeping medication that has been banned in Canada and the United States since sometime in the 1980's. It is highly addicting, has unpleasant side effects including visual disturbance with visual blurring and occasionally hallucinations. It is nasty stuff and other than some very small amounts for scientific research its manufacturer was allowed to distribute only very small amounts to research labs. No wonder the lab in Vancouver had relegated it to the back shelves years ago.

What the hell am I going to tell Amy Pham tomorrow or even worse, what am I going to ask her? She's going to think I'm nuts. Also, sometime I'm going to have to decide who else I tell. Someone tried to put Amy out of commission just when she was starting the audit. That was scary. Too scary for me to even think about. I headed home for what I knew was going to be a restless night and tried to make some sense of what I thought I knew.

14

The road was clear and dry when I headed out in the dark for the hour and half drive to Fort Mac. Luckily it was early in the morning and there were fewer trucks than usual on the two lane road. The other danger I was alert for was an errant moose wandering out for a stroll but it was a little early so I wasn't taking much of a risk as I pushed the jeep to a hundred twenty klicks. I figured I could get there early enough for breakfast and then figure out how I was going to deal with this at that time.

My mind kept flashing back to the events of the last few months and I thought there were too many coincidences happening too close together. I'm not a conspiracy theorist but this stuff should make for a good movie if it wasn't so scary in real life. Someone was actually trying to harm the young accountant I was speeding off to meet. And if the information I had ever became known then I might have to go into hiding. I thought again about the truck that demolished the church. Was it a coincidence that a couple of undocumented characters should lose a wheel coming into town and crash a rented truck? I hadn't heard any more about the investigation. Nobody was talking but the truckers all had their theories and they all pointed to one thing. Sabotage!

Abrahms and Abrahms had an office at a downtown location just east of the Athabasca River, It was easy to find and parking was little problem. I still had an hour before my meet so I stopped at Smitty's for breakfast. They always had papers to read so I grabbed one as I waited for my omelet to arrive. There was a story about vandalism at the new mosque and the terrorist panic was still gaining traction. I read another story about the guy that was detained at the Vancouver airport. Evidently the cops were focusing on his uncle in Kashmir. The company that employed the young engineer swore to his patriotism and reliability and harshly criticized the gossip that was going through the community. Yet there were letters speculating that all Muslims should be watched and deported if they even looked suspicious. This place was getting ugly.

I was told to wait when I asked the lady at the reception desk if Ms. Pham was available. I was about ten minutes early but I didn't want to miss coffee. She suddenly appeared in front of me with her megawatt smile and teasing voice but I sensed a bit of cautious reserve as she guided me into her office and closed the door.

"You don't get coffee until you tell me what this is all about." I didn't know if she was still teasing or if she was half serious. I wasn't about to take a chance so I simply said

"I'm sorry to frighten you but I need to find some stuff out before I know if it is serious."

I sat without asking permission and said. "That blood test showed you had a large amount of sleeping medication on board when you crashed."

"Are you out of your mind?" she cried. "That's crazy. I never use sleeping pills."

I tried my best to play the thing down but I didn't have a lot of wiggle room.

"Amy, the stuff they found has not been available in North America for twenty five years. I have no idea how it showed up in your blood test unless you can tell me."

She sat and shook her head a few times and said, "This is nuts." She went on. "I had a sandwich at the pub where I met you. That was about noon and I never had anything else after...uh oh."

"What?" I asked. "Why the uh oh?"

"I don't know if this had anything to do with it but before I left, the chief's secretary made me a cup of tea. It tasted a little bitter but I thought she was just trying to be nice so of course I didn't say anything." A look of puzzlement mixed with a sudden look of fear clouded over her face. "You don't think she spiked the tea with anything do you? Holy shit!"

She didn't look ready to cry but more like she was ready to kill. Remind me never to piss her off.

"Amy, I came down here to tell you myself because I don't know what to do with this. I should turn it over to the cops but which ones and what happens then? What are you going to do if the chief asks you to do the audit? Has he asked you to come back?"

I wasn't about to tell her about my talk with the chief. I was in deep enough already.

"No but if someone is trying to screw around with me I'm not going to run away." The fire in those sparkling green grey eyes was frightening and I thought to myself that this lady better be careful. This is not reality TV.

We kicked it around for an hour reviewing all the events then she showed me the spread sheets she had emailed to her office and went through her suspicions. By the time we were finished I knew that something dirty was going on but I still was at a loss to figure out what to do. It was getting close to noon so she suggested we skip out for the rest of the afternoon and grab a meal at a quiet pub that she sometimes frequented. Knowing I had to drive home I wasn't keen on loading up on beer so I said OK to the food but begged off the booze. If I wasn't expected back until tomorrow afternoon I could have blissfully settled in with the gorgeous Ms. Pham and seen where the afternoon took us. I hated to dump this news on her and then leave her in the lurch. She looked like she could handle herself but this was big stuff and she might be more at risk than either of us realized.

We seemed to be hitting it off pretty good and the meal was better than most pub food. Instead of talking about the real reason we were here we spent the time talking about our respective lives. She was easy to talk to but she had a little reserve and didn't volunteer much about her life. As a matter of fact it was like pulling teeth to get any personal information out of her. I did find out she wasn't with anyone but that she had been seeing someone up to a half a year ago. However, it flamed out when he got transferred back to eastern Canada. She was curious about my answer when she asked me if I was married.

"I am and I'm not." I was reluctant to dump a bunch of personal stuff on her but next thing I knew I was telling her about running away to Burning Lake to do what I wanted to do most. It sounded selfish and cheesy. She didn't miss a beat.

"Better to find out what you want to do early on and get it out of your system than live in quiet desperation the rest of your life."

Wow! Was she an accountant or a shrink? I filled her in on my situation but brushed around the edges a bit so she wouldn't think I was trolling for sympathy. All I knew about her was that she was smart, tough and gorgeous and maybe even available. I should be so lucky!

It was getting late and I didn't want to leave but caution got the best of me and I stood to go.

"Thanks so much Paul, for coming to my rescue. I know there is something serious happening and I'll be careful. If the chief phones I'll definitely accept. Those crooks are going to find out that I don't scare easily." I didn't want to say "But I do." I didn't want her to find out I'm a wimp.

The drive home was uneventful but I couldn't get my mind off the fact that someone had deliberately tried to kill this gorgeous lady. I started to get mad. Time to go active. A plan started to form in my mind.

* * *

The work that Jeremy Butler did often brought him into contact with all sorts of people involved in security and criminal investigation. He also associated with a lot of cops who were involved in criminal conspiracies. I guessed this included threats to national security. Canada doesn't have a CIA like the states but has an agency called Canadian Security Intelligence Service or CSIS. CSIS is Canada's agency on national security matters. It is responsible for conducting national security investigations and security intelligence collection. Also it has a role in covert activities both in Canada as well as in other parts of the globe. In this way its mission is a little different than the mission of the CIA.

It occurred to me that Jeremy would be my best bet in figuring what to do next but this wasn't something that could be handled over the phone or risked to the insecurities of email. And then another thought struck me. If I could talk Amy into coming to Vancouver with me maybe we could meet someone to help us fix this mess. Was that my motive or was I just trying to talk myself into pursuing this gorgeous lady. Who cares? It still looked like a good idea. Until then I resolved not to talk to the local cops.

The thought of getting away for a few days particularly with an interesting and attractive travel companion got my juices flowing and next thing I noticed I was flying along at about thirty klicks over the speed limit. Slow down Paul boy! This is no time to hit a moose or a tanker. I made a mental list of the things I had to do to make this work.

It was dark when I got back to Burning Lake so I headed straight to my place anxious to get a good night sleep so I could work out this plan with a clear head. In spite of the potential danger from unknown evil bad guys I felt an energy that had been missing in my life since I left Riyadh.

Next morning I was in my office well before the morning parade of ill or anxious or both.

Jeremy was easy to track down and he agreed to meet with me and told me to let him know when I would be arriving so he could pick me up. I didn't let him know I might have a traveling companion. Next I chased down Jordan Aziz and after some small talk I told him that Amy had surfaced and thanked him for his good work. I didn't let him know about the blood work. The less said the better. We didn't need a long list of speculators. Jordan actually was able to arrange to be free all next week and was more than agreeable to cover for me. I think he liked the rural practice and the surface tranquility of my community. Good thing he didn't know the full story.

Now for the big challenge. How am I going to talk Amy Pham into picking up and heading to Vancouver with me? What if she tells me to get lost? What if she thinks I have an ulterior motive or two? I can just see it now.

"Hi Amy. Paul here. Do you want to come to Vancouver with me? Drop everything you've got going and pack your bags. Oh, shall I get one hotel room or two?" Suddenly I was getting cold feet. What can I say to her to make this thing work?

I learned a long time ago that the best way to deal with a crisis honestly is to be honest. She could draw whatever conclusions she wanted to. It still didn't change the urgency of countering the real threat. My hands were already sweating when I picked up the phone.

* * *

Amy Pham was in her office early and continued to pour over the spread sheets she had emailed to her office before the whole project went off the rail. She couldn't believe someone had tried to kill her. Was that right or was it just a crazy mistaken conclusion bolstered by an incorrect blood sample. She wasn't about to be stampeded into leaving town or running away but Paul was right. They couldn't go to the cops without more evidence and so far all she had were suspicions based on some unexplained entries over several weeks. Fairly inconsequential sums had popped up where there was no explanation for either their original source or ultimate destination. Perhaps she could combine them and maybe aggregate them into groups…or maybe list them by dates and look for a pattern…or maybe look for duplications that could not be explained. She couldn't spend all her time on this without a further commitment from the Indian Band. That wouldn't be fair to her company. But without more study she had no evidence or clues. This was not just an accounting problem. It could be a life and death challenge.

She was just getting up to get a coffee when her phone rang. "Now what?" She was in no mood to be interrupted.

"Hello" she growled in to the phone, immediately regretting her lack of professional voice.

"Maybe I should hang up and phone when you're in a better mood." Paul, she thought. Why is he phoning so soon?

"No, don't hang up! I'm sorry. I was thinking about what these damn spread sheets mean. There's something there but I can't see it. It's so damn frustrating."

"Hi Amy. I didn't mean to kid you. We are both in a rut over this stuff but I thought maybe we could come at it from a different angle."

"What do you mean? What angle" Did he have more info?

"Are you up for some adventure and open to a crazy idea?" He sounded enthused and just a little shy, she thought.

"Sure if it doesn't involve crashing my car again. What are you thinking?"

"Would you like to visit Vancouver?"

What the heck? What's going through that brain of his? She waited a few seconds and heard "Amy. You still there?"

"Yeah Paul I'm still here. I'm wondering what me going to Vancouver would prove. Isn't that where you sent my blood sample? What, do they want more blood? Couldn't someone here take the sample and send it to Vancouver?" This was getting weirder every minute.

He answered in what she thought was a more careful tone of voice than was necessary.

"I thought maybe we should go together and talk to someone"

What the heck is he proposing? Talk to someone? Who? Does he think I'm nuts? Is he hitting on me? Not that that would be such a bad thing.

She took a deep breath and answered as carefully as she could. She didn't want to give him any wrong ideas. "Paul, what do you have in mind? Who do you want us to talk to?"

Over the next several minutes he described his conversation with his pathologist friend then carefully explained a plan that would put them in touch with people concerned with national security and if this was considered only a criminal matter then those people could line them up with RCMP investigators on the Q.T. One way or other they had to chase this thing down or she would be looking over her shoulder for a long time.

"When do you think we should go?" she asked. There, she didn't say no. Would he read something into her answer she didn't intend or did she intend something unintentionally? Shit! This was getting too complicated too fast.

"I think I can get a locum doctor down here next week and we could set it up for Monday morning. Jeremy already promised me he would pick me up and take me to one of his contacts in CSIS. I didn't mention your name or that you might be coming with me. I didn't want to presume something and then go down in flames."

She laughed a little then said, "OK we go dutch all the way and I get my own room."

"Absolutely," he replied, breathing a sigh of relief. Already his mind was spinning to the next few steps he had to take. That damn chief better get her back on the payroll. This was not going to be a cheap adventure. He wondered what she knew about Vancouver or if she liked hockey.

Part IV

15

We landed in Vancouver with time change about a half hour after leaving Edmonton. The flight from Fort Mac was uneventful though a little strained as we made small talk and tried to figure out where we were heading and not a little apprehensive of where we were heading personally. There had only been a half hour wait between landing in Edmonton before boarding for Vancouver so there was little time to waste but we managed to grab a coffee and find a quiet corner free of prying ears. I listened carefully to Amy's analysis of the spread sheets though I know nothing about accounting except the fees the numbers guys charge me each year for my professional corporation. I had a hard time following her and had to butt in too frequently for my own comfort. She must have thought I was the most dense person she had ever met.

"How do you balance your own bank account?" she teased as she launched into yet another explanation about the difference between debit and credit. Everything seemed backward to what I had always believed. However I was extremely impressed with what she knew and what she had learned so far. The Indians were going to get a good deal if they ever got their act together. The bad guys had reason to fear her. Maybe that alone was a clue. Find the crooks on the sheet and we'd find the crooks who drugged her. I felt a growing urge to catch those guys and beat the shit out of them. Careful, Cross. You're taking this too personally. Besides you haven't been in a fight since midget hockey and you lost most of those.

The sky was clear and the flight over the mountains was stunning. She had talked me into taking the window seat because of her T.B. (that's tiny bladder to you non travelers.) I didn't mind and besides she kept leaning over me to get a look out the window and I kept getting dizzy from hyperventilating from her perfume and other things. Flying in the intimate privacy of an aircraft miles above the earth in the company of a beautiful woman is a thrilling and exciting experience. I hoped I didn't have to answer the call of nature anytime soon.

Before we left I called Jeremy and clued him in. He arranged for two rooms at the Airport Fairmont but was only able to get the rooms on two different floors. I wonder if he was protecting me from myself or just had a cruel sense of humor. We got off the plane and because we didn't think we'd actually be in Vancouver for long we had only brought carry-ons. I was impressed that I had met a woman who could go on a trip without taking all her possessions with her. Wisely I kept my comments to myself.

After registering at the hotel we headed for our rooms and agreed to meet in the bar in a half an hour. Jeremy would meet us there. I headed for my room for a quick shower and a chance to calm myself down and thought ahead to the unknown. I've chased a lot of adventures in the last five years but this one left me with a sense of high anticipation though a dark foreboding dread.

Jeremy was sitting in the bar nursing a single malt and Amy was nowhere to be seen. He had changed little since I had last seen him. Always a bit eccentric he was dressed in wrinkled Dockers and a black biker leather jacket was strewn sloppily over a chair. The painted tee he had chosen for the occasion read "Always be yourself unless you can be Batman then always be Batman." I'd seen that before a few times but the irony was not lost on me. I sat down and ordered my own single malt and we exchanged a few insults before we got into the reason we were here. I had my back to the entrance to the bar and was trying to spell out the problem in a little more detail when he looked up and let loose a low whistle.

"Holy shit Paul! Does she belong to you?" I turned and Amy was strolling over to where we were sitting and I gasped. She had travelled in a pair of jeans with a loose turtleneck and some sort of curling jacket and I wasn't prepared for the apparition that came out of her carry on.

Her long legs carried stylish gray green dress pants and she had a knitted onyx top with sleeves just past her elbows. The alternating shades of black and brown gave off a luminance that was offset by the broad gold necklace of vertical bands circling the front of her neck. She was stunning. I was too scared to talk because I knew I would stutter but before I could recover she reached the table, pulled out a chair and said "You must be Jeremy. Hi, I'm Amy".

I was relieved to see that my buddy was equally stunned and his high usually pale forehead was blushing deep red. In such a scenario the macho dudes usually drink single malts and the eye candy sips some white house wine. Not Amy. She signaled the waitress over and said "I heard you stock seventeen year Macallans. I haven't had that for a couple of years. My friend is paying so I'll have a double." I just about choked and Jeremy laughed so hard he just about spilled his drink.

"Were you two talking about me behind my back before I got here?" she queried with batting innocent eyes.

I thought I had better get this into a serious mode before the Amy show got out of hand.

"As a matter of fact we were. Jeremy said you must have had about a gram of that stuff on board to still have the level you tested at when the blood was drawn." You could probably have slept it off but it's pretty hard to drive a car in that condition. Those assholes really mean business."

Jeremy chimed in.

"After your call last week I got ahold of my CSIS friend and let him know what was going on. He is really interested and has come up with some intriguing stuff. Did you guys hear about the young Kashmiri engineer that was held up in customs here several weeks ago?" We both nodded wondering what that had to do with us. It had been in the news and mentioned a few times the latest after the vandalism at the Fort Mac Mosque.

"Anyhow," he went on, "They traced his trip from Delhi to Frankfurt and discovered that his seat mate was traveling under an assumed name on a forged passport. Surveillance identified him as Roberto Rubinowich and he is well known to Interpol as a prominent member of ELF." Amy and I stared at each other and she said, "You mean the Earth Liberation Front? What's that got to do with us?"

"I don't know but our friend from CSIS might be able to fill you guys in."

I knew that the CSIS office was over forty minutes away in Burnaby and already Jeremy was facing another couple of hours away from his work so I suggested that we would rent a car and head for the office ourselves. I think he was relieved not to have to kill a good chunk of the day playing limo driver for us so he answered. "Great idea. Thanks. My contact said you would be meeting a CSIS Intelligence analyst named Kelly

Fitzpatrick. I don't know anything about him but they know you are coming. Your meet is about an hour from now." He shook my hand, took a moment to feast his eyes on Amy once more, mumbled something about making me behave then turned and headed out.

Amy had to head back to her room for her coat, computer and documents so I headed to the desk to arrange the rental. My gorgeous companion wasn't kidding. She made me get the check.

* * *

Vancouver in the winter is often a crapshoot for weather and driving conditions but we were from north central Alberta and we were not easily intimidated. Traffic was heavy but not insane and we got to the Burnaby CSIS location and found ourselves being ushered into a small conference room to await the arrival of Officer Fitzpatrick. Unlike the US, Canada's feds are called officers, not agents; same breed, different kennels. We took a look at our materials and chatted about what was to come but we were still puzzled about the curveball we heard from Jeremy about ELF and the kid returning from Kashmir. What the hell did that have to do with anything?

The door opened and a slight young lady in business suit came in and said "Hi. I'm Kelly Fitzpatrick. I've just come from a briefing on this matter and I understand you folks have some important information for me."

Amy and I looked at each other, both thinking the same thing. What the hell have we gotten into? Because Amy had the papers and was the victim of the spiked drink we had decided beforehand that she should take the lead.

"I'm Amy Pham and this is Dr. Paul Cross. We have just arrived in Vancouver this morning at the suggestion of Dr. Jeremy Porter. I think your agency is familiar with him."

Officer Fitzpatrick replied, "Oh yeah. Jeremy. He keeps digging up weird info that we have to sort out. We always pay attention to his stuff because he has never sent us on a wild goose chase."

Like most people I have watched my share of spy thrillers and read the pop literature about the CIA and MI6 but this was not my idea of a super spy licensed to kill. I wondered what this plain Jane bureaucrat could do for us and she read my thoughts. "Yeah I know. You don't have to say it. I'm an intelligence analyst not a covert operator licensed to kill. I have never shot anyone and don't ever intend to. I'll leave that to the SWAT gorillas."

Amy didn't seem to be hesitant about spilling the story and she outlined the whole tale from beginning to end including the stuff about the reserve audit. I thought that stuff was supposed to be confidential but I guess it's not a good idea to hold back on the feds once you've dragged them onto the scene. When she finished she added, "The only thing that confuses us right now is what ELF has to do with our problem?" Ms. Fitzpatrick paused to digest the stuff she had just been told then said almost too nonchalantly, "Yeah, me too".

"What do you mean 'me too'?" I asked. "I thought you guys had this all figured out."

Kelly Fitzpatrick looked at me and asked "What's your stake in this? What's a doc got to do with criminal or terrorist investigations? How come you're here at all?"

She sort of pissed me off with her dismissal and my macho got the best of me and I barked, "If it hadn't been for me and my curiosity and suspicious nature neither of us would be here and you guys would have no idea that anything might be happening."

Amy sensed my annoyance and came to my rescue before I said anything stupid.

"Some bad guys tried to kill me when I was starting a forensic audit in a place where we are up to our necks in aboriginal against Muslim tensions. We thought you might be interested. If you don't think you are interested we'll just go back and tell what we know to the local RCMP constable and let the cops sort it out." She started to get up and gather up her things. Afraid that I was going to have to be a referee in a feminist pissing match I cut in.

"Maybe we should start over again. There are political tensions on the reserves back where we are from and it occurred to us that someone was trying to exploit the confusion for personal gain. We know that the reserve got screwed in the contract they signed with this Midnight Sun organization but we don't know if Midnight Sun is a player or just a victim like Amy." I added "The reason we are here is because we are not confident that just reporting our suspicions to the cops will keep us safe. We also are not confident that there is no overseas interest in disrupting the oil sands operations."

By this time Amy was sitting down again and appeared to have calmed down a little.

"Is the emergence of a possible link between a Canadian born Engineer from the Muslim community and a known ecoterrorist raise any questions in the CSIS world?" she asked. "And if so, is that linked even peripherally to our situation? If it isn't then you will have no trouble assuring us that I got caught up in a local criminal matter and we can turn this stuff over to the RCMP for further investigation."

Ms. Fitzpatrick pondered for a few minutes then said "Maybe we should make more inquiries before you do that. Would it be possible for you to proceed with your audit on the Q.T. but keep us in the loop?" She already knew the answer to that. There was no way a pro would sign a confidentiality agreement then pass all the info over to a spy agency.

Amy was way ahead of her on that. "How about you sending an officer to the chief of the Indian band and let him know your concerns and ask him for cooperation. I understand

you guys have an office in Edmonton. It shouldn't be too hard
to set that up. In the meantime, if he wants me to proceed and
also cooperate with CSIS then everyone is covered and we can
find these bad guys and gut them." The mental imagery was not
lost on either Ms. Fitzpatrick or me. Like I said, I'm not about
to piss off Amy Pham anytime soon.

Ms. Fitzpatrick pondered for a few seconds then replied,
"That sounds reasonable but I have to clear it with some of my
people. In the meantime I think I should tell you that we have
uncovered a tenuous connection between that ecoterrorist
Roberto Rubinowich and a security firm operating out of
Seattle. They have a satellite office in Vancouver and for some
time we have had them on a watch list."

"Huh" I exclaimed. "What the hell does that mean? Who
are these guys and what are they after?"

"We aren't sure. Their name keeps cropping up in a number
of our open files but so far they appear clean. This attempt on
Ms. Pham's life raises some questions that may give us an
opportunity to exploit. I can't give you any more info than that
because it is all classified but the firm listing in Seattle is public
knowledge that you could get from anywhere so I don't mind
telling you that for your own information. Just don't spread it
around that you got it from me."

She found the info and wrote it down and gave it to Amy
who looked at it but didn't comment. She then got our contact
info and promised to keep us in the loop through Amy. I guess

the ladies were bonding and keeping ol' Paul on the sidelines so he couldn't screw anything up.

It was getting late so we grabbed our rental and headed back to our hotel through Vancouver rush hour traffic. Not wanting to miss an opportunity to lighten the mood I swung off in the direction of downtown Vancouver with its teeming night life, good restaurants and some live music. When I was last here I had a great meal at a four star sushi place on the waterfront. It wasn't cheap but the average $90.00 buck tab seemed like a small price to pay for the chance to spend an evening with an exotic woman in an exotic place. Amy asked where I was headed so I lied and said I thought it was a shortcut to the airport. I could tell that she wasn't buying it but neither did she object. It's easier to get into the downtown than out of it during rush hour so we were soon parking the rental in a parking high rise and walking to the sushi bar. On the way she grabbed my hand and held it as we strolled in the mist through the tourists and townspeople all out looking for a good time. I didn't have to look. I had found my good time.

The meal was good, the service great and the setting was idyllic. After a couple of hours of eating and drinking we proceeded to be merry as we walked along the waterfront looking at the yachts and sailboats moored at their berths. Out in the bay there was an assortment of small craft with navigation lights twinkling like a cluster of stars in a winter's night. Every once in a while a float plane would land or take off amid a roar of the props as the little craft grabbed the sky. In this setting it was easy to forget the real purpose of us being here but neither of us seemed keen to get back into reality mode just yet. We talked about our backgrounds and our hopes and plans for the future. This was our first chance to talk about anything not related to the drama that was playing itself out in our lives and I felt a little shy and hesitant as we strolled the Greenway towards the Seawall. Every once in a while she gave my hand a reassuring squeeze and I felt a hit of euphoria I've only rarely experienced before.

We ambled along for about an hour then headed back to reality, found our ride and headed for the airport and the Fairmont. I wasn't sure what the rest of the night would bring but I hoped that whatever it was I'd be up to it. Amy left me at the third floor wishing me good night and giving my hand a squeeze. Any fantasy I had concocted on the way back shattered into pieces and I was left with nothing to look forward to but the shot bottles of scotch in the little bar in the room. It took two of them before I found sleep, tossing and turning with dreams that didn't make sense.

I woke up early the next morning after tossing and turning most of the night. Getting rid of a forensic audit to cover up a fraud was understandable but where did ecoterrorists and racial conflict fit in? I looked at the name and address of the Seattle security firm that the CSIS officer had given us but I couldn't connect any of that to a Canadian engineer with a Muslim background or a spiked drink supplied to a forensic auditor. Where was the connection? I kept turning over in my mind the events of the past several weeks and remembered the two illegal aliens driving the truck that was wrecked resulting in the destroyed landmark at Burning Lake. Who profits? It was still too early to call down to Amy so I phoned back to Fort Mac and reached Constable Porter, the RCMP officer involved in the ongoing investigation of the wrecked tanker.

Constable Porter remembered me but wasn't able to add anything I already knew. He confirmed that a blown tire had caused the wreck. However, he said there were a few anomalies that have yet to be sorted out.

"What do you mean by a few anomalies?" I asked.

He countered with, "Just what is your interest in the case? Do you have any information about the wreck?"

I didn't want to tell him about our suspicions about a connection between Amy's car crash and some of the weird happenings in and around Burning Lake.

He then went on to ask, "Where are you phoning from? The caller ID says Vancouver. What's so important that you have to phone from Vancouver about a truck crash? What has that got to do with being a Dr.?" Thinking fast I said "I'm out here visiting a colleague and last night we got talking about our jobs. I told him about all the stuff that's been happening back home and he asked me why a truck driven by a couple of undocumented people using forged licenses would blow a tire while coming into town. I guess his suspicious nature comes from his association with the RCMP during criminal investigations. He's a pathologist specializing in investigation of criminal stuff like poisoning or intoxication or drug impairment. His question got me to thinking I hadn't heard any more about the crash and I guess I just got curious. We're meeting a little later today for lunch and I just thought I'd like to be able to give him an answer." I hope he buys this tale. I felt foolish making up a bull shit story to feed to a cop. Guys go to jail for this stuff.

"Doc" he replied "I think you're feeding me a line but you've got a good rep. around here so I'll let it go for now. On the Q.T. you can tell your friend that preliminary evidence suggests that a small explosive charge was involved in blowing the tire but we haven't even let that out to the media so if you have any information to share we expect you to share it. When are you coming back?"

His reply shook me and I had to sit down before I fell down. What the hell now? Are these incidents connected and am I guilty of withholding evidence?

"Doc, you still there?"

"Constable Porter I don't know if I know anything connected to your case so I don't know if I can help you. I'll be back in Burning Lake in a couple of days and I'll call you as soon as I arrive."

He said "OK Doc. We'll let it go for now. Oh by the way, that info about the blow out is classified. You didn't get it from me. Be careful what you tell your buddy but tell him it's classified. He'll know how important it is to keep it under wraps. If it gets out I'll know who to look for."

He hung up leaving me dazed and confused. How the hell am I going to break this to Amy? This is getting way out of control!

I looked again at the Seattle address and a thought began to form somewhere in the back of my brain. What kind of security firm is it? Why should it be connected to a nut that blows up pipelines and spikes trees so they won't get cut down? I think I need someone more devious than me so I picked up the phone and dialed Amy's room.

16

We agreed to meet in the dining room for a quick breakfast and then figure out our next moves. It took me about twenty minutes to shampoo, shower and shave and then I headed downstairs wondering how I was going to pull off what I had been tossing around in my head for the last hour. Amy was already there looking as sensational as ever but somewhat restless. She looked like she'd been awake most of the night. Welcome to the club!

"What now James Bond" she greeted me. I poured a coffee and took a long drink of the really strong brew, not noticing that it was so hot it almost fried my lips. I needed the kick to clear the cobwebs and put my brain into high gear.

"What I'm going to tell you is classified and if you let it out we'll both be in big trouble". I hoped that would set the tone for the next few minutes.

"Who have you been talking to?" she queried? Then that little grin. "Or have you been hearing voices?"

"Be serious" I muttered. "This is serious stuff. I called the Mounties this morning."

"You what?" she almost shouted. "Why the hell did you do that?"

Now that I had her attention I began to fill her in.

"Remember that truck that demolished the church?"

"How could I forget?"

"Well I called our Constable Porter of the pony soldiers and he told me the front wheel was blown with an explosive charge that was probably set off by a remote device. Do you know what that means? It means a bad guy or two were on the scene watching that truck come down the highway. That means it was a set up."

"You're kidding. Holy shit!"

"Yeah, holy shit!"

"Paul! What are we going to do?"

"I need to get that devious mind of yours into high gear and help me on this. Someone deliberately sabotaged that truck and I think it was to kick up trouble between the East Indians working that road project and the reserve Indians. You know, Indians and Indians instead of cowboys and Indians."

"But why would they do that?"

Why indeed, I continue to wonder but I think better after eating so I got up and wandered over to the buffet to fill my plate. I loaded up on bacon, eggs, pancakes, toast and strawberry jam. She looked at the load and wrinkled her nose in mock distaste. Naturally she took a small dish of fruit salad. No wonder she looked so lean and mean.

We headed back to the table and in between bites I surmised, "Suppose someone figured that if the Indians started to raise hell and look for scalps, Midnight Sun would bring in a bunch of security guys. Suppose further they slipped in one or two guys as security people who were actually ecoterrorists then that would tie this whole thing up in a nice neat bundle."

"But no big company would do that to their own project. It would be too easy to get caught. They'd get kicked off and someone would go to jail."

"But what if Midnight Sun didn't know anything about it?"

"You mean an inside job without the knowledge of the management?"

She looked at me as if I'd been smoking something and exclaimed, "You've been reading too many cheap thrillers!"

"Hey those thrillers are not cheap. Have you seen the price they charge in the gift shop?"

"So if you are even close to being right, what do we do next?"

"I've been thinking. That Seattle firm the CSIS lady mentioned yesterday has a satellite office here in Vancouver. How about we pay them a little visit?" She looked at me again like I had one too many tokes.

* * *

Watts Domain Management is listed as a security solutions firm specializing in design and delivery of strategies for protecting private and personal property from exploitation. It has offices in Seattle and South Carolina and curiously enough recently opened a satellite office in Vancouver. It was this name that the CSIS officer gave to us and Amy and I are looking at the innocent looking storefront location just off East Broadway. I thumb the phone number into my mobile and two rings in it is answered by a male with what sounds like a Middle East accent.

"Watts Domain. How can I help?"

We've gone over our monologue a bunch of times and worked out most of the wrinkles but here in real time my palms are sweating and my heart beat sounds like a trip hammer.

"Good morning. I have been referred to your firm by some colleagues of ours who told us what a great service you performed for them several years ago in Seattle. They informed me that your firm has opened a satellite in Canada and we are interested in meeting with you to see if you could assist us with a project." Mr. Cool. I wonder if they already have us pegged as frauds.

"Please who is speaking?"

"My name is Rufus Eagletail. My wife and I are acting for a small First Nations Community in Northern British Columbia who are concerned that our community will disappear if that pipeline comes through our land. We are looking for expert help and consultation to design a strategy to provide opposition." More bullshit. By this time Amy was rolling her eyes and shaking her head. After an unusually long pause the heavily accented voice came on again. "Are you in Vancouver or do we have to come to your reserve?"

"As a matter of fact we are in Vancouver meeting with some advocacy groups but we could be free later this afternoon."

"If you could give me the name of your client we could see you at three this afternoon."

"I'm sure we could be free by then but we cannot tell you anything about our client until we have preliminary discussions. I'm sure you understand."

Again that extra-long pause. I hoped he wasn't looking out the window at our rental a half a block away. I made sure caller ID was blocked so he couldn't easily find our location in a hurry but if his security company was worth a damn he probably had tech resources I'd never heard of. I wanted to get the hell off the phone so I continued.

"I have your address just off East Broadway but it will take us a while to get there after our meeting. Would three thirty be convenient?" Mr. Bullshit coordinator.

"Very well Mr. ah Eagleclaw?"

"Eagletail," I corrected. "We will be there at three thirty."

We had a bunch of time to kill so we headed back to the waterfront and found another parkade to stash our rental. We sat there for a while working out a plan for three thirty but all of our plans seemed amateurish and transparent and I wondered if I had talked us into a blind canyon. This whole thing could blow up in our faces if we weren't careful. Amy got on her phone and found a pub not far from where we were parked so we took off through the drizzle for some lunch and a beer. Maybe we could think straighter if we were half pissed.

We found an upscale Irish pub at Burrard Landing that was just opening for the day so we ducked in there. I looked at the decor and the menu and decided that we needed a sponsor for this gig. The price tag was starting to skyrocket. Then I looked at Amy again and thought it was worth it.

The food was good and we of course split a meal of Guinness infused something as well as a pint of Guinness each. As we chewed the food we chewed over our plight but it didn't get any more clear. Finally I said,

"Look. No way can we let these guys see you. If they have anything to do with the stuff going on they may spot you if you get back with the two chiefs. I should go in myself. It's unlikely anyone from here will show up in my office." I hoped!

Amy asked "Do you have any idea what you are after or are you just going to wing it and hope some pieces fall into place?"

What's this? Another controlling woman coming into my life? I swallowed a smart ass retort and replied "I want to see how they will react if I propose some close to the wire activist activity. I know they'll dodge the question but I wonder how hungry they are."

"So what do we do if they seem like they sponsor mayhem? Have you thought of that? And where do we get our finances and who are our clients and where is the reserve?" She was on a roll and made a lot of sense but I still felt I wanted to know more about the company. The CSIS contact didn't give us the name just for conversation. Maybe they wanted to see what we would do with the lead. I changed the topic a little and asked her if she was still keen to chase the numbers.

"Paul, I'm not letting those crooks wreck my car and almost kill me. I'll do the job for nothing if I have to." I stared at the bill we were running up and observed,

"Better not do it for free. This is getting costly. By the way we were supposed to be going Dutch and I got stuck with the bill yesterday." She picked up the check and headed for the till. I think I might have pulled her chain a little too sharply. However as we headed out the door she grabbed my hand again and said "Thanks for looking after me." I felt like a jerk.

We wandered a little and looked in windows and traded comments about the town, the stores, the homeless, the traffic and the weather. We touched on everything except the most important subject; us. I resolved to be extra careful when I met the security guys. I didn't want any stupid recklessness to splash back on this beautiful lady.

By now it was close to three p.m. so we headed back to get the car and drive back to Watts Domain Management. We found a parking spot about two blocks away and promising to be careful, I left her sitting in the locked rental with a warning not to go strolling in this part of town. It never occurred to me that they may have me followed back to my car or take a picture of the car and license plate. When the thought did hit me between the eyes it was too late to change course. I hoped our luck would hold.

Watts Domain Management occupied a small conservatively furnished office. When I stepped through the door I saw a young lady sitting at the reception counter wearing some earphone and mike contraption while staring at a computer. She looked up at me, down at her screen and asked;

"Mr. Eagletail?"

"Yes" I replied, wondering what happened to the guy that took my call. I jumped right in with a clever observation. "You're not the guy who I talked to earlier."

She laughed and said "That's OK You don't look like a guy with the name of Eagletail." Score one for her side. I thought quickly about my cover. We had anticipated this but not so quickly. "My grandfather was Rufus Eagletail from the Shuswap Nation before it was a nation. He married a

Norwegian woman who became my grandmother and they had a bunch of kids. Half of them looked Norwegian. My dad was one of them and he married a German from North Dakota." By this time she was laughing and I didn't have a clue if she bought it or not. It didn't really matter though because I'd be long gone before they could begin to sort out that mess.

"Mr. Watts will be with you in a couple of minutes. Can I get you a coffee?"

"Black, thanks" and I took a chair in the comfortable reception area, relieved I might have survived the first test. "Is Mr. Watts the gentleman with the accent who answered the phone?" Sometimes I marvel at my perceptiveness.

Again she laughed "No Mr. Watts is the grandson of our founder. He's just breaking into the business. The man who answered was just minding the phone while I was taking my coffee break. He's Albert Kahn, one of our security operatives. He's only been back from Afghanistan a few months and is training with us to provide security and protection. He grew up in Pakistan but immigrated to Canada about five years ago."

Just then, a trim fit looking young guy wearing a thousand dollar suit came out of an office, looked me up and down and asked? "Mr. Eagletail" with a quizzical frown on his face. I looked at the receptionist and she started to laugh. He glanced back at her and she said

"We just went through that," and went back to her computer. He shook hands with me and said "Jonathan Watts.

Let's go into my office and you can tell me the story". He led me down a short hallway on a good quality industrial grade carpet to a moderate sized office with a small couch and coffee table in the corner just off to the side of his rich looking gleaming cherry wood desk empty of everything but a simple file folder. Behind him on a built-in credenza was an assortment of IMac's extra monitors and what looked like a combination printer fax of some sort. Curiously there were four clocks on the wall each showing time in four areas of the globe. It was puzzling why Alberta was displayed alongside New York, Frankfurt and New Delhi. I guess he already knew the time in Vancouver and Seattle.

"Tell me, Mr. Eagletail, What sort of work do you do?"

I wasn't about to get into a game of chip and chase with a pro so I answered,

"I think probably a similar game as you are in but you guys are the pros. That's why I'm here. We have been working with a number of small First Nations bands the last eighteen months trying to shore up their business plans and helping them to understand their short and long range opportunities."

"Oh? What bands have you been working with?" This guy was attacking early and I just got into the game.

"Of course you realize that our activities are confidential. We're here to outline some challenges we face and examine what resources you can provide to help overcome those challenges."

"That's pretty vague Mr. Eagletail. In this business two way confidentiality is a must and we don't enter into any blind contracts. Maybe you could outline some of those challenges you face."

He may be young looking but I now knew I was up against a pro with experience. What I didn't know is if he or his group was dirty. Knowing that CSIS had a better chance at finding that out I decided to call time out.

"Mr. Watts, I know from my contacts in the environmental movement that your group was instrumental in staging at least a little of the action in the '99 Seattle events. You look too young to have been a part of that but I'm sure you and your firm have plenty of experience in providing security to those in the movement who sometimes take their activism a little too seriously. Some of my clients, one group in particular, have significant resources and are willing to act aggressively and take some reasonable risk. They have asked me to explore opportunities to mitigate that risk. I need to know what manner of resources you can bring to the table and what financing I would have to assemble." If he couldn't read between those lines then I'm whistling in the wind.

"OK Mr. Eagletail we'll lay our cards on the table. We can supply highly trained special forces mercenaries who are loyal to us and who know how to work within the law and make sure that all they do appears to be law abiding." Now we were getting somewhere.

I tried another tack. "One of our groups is looking to install two security operatives into the security group contracted to the company with whom we are negotiating. We are interested in determining the security plans of our Client's corporate adversary."

"Within the limits of the law we can provide you with such a strategy and provide operative support. It will be costly but I'm sure you already appreciate that. However this isn't the first time we have been faced with this challenge and operation protocols already exist. I must warn you that before we enter into any contract I will have to meet with the band member most responsible for this operation and survey the environment personally. This is necessary to insure that we all understand the extent of our mutual rules of operation and the consequences for breaching those rules." Now I was really getting uneasy. Was I getting a not so subtle warning not to screw him? I decided to wrap it up.

"Mr. Watts, I have to report back to my chief and carry your message to him. That will happen before the end of the week. When I have a decision I will contact you to set up a meeting at a time and place agreeable to the both of you." I got up to go and he held out his hand but not to shake mine. It was a palm down gesture for me to pause.

"Mr. Eagletail, our firm has been in this business for over forty five years and we have remained successful by being very careful. We provide a very good service but we do not tolerate disloyalty either from our operatives or our clients. I hope you understand that and make that clear to your client. The stakes are extremely high." He turned and headed for the door. Then he turned back and added "Someday I would like to know how a blond white guy gets the name Eagletail" I just about wet my pants. He exited the room and headed to the back of the building leaving me to show myself out. I walked to the front and a dark-skinned tough looking guy in his mid-forties was sitting at the desk. He said in a rich Middle East accent,

"You must be Mr. Eagletail. We met on the phone yesterday. I hope you had a nice talk with my boss." There was no sign of the young lady that was there when I came in and I wasn't about to ask. It occurred to me that I was already under surveillance and I might be screwed.

A thought hit me like a ton of bricks. How was I going to get back to Amy without being seen?

I left the office and turned up toward Broadway looking for a cab. As luck would have it one was cruising by and I hailed it. Jumping into the back I said "The Convention center at Burrard landing." I then thumbed my cell phone to call Amy and when she answered I said, "Don't talk. Just listen. Take the car to the parking place we used this morning and walk to the restaurant. I'm heading there now. Get a table and I'll meet you." Hoping that the cab driver wasn't in the pay of Watts Domain I settled in and looked around. No cars pulled out of the parking lot at

Watts and I didn't see anyone following but what do I know about surveillance.

I kept looking over my shoulder in both directions but no single car seemed to be on our tail. The cab dropped me at the convention center entrance and I wandered in, turned and watched the doors. After a full five minutes I was convinced no one was interested in me. I knew that if I had been followed I would have had little or no chance of shaking a tail. I hoped I was lucky.

Playing tourist I wandered along and eventually got to the pub and found Amy sitting alone at a table looking pissed.

"What the hell was that all about?" she demanded.

I said, "Not here. I think everything is OK I just wanted to make sure I wasn't followed. Let's get a drink then head back to the hotel. We have to talk."

"Bloody rights we have to talk! You're scaring me again. What the hell happened in there? What did you find out? What did you get us into?"

She was seething and I didn't blame her but I still wasn't sure it was safe to talk here. I looked around nervously. Only three people saw me in that office and I didn't see any of them in here but, shit, they could have picked me up on a surveillance camera. Any one or two of these people could be following me. The place was almost full and everyone seemed busy with their meals and drinks and no one seemed interested in us but again what do I know about tails. I must be getting more paranoid. This was a stupid idea. I wonder if Amy wants to go to Riyadh?

We ordered a plate of nachos and a couple of light beers and finally I told her a little of our conversation. Because we had gone over the theme really carefully before the meeting she had some idea of what I was going to say. But it was soon evident that she was shocked at how far I had gone. However to her credit she saw how shook I was and she didn't chew me out too much.

The walk back to the car park was going to take about ten minutes but it was still light out so I was confident we could get back to the hotel without incident. I suggested we finish our beer and get the hell out of Dodge.

17

Because Amy still had the keys to the rental I asked her to drive while I worked my phone. My first call was to Jeremy who picked up and said, "You still here in town? I thought they might have locked you up by now? What did the CSIS contact have to say?"

I let his jab go and asked "How well do you know that CSIS officer?"

"Which one? I don't know which one they hooked you up with. I'm just a humble go-between."

"Kelly Fitzpatrick."

"Don't think I know him."

"Her" I answered. She certainly seemed to know of him. "You told me the contact was a man and you didn't know him."

Jeremy laughed and countered, "Yeah I know her. Just pulling your leg. She's OK. Pretty young but pretty sure of herself. If you got in and out without her threatening to put you in jail then you passed the test."

"Can I trust her?" Can any sane person trust a friggin spy?

"Depends what you are trusting her with. She'll just tell you enough to make you spill everything you know. If you don't know anything she'll just talk about the weather unless you look hot but lonely. Then she may tease you a little. She's actually married and has a couple of kids. How come you're asking?"

I wasn't sure myself but I couldn't figure why she gave me the security lead. I told him what she had done and what I had done and asked him what I should do now.

"Holy crap Cross. You went into a bad guy's cave and tried to con him? Are you nuts? These guys play for keeps. They'll probably put a bomb in your suitcase." He paused a beat then more seriously suggested. "You may be right. They may have a tail on you to see if you are legit. Let me phone some people and get back to you. In the meantime be careful and stay at the hotel."

He cut the connection leaving me wondering if we'd get through this nightmare in one piece. Amy was doing a great job of piloting through the rush hour traffic and I was looking behind me doing a lousy imitation of Jason Bourne checking for tails. I couldn't wait to get back to Sleepy Hollow and my cozy cabin. We found a spot in the parking lot and beat a line for the lobby so we could scan the doors for suspicious people and wait for Jeremy's call. There was a quiet lounge with a piano bar and a young girl looking no more than sixteen was playing some jazz. The whole scene was surreal. Another time I would have settled back with my favorite scotch and watched the logs burn in the fireplace. Amy had said little during the drive back but now she started with the first degree.

"When did you first suspect that you might be under surveillance? Did something happen in there to make you think you'd been made?"

"It hit me like a brick when I stood up to go. I thought that if he was tailing me then I would lead him to you and he'd naturally think that we were bogus and running some kind of scam." I waited to see her reaction and when she didn't speak I continued. "I thought that if someone was tailing me I would get a better chance spotting them if I was in a cab. I dunno. I guess I was spooked."

"No, it was a good thought. I'm impressed. What made you think he suspected something anyhow? Was it something he said or did or something else?"

"All of the above. I just thought I was in way over my head. But when he revealed that they had encountered the same problem before and had operational plans to deal with it I thought maybe I'd gotten him to reveal something he might otherwise not have intended."

Just then my phone vibrated and Jeremy's name flashed on the screen.

"Hey Jer. What did you find out?"

"Are you guys staying there for a while? You should be receiving a couple of visitors in about thirty minutes. I talked to Kelly and she and another officer that I only know as Kermit are heading your way. Because I didn't know Ms. Pham's room number I gave them yours. You'd better get up there and make sure it's presentable."

"What the hell do they want?" I asked, *like I didn't already know.*

"Be cool. Just answer their questions truthfully and don't try to BS them. They're better at this than you."

I told Amy I was heading to the room to make sure it looked OK and she said she was going to her room and would be up later. I desperately needed a cold shower and another drink.

* * *

The cold shower quickly turned into a hot shower followed by a vigorous toweling off and I was just tying my shoes when there was a hesitant knock on the door. Thinking it was Amy I opened the door and was confronted with an NFL linebacker looking about six foot seven and weighing over three hundred pounds. He was dressed in an expensive and well-fitting suit and shirt with a stylish looking tie that must have cost a couple of hundred dollars. He offered a broad grin with a booming greeting, "Hi, I'm Kermit" and he pushed past me into the room. Standing behind him and well hidden by his bulk was the diminutive Ms. Fitzpatrick who followed him into the room. They were well inside the room before I could stammer "Come in," like they needed an invitation. As intimidating as the giant Kermit appeared he actually sounded polite and friendly. Ms. Fitzpatrick looked the same as she did yesterday.

"This is Tony Archangelo but he likes to be called Kermit. That's what his mother used to call him." She gave him a wink but there was no doubting who was in charge.

She took a long look at me and began what I thought would be a well-deserved chewing out. Curiously, she was reasonably calm.

"When I told you about that Seattle firm I didn't figure you as a wise guy with more balls than brains." Her rebuke took me back just a little but it puzzled me.

"What do you mean?" Mr. naively innocent.

"We didn't figure you would stumble into their shop and try to con them into confessing their sins. We just wanted to impress you that there was something going on that went deeper than you seemed to understand." She went on. "You probably took them by surprise. I don't think they had time to mount a surveillance so you probably got away with it." However, now they know what you and Ms. Pham look like so your usefulness is probably compromised.

"How would they know what Amy would look like? She wasn't even there."

They looked at each other and Kermit said "Your snitch didn't tell us that."

She flared a little then answered calmly, "He's not a snitch. He's a confidential informant and a professional colleague."

He grunted, "Yeah, a snitch." She glared at him for a moment then started to laugh. "Kermit, you gotta drop that cop slang and get with the program. We need these people to help us a little."

"Sorry Doc," he said. How did he know I was a doctor?

"Sometimes I can't resist pulling the Kel's chain a little." He added. This guy still scared the shit out of me but I was beginning to warm to him a little. Just wait until Amy saw him.

The wait wasn't going to be long because at that moment there was another knock at the door. I let Amy in and the big guy stared at her, in approval, I hoped. At least now he knew she didn't have a key card and I wouldn't have to explain we didn't share a room.

Ms. Fitzpatrick introduced Kermit without an explanation and Amy looked at me with raised eyebrows. It wasn't up to me to explain his name. I guess they had tired a little of the banter and they decided to get right to it.

Kermit started in. "The snitch, er sorry Kel, Doctor Butler said that the subject said a few things that raised your suspicions that he might be operating on the fringe. What did he say?"

"I suggested to him that my clients were anxious to effectively oppose a project that may interfere with the sovereignty of their land and that they did not rule out activism that may skirt the laws. He replied they were a law abiding corporation and they provided good service within the boundaries of the law."

Kelly Fitzpatrick jumped in. "So how is that suspicious?"

I replied, "He went on to say that his operatives and his clients were always loyal to the company and that those who became disloyal soon came to regret it."

She frowned and queried "So how is that evidence of wrong doing?"

"I don't take kindly to threats and to me that was a threat, not just a positive claim to ethical purity." I ventured, "The guy creeped me out. You had to be there." I went on. "He then said that the job would be a little simpler than we might expect because this was not the first time they had to deal with this challenge and they had protocols to deal with the necessary rules of engagement. The job he was referring to was my hint that we wanted to insert a couple of security people into the security organization contracted to the corporation looking to cross our client's land. I guess that's when the penny dropped because back home the band we represent is being told that the company working on the roads wanted to bring in their own security."

I could see that I might have struck pay dirt. Up to this point Amy had been quiet but now she spoke up. "Honestly, you guys, Paul was so shook up he made me drive. He must have really been scared." Thanks Amy, now they know I'm a wimp!

We kicked around the various bits of information Amy and I had provided and tried to make some sense of it all but it was still pretty thin. The CSIS crew still seemed interested but their enthusiasm had lessened somewhat. They cautioned us to have no more to do with Watts Domain Management but I needed no urging. I never wanted to see those guys again. After a while we ran out of things to say to each other and the two officers gave us their contact info and we promised to keep in touch. No one brought up Amy's spiked tea so I thought it best not to mention it again. We all shook hands and resisted a group hug and they left with Kermit obediently trailing behind Ms. Fitzpatrick. I guess he only goes first when there is a door to go through.

It was now well past eight p.m. and we were getting hungry so we headed downstairs to grab a bite. We hadn't made any firm plans for a return flight yet so that was something else we had to discuss. Amy solved my worry before I could bring it up.

"There's a milk run flight to Edmonton at eleven thirty tonight. I'd like to check out after dinner and get back. We can sleep on the plane and get the first flight from Edmonton to Fort Mac in the morning."

I wondered if she realized milk run meant a landing at Kelowna and Calgary. We'd be a wreck by the time we got back to Fort Mac. However I wasn't in a mood to argue and we weren't going to get any more info hanging around here. Any other time the thought of hanging out with Ms. Pham in Vancouver for a few days would light my fire but she was right. The sooner we got out of here the safer I would feel. We had a burger and beer in a restaurant nearby and I gave her my credit card so she could arrange the flights while I headed out to turn in the rental. I hoped she remembered this was supposed to be "Dutch treat".

Part V

18

With liftoff around midnight I started to relax as we climbed and turned to the northeast and home. The aircraft was less than half full so Amy moved across the aisle to stretch out in two unoccupied seats and within minutes was asleep. I leaned back and tried to tie together the events of the last forty-eight hours but I was still unable to figure out the end game. Who benefits in a fight between Muslims and aboriginals? Who benefits in a conspiracy involving an Indian band and a seemingly respectable energy company? We were only just beginning but I was convinced we were on the right track. That audit is the most logical as well as the most urgent next step. With that conclusion I drifted into a fitful sleep.

I woke up with someone holding my hand and a warm body snuggled up next to me. If this was a dream I wanted to go back to sleep and continue it. The dream became reality and I heard Amy say,

"Wake up sleepy head. We're landing in Kelowna in a couple of minutes."

Amy had evidently woken up sometime and crawled back into the seat.

She continued, "We'll be here about a half an hour but we don't have to get off. Next stop Calgary. Milk run special."

I hate flying milk runs. Take off, feed me, entertain me then land me. That's the way it used to be before the crazies started to hijack planes or blow them up. Now we spend more time in airports or on the tarmac waiting for whatever. My three quarter hour power nap had somewhat reenergized me but I was tired of struggling with our dilemma and just wanted some quiet pleasant conversation. Amy just wanted to sleep and she snuggled in a little more. Any more and she would be in my lap but that was OK too. She dozed off and gently snored and I sat still, not wanting to disturb her and break the mood. I could sit like this all the way back to Edmonton.

After loading a dozen or so passengers we took off again. Next stop Calgary. We had to change planes there. Because it was the middle of the night we missed the spectacular view of the mountains but the sky was clear and with a bright full moon we could just make out the ghostly site of the snow covered peaks at twenty-four thousand feet. The ride was smooth and the chinook winds that often accompany a bumpy landing in

Calgary were not in the forecast so I put my head back and let myself sink into pleasant oblivion.

The announcement that the aircraft was on final approach to Calgary woke me out of a deep sleep and the first thing I noticed was that the seat next to me was empty. Disoriented and a little anxious I sat up and noticed Amy winding her way back down the aisle obviously returning from the lavatory. In spite of a hectic day and disrupted sleep she still looked fabulous and I wondered if I was way out of my depth. What if we got off the plane at Fort Mac and she said thanks but no thanks? What if she panicked and pulled up stakes and moved away? Should I make a move or would that put her into full flight? Yet she does not seemed to be discouraging me from making a move to a relationship on a higher level. *Better get your ass in gear, Cross, or you'll lose something great without making a fight for it.* Watching her walk down that aisle I felt my legs turn to jelly and my tongue become paralyzed. Two more take offs and landings before we split up. Don't screw it up!

Amy sat down beside me leaned her head back and let out a barely audible sigh. We sat in silence for a few minutes, neither of us wanting to say anything. The aircraft drifted lower and then we were skimming the runway and landing. We had to change planes and ride what seemed to be a puddle jumper after the 767 that had just delivered us. We were booked on a Q400 that is not as noisy as the older turboprop jobs but it is no 747. I didn't think we'd get much sleep for the rest of the trip. With the switch of aircraft we also got a switch of gate which meant we had time to grab something to drink while we waited for boarding. Coffee didn't make much sense at that time of night so we settled for a bottle of orange juice and a sandwich. We grabbed our snack and headed for the gate to wait with all the other sleepy eyed travelers. The place was quiet. Thumbs on iPhones don't make much noise. Time to break the ice.

"Hey Amy."

"Yeah?"

"Where are we going?" Brilliant conversationalist.

"Edmonton then Fort McMurray. Why"

"I mean where do you and I go after we get there?" She turned to look at me.

"Gee Paul, are you asking if you can crash at my place for the night?" That little teasing grin again. I fought through my tongue tie and stammered,

"No. I mean no, that's not what I meant."

"What did you mean, Paul?" Shit, she was doing it to me. It was like being at a grade ten dance all over again.

I swallowed a couple of times and the words came tumbling out.

"Amy, I have never known anyone like you before and I want to be with you more." There, I've said it.

"You mean you want to crash for a few days?" She wasn't making this easy.

I took a deep breath and said, "You know damn well what I mean. Don't make it so hard!" She started to laugh so much she just about spilled her juice.

That undid me. I just shook my head a few times and next thing I knew we were both laughing like a couple of idiots. Then she sobered and looked right at me and said,

"If you have any ideas of leaving me in the lurch and not seeing me again I will hunt you down and strangle you." Sleep deprivation does funny things to people but somehow I knew this was real. My world just took an abrupt turn and a feeling I never experience before flooded over me. I said the only thing I knew that would make sense.

"I'm not going to get all tender and mushy in an airport lounge but you just made me as happy as I have ever been." She reached over and shyly kissed me on the cheek and settled back with a smile, grabbed my hand and I knew then that there was more to come.

Who was this woman whom I hardly knew but had me feeling like a kid just plunged into a high school romance? There was so much I wanted to ask her, so much I wanted to tell her and so much I wanted to be with her and now I realized that she was feeling the same.

They called our boarding announcement and we headed down the long corridor to the aircraft and found our seats, snuggled in to the extent a couple can snuggle in a pair of

economy seats, saying nothing but dreaming of the time ahead
of us.

* * *

The two men sitting in the departure lounge watched the
guy and the Asian girl head through the boarding gate and then
one of them took out his phone, said a few words and replaced
it in his pocket.

"They'll be met in Edmonton but they won't know it. We
now know for sure that was a line of B.S. he peddled to the
boss in Vancouver. There's no reason for them to be heading
for Fort Mac unless they are from there in the first place. I
wonder what they're after."

The other man shrugged and answered "Who cares. That's
above our pay grade. We just called it in and now we can get
back to bed for a few hours. That Asian broad will be easy to
spot at Edmonton if they leave the terminal but I'm betting
they'll stay on until they land at Fort Mac."

His partner nodded and they left the gate, and exited
through security. The rent a cop creds. come in handy once in a
while.

Watts Domain Management was a relatively small
organization but they had operatives on call in all the major
cities in western Canada. Most of them were retired cops or
army intelligence people who didn't mind getting their hands

dirty once in a while to supplement their pensions. Like the man in Vancouver said, they were loyal to the man and well aware of the consequences of disloyalty. The subject and his Asian girlfriend were well under wraps and would stay that way.

* * *

Amy Pham settled in for the short hop to Edmonton International and thought about the future. Who was trying to kill her? Was she on the trail of something a little more serious than a little bribery? Should she push it or tell the Indians she was no longer interested. Part of her wanted to let it go and get back to her old dull routine of number crunching but there was a deeper part of her that wanted to find these scumbags and put them out of business. She resolved to get back to the chief and persuade him to go ahead with the audit but first she had to get more evidence to show him.

She thought of the man beside her. It was the first time in a long time that she felt either the need of a relationship or even the desire for one. Her last involvement ended easily without rancor. The guy was OK but about as interesting as last week's news. She knew there had to be more to life and had resolved to pull up stakes and move back east to Toronto where she could be closer to her family. That was before the audit and the crash. And now this exciting and interesting man had crossed her path and lit her on fire. She dozed fitfully while the oversized puddle jumper plodded noisily through the predawn darkness toward yet another landing. She was beginning to regret her hasty decision to get out of Vancouver. A day or two enjoying the west coast oasis then a nonstop flight home would have been a hell of a lot smarter. The good Dr. Cross must think I'm a silly neurotic female. Hope I didn't turn him off. He just seemed to be warming up to me. Where the hell did that hackneyed phrase "the good doctor" come from. I better stop reading those magazines and get a life!

The landing in Edmonton was uneventful and after dumping most of the passengers and picking up some oil patch regulars the plane took off for the final leg. God it would feel good to stretch out in her own bed for a few hours. The last thing she remembered as she drifted off to sleep was thinking she had to start back to her old routine of jogging and Yoga. She also resolved to call her father and make sure he was OK and not still mad at her for moving so far away.

Landing in Fort McMurray about an hour later in a light snowfall, the plane soon emptied and the passengers headed for their rides leaving only a few customers for the sleepy cab drivers.

Amy signaled the lead cab and they piled into the back along with their carry-ons. Amy gave her address to the cabbie without asking Paul and they rode in silence for the few blocks to her condo.

"There's no way you are heading back to Burning Lake in the middle of the night in a snow storm," she told Paul. She then smiled and added, "Don't get any ideas. You get the couch and have to make coffee when you wake up. I'm beat. I think I'll sleep until happy hour." They were both sound asleep within fifteen minutes.

Down the street a lone figure sat in a black SUV, watching the condo until the lights went out. He then took his phone, thumbed a number and said,

"They're shacked up in a condo and the lights are out. Do you want me to keep watch or take off?" The answer must have been no because he put the idling vehicle in gear and drove away.

19

I woke up to the smell of fresh coffee and heard the shower running. The sun was shining through the window and blue sky peeked through the curtains.

"I thought I was supposed to make the coffee," I called to the closed bathroom door. There was no answer so I must have been drowned out by the sound of the shower. I got up, padded into the kitchen and spotted some thawing cinnamon rolls and a pitcher of orange juice on the table. I poured a coffee and juice and popped one of the buns into the microwave. I was starved and needed the jolt of caffeine to get my brain working again. I heard the shower stop and shortly after the bathroom door opened and a voice called out, "Don't eat all the buns." Then I heard the bedroom door close. I turned the TV on and caught a news channel to get the latest and the weather report. There was one of those electronic thermometers attached to the outside window showing minus twelve Celsius. It looked calm outside so my trip home should be OK but Amy had other ideas.

She came through the door in a casual pair of slacks and a dark wool pullover long sleeve turtleneck sweater and as usual she was gorgeous.

"Do you look like this every morning when you just get up?" I asked.

"Only after I have a chance to put myself together. Other than needing a shave you look pretty good yourself," she said giving me a chaste little peck on the cheek.

I was just preparing myself for an awkward moment when she added, "I know you are off for a couple more days so I figure you can help me with a little sleuthing. I've got those reports here and I need to go over them line by line to look for clues. I'll show you what to look for after breakfast. We should be done in a couple of hours and if I find anything that makes sense I'll write it up so I'll have something to give the chief."

"When do you see him?" I asked with a puzzled voice.

"Whenever we get there," she replied. I'll ride back with you and on the way we can talk."

I wonder if this woman ever hesitates before making a decision. I always seem to be two steps behind her. She would have a tough time being an Arab or a Dene wife. She doesn't look like someone who trailed behind anyone. The next while should be fun while we both maneuvered to fit on the alpha throne.

"OK I replied. Is a cinnamon bun all I get for breakfast or does one of us cook bacon and eggs?"

"You can cook if you want. There's stuff in the fridge. In the meantime I want to get to work on this stuff." Little miss take charge! I got up and rinsed my coffee cup off in the sink while glancing out the window. There was a black SUV tucked in behind a four by four a little way down the street. I could see the exhaust curling out from under the back bumper.

"Is there a school near here?" I asked.

"No," she replied looking at me with a raised eyebrow.

"Looks like one of those photo radar vans down the street. It's pretty cold to be sitting there. I hope the driver doesn't freeze to death."

She walked over to the sink and butted me out of the way with her sexy butt and craned her head to look at what I saw. She said,

"That's not a photo radar trap. They are usually little jeeps." We looked at each other and both thought of the same thing at the same time.

"Shit! Someone is watching us."

"Are you sure?" she asked me. "How would they have tracked us here? They don't even know who we are."

"There's one way to find out. Do you want to go out for breakfast?"

I grabbed my backpack and headed for the bathroom to clean up and shave.

"I'll only be a few minutes, Keep an eye on that guy and let me know if he leaves."

When you are a doc you get used to showering and shaving in under ten minutes and I was soon heading out the door with her to the parking lot and her car. There wasn't a lot of snow on the ground and from the tire tracks it didn't look like there had been much traffic in the last little while. I wondered how long the tail had been watching the house. We brushed her car off and headed downtown to get breakfast. Two corners later we didn't see anyone following so we relaxed and headed to the nearest Smitty's for breakfast.

We were into the breakfast special and coffee and were tossing around the events of the last twenty four hours, trying to make some sense of them when I glanced out the window and saw a familiar SUV cruise slowly by. What the hell... how did they know where we were? I didn't say anything to Amy but kept an eye on the window and a few minutes later there it was again.

"What are you staring at?" she suddenly asked as she glanced out the window. By that time the car had disappeared.

"I think our friend has picked us up. That's twice I've seen that SUV and I'm sure it's the same one I saw outside your place."

"But I'm sure we weren't followed by him whoever he is."

I wonder if it occurred to her that the he could be a she but then she didn't seem much into political correctness and gender equality. My kind of girl. But she had a point. Who the hell was that and were we in any immediate danger? My plate was still half full and I was starved so even if the SUV was actually a tail it wasn't going to leave us before I finished my coffee.

We continued our breakfast but kept an eye on the window in case our friend showed up again.

"Do you need an oil change?"

Amy looked at me wondering no doubt if I had ever been subject to ADHD and it was surfacing again. "What's that got to do with anything?" she asked.

"I'd like to look under your car and see if there is anything there that shouldn't be".

"Like a bomb?" her horrified eyes widening.

"No. A tracking device. If nothing is there then he must have got into one of our cell phones and tracked us. I've heard of that but that's pretty far out technology."

"Not so far out." she mused then asked, "Paul, do you remember that Muslim kid who was picked up in Vancouver at the boarder when he was coming home here. I think he is the son of a guy we sometimes do business with. His father, our client, owns an IT company specializing in GPS and recreational drone manufacture. They have branches in Calgary, Edmonton, Vancouver and London, Ontario."

I looked at her, wondering where she was going with this.

She went on. "I've never met him but I know my boss has. He's even spent some time with him once in a while in Edmonton. I bet he or his son could help us."

"Amy, I've just gotten off a friggin airplane. I'm not getting on another one for a while!"

"No, dummy," she laughed. "I think we should locate his son and see if he can help us. He lives and works right here in Fort Mac."

"Why would he help us and what could we safely tell him to make him want to help us?" I ask somewhat skeptically?

"Look, he must have been shook up and pissed off at his experience. Now we seem to be in a similar situation with Vancouver connections. We should try to meet him, figure out if we can trust him then suggest pooling our resources. We know he was targeted by a scumbag who has connections to Watts assholes. Do I make sense?"

"Maybe" I mumble "but I think it's a pretty long shot. In the meantime I think you need an oil change." She thought for a minute then her face brightened in a smile and she said,

"I think I know just the guy to do it."

We (Me) paid the bill and headed for the car. Good thing I know an accountant who can sort out this Dutch treat thing. She pulled out of the parking spot and headed to a back street and pulled up to a rundown looking building with a garage door and greasy looking dirty windows. The beat up door had a sign that read *"Al's Autos"*. I wonder who Al is.

We headed into the shop and I stared in amazement. You could eat off the floor. The walls had neat pegboards full of tools all neatly arranged. Three gleaming lifts were front and center, two of which had sixties muscle classics on their ramps. Three or four other vehicles were parked in various stages of repair and a couple of technicians (they used to call them mechanics) were busy at their tasks. Playing in the background was some sort of piano classic that sounded vaguely familiar. This had to be the weirdest shop I've ever seen.

A giant of a man looking in good shape and probably in his mid-sixties looked up from the gleaming Road Runner he was working on and his face lit up.

"Amy Pham! Great to see you." He looked at me. "Another customer?"

"Maybe." she answered. "If you can put up with him." She turned to me.

"Al's pretty particular about who his customers are".

I mumbled something like "Hi Al" and shook his hand, looking at Amy in confusion.

"Al. This is in absolute confidence. Don't share with anyone including your techies".

"Wow!" he whispered in a conspiratorial whisper. "Something sleazy going on?"

Who the hell was this guy? Reading my mind she said,

"Can we talk in your office?"

Al led us to his office down a little hall. Like the shop, it was neat, orderly and immaculate. A glass case was hanging on one wall and in it was an assortment of trophies and plaques attesting to some expertise in the world of cars. What's her connection to this guy?

She turned to me and said,

"Al's an old client and a good friend. A couple of years ago some business partners tried to rip him off and I helped him get the goods on them and turn the tables."

He chimed in. "If it wasn't for this gorgeous lady I wouldn't have all this. I owe her big time!"

"No such thing," she returned. "But I do need a little favour in confidence and I need you to do it personally. If anyone asks, I was in here getting an oil change and looking for a rattle that was driving me nuts".

He stared hat her with concern and asked, "What's up Amy? What are you into?"

"I think I've got some kind of tracking device on my car and I need to see if there is one, and if so, who stuck it there."

"You're not kidding me?"

"Sometimes but not this time."

"Goddamit, Amy, if any scuzzballs are chasing you I'll tear them apart myself!"

"Whoa, cowboy, I can look after myself. I just need to look for that toy".

His concern seemed to be growing as he looked at his friend and then me, obviously wondering where I fit in.

"Who the hell are you and what the hell have you got to do with this?"

"Easy Al. He's a friend. Besides I think he's harmless." That little half grin again. How come she keeps pulling my chain at the oddest times?

Suddenly a new thought seemed to strike the man mountain and he blurted,

"Does this have anything to do with you wrecking your car a few months ago?"

"Maybe" she replied cautiously. "Maybe not. I dunno."

Again he looked at me trying to figure out where I fit in. I decided it was time to break into their back and forth.

"I'm a friend of Amy's. I met her a while back down in Burning Lake and helped her with some medical stuff. I'm a doc down there."

Again the concern. "What medical stuff? You sure you're OK, Doll?"

"Yeah I'm OK. There's nothing wrong with me. This is something different. Has to do with a case I'm working on. That's why I need absolute confidentiality. No records except an oil change. No description of inspection of the frame or undercarriage. It may be nothing but then again we have to play it safe for all of us."

"Let's get that crate on a hoist." he ordered, walking away and shaking his head, muttering under his breath.

Amy whispered to me, "Sometimes Al gets a little over protective. He was going to kick the shit out of his former partners because they had threatened me. I convinced him my way was better." She turned and walked out to her car to drive it into the shop.

Before conducting a search Al was obliged to wash the undercarriage in his wash stall. He had a sophisticated spray set up for cleaning mud, salt and debris from beneath his clients' vehicles, some of which were worth a good deal more than the average car on the street. He told us that the process was going to take a few hours before the vehicle was dry enough to search thoroughly. He tossed a set of keys to Amy and told her that they were for a spare car behind the shop. It was a seven year old ford in good shape but covered with the street grime of the last few days. It would do nicely. We drove back to her office and parked in the public lot and slipped in through the back door. I remembered her office from my last visit that seemed like years ago.

She pointed me at the coffee pot while she brought up a couple of spreadsheets on each of two large screen monitors. I get glassy eyed just looking at my bank statement and my income tax return is a total mystery. How the heck was I going to help her with this stuff? But I could make a good cup of coffee. We both got busy at what we knew how to do and I

settled into a comfortable chair with a fresh cup of better than
Starbucks stuff and waited for her to tell me what to do.

After about a half an hour she got up and grabbed a coffee
and signaled me over to one of the monitors.

"This is a blowup of all disbursements by the band council
over the last two years. I need you to flag any disbursement that
looks suspicious or is not clearly identified. I've given you a
key to match each one with a series of standards that each
disbursement must meet. When in doubt flag it as suspicious.
Time to get to work."

Did she actually think I could read every single line on this
record and analyze it and flag it without screwing up and
missing something important? My eyes glazed over and I
reached for my now cold coffee. She took it from me and
poured it into the bar sink.

"No drinks around the hardware. You can't back up rust or
short circuits." What a friggin martinet!

With no reasonable choice available to me I sighed and
reached for the mouse. What an irony. Sending a mouse to
catch a rat. I started to giggle and she looked over and rolled
her eyes.

After a few minutes and some experimentation her key
started to make some sense and I soon got into the rhythm. If
the chiefs at the band office knew that I was looking at two
years of business they would crap and howl and we'd probably
both go to jail. I suddenly realized how much she trusted me. I

immediately felt subdued and a lot less cocky. We worked for a solid two hours with only a few comments between us and she finally signaled for a break. It was early afternoon and neither of us had eaten any lunch and we still had to go back to Al's so we elected to hit an A&W for a snack then swing by Al's. I was starting to be comfortable in the presence of this lady and my big head was finally taking over from my little head to let me actually think of our predicament.

"What are we going to do if we find some bug on your heap?" I asked.

"Simple. We find out what it is, what it can do and then we look for who could have put it there."

"Amy! Are you out of your mind? That's something for the pros. We're pretty smart but we're not pros."

"We're not pros but we've got pros in our corner; the Mountie in Burning Lake, the CSIS crew in Vancouver, and maybe even the guy we talked about earlier. I still think we should talk to him first before talking to anyone else if we find a bug."

What she said made some sense but it would take us to a whole new level of action that we had neither the skill nor experience to tackle. How do I rein this headstrong filly in before she gets us both killed? I decided to take one thing at a time and the closest thing was my stomach.

"Where's the nearest A&W?"

We grabbed a couple of meals and switched to root beer instead of coffee so we wouldn't be too wired and found a quiet corner.

I had my face full of onion rings and hamburger when Amy reached over, took my free hand in hers and quietly said to me,

"Paul you have been fantastic through this. I couldn't have faced all this myself. We have to get control of the whole affair then maybe we can take a real break and have some fun."

Putty in her hands. Mr. softie. Ever try to talk seriously with a mouth full of onions? I didn't even try. Just kept chewing and hoping that she wouldn't let go...ever.

We finished our meal and headed back to our borrowed ride. There were no suspicious SUV's lurking nearby and no one pulled out from a dark alley to follow us so either our friend was still watching Al's or he got tired and left. Amy drove slowly and took a different route to the back street and as soon as we turned on to it we spotted the tail about a block ahead with exhaust still curling out from under it. She quickly hung a right and found a small parking lot about a half a block down and out of sight of the watcher. Grabbing her phone she soon had Al talking to her.

"Where are you guys? I hit pay dirt. The device is small and attached to the frame with a magnet. I left it where it is so we could talk about what next."

"Al, the guy is about a block from your place, pulled into the curb, just sitting and watching. We didn't get close. What should we do?"

"Don't worry. Stay put. I've got it covered. I'll call you back in a half an hour. Don't go near him and don't let him see you."

The half hour seemed like forever and we were getting restless. The car heater was doing its job and I was just starting to doze off when Amy's phone vibrated.

"Are you some place where you can see your tail?" Al asked when Amy said hello.

"No. we are hidden around a corner."

"Ease up to the corner and see if he is still there and watch." He disconnected and Amy slowly moved the car out of the parking lot and back to the corner where we could see the SUV. A couple of minutes later it took off to the end of the street, turned a corner and disappeared. A few seconds later Amy's phone vibrated and she said hello to a chuckling Al.

"What's so funny?" she answered into the phone, listened and started laughing herself, thumbed off and turns to me.

"You're going to love this. He had a Mountie car behind his shop that he had just finished and before the cop arrived to pick it up he transferred the bug to his patrol car. The cop just picked it up and left."

"Amy, we need that bug!" I objected.

"Don't worry. The cop is heading out toward Fort Chip and back and will come back here in a couple of days. The road ends about fifty miles from Fort Mac but there's a winter ice road that goes the rest of the way into Fort Chip. The cops don't regularly patrol that far out unless there is an emergency. He doesn't know about the bug and chances are the slime ball will hang back out of sight and follow the beep. He won't even know it's on a cop car. When the cops return in two days they have to bring their patrol car back to have the wheels torqued and Al will remove it then and hold it for us."

I shook my head and a thousand what ifs poured through my brain but done is done so we drove to Al's for giggles and hugs, gave him back his heap, collected ours and left. This was starting to read like a second rate movie. I wonder how much deeper into this mess we're about to sink.

After a quick stop at the office to gather some papers and Amy's notebook we swung by her condo, approaching cautiously in case there were more watchers. The street was empty so we parked in her spot and went in so she could quickly stuff some things into her backpack while I grabbed my stuff. We decided to leave my jeep and take her Murano. I still had a couple of free days left and we had to get back here to finish looking at the rest of the spreadsheets. Next stop, Burning Lake.

20

Winter driving conditions were pretty good. The recent snow had for the most part been either compacted or worn off in the driving lanes. There had been no melting so icy conditions did not seem to be a problem yet. Because we weren't in a huge hurry and it would be dark anyhow before we got to Burning Lake, Amy trundled along at eighty-five to ninety klicks or at about fifty mph. as they say south of the border. She was a good driver and I sensed she was in the mood for conversation. I decided to help her along.

"I think it's time to compare notes. Do you want me to start or do you feel like talking while you drive?"

She glanced over at me then back to the road and replied,

"Compare notes about what? We both know the same things about this stuff."

"That's not the stuff I'm talking about. I'm talking about us. Who are you? Who am I? We haven't talked about that yet."

She drove on for a minute or so then spoke.

"There's not a lot about me to know; grew up in Hamilton Ontario, have a father and a kid brother, went to Saskatoon to the U. of S., went back to Hamilton for two years then came out to Fort Mac."

"You forgot to mention the boyfriend who pulled up and left about ten months ago. He must have been nuts."

"No. I think he knew it wasn't going anywhere so he finally took the hint and pulled the plug."

"What did he do?" I asked, just to keep the conversation going.

"He was a tech consultant for Shell working with the engineers on some of their extraction problems. Look, why are you so interested in him? There wasn't much there and there's nothing there now." Wow. I hit a nerve. I decided to change tack.

"How old's your brother? What's he like? Is he as smart as you?"

"He's about nine years younger than me, almost finished his last year of university, plays a mean game of squash, doesn't have a girlfriend and thinks I'm the best person in the world. Too bad it doesn't run in the family."

That got my attention. Did I open up a sore?

"Care to talk about it?" my Mr. psychotherapist training coming through.

"No." She continued to plod along at the same speed and no one spoke for a while. I was smart enough to let her decide what she wanted to tell me. A few minutes passed and she started to speak.

"When we first met you told me you were sort of married and that you were running away from your life. Since then you've said zilch about yourself. I know you are a good person and probably a pretty good doc but nothing else. Yet here we are dancing on the rim of a relationship and neither one of us seem to be comfortable talking about our pasts. Is that what you meant by comparing notes?"

"Sort of, I guess. You are the most attractive person I have ever met. I mean attractive in every way. I'm sure you've got an interesting past and I'm a sponge for good stories. I want to know everything about you; how you think, what's important to you, who's important to you, what pisses you off, and a whole bunch more."

"Ask me about anything you like. Just don't try and get me to talk about my father or any of my past boyfriends."

I tried to make a light joke about this. "Why not your boyfriends? Did you actually have boyfriends sometime? You only mentioned one."

She glared at me then grinned and muttered "Asshole".

We seemed to be getting somewhere but I wasn't sure I was going to like it. It was obvious that something in the past had affected her but she wasn't ready to bring it up. I took a new tack.

"My past probably isn't as dark or mysterious as yours. I grew up in Calgary, went to school, played hockey, was a bus boy in a couple of restaurants, became a ski bum for a year then got serious and went back to school. I have a married older sister with two kids living in the states. My folks are retired and spend half their life in Phoenix. We keep in touch but rarely see each other. There weren't a lot of girlfriends and my marriage was probably an impulsive act of insanity after living in the Middle East for three years. The first day you and I met I was wondering what the hell I was doing with my life. I was just drifting along in yet another adventure. You were the first interesting thing to come into my life in a long time."

"An interesting thing? How romantic!"

She had a way of teasing that was pleasant but perceptive. I stumbled on.

"When I was a kid I was incredibly shy. Girls were best avoided because they scared me. That seemed to ease up when the hormones kicked in but I'm still a little wary around them. It takes more than a little eye candy to get me interested. That's why my impulsive marriage is so confusing. That's probably why I ran away instead of facing up and ending it." Wow! This woman should be the doc. I've never said that to anyone else in my life.

We drove on through the now darkened countryside, neither one of us talking. There was a full moon and the road was dry in the driving lanes though there were a few packed icy patches especially on the curves. She was a good driver and the hypnotic effect of motor noise and quiet background music was making me sleepy. I was just dozing off when she suddenly slowed down and said, "Here's where all this started." I woke with a start and looked out at a curving road surrounded by bush on either side. Nothing spectacular.

"What started?"

"This is where I hit the ditch. God, I still remember that phantom like thing coming out of the ditch at me."

We were about twenty miles from home and I had told Marla I would call her just before we got there so we could arrange to take Amy to her place for the night. I grabbed my phone and thumbed her number. She was out a few miles from the other end of town seeing one of her palliative care patients and would not be back for an hour so I told her we would meet her when she got home.

"I've got a frozen pizza and a bottle of cheap wine in my cupboard if you want me to cook you supper."

"Sure. I'd love to see your cabin, see if you are a neat freak or a slob."

I'm far from a neat freak but I did clean up a bit before I left
town so I hoped I wouldn't embarrass myself too much. About
a half hour later we were tramping through the thin crust of
fallen snow to my cabin and my pulse was starting to race a
little.

"Oh, I love it," she exclaimed as I opened the door and
turned on the light. She spun around, took in the fireplace, had
a long look at the *Calle* on the wall and plopped into my couch.

I told her, "Pizza's in the freezer in the fridge. The oven is
easy to figure out. I'm going to light the fire."

"What kind of a date is this? I thought you were cooking."
she teased as she unwound, came over and gave me a light hug
and turned to the kitchen. By then I was wound tight and not
thinking a hell of a lot about pizza. I grabbed her from behind
and turned her around and she didn't resist, just melted and
kissed me like I've never been kissed before. She then gently
pushed me away and whispered,

"Careful big boy. We only have a little over three-quarters
of an hour before we head for Marla's and I'm not into quickies
with a married man."

Damn! What do I do now? She just summed up one more
chaotic muddle in my so far aimless life. She continued on into
the kitchen and I opened the wood box and started to pile
kindling onto the grate. The wood was dry and I soon had a
pretty good flame going. I rose to go to the kitchen and she met
me at the door with two glasses of Chateauneuf du Pape.

"I thought you said you had cheap wine. This stuff is not cheap."

I mumbled something cheesy like "Only the best for the best," My tongue tie was coming back. We sat comfortably on the couch while the Pizza cooked and she asked me about the *Calle.*

"I didn't know you were an art fan. I love that picture. I've always wanted one of those but I could never bring myself to spend that much money for a picture."

I told her that it wasn't mine originally and that it came with the cabin. Maybe she's right. Collecting art might be a good pastime. By this time I had gotten control of my hormone rush and we chatted about my work and this little town I found myself in. The pizza finished baking and we cut it up and wolfed it down like we hadn't eaten in a week. The wine didn't last long. She had an amazing capacity for the stuff and out drank me two to one. Good thing I could do the driving. We got to Marla's about an hour later and I reluctantly left Amy in her care and headed home.

Next morning I arrived early at the clinic to catch up on paper work and stuff. Jordan Aziz still had two days left but he had not yet arrived for the morning. I had offered him my cabin but I guess he was shy or something because he opted for a B&B at the other end of town. I guess he wanted to be waited on. Though I had talked to him by phone a few times I had yet to meet him in person and I was looking forward to his arrival with interest. I had never met a *Doogie Howser* before. Louise was the first arrival and when she saw me she mumbled

"I thought we got rid of you for a while. What's the matter, don't you trust the newbie?"

Then she turned on her thousand watt smile and added "Good to see you back, not that we really needed you. Your locum is a good guy."

At that moment the door opened and a slim looking Middle Eastern teenager walked in. He took one look at me, glanced at Louise and walked over and offered me his hand.

"Nice to meet you at last. I'm Jordan"

I did a double take. I knew he was young but I thought he must have, at least grown up enough to get a medical degree. This guy looked like a high school student without zits.

"I know," he added. "I often get that look. How come you're back so early?"

I finally found my tongue and stammered,

"I, er, we got in late last night. Amy bunked in with Marla. They should be here any minute now."

Louise looked at me with a "What's going on" look and sat down and started to go through the day's schedule, all the while glancing at me every few seconds and shaking her head.

I said to her, "I'll fill you in, but right now I have to talk to Dr. Aziz," and I herded him into my office and closed the door.

"Sorry for all the confusion," I apologized. "Louise doesn't know what's going on yet. I've sort of kept stuff to a need to know but there are some things you should know."

He sat quietly and his face was expressionless. I've heard of inscrutable Orientals before but have never encountered it in people from the Middle East.

I went on. "You will remember Amy Pham. You did a great job for her when she wrecked her car and bust her arm but you pulled blood for alcohol and drugs and they came up negative. What you don't know is we kept duplicate samples as part of our backup routine and I sent the sample to a forensic pathologist buddy of mine in Vancouver and all hell broke loose." I had his attention now.

"The sample came up testing for Doriden."

"What the hell is Doriden?" he asked. I've never heard a Muslim curse before. He must have been working in Fort Mac too long.

"It's a hypnotic popular in the late 70's but it's been banned in North America for over 20 years. You can't even buy it any more."

"I've always been curious why a normally sane person would suddenly run off the road and talk about ghosts coming out of the ditch. I was thinking she was an early schizophrenic but she certainly didn't sound psychotic when they brought her in. Does that stuff cause hallucinations?"

"I understand it can. It was banned long before I started to practice so all I know is what I read on the net. It was only luck that my buddy was able to chase it down."

He caught on right away. "Someone is trying to harm her! Why?"

"We don't know but we suspect she knows something or is going to find out something from one of her audits. That's why we headed to Vancouver. I can't tell you anything more right now. This has turned into a classified investigation by the Mounties and CSIS."

"Holy shit," he exclaimed. Again the Muslim cursing. This guy was quickly going native.

I asked him if he could stay through to the weekend because we had some business here and then had to go back to Fort Mac to see some people and I had to pick up my jeep.

"No problem," he assured me. "This place is fun to work at. You got good staff and the people are great. Do you want to trade jobs?"

"Not on your life!" I replied. "Been there, done that." The old cliché was out before I could help myself. I didn't realize until just then how glad I was to be out of the ER with all the adrenalin junkies.

While we were talking I was listening for Amy and Marla's arrival. The chatter behind my door suddenly increased so I got up and opened it to see Amy and Louise exchanging hugs and hello again so we got up and joined them. Jordan headed for his first patient in an examining room so I herded Louise and Amy into my room and closed the door.

"Louise," I said, "Amy is going to fill you in on what's going on but it is critical that none of it leaves this place. Amy's life and maybe mine too depends on secrecy. Besides it's sort of classified information and has the attention of CSIS, our spy agency and they would not be pleased if leaks were traced back to here." She nodded her understanding and did a zipper thing across her lips.

"I've got to talk to Chief Wah-Shee but I think it best if I get him to meet me somewhere rather than his office so I'm going to see if he can come here. In the meantime it's business as usual with Jordan." Louise went back to her work and I shut the door and picked up the phone.

Amy was looking at me with a questioning look.

"Best you fill him in here and see if you can talk him into opening up the audit again. I'll stay out of it for the time being." I suggested. She nodded agreement as I punched in the number of the band office. After a couple of rings the flat somewhat sullen voice of his secretary answered.

"This is Dr. Cross over at the clinic in town. Can the Chief come to the phone?"

"Hold on." His staff was just dripping with personality.

After a couple of minutes the chief answered. I started with my story.

"Chief, sorry to bother you. I've just gotten back to town from Fort Mac and we are looking at expanding our community services program but I need your advice on how to make sure reserve residents can be included. We've got to get a grant proposal in ASAP but I don't want to move ahead until I talk to you. Any chance you can slip over this morning so I can fill you in?" Bullshit 101. I was hoping he would smell money and programs he could get some credit for.

"Sure Doc," he replied. "It's quiet here right now. You got the coffee pot on?" He said he would be here in about a half hour.

One more call to make.

"Constable Porter please. Tell him it's Dr. Cross at the clinic returning his call."

The Mountie dispatch operator told me Porter was out on patrol but would be back about noon. I made a date to meet Porter at the pub for lunch. I think I may be in deep caca with the cops for concealing evidence in a criminal case but as far as I know there isn't a criminal case yet so maybe I can BS my way clear. There was nothing more to do now but wait. I turn to Amy.

"How did you and Marla get along?"

"Oh she's pretty sweet. She kept fussing over me wanting to make me tea and feed me. She's not a bit nosy but I thought I should clue her in a little more. She only knows that we were seeing if we could find out more about my accident. I told her there was more to it than she thought but I swore her to secrecy. I think we can trust her but there are too many people in the loop. Someone is bound to slip up."

"Yeah I worry about that too" I admit. "I think this whole operation should be moved to your office at Fort Mac. You should deal only with the chief and I'll try and keep the cops out of it for now. Best they don't interview you yet. I just hope Porter goes along with it. If he gets gung ho about it he may want to start an investigation and will have to drag in the whole RCMP apparatus. I'm hoping to get the CSIS guys to have a talk with him. I'll give him Fitzpatrick and her pet Kermit and maybe he will see the light."

I can hardly wait to get my hands on whoever is screwing with Amy's life. Also, it's getting personal. I can just feel a little rage starting to build. Amy had her notebook with her so she opened up the program and clicked on the summary of our suspicions so far. We only had one monitor and it was not all that big so we had to huddle together to read it. As we nestle together on a couple of chairs I catch a whiff of her clean hair and lightly perfumed neck and find myself losing interest in detective work. I remind myself that I have some personal stuff to work out and I reluctantly focus on the screen and her voice again.

We quickly scan through the entries she's selected and look again at the pattern of transactions that don't make sense.

"The chief should be able to get us copies of minutes of meetings that decided this stuff. I hope they kept minutes and haven't shredded them. They have to report most of this stuff to Indian Affairs through some program or other. He'll have to dig them out himself. I don't trust his office staff. Remember, that Dawn girl is connected to the old chief through family and she possibly knew she was spiking my tea."

"All the more reason for meeting you here." I replied. "You should probably let him know that CSIS is now involved and to keep quiet about it. I don't know if he can be trusted to keep it from the reserve police chief. If it gets out in the community it will spread like wild fire and his job won't be worth getting up for in the morning."

I change the subject. "After I meet with Porter and you finish with the chief we should get back to Fort Mac. We have to get that bug and I have to pick up my Jeep. I wouldn't tell the chief about the bug and I certainly won't tell Porter about it. I don't want to get Big Al into shit with the cops."

She nodded in agreement and added somewhat hesitantly, "That will mean I'll be in Fort Mac and you'll be down here and we won't be seeing each other for a while."

"Phones and texting will keep us close. Maybe we could brush up on sexting," I kinda joked. She punched me on the arm, got up and headed for a coffee while we waited for the chief. I had some stuff I had to look at before I headed out to meet Constable Porter so I busied myself with learning a little

more about the stuff that put Amy in the ditch. There was lots
of information on the net but none of it particularly helpful.
Nevertheless I wanted to impress Porter that I probably knew
what I was talking about. I got the sense that bullshit baffles
brains would not work with him. I was busy reading about the
reasons the stuff had been pulled from the market when Chief
Wah-Shee walked in. Louise showed him right in to my little
office and I motioned her to chase Amy in also. I got right to it.

"Chief, some strange things have happened here the last
couple of months and they've got me worried. Amy has been
telling me that she thinks her trip into the ditch might not have
been an accident." I didn't mention the spiked drink because I
didn't know whether or not he could keep it to himself. He
looked from me to Amy with puzzlement and asked,

"What makes you think that?"

Before Amy could answer I cut in.

"Usually when someone loses control of a car unexpectedly
we check out a number of things. We checked her for booze
and epilepsy and diabetes as well as heart disease and risk of
stroke. All those things came up negative. Yet neither I nor the
doc who saw her can explain her sudden loss of
consciousness."

"What's that got to do with me?"

"I guess nothing I'm sure but I keep wondering if it has
anything to do with her work for your band." His face clouded
over and he angrily asked,

"Now wait a minute! Are you accusing me of something?"

"Absolutely not." I countered. "I think you and Amy may be at risk because of what you two were looking for. I'm not breaking any confidences because it was you who first asked Louise and me if we knew of anyone with accounting skills who could help you out. I wonder if the word got out that you guys were nosing into the Midnight Sun Contract. You didn't actually hide the fact that you were royally pissed at the old chief and council for signing it."

He seemed to calm down but his anger was replaced by a look of deep concern. That was Amy's cue to jump in.

"Chief, the documents you got me to look at just before my crash had a few anomalies that raised my suspicions but there was nothing there to take to the bank. I know you wanted to pull back on this but I think I can help you and your people with this. Also, if someone is after me I'd like to nail them to the wall!" I think we finally connected. He seemed to ponder for a few minutes then asked Amy,

"What kind of anomalies? What did you find?"

She shifted gears and seemed to take control of the meeting and I cut in to clear the way.

"Chief, if there's anything ugly going on it would probably be best if you guys didn't meet at the band office. How about I make myself scarce and let you two sort it out here in my office and come up with a plan. I've got a lunch date and then we have to head back to Fort Mac so I can pick up my Jeep and see some of the public health people about one of our projects."

He seemed to think that this was reasonable so he nodded his head OK. I grabbed some stuff off my desk and shoved it into my backpack. I used to use a briefcase but since I've come here I've tried to avoid looking like a bureaucrat. They all wear ties and carry briefcases and water bottles or Starbucks cups or both if they can find a third hand. I left Amy to try out our proposal that we came up with on the way here last night. I hope the Chief bites. I couldn't see Jordan so I waved goodbye to Louise and Marla as I passed through and headed for the pub and an early lunch. I'll probably skip the beer because I'm meeting with the pony soldier.

* * *

It was almost an hour before the usual lunch hour and there were only a couple of regulars sitting and sipping when I walked into the pub. This is the first time in days that I have had a few moments of solitude to myself. I sit and think of the possible shit storm that I might be stirring up by talking to the cops. They have their protocols and policies and Porter will undoubtedly have to document our meeting somewhere. I try to think how to talk to him without creating a public issue with all the usual media nonsense. So far nothing is coming to mind. I'm an emergency doc not a political science spin doctor junkie.

I'm way out of my element. How do I take the offensive without being offensive? I decide to play the naive amateur. That shouldn't be too hard because that is what I really am.

The pub food here is pretty good and I'm famished. The snacking and grazing of the last week is taking its toll. I haven't spent a minute of brainless physical exercise and I'm starting to feel it. Maybe after Amy gets back to Fort Mac and I get back to work I can start working out. I hear that snowshoeing is great training for marathons. I remember a guy that was in residency with me who was a runner but had never snowshoed before. They don't have a lot of snow in Jamaica. He was a riot to watch in the first couple of weeks but within a couple of months he was motoring pretty good and even won a couple of races before the spring wiped out the snow.

I was into my second coffee when Constable Porter walked in. He had some guy dressed in civilian casual who looked like a reformed biker. Now what? I'm sitting at a table for four over in a quiet corner and they amble over and sit down like they owned the place. Looks like I'm in for an interesting time. Porter doesn't waste any time. He introduces his buddy as Don something and I don't ask him to spell the last name.

"Don's with an agency in Edmonton that's interested in some of the stuff that's been happening around here. Maybe we can get back to our last phone conversation a few days ago."

So much for easing into the issue. I decide to go for it. I looked at the ex-biker and said,

"Who the hell did you say you are and how did you get into this conversation anyhow?"

"Easy doc," Porter cautioned. "Your lady friend put a bug in the ear of a CSIS officer a few days ago suggesting they get someone from their office in Edmonton to talk with the RCMP office in Edmonton. They did and Don got assigned to team up with me. I already know about the drugging of Ms. Pham. Actually you got me out of a tough spot with my bosses by getting them to open the investigation. You're in the clear. Unlike our friends across the border we actually talk to each other up here."

Don somebody or other then chimed in. "I hear you had a little talk with the Watts organization. Maybe we can talk about that for a bit." These guys were way ahead of me.

"Hey, I lost my head on that one," I protested. "Those guys scared me. I felt like I had a big bullseye on my back ever since."

He seemed to be in a listening mood so I go over my visit in detail and as I talk I think I must sound like some wannabe amateur sleuth. They must be laughing up their sleeves. But they remain quiet and I don't get any sense that they've pegged me for a wing nut. Like most spook organizations they don't give much and after our tete-a-tete I still didn't see a connection between Indian band graft and international ecoterrorism. Don whatshisname gave me a card that stated he was Donald Palamarchuk, Canadian Security Intelligence Service and listed a mobile phone and email address. Also it listed the CSIS office number in Edmonton. He didn't say 'Ask and you shall receive.' I guess I expect too much.

A sudden thought hits me and I ask spook Donald,

"In my little brush with Watts and Co. I suggested that maybe they could help our client inject a couple of moles into the security team of the energy company looking to do business. The main guy said they had done that before so it should be no problem. I wonder if they have ever had any business with Midnight Sun." The Donald thought for a few seconds then said,

"Maybe that's worth looking into." Maybe he's just trying to humor me. I let it go.

We scanned the menu and signaled the barkeep over. Don informed him we needed separate checks. He must be on a career path with a small expense account. Or maybe he's Dutch and not Ukrainian. We ordered steak sandwiches and Don and I ordered a beer. Porter must be driving. I was anxious to get back and see how Amy made out with the chief and I wanted to get back to Fort Mac and get my car. It was then that Porter hit me with the biggie.

"Did you guys know you were under surveillance as soon as you landed in Calgary?"

I must have looked like the proverbial deer in the headlights. Don laughed and said to Porter, "Told you that would unhinge him."

Constable Porter smiled and countered with, "Don't be too rough on him. He's just a rookie."

The Donald scratched his head and said, "Funny thing though, I still can't figure out why the tail left suddenly and headed half way to Fort Chip. I guess that will remain a mystery unless we pick those guys up and sweat them a little."

Did they know about Big Al's little stunt or were they really mystified. At this point I'm not about to spill the beans so I pretended shock and asked,

"What makes you think we were tailed? What the hell's going on here? Who's tailing us?"

Don replied. "We had a guy look for you in Calgary when you left unexpectedly from Vancouver. When he spotted you he also spotted your tail so he called our guys in Edmonton and we watched you get off at Edmonton International and back on again for Fort Mac. We didn't have a guy in Fort Mac so we talked to the Mounties there and they set up a watch for you there. That's when we saw the surveillance on you two as you went to your lady friend's home, then her office, then finally to her mechanic's to get her car serviced. That's when they took off like a bat out of hell and headed for Fort Chip."

I try not to give anything away. These guys are good and maybe they'll find out about Big Al but it won't be from me. I don't need any obstruction to justice charges. I decide to change the subject.

"How come you guys were tailing us? Should I be pissed off or relieved?"

"Just doing our job." Don the biker was back in his twilight zone, ready to do battle with the jihadists and ecoterrorists. Unlike the CIA, CSIS can operate both inside and outside Canada. I don't know if that's a comfort or something to worry about. Can you be paranoid and right at the same time? All I know is I'll be dizzy for the next few months looking over my shoulder. However I did feel some comfort that someone was actually taking us seriously and investigating our concerns. All I have to do now is go back to work, break up with my estranged wife; get some free time with my new love in between her regular work and freelance stuff with the Indians and save the world. No that's for someone else to do. We finished our meal and headed for the bar to pay our bills. I noticed Don paid cash. I guess he wasn't here if anything came up.

Driving back to the clinic to meet up with Amy I wondered how much of this I should tell her. I don't like keeping stuff from her but the less she knows the safer she will probably be. I make a note to have my new spymaster buddy keep an eye on her in Fort Mac. I found the chief gone and Amy sharing Pizza with Jordan and the ladies. They were in a good mood and seemed to be getting along so I sat with them and had a coffee then Amy and I hit the road once more to Fort Mac. We could talk about what's next on the road back. This thing was taking on a new life and I wanted to be clear that we both agreed on what we were seeing.

21

Our luck seemed to be holding and other than a few flurries of fluffy snow the conditions were OK. I sat quietly as we got out of town and headed up the highway. It was early afternoon and I expected to get to Fort Mac before dark. Amy seemed surprisingly quiet and I'm wondering where she is with the Indians.

"I had an interesting talk with Chief Wah-Shee. He was pretty guarded but I went over the last several days with him and I could see he was beginning to think about the big picture. He obviously knows that his office is not secure and also is aware that he could take a lot of heat from some of his band members."

I was curious about their approach to an audit now that it was obvious that some bad stuff might be in store for us. This was her game so I tried my best not to come on like gangbusters but I also didn't want to sit around twiddling my thumbs and wondering what next was coming our way. I edged my way in to the conversation very carefully. Well not that carefully.

"So what did you two come up with?" Subtle and low key. She didn't take her eyes off the road as we passed her crash location.

"He's going to pull out the Council minutes going back four years and review them carefully and any place the issue of Reserve exploration or Midnight Sun comes up he's going to scan them and send them. I cautioned him to delete the record of scanning and any emails to me after he saves them on a stick. That way any snoop won't have a way of knowing what we are doing."

"Good thinking," I commented. "There probably won't be too many clues but we might see some patterns develop."

"What do you mean 'We' white man?" she countered. "This stuff is all confidential client/consultant work product. If I show it to you I'll have to shoot you."

I'm about to press through her banter and object when I realize she's right. The only way I was legally involved was through the suspicious blood test. It wasn't even my car that was bugged. That sucks but I really don't need all that aggravation so I shut up and wait for her to continue. She's more serious when she starts out again and seems to be ready to dive in and get some answers.

"I think he trusts you and is happy to have an ally in the white man's world. He was glad that you suggested working together at long range. I guess we'll be so busy working on this that I won't be able to talk to you very much." This woman never stops teasing.

"That's OK" I reply. "I'll probably be busy with all the locals and having fun at the pub every night and maybe flying to Mexico for some sun and sand." Two can play at the same game.

"Seriously," she says, "I'll need a shoulder to lean on through this stuff. It is scary and I'm scared. When it's all over I'm going to get a job keeping books for a dog kennel or something. What do you think we should do first when we get to Fort Mac?"

I have a suggestion but I don't think she had that in mind.

"We have to see if Big Al got that bug back and then make contact with that Mir guy or have you changed your mind about getting him involved?"

"No," she mused. "If we can meet him and just talk to him in general about the action around here and his own experience maybe we can get a feel for him. Then if he seems legit we can see if he can help with the bug. That could help us piece together any connections with our Midnight Sun audit."

I'm about to bring up my resolve to sort out my own marital status ASAP but I change my mind. This is not the time to bring that little problem into the mix. I file it away for another time and settle back to watch the road. The next hour seems to slip by pretty quickly and I doze on and off as she makes her way through a few more squalls of snow and finds the outskirts of Fort Mac. It is late afternoon as we thread our way along increasingly slippery side roads and I realize that she is heading right for Al's Autos. I hope we get a break with this bug thing. Again, I get the uneasy feeling we may be skirting the obstruction of justice process but we don't have much choice. All we need is a name for CSIS. We don't have to tell them how we got it…or do we?

Al's Autos was just as cruddy looking from the outside as it was the last time I saw it. We pulled into a parking space out front and headed for the door. The shop looked pretty busy and right in the center, up on a hoist, was a dirty RCMP cruiser. Al was standing under it with a trouble light when we walked up.

"Nice timing," he said. "They are coming for this rig in about a half hour from now so we got lots of time." The other shop guys were over at a corner hoist huddled around some expensive looking muscle car with the hood up. Al motioned us closer.

"See this little baby?" he whispered. He pointed to a small electronic gadget attached to the rocker panel on the passenger side. "It'll just take me a minute to pull this off. I'll wait until after the cops pick this rig up then we can clean it up and see if we can sabotage it so you can move it." He fiddles around for a couple of minutes, gets it popped off and says, "Let's go have coffee. They'll be here pretty soon and I want to keep you guys out of sight in my office."

We head down the hallway to his man cave style office and settle in for the wait. Al leaves us alone and pulls the door shut. This is the first time I've been alone with Amy since we were at my place last night except when she was driving me back here. I could feel the tension starting to rise. It was exciting but seriously frustrating. How do you separate horny from just plain being in love? This was not a familiar feeling. I knew that she was feeling the same way because as soon as Al pulls the door shut we are in each other's arms with only a faint awareness of restraint. Good thing she can think with her head because my big head was arguing with my little head and was losing.

We pull apart after a moment or two of passionate exploration…her idea to pull back, not mine, and sit holding hands, trying to catch our breath. Somehow I don't think that this chaste resolve is going to outlast the divorce process.

Trying to change the direction of our half hour wait I ask, "Do you remember that Muslim kid's name that we talked about before?"

"I've got it right here. I wrote it down and got his phone number in case we needed it," she replies.

I suggest to her that maybe we should contact him as soon as we left here and see if we could talk to him.

"You could probably talk him into seeing us without making him too suspicious. Something like 'Hello I'm an accountant working for the Indians and a bunch of weirdos are trying to kill me and I think they hate Muslims. Can you help us'?"

She makes a face and pulls out her phone.

While she was calling I wandered down the hall and peeked into the shop. The lift was empty and the patrol car was gone. Al was just heading toward me.

"They didn't suspect a thing," he grinned as he handed me the device. "I think the battery is dead otherwise it looks OK. I cleaned it up the best I could." This guy has been around the block a few times. He led the way back down the hall to his office where Amy was just finishing her call. After giving Amy a fatherly hug he shook my hand and warned me,

"If anything happens to this lady you'll be in a shitload of hurt." I believed him! I sure as hell don't want him gunning for me.

* * *

Adam Mir Lives in a house not far from downtown about five minutes from Al's. Amy told me that he was very cautious and suspicious but once she mentioned his father and the connection to her he loosened up a little. He invited us right over. We are now sitting in a pleasant living room of a neat and fashionably decorated home. The walls are filled with photographs of every description, artfully arranged, and looking like the room was built for them. He is a pleasant very good looking young man and has greeted us in a formal and polite manner.

"Please tell me what you want of me," he began. "I did not quite understand what you were telling me."

"Mr. Mir, as I told you on the phone, I heard about your incident at the Vancouver airport and recognized your name. My boss has sometimes done business with your father so I guessed that you might be able to help us with a problem."

Amy wasn't giving anything away just yet. This guy could be a victim or he could be a terrorist. I couldn't decide which so I stayed quiet and she continued.

"About the time you were targeted and the Mosque was being vandalized, a truck driven by two undocumented Pakistani youths crashed into a church in Dr. Cross's village and burned it. We have reason to believe it was sabotaged. We are not sure but we think that someone is trying to stir up trouble between the Muslim community and some of the First Nations bands. We don't know why but for a couple of reasons we have been dragged into the middle of it. That's about all we can tell you right now, mostly because that's all we know. If there is something more to this than coincidence then it could become a federal security matter and there is a theoretical

possibility we might be in danger." Theoretical, my ass! I
thought. Yet she was doing a good job setting this up.

He sat very still not saying a word then asked, "Would you
like some tea?"

Tea wasn't at the top of my list but remembering that he
was Muslim and recalling their culture of hospitality I replied.

"That would be great. We'd love some."

While he headed for the kitchen for the tea I got up and
examined the photographs. Each one was unique and
exquisitely presented and made more striking by a simple frame
that matched the colors of the subject. I saw simple scenes of
bush and woodlands, narrow meandering streams, Strong
scaffolds of industrial plants and a simple highway pushing
straight through the landscape as if it had an immediate
destination and couldn't wait to get there. One particular scene
stood out. It was a small lake with a moose near the shore
looking straight into the camera as if daring it to blink. The
colors were vivid and the shadows framed the animal. Whoever
took these was a talented artist. I wished I could swipe a couple
to keep my *Calle* company.

Adam came into the room carrying a tray with tea and three
small cups. Three small pastries were arranged on a small plate
and three real cloth napkins were artfully arranged on the tray.
It didn't take a genius to figure out who did the photos. He
poured out two cups and handed one to each of us and then
passed us the plate of pastries. All the while he said nothing.

When we finished taking a sip of a very pleasant tea he began to speak.

"This affair is very painful to me. I am a Canadian born citizen with an Irish mother. I was treated shamefully by our border services and I have heard nothing from the authorities. I realize that mistakes can happen but even though I'm positive I was framed I have no idea by whom or why."

Amy and I looked at each other and wondered what we could reveal. The stuff we had from CSIS was confidential and if we spilled it we could lose any trust we might have with that agency.

I asked Adam to clarify.

"Why do you think you were framed and this was not just a mistake?"

He replied quite candidly,

"The lawyer who got me released told me that the cops had learned that the guy that sat next to me called the Vancouver based Border Services office and reported that I was looking suspicious and carried suspicious documents and plans. They didn't know who he was."

I agreed that he probably was framed but did not let on we knew who the perp was. Amy remained silent.

"Do you think if I help you with your problem it will help me with mine?" he asked. I was in no position to make promises but I told him that if I found out anything about his circumstances I would let him know as long as I was not breaking any laws. He seemed puzzled by my reply but seemed to sense that I was not about to say more.

Amy got me off the hook.

"I understand that your father manufactures recreational drones and GPS tracking devices. Our company has had occasion to consult with his company on behalf of some of our clients. One such devise has come into our possession but I'm afraid I can't explain further. I can only explain that CSIS has been in contact with us regarding our involvement with this affair. We are not under investigation nor are we suspected of breaking any laws. At this time they are not aware of this device but we intend to inform them as soon as we learn a little more about it."

In order to ease his suspicions Amy advised Mr. Mir to contact his father and have him call Abrahms and Abrahms and ask for a reference for her. She then produced several pictures of the device and gave them to our friend. She said she would turn over the device to him when he was satisfied that we were who we said we were. If this guy was a jihadi then we were playing with fire. But sometimes you have to trust your gut. Anyone who could take pictures like that was probably OK. Besides I intended to tell Kermit and his friend about our contact. I just wasn't ready to admit to the tracking device yet.

In order to lighten the mood a bit, I changed the subject.

"Mr. Mir, you mentioned that the stranger on the plane claimed that you might be carrying suspicious material. Did that include any photographs?"

"Yeah. They said I was photographing images that posed a security risk to Canada's vital energy infrastructure. What a bunch of B.S.! That stuff was part of a portfolio showing the places I work. They said I was providing those pictures to persons in India who were a security risk. I showed them to my uncle and told him I was publishing a coffee table book of photo art. That's my hobby for god sakes!" I guess I didn't lighten the mood much. I tried again.

"I was looking at all these pictures on your walls. They're incredible. I'm not much of an art critic but they're beautiful. Did you take all those photos?"

He answered with not a little pride. "I've been taking pictures since I got my first camera when I was 5 years old. There weren't very many digital cameras around then. I think some of them may be good enough to publish in my book but I'm still not confident that they show the excellence that I'm looking for."

"Do you mind if I ask you what kind of work you do when you are not producing these excellent pictures?" I hope I didn't piss him off. He seems to be warming a little and may be willing to talk a little more.

"Not at all. I'm a Geological Engineer. I graduated three years ago from the University of Saskatchewan."

"That's incredible." Amy exclaimed. "That's where I went to school. It's a great school that seems to float below the radar."

They spent the next several minutes comparing notes and I could see that they might be bonding so I sat back with my cooling tea and listened to the to and fro of their conversation. This guy was either a superbly skilled actor or was actually who he said he was. I sincerely hoped that it was the latter. He might actually be able to help us by giving some insights into the Muslim community at Fort Mac. Besides, I'd like to con him out of a few of his pictures. Just kidding.

After a few minutes I suggested that we should give him a few days to think about hooking up with us. In the meantime he should call his father and talk to him about some of the things we discussed. I'm certain Amy's boss will get a call. If that goes OK she can then handle the issue of the tracking device. She doesn't need me for that and I can get back to my quiet life in Burning Lake while she does the heavy lifting with the Indian band. I can't see that we are any closer to the crooks that spiked her tea but that is for the cops to figure out if and when they get around to it.

We left the young Mr. Mir with some pictures of the tracking device and Amy's contact info and probably a few questions about who these two nut cases were who just showed up and stirred up some old news. My Jeep was over at Amy's condo and it was well past dark so I didn't feel much like heading down the road. But I also didn't feel much like lying awake all night in a frustrated fugue. Adam Mir's two little pastries didn't quite match my mood for supper so I suggested that we find a steak house and splurge. Amy said "My treat". How could I argue with that? She headed for the Keg and I did my best to put the bill over her credit limit. Our Dutch treat account needed some adjusting.

After a great dinner and a few more drinks than was prudent for me we headed back to her place. She knew she had to drive so she limited herself to a glass of wine. We got to the condo OK and she pushed me through the door over my objections…well not quite over my objections… and there we were again, alone, in love and all likkered up. Actually, she only had one glass of wine. If this is a test or something I hope I passed because I'll remember that night the rest of my life. The booze didn't hurt me one bit.

Next morning we fired up both cars and met downtown for breakfast. She was anxious to get back to work and I was anxious to…well anyhow I did have to get home and clean house or do the laundry or read my mail or something. Did last night really happen?

Part VI

22

Midnight Sun is a resources service company that is involved with road building, camp facility provision and operation. Its fortunes depend on the overall activity in the energy sector at any one period of time. As exploration, production and distribution are ramped up, the resource service companies thrive. Right now Midnight Sun is up to its neck in contracts and business is thriving. Because Burning Lake is located in an area that is largely covered with muskeg and swamps, resource companies require stable roads to extend the exploration and production season. This is achieved through a process known as matting whereby materials such as pine planks from salvaged pine beetle infestation are laminated into mats held together by steel rods or bolts and placed over the surface of the road or rig location.

It is this activity that the Prairie Dene reserves contracted for and were expecting to receive. Oil sand deposits were not especially rich in and around the southern half of the reserve so there was little expectation by the band that exploration companies would be interested in locating huge projects in that area. However the prospect of having a network of access roads for most of the year was inviting and the long term investment was hoped to be offset by revenue from royalties derived from projects elsewhere that abutted or extended onto reserve land in the northern sector. The agreement between Midnight Sun and the reserve council was regarded as a win win for the First Nations people. It was only after the defeat of the former chief and council that suspicions of fraud began to surface. Whispers of a different agenda continued to pop up in and around the local area. Was there more to the agreement between the band and Midnight Sun than just the construction of an all season road access system?

I'm sitting along with Mara, our public health nurse and recently radicalized community organizer in a meeting with the health services people and some elders of the Prairie Dene. We are hashing over the increasingly alarming issue of substance abuse both in the adult population as well as the adolescents and teen agers. Everyone has a solution as long as someone else will pay for it. The discussion goes round and round and I find myself losing interest and letting my mind wander to Amy and her forensic audit project. So far the public seem to be unaware of the activity and my daily calls and texts to Amy remain personal and don't intrude into her confidential business. As the meeting drags on I find myself trying to piece together all the elements of the past few months that are even remotely connected to Amy's mysterious drugging. Who gains? What do they gain? What was she onto? What is out there that we still don't know about? Why is CSIS interested in some local criminal activity and where does a known ecoterrorist fit into the puzzle?

In the meantime I keep telling myself to get off my ass and sort out my marital status. I've been so busy I haven't had a chance to get back to Calgary and talk to a divorce lawyer. I was kind of hoping that my soon to be ex-wife would start the process. She didn't particularly seem too upset when I pulled up stakes and headed north. With Amy up to her neck in spread sheets and band council minutes and Carol chasing her career ambitions I'm finding that I've been shunted to the sidelines for most of my life since I got back from Saudi country. Poor me! I hate that feeling.

My mind returns to the meeting and I catch a comment that the young guns on the reserve would be more likely to try for jobs with Midnight Sun if there wasn't so much racial conflict out in the field. Some guy is going on about the increased security force at Midnight Sun and the tactics they were using against the natives on their own property. The meeting was just breaking up and I grab the elder who was complaining about the security force and try to coax some information out of him. It's obvious he doesn't know much but he talks about some questionable excessive tactics used against his two nephews who were trying to get on with the crew. The Elder said it didn't use to be that way when the company first started but ever since the two bullies recently hired by the company showed up there have been more complaints from the reserve folks. He seemed to think the company was going out of its way to piss off the population.

Where did I hear that before? My mind flashes back to my encounter with the slime ball security firm in Vancouver and I recall the head honcho saying that they already had protocols in play for seeding dissension in aboriginal bands. Was this what he was talking about? An idea started to form in the back of my mind.

* * *

Carl Reimer was sitting in his truck monitoring the progress of the matting installation process by the Midnight Sun Crew. As an employee of the emerging Chinese resource company Wu Zaho, he was liaison between his masters and Midnight Sun and was responsible for assuring his masters that Midnight Sun was living up to the terms of their contract. In effect he was the on-site quality officer. While Midnight Sun held the development contract with the First Nations band, it was in turn contracted to the Asian Canadian joint venture who was essentially the parent or lead company responsible for the project. Carl had worked at the same level for a number of companies over the last few years but this arrangement was the most complex and perplexing challenge in which he had ever been involved. He was working with the Canadian company when the Wu Zhao group moved in to form a joint venture by investing a huge sum of cash. He was subsequently seconded to Wu Zhao who then became his bosses. The Midnight Sun crew were well experienced and competent but there seemed to be a frequent dispute between the joint venture company and Midnight Sun regarding priorities and goals. In addition there was increasing hostility between the Lebanese workers and various members of the Midnight Sun security branch. This was something new and seemed to have started after the arrival of two new hires. The security bunch were mostly rent a cop hires with some on-site training but these new hires seemed more like third world special forces mercenaries. He had the uneasy feeling that trouble was brewing.

Last week two young fellows from the band appeared looking for a job and the security guys hustled them off the site saying that they weren't hiring no Indians if they could help it. Since his accident with his hand and the prompt care he got at Burning Lake and the courteous and careful transport he was subjected to during that snowstorm he had no fight with the natives and was a little pissed at the rent a cops for their behaviour. Though that had nothing to do with his duties he worried that insulting the locals could backfire and eventually affect the quality of work and then it was his business. For the

time being he put it out of his mind. Carl could not for the life
of him figure out why the Asians were interested in a little road
building project in a small corner of a minor First Nation
Reserve. What was their stake? Shaking his head he made his
way back to the camp for his five o'clock meeting and report.

23

Eli Watts was sitting at his desk in Seattle when his secretary buzzed him that a Mr. Laszlo was calling from Vancouver and was anxious to reach him. Wondering what was in the wind he told her to put him through. Usually he only heard from Laszlo when there was a problem. Usually Eli's son Jonathan looked after their dealings through the Vancouver office. Something must be up. Jonathan had proven his competence a number of times and though he sometimes went out on a limb a little too often he usually had everything under control. The company had flourished over the past ten years and there continued to be a demand for high level security services in the Middle East and South America. Jonathan had tapped into the lucrative tar sands market and things had gone pretty smoothly. Though most of their work was legit and up front, a few times they had to go under the table and give a nudge to some of their clients. That was OK as long as they didn't push their luck. The Seattle experience had been profitable but had the unfortunate effect of focusing a little more heat on them than they anticipated. That wasn't Jonathan's fault. He had cautioned Eli to be careful. However some of the folks from Greenpeace and their friends at Elf had gotten a little careless and they had to lay low for a couple of years.

Sensing that he better talk to Laszlo he picked up the phone.

"Good afternoon Jozeph. What can I do for you?" Eli never wasted time on chit chat even when an important client was calling.

"Eli. I'm glad you're in the office and not holidaying someplace exotic."

Eli Watts felt a twinge of annoyance at the subtle impertinence. This guy may be an important client but he was still a sleaze ball shyster and Eli didn't trust him.

"What's on your mind Jozeph?"

"We might have a problem with one of our projects up in the tar sands."

"I thought we only had one project up there and it was a low level opportunity that had good potential for the long term. Your words, Jozeph. When we became involved in this 'low level' opportunity I thought we agreed that Jonathan would manage it. Why are you calling me now?"

"Actually I'm calling from Jonathan's office on my cell phone. He's sitting here with me."

That made Eli sit up and pay attention.

"Go ahead Jozeph." This had better be good he thought.

"I've asked Jonathan to come with me to Seattle and discuss our Canadian venture directly with you. It is secure and on schedule but our arrangement with Midnight Sun is being questioned by the new chief and council and now we think they are looking at it more closely. Our plan to distract the locals by stirring up trouble between the Muslims and local Indians seems to be working OK but we think the chief has brought in some outside help to look at Midnight Sun's agreement. We're certain that we covered all the bases but the accountant was still sniffing around and last week she and her boyfriend showed up in Vancouver and told Jonathan a bullshit story about hiring us for a job in the interior B.C. We are still hoping the chief will back off after he has to worry about trouble with the Muslims working on the reserve and taking jobs from the natives in Fort Mac. The boyfriend is an amateur working in Burning Lake and the accountant has gone back to Fort Mac. We have two of your operatives on the Midnight Sun security force and things seem to have quieted down."

"So what's the trouble? Why bother me with operational issues? How come you are calling instead of my son?"

"I insisted on talking to you personally. He was good enough to cooperate. I wanted to fill you in myself before he

talked to you. We want a meeting with you in Seattle as soon as
we can."

Sighing in exasperation, Eli said "Put him on." This lawyer
was getting to be a dangerous nuisance.

Following a frosty exchange between father and son an
agreement was reached and the Seattle meeting was set to be
held in a couple of days.

Eli broke the connection and buzzed his secretary. "Get me
Rubinowich. I want to see him first thing in the morning if he is
in the country."

* * *

Northeastern Alberta and her neighboring province of
Saskatchewan share a vast area of mineral wealth that is just
beginning to be exploited. In addition to the vast reserves of the
oil sands, the area is thought to be rich in uranium and yet
unproven deposits of diamonds trapped in kimberlite rock
formations. Though Canada has become the third largest
producer of diamonds, the area of northeastern Alberta as well
as western Saskatchewan and the Yukon Territories has only
recently been the renewed focus of exploration for these
minerals.

Eli Watts unlocked a lower drawer in his desk and retrieved
a document marked confidential. It had been prepared at
significant expense by a small geologic exploration firm that,

not coincidentally, named Eli as a significant shareholder and
Executive Vice President Strategic Matters. While the
document outlined in detail the potential for oil sands deposits
it also documented preliminary findings of uranium and
diamond bearing kimberlite in significant quantities. The center
of concentration of the latter two minerals was located in an
area of Wood Buffalo on the southern half of a First Nations
reservation. The report stressed that commercial deposits of oil
sands deposits were sparse in that area and further exploration
or exploitation was not recommended. Curiously absent from
the report was any recommendation concerning uranium and
diamonds. The report had been prepared for Wu Zhao
Resources, a Chinese Resource company anxious to make
inroads into the resource rich area of the Canadian province.
The Asian folks had mountains of cash but little expertise in
mining and even less familiarity with Canada culture or law.
However, uranium and diamonds were tempting prizes. First
Nations reserves hold mineral rights to resources but
unfortunately the revenue from exploitation does not always
trickle down to the community. Royalty agreements between
mining resource companies and band councils have been
known to benefit the company and band leaders to the
exclusion of the band itself.

   At the urging of Wu Zhao Resources, Midnight Sun found
themselves in a joint venture agreement crafted by Jozeph
Laszlo that contracted them to carry out surveys and prepare a

road network for the Prairie Dene. Hidden in the agreement was a provision that gave Midnight Sun and their affiliates first rights to all resources exploited within the boundaries of the reserve. It was this provision that Chief Wah-Shee had stumbled upon while carefully reading the fine print in the agreement. Fortunately there was no mention of the potential for uranium or diamonds in the agreement. A large amount of cash in the form of finders fees had already been paid to Laszlo and the ex chief's brother, Wilfred Natannah. If a forensic audit turned up any evidence that the finders fees had been fraudulently buried then the agreement itself could be at risk. The Asian partners could find themselves out of the picture. For the first time Eli felt a shiver go down his spine. Those Asian guys were not above playing dirty. Watts Domain Management had provided security services for them in the past and through their involvement had discovered Wu Zhao's involvement with cybercrime and arms dealing. Perhaps he should look at this whole mess a little more closely.

Two days later Jonathan Watts and his Father Eli Watts sat in a meeting with Jozeph Laszlo. Also present at the meeting was Roberto Rubinowich a senior security consultant for Watts Domain. Rubinowich was well acquainted with black ops and the wet work that went with them. Originally from Cuba, the son of a Cuban mother and Russian father he was trained by the KGB and after the breakup of the Soviet empire he found himself unemployed but in a unique position to freelance as a mercenary to the highest bidder. He found a home with Watts and rose to the position of Director of Operations. The meeting lasted most of the morning and contingencies were adopted to deal with any emerging threats earlier rather than later when they could do greater damage. It was decided that Roberto would travel to Fort McMurray at the slightest suggestion that the flawed agreement was becoming a dangerous liability. Jozeph Laszlo left Seattle feeling somewhat assured that they had dealt with the threat effectively.

* * *

Returning to Edmonton and Midnight Sun, Jozeph Laszlo called in his two new security goons and brought them up to date. There had been no more meetings between Chief Wah-Shee and the Asian broad but just to be safe they decided to keep an eye on her. The band council mole reported that all seemed quiet. Wah-Shee was up to his ass in alligators with the racial unrest as well as the recent murders. Those were just a coincidence but they muddied the water nicely. The road work by Midnight Sun was proceeding without incident. Reserve sentiment was somewhere between concern and outrage and the young chief continued to feel the heat. Reserve police were increasingly occupied with confrontations between Midnight Sun employees and Reserve citizens. Whenever things started to settle down the security goons stirred the pot a little to raise the heat on Wah-Shee. He still had more than a year to go before reelection but in the meantime he would be kept too busy to worry about forensic audits. If things got too quiet the gang from Hobbema could always ramp up their operations on the reserve and have the two chiefs chasing their tails.

24

Spring came to Wood Buffalo early and with it came the sudden downturn of commodity prices. Major projects were under review and the mad rush for oil patch workers was cooling. Every second day some guru or other was either predicting the collapse of the industry or a renewed frenzy of investment just over the hill. Meanwhile the road work on the Reserve chugged slowly forward and the folks at Burning Lake did what they always did. While business wasn't exactly booming it was steady and traffic along the highway remained brisk.

I'm sitting with Marla and Louise reviewing plans for the next quarter and trying to guess what we would need to continue operating. There was plenty of need for health and social programs and poverty in the area was still a problem even amidst the immense wealth created by oil sands

exploitation. Marla's diabetes community program was
flourishing and even attracting attention in other areas of the
province. It wasn't exactly rocket science… just good
promotion and care and attention. We were kicking around a
renewed plan to do the same thing with substance abuse. The
Reserve police seemed to be busier all the time chasing dealers
and charging users. It seemed that more and more the dealers
and product were showing up from central Alberta especially
the Hobbema area. David Wah-Shee and his police chief
brother seemed to be constantly complaining about manpower
shortages and lack of intelligence and the RCMP had their
hands full with a slowly escalating rate of major crime in the
area. Drugs, assaults, thefts as well as missing persons were a
little more common as the area celebrated the end of another
winter.

"Any word from the planners at Health Services about our
community drug prevention proposal?" This from Marla.
"They've had enough time to think it over. It's not like it's a lot
of money." Marla had the bit in her teeth and was on the verge
of saying 'Screw the suits. Let's just go ahead and see how long
it takes them to find out.' I had been thinking about Amy's
dealings with the Indians and was not exactly paying attention.
Now I shake my head and try to get back on track.

"What have you got in mind?" I ask her.

"Look Doc," she begins, "If we wait for all that stake holder
and best practices BS the kids that are starting to use will be

full-fledged dealers in some remand center." she went on. "Don't you know someone who can goose the money people and get them off their butts?"

I'm constantly amazed at this little mousy firebrand who can't seem to take a no when yes is the better answer.

"How many kids in middle school do you know?" I ask. "How well do you know the teachers?" She immediately gets what I'm suggesting and replies, "That's why we need some funding. We already showed that community support and organization is the key to solving these problems. You said the same things yourself when you talked me into starting this stuff."

"So you want to grow the bureaucracy." I challenge. Sometimes I can be a real asshole.

She laughs. "What are you? Some right wing weirdo?"

Louise, who is sitting back chuckling at our to and fro shook her head and headed for the coffee and donuts muttering to herself, "Just do it!"

"Do what?" I ask.

"Look," she replies. "I know every one of those kids and their mothers and at some time or other I probably went out with most of their fathers. They're easy to talk to. Easier to motivate with the right rumor."

I sit thinking 'I've got a political action groupie here' and I say "Jeez Louise, you dated most of the men in this town?" She

threw her notepad at me and admonished "Can't you be
serious?"

Time to start seeing the morning's patients who were
starting to back up. I have a good crew here and with a little
help and encouragement from their organization they could do
some good things. I say "Let's talk about this tomorrow. I've
got some calls to make." I just know that Marla is way ahead of
me and by tomorrow she'll have most of the community
organized into a MADD like committee ready to take on the
dealers. She's right, though. I've got to get her some help. I
head for my first patient wondering what the day had in store
for me. I desperately need an Amy hit. It's Thursday and
tomorrow I'm heading for Fort Mac as soon as the office
closes.

* * *

Amy Pham was sitting at her desk reading a brief email
from Adam Mir. Over the past few weeks she has been talking
to him on the phone but they have kept email communications
at a minimum. She had given him the tracking device and he
had sent it to his father as promised. Turns out it is a state of the
art device that not only transmits a signal but it also stores data.
Adam's latest email informed her that his father's technicians
were in the process of trying to break through the encryption
and learn more about where the device had been before being

stuck on her vehicle. The evil goons must be a little worried about their missing toy. Hopefully they would think the magnet failed and it was lost on the road to Fort Chip where it was last heard from.

She was pretty busy with the stuff her firm was dealing with and her audit was dragging along. Each step seemed to depend on information she got from the Band minutes and memos that Chief Wah-Shee sent to her. He must be pretty busy because the flow of info had been reduced to a trickle and her frustration was mounting. She needed a break. Oh well, Paul was coming tomorrow evening. He hadn't been here for two weeks and she was restless just thinking of him and wishing he was here. They had been seeing each other almost weekly for the past while and their love and affection for each other was electric! He told her that he was in contact with a lawyer in Calgary but his wife was being difficult. Amy sighed. Her life depended on lawyers and control freaks. She was starting to lose her patience.

While she was sitting there daydreaming about her love affair and thinking ahead to the weekend her phone line lit up.

"Amy Pham here. Can I help you?"

The now familiar voice of David Wah-Shee brought her abruptly out of her reverie.

"Ms. Pham I've come across some information that might be useful to you. I don't want to discuss it over the phone but I'm scanning to you a pile of documents I've just uncovered while going through a bunch of three year old invoices."

"Do you need my opinion urgently or can it wait until next week? I'm kinda backed up here right now but if it's urgent I'll put some other stuff on hold and get back to you."

"You might want to see this stuff. It looks awfully suspicious to me. It might be what we are looking for."

That got her attention! "Soon as it gets here I'll look it over and get right back to you. Where will you be?"

"Phone me on my cell. I'll be out on a hotshot run into Fort Mac and have to get back to the Midnight Sun camp with some parts they need but I can stop for a few minutes if you are free."

He sounded excited so Amy told him to come right over as soon as he got to Fort Mac. Time to get some lunch and get back to the grind. She grabbed her coat and made for the parking lot. Lunch would have to be quick because she had a ton of work to get at. As she drove out of the lot she didn't see the lone guy in jeans and a hoodie sitting in the little take out shop downstairs. He paid his bill and jumped into his car that was parked out front and slid into the noon hour traffic a few cars behind her. This was the fourth day he had been staked out keeping an eye on her. None of the clients that went up to Abrahms and Abrahms looked familiar but you never know…sometimes she went home for lunch and on a couple of occasions she grabbed a sandwich downstairs. Guess she was getting tired of the routine and decided to try somewhere else. Where the hell was she going? He followed the Murano to a local garage. When he was briefed on this surveillance he was told about losing their tracking device shortly after her visit to a mechanic shop. Maybe this was the shop. He quickly texted a few words to a number and settled in to wait for her to come back out of the shop. Wonder what she's up to.

* * *

"Hey Doll. What's up?" Al was standing at a bench adjusting a carburetor like it was a Swiss watch.

"Thought I'd drop by and tell you. We got a hit on that tracker. It's loaded with data…where it's been…when it was there…all sorts of stuff."

"That's pretty high tech. Any idea who it belongs to?"

"No, unfortunately. Did you get any grief from the Mounties?"

Al laughed. "They never knew it was there." They both laughed then Amy said,

"I owe you, Al. Just thought I'd drop by and remind you to keep it under wraps. We'll probably turn it over to somebody soon."

"No problem, Girl. I hope you nail those guys. Anything else I can help you with?"

"Not right now. I'm just killing time, waiting for a client to show up. He's coming up from Burning Lake on a hotshot run. Should be here in a little while." She turned and made her way out of the shop and back to her car.

Figuring that that she was heading back to her office, the tail waited a few minutes then walked over to the shop and went inside. Al looked up and greeted him.

"Hi. What can I do for you?"

Hooded guy replied, "Friend of mine said you give good service and recommended you. When can you do a tune up for me?"

Al wiped his hands and said, "Let's go look." He walked into the office and grabbed the book to look.

Hooded guy continued. "My friend said she was in for a service a month ago. Drives a Murano, real nice ride."

Al looked at the guy. He didn't look like anyone Amy would know so he countered,

"Lots of Muranos come through here. Who's your friend?"

"She's some sort of accountant across town. I think she's Chinese."

Al's guard went up and looked the guy up and down. "Don't remember any Chinese customers. You sure you got the right shop?"

"Maybe I'm mistaken. She might have meant another shop. Maybe I'll check with her and get back to you." With that he turned and left. Al beat it into the office, grabbed his binoculars and just managed to get the last three numbers of his plate as he shot out of the parking lot. Grabbing his cell he thumbed the directory and when Amy's name came up he punched it in.

"Hi Al. Didn't I just talk to you?"

"Amy. Some shady shithead was just in asking about you. Do you think he might have tailed you here?"

"Got no idea. What did he look like?"

"Nothing special. Mid-twenties, a little rough, jeans and a hoodie."

"Al, that could be ninety percent of the males in Fort Mac. What did he want?"

"He wanted a tune up. Said you recommended him. Described you and your car but never said your name. By the way, he thought you were Chinese."

Amy laughed, "I get that once in a while. I wonder if it's the eyes."

"Whatever" Al returned. "Just be careful. Someone is interested in you and it's not your boyfriend."

"I hope my boyfriend is interested in me too. But Al, what do you think he was looking for?"

"He was probably the tail you had before and he was sniffing around. I got part of his plate. It was Alberta but I couldn't get it all. It was a dark SUV. Probably a piece of shit, Ford."

He gave her the three numbers and warned her again to be careful and call if she needed help. Thanking him again she signed off and climbed the two floors to her office. Now what? Call the cops, call Kermit or his partner, call Paul, then what? She jotted down the numbers and settled in to wait for the chief.

* * *

David Wah-Shee arrived about an hour later and immediately advised her, "I've got to get back with these parts so I only have a few minutes."

Amy had his scanned email open and was studying it but couldn't see what it had to do with anything. She looked inquiringly at the Chief. "What am I missing here?"

"Those invoices you are looking at represent a series of payments made over a six month period two years ago. They are for upgrades to drainage ditches, reserve road upgrades, provision of two portable school rooms and salaries for two teachers for a full year."

"Yeah? So What?"

"Ms. Pham, I've lived on that Reserve all my life. None of those things ever happened."

"You mean these funds went elsewhere? Where? Who did they get paid to?"

"The companies and the teachers are bogus. The payments are electronic into bank accounts that we only have deposit authority for. I bet that if you checked the teacher's accounts you would find bogus SIN information. I bet further that the payroll accounts will not list those teachers."

"Holy shit! Pardon my French. That's nearly a million dollars."

"I also bet that if you are able to get banking information you'll find that those accounts have disappeared."

"Chief, this stuff is dynamite. If this gets out neither of our lives will be worth anything. Are these all the bogus invoices? Do you think there are any more? Are you able to go back a couple of years without raising suspicion?"

"The thing is, Ms. Pham, I tried that and all the invoices further back have disappeared."

"We've got to get this stuff to the Mounties commercial crime guys but how can we do that without getting it out into the public. They'll just walk in and box up everything you've got."

"Not on the Reserve. They need permission from Indian Affairs and a directive from the Minister of Justice to open an inquiry." He paused then added, "Or the Chief and Council can ask for an investigation to be opened but I don't think I can get the Council to go along with that."

"Chief, I'm not sure how much further I can go without bank info that only can come by subpoena."

"How about I disappear all the invoices up to this fiscal year and get them to you. It'll be a lot of grunt work but with what we've got couldn't you spot bogus invoices?"

"Not without help. Like your help or someone from the Reserve who you trust and who knows a little accounting."

Chief Wah-Shee thought for a moment then mused, "Does your firm ever hire summer students for sessional work while they go to school?"

"Sometimes. What are you thinking?"

"Why don't we beat these guys at their own game? We have a few students in Keyano College enrolled in trades but my wife's younger brother is studying accounting there and will be looking for a summer job or some sort of internship or apprenticeship. What if you guys were to hire him? Could that be arranged?"

Amy thought about it for a minute and replied, "I'm not sure I can talk my group into going along with that. Too many potential conflicts of interest. But leave it with me to see what I can do. In the meantime for god sakes don't mention this to your wife or her brother or anyone else. That includes your brother the police chief. If you do, he is obliged to open an investigation and bring in the Mounties. And most of all don't raise any suspicions. If you get those invoices make sure you don't get found out. You could put yourself at risk for a conspiracy charge or obstruction of justice charge which would never stick but would compromise you as Chief. Also, these guys, whoever they are, may play rough.

You remember when Dr. Cross told you that my accident may not have been an accident. Well, I know this is sensitive but I think I may have been drugged just before I left your office. I don't know if your staff was knowingly involved or not. We haven't said anything because we don't want to tip our hands but I think you have both a need and a right to know. Your staff might not even know that they could be involved but I can't emphasize too much that this is highly confidential and no matter how much you trust someone you must not let them know of our suspicions. My life may depend on it."

David Wah-Shee sat with a stunned look on his face. He started to reply then paused and swallowed a few times then finally spoke.

"I don't know whether to be scared or royally pissed off or both. Do you know what you are accusing me or us of doing? Do you know how this is going to look if it gets out? I'm wondering if I need to talk to a lawyer or even start a lawsuit against you or Dr. Cross and his clinic. I've known my staff since I was a kid in school. Hell, Dawn was in my grade through high school. I know her old man is not my biggest fan and I suspect he bankrolled his brother when I ran against him for Chief but I can't believe she would have anything to do with this!"

"I'm so sorry Chief Wah-Shee. It's not my intention to badmouth you or any of your family or staff. That's not my style. I respect you too much. It's just I have proof that I was drugged and I'm scared as hell that there might be a next time. We both know that something evil is going on and we may both be in danger. The danger may be worse if we don't get more proof before we go public. Just give us, you and me, time to look into this further. Please."

The Chief sat shaking his head back and forth and looking like he'd been kneed in the groin. "I guess I don't have much choice. We're both in too deep to back out now. I'll keep my mouth shut. If this gets out it will be someone else's doing. That's a promise! Sorry about threatening to sue you. I sometimes get mad and shoot my face off. But even though I want you for a friend you sure as hell don't want me for an enemy!

Anyhow I've got to get those parts back to the guys at Midnight Sun. Are they crooked or is there someone in their organization crooked? I can't believe a company like that would be involved in a fraud."

Amy replied "I don't know. Sometimes crooks flourish behind those corporate doors. I remember a big Canadian engineering firm getting mixed up in dirty dealings over in the Middle East and we were all shocked and surprised. Turns out it wasn't the company but some of the people who worked for them. Just be careful and don't put yourself at risk."

"In the meantime I'll think about your wife's brother. I sure need the help. If we can swing it he'll have to be read into this mess and I sure as hell don't want to put an unsuspecting youngster in danger. His sister would probably kill both of us."

Showing the chief to the door she returned to her desk and sat down. Her heart was going a million miles an hour and she was sweating. 'What do I tell Paul? Dare I tell him anything? This stuff is all confidential client product.' She could go to jail if she spilled any of this to him. 'Oh shit' she thought. 'I got to talk to someone. I can't handle this by myself.'

Part VII

25

October 1978

Hai Hong…a bucket of filth…a bucket of hope. Home and hell for weeks on end. Pham Hau Lanh, a late deserter from the ARVN (Army of the Republic of Vietnam) found himself near the front of the line waiting to be interviewed or processed or both by a Canadian immigration officer. Hau Lanh knew that Canada was somewhere near the United States and, though he was anxious to take his young wife to Malaysia and start a family he was told that if he was accepted in Malaysia he could spend several years in a refugee camp.

The Hai Hong was a rust bucket soon to be scrapped, that had loaded 2500 paying passengers, mostly recently expelled Chinese, in a port in Vietnam and set off for Malaysia October 24, 1978. Bad weather took her off course but she finally found herself in Malaysian waters where she anchored November 9, 1978. Among the passengers were Pham Hau Lanh and his

young wife A'nh Phuong. Also aboard were their benefactor,
Hau Lanh's Chinese adoptive father and his wife who had been
expelled from their land in the Mekong Delta.

Little did Hau Lanh know that the overladen ship was the
center of an international drama being played out on the world
stage. All he knew was that he had managed to get into a line
where an unknown number of refugees were to be selected to
travel to Canada. His adoptive parents were not in the lineup.
As he stood waiting patiently for his turn to be interviewed his
mind drifted back to April 1975 and those terrifying two weeks
as he made his way from a few km. north of Saigon to the home
of his youth in the Mekong Delta. The final few days of
fighting was terrifying with chaos all around him. With his
senior officers deserting and his comrades dying he acted on an
impulse to slip into the bush and discard his rifle and uniform.
In his kit he had a suit of civilian clothes which he donned.
Then abandoning all effects save his dog tags which he hid in
his shoe he began to ease his way from the front lines as he
cautiously headed west and the Cambodian border. Two weeks
later he found himself at the home of his adoptive parent,
exhausted, dirty and starving. He was quickly taken in and for
the next three years he toiled as a laborer for his father always
fearful that he would be identified as an ARVN deserter and
executed or imprisoned. Always resourceful and hardworking,
he became well known in the village and caught the eye of the

nineteen year old daughter of one of his father's employees. They were married in the fall of 1977.

Relations between China and Vietnam had been deteriorating for the past two years and Chinese land owners were being rounded up and expelled or imprisoned. It was in this environment of despair that Hau Lanh and his adoptive parents and his new wife arranged passage on the Hai Hong, not knowing what the future held for them. The journey was terrifying with storms and sea sickness while all the while they were bathed in uncertainty of where or when they would arrive.

Pham Hau Lanh found himself at the front of the line answering questions through an interpreter completely unaware that he and his wife would be two of only 604 persons selected to journey to Canada. He was equally unaware that over the next few years almost a million Vietnamese would attempt to find a new home and tragically hundreds of thousands would perish at sea or at the hands of pirates. Ironically, his young wife, A'nh Phuong had been named Phuong meaning Phoenix, the mythical bird that continued to arise from the dead. Certainly they had both escaped death countless times in the past three or so years. Shortly after leaving the Hai Hong they found themselves in Hamilton, Ontario sponsored by a church organization they had never heard of. In 1983 A'nh Phuong gave birth to their first child, a baby girl they named A'nh Hoa. It wasn't long before their new friends and neighbors were calling her Amy.

Hau Lanh, now known as Lanny loved his beautiful little daughter but as a traditional Vietnamese male he would have valued her far more had she been born male. That barrier would haunt her throughout her childhood and into adulthood. Nine years after Amy was born A'nh Phuong presented her joyous husband with a new born son. Things were never again the same between Amy and her father. Now the successful owner of a moving and storage company, Lanny Pham relentlessly badgered his daughter to get an education and a husband. His son, he indulged but was fortunate enough to have a son who enjoyed learning and studying.

In 2006 tragedy struck and A'nh Phuong developed a particularly aggressive cancer of the lung and died leaving Lanny with his two grown up children and a successful business. He was devastated. His son was in high school and Amy was completing her final year of her master's degree at Saskatchewan and was dating a man that Lanny had yet to meet. He should have been comforted in his grief that his children were growing into successful adults but Amy had not informed him that her boyfriend was black. Living in Hamilton, just across from Detroit, Lanny had developed a dislike and distrust of black America and was not easily dissuaded from his prejudice. When he discovered the truth about her boyfriend he confronted her and the years of tension over her value in the eyes of her father boiled over into an ugly fight that ended with her accepting a job halfway across the country at a frontier city in Alberta's oil sands; Fort McMurray.

* * *

The present

Sitting at her desk and collecting her thoughts after Chief Wah-Shee's departure Amy turned her mind to her brother and father. She had not spoken to her father since she moved to Fort Mac but called her brother every couple of months to see how school was going and to ask about her father's health. Even after six years she continued to grieve the loss of her mother yet she was not able to get over the deep resentment she felt toward her father. Growing up in Canada she could not understand why her father could not overcome his very rigid traditionalist attitude toward girls. Although he had treated his wife with the greatest respect he had not outwardly shown affection toward either her or his daughter. His world revolved around his son. He would never change.

Now she thought of Andy, her brother as he was called by all his friends. Named Anh Dung at birth by his parents, only his father continued to refer to him by his Vietnamese name. Though almost nine years separated Amy from her brother she found him easy to talk to and a comfort that more resembled an older brother. Grabbing her phone she fired off a text. 'Andy, phone me. I need to talk to you.' She never knew where he would be but she knew that the phone would ring in a couple of minutes and her baby brother all grown up would be there for her. Andy was in his last year of law at Queens University. In his third year of Commerce he applied to the combined BComm/JD program and was accepted. He looked forward to graduating in the spring. Business law had always fascinated him and he secretly harbored a dream to travel to Vietnam as a visiting academic. He had never discussed his dream with his father. He knew better than to awaken his father's intense hatred of the Vietnamese regime.

The silent vibration of her phone brought her out of her daydream and her screen, as expected, displayed "Andy"

"Hey Sis. What's up? You sound serious."

"Just lonely, I guess. I needed to hear from someone who doesn't mind listening to a frustrated old maid vent."

"Whoa! What do you mean, frustrated old maid? I thought you had the hots for some doc out there. What's the matter? Did he find out what a bitch you can be when you don't get your own way?"

"Andy! What a shitty thing to say!"

"Sorry. It's just unlike you to put yourself down. What's up?"

"I'm in trouble. Somebody is trying to kill me and if I find out what I'm looking for they'll kill me for sure."

"Hold it. Back up. Are you serious or just hysterical?"

"A little of both. I'm in the middle of a forensic audit and I've discovered a huge fraud with possible national security significance."

"Hey, sounds like you need a lawyer not a school kid. I'll help where I can but that is way out of my league."

"I know Andy. I just needed to talk to someone I trust."

"Look, Amy. I'm just about due to head into a class that I can't skip. Let me call you back in a couple of hours. Can I call you there at the office? Is this something we can talk about on the phone?"

"Actually I was thinking about taking a couple of weeks off and coming home for a visit. I miss you and home and I don't know what to do about Dad. I can't let this go on without making things right. How do you think he'd react if I called him and told him I wanted to come home for a visit?"

"That's easy. He'd send you the ticket first class and pick you up and take you for dinner. He might even let you order. He misses you Amy. You know what? I've got exams and then a semester break after the middle of next week. Why don't you come out on Monday and I'll drive home on Wednesday and we can catch up?"

"Andy, that's perfect. You're the big brother I never had. I'll call him and set things up and see you middle of next week. And Andy...Thanks. I feel better already."

"Hang in there Sis. Gotta go. Call you later."

The line went dead and Amy leaned back and took a few deep breaths. Where did that come from? Going back to Hamilton was the last thing on her mind twenty minutes ago but now it was something she wanted to do more than anything. Paul! What would she tell him? How would he react? He'd know something was up for sure. She wondered if she could survive the stress of the coming weekend without going nuts.

* * *

It's Thursday afternoon and especially busy this afternoon. Louise and I are running the show alone. Marla is out doing her home care rounds and Louise and I have both been conscripted into well baby visits and immunization tasks. Thankfully 'flu season is over or we'd be up to our neck in flu shots. I've got a few new patients from outside our usual drawing area and I'm beginning to wonder if we might be getting a little too successful. Certainly I'm becoming an expert at looking after pregnant women even if I don't deliver babies. We have a couple of midwives floating around and they do a pretty good job of bringing babies into the world. If anything serious comes up we can always load them into an ambulance and send them to Fort Mac. I'm trying to overload today because I want to get away early in the afternoon tomorrow and get up to Fort Mac to see Amy. We've got lots to talk about and I'm beyond curious about her progress. I'm actually a little upset that she isn't keeping me in the loop. I understand all this confidentiality stuff but if it wasn't for me she wouldn't even be involved.

Wondering if she has made any progress I resist the urge to call David Wah-Shee. Who knows who might get curious about our relationship? What we don't need is a bunch of rumors floating around. Things have been pretty quiet and even the cops are crossing their fingers and hoping for peace in the park. Changing gears I head for my next patient.

26

Jozeph Laszlo was not used to meeting with front line workers but the stakes were too high to leave this with a hired hand. Sitting with him in the hotel room in Fort McMurray were two heavy weights from Watts Domain Management and these guys were scary. He remembered The Cuban guy Rubinowich from the Seattle meeting but this was the first time he had seen the Pakistani operative from Watts's Vancouver operation. However he had a complete file on both of them and he was impressed. When he had first talked to Midnight Sun's Asian partners he got the impression that they were not above playing dirty if necessary. He wasn't sure of the connection between Watts and Wu Zhao but he suspected that Watts supplied muscle when necessary to the Asians. Thinking about the stuff they had been involved in while in Nigeria he shivered a little and for the first time wondered if he was playing with fire. It was probably OK when they had supplied him with that damn drug that started all this but he stupidly had thought that the accountant would be killed and that would settle things. He wasn't concerned too much about a body count. When he was a kid growing up behind the iron curtain he had his share of wet work in the gang he ran with before he eventually emigrated with his parents to Canada. Going to school in Toronto and eventually to law school at McGill he was usually at the top of his class but he was a loner with few friends. It was only natural that he straddled both sides of the fence as his career advanced. Now he was chief counsel for Midnight Sun and his offshore accounts were growing at an impressive rate. Soon he would be able to get out of the game and find a warmer climate for retirement. His childless marriage was a shambles but he wasn't quite ready to split his fortune in a divorce. When he was ready he would just disappear.

Also at the meeting were the two goons from Midnight Sun's security force and a couple of local foot soldiers on contract to Watts. The main item on the agenda, indeed the only item was that damn nuisance of an accountant. Getting rid of the Indian would cause too many complications but the woman should be no problem if they handled it right.

Rubinowich was pretty closed mouth. Jozeph noticed that he didn't give out any details about the Midnight Sun contract with the Indians. No doubt he knew that Jozeph and the ex chief had been paid well to set up the scam but there was no use letting the locals know about the eventual prize. No one was mentioning diamonds or uranium. That was good. Only the Cuban and the Pakistani knew anything about the geological report that had induced Wu Zhao to partner with Midnight Sun.

Recalling some of the preliminary information from that report Jozeph now spoke up.

"I don't know if any of you are aware but our company owns the rights to a large piece of land somewhere north east of here up near the Yukon border. There's a couple of old abandoned uranium mines there. It wouldn't take much to fix up one of those mines in case we needed somewhere remote to disappear someone."

"You mean someone like a nosey accountant?" Rubinowich asked. "Tell me more."

Jozeph paused a bit then carefully continued. "I'm not into planning campaigns. That's why we have people like you. I know this is not new territory for you. What I don't know can't hurt you. I know all of you have had more than a few brushes with the law and I also know that there is a lot of stuff the cops still don't know about so I'm not worried about turncoats. You people have all been paid well and I am confident in your loyalty."

Roberto Rubinowich looked at his Pakistani partner, gave a slight nod then replied,

"What you're saying is that you will say when and show us where and leave the how to us. Like you say, what you don't know can't hurt us. That's good thinking. In the meantime we just keep an eye on that woman and see who she meets with and how often. It would be helpful if we could get a bug on her home phone. The office phone would be too complicated. By the way," he asked, turning to the locals, "Did you guys ever figure out what they were doing on the road to Fort Chip that time you lost contact?"

Albert Kahn, the Vancouver Watts Pakistani operative had been sitting silently through the conversation but now spoke up.

"That bug should have lasted at least another week. If you guys attached it the way I told you it should have worked perfectly. Are you sure you attached it correctly?"

The older of the locals squirmed a little and stammered "We did exactly as you said. When I stuck it on I gave it a few good tugs and there was no way I could pull it off. Maybe it got knocked off on the road."

"Or maybe they discovered it and ditched it after disabling it." added one of the Midnight Sun goons.

"How would they discover it?" queried Kahn. "Why would they think they were bugged in the first place?"

Jozeph cut into the conversation fearing that it was about to get heated.

"No sense fussing about it now. Maybe they spotted the tail and got suspicious. At any rate we have to assume that they might know someone is looking at them. But they must have been suspicious before that because you didn't bug their car until after they got back from Vancouver. Whatever it means we better go ahead and get that mine operational because we may need it sooner than later."

The meeting lasted for another couple of hours and then they left leaving Jozeph a little less confident than he felt when he left Seattle. Too many things could go wrong here. Maybe it's time to start thinking about an exit strategy.

27

Winter driving conditions were pretty good. A small skiff of snow had fallen overnight but the traffic on the road had taken care of that and the driving lanes were largely clear. I finished up at the clinic earlier in the afternoon and I'm now driving up the highway to Fort Mac. I've driven this road so many times in the past few weeks that I think my jeep could do it without me. Right now the furthest things from my mind are terrorists and crooks and First Nation politics. I've been talking back and forth with lawyers trying to get some progress on regaining my bachelorhood. I can't understand why such a simple thing as pulling the plug on a couple of years of marriage can be so complicated. It's not that I have a lot of assets. My small retirement fund and an equally small investment portfolio is about the same as it was when I first got married. Carol was the one with the bucks. Her daddy was loaded and she seemed to be well off too. I never got into that with her. I could care less about her finances. Yet she or at least her friggin' lawyer always seemed to find some stupid thing to delay the process.

I'm mulling this over and trying to think of some way to speed up the process when my phone rings. Like a good upstanding safety conscious doctor I pull off to the shoulder and say "Hello."

"Are you going to be here soon? I need to talk to you." Amy sounds a little strange and strained.

"What's up, doll?" I ask. "Something wrong? You OK?"

"Nothing new. Just same old stuff. I miss you. This stuff is getting to me. I wish I could talk to you about it but all this stuff is confidential. My profession frowns on pillow talk."

"If I ever get near a pillow to talk to you we sure as hell won't be talking about crooks and Indians." Mr. empathy and concern.

"How long before you get here?" she asks.

"I'm just about a half hour out. Where do you want to go for dinner?"

"Dinner's in the oven and the wine is breathing. No Scotch tonight for you though. I need you with a clear head."

"You sound different. Something's got to be bugging you. This confidentiality crap is going a little too far. How can I help if you won't tell me where you are in all this?"

"Just get here as soon as you can. Drive carefully." I wonder if she sees the irony in that last comment. Careful driving on a winter road at dusk and getting there in a hurry doesn't quite compute. I punch end call, pull back onto the highway and push the jeep until that shimmy at 140 klicks kicks in. I wonder what's up now.

For the past few weeks I've tried to pry some progress report from her regarding the audit research but all she says is "It's confidential. Don't ask."

What the hell am I in this stuff? I never should have sent those damn blood samples in! If anything happens to this gorgeous lady because of that I'll never get over my guilt trip. I feel my rage starting to build again. I'd like to get my hands on the creeps that set her up in the first place. It seems I'm waiting for everything…waiting for her to finish her research…waiting for the cops to find out who drugged her…waiting for my lawyer to get me free of my past and waiting for my life to settle back into a simple routine. I stepped on it but the shimmy got worse and the speedometer was reading 150 klicks. '*Easy, Cross,*' I admonished myself. '*Don't get yourself killed just because you're pissed off.*' I backed off a bit and settled in for the last half hour of the trip.

Amy met me at the door and grabbed me and kissed me like we had been apart for years then she started to sob with great heaving sobs. What the hell is going on? The kisses I could handle. The sobs…that was different.

"Paul, promise me you won't ask. Promise me that you'll put up with me! Promise me you'll stick by me and try to understand me!"

"Hey, whoa! What's the matter? What happened today? What shouldn't I ask?"

I lead her to the couch and we both collapse onto it. Falling onto a couch with a horny woman is one thing. That's something I can handle. A near hysterical woman is altogether different. I've never had that happen before. She finally slows down to a little whimper then just lies there in my arms while her breathing slows back to normal. Do I let nature take its course or do I wait for her to take the lead? Another thing to add to all the stuff I was waiting for already. She didn't keep me waiting, though. She gently pushed us apart, sniffed a couple of times, straightened up and sat there staring straight ahead. I'm pretty good at dealing with hysteria and crying people. You get a lot of that in an emergency department. I learned a long time ago that a period of silence is often the best tactic in defusing a crisis. Most people can't sit silent for a prolonged period of time and eventually the non psychotic ones will try to talk themselves out of their misery. Eventually she started to talk.

"I phoned my brother today. I needed to talk to someone. He's just a kid but in many ways he's the big brother I've never had. I told him about some of this stuff that's happening but just gave him a few hints that it was serious. Paul, I'm going home!"

That hit me like a ton of bricks.

"Home! What do you mean home?"

"Just for a quick visit. I have to get away. I have to make up with my father. I need to figure out what to do next."

Something about all this wasn't adding up.

"Amy, has something happened to you? Has anyone..."

"No, Paul. Nothing more has happened to me. The Chief was here today and brought me some stuff that will help with my audit but it's really scary. Big stuff! Years in prison stuff! Don't ask me. Please! If the Chief wants to fill you in that's OK but I can't. Please don't push me."

I liked it far better when she was clinging and sobbing. We stood up and straightened ourselves out. She headed for the bathroom and I headed for the Scotch in spite of what she had said. A few minutes later she came out of the bathroom. No more tears, no more red eyes, perfect minimal make up and her million dollar smile.

"I'm glad you found the booze. Where's my wine?"

I poured her a full glass of Amarone. The girl knows good wine. She grabbed it and started toward the kitchen. I followed with my scotch and my puzzled look. Somehow I felt that this whole thing could blow up in my face if I started to prod but I wasn't in the mood for small talk.

"Tell me about your brother. What's he doing now?" She's never told me anything about him other than that he was a law student. I thought at least that was a safe subject. Her father was another matter.

Over the next two hours and a great meal and a full bottle of Amarone she told me the whole story about her rigid traditionalist father and his racist beliefs. She told me how he had never accepted the fact that she was a girl and how she had always felt undervalued though not unloved. She stressed that he was a good man but didn't know shit about women. She described how her brother had assumed the dominant position in her family since her mother's death. Now we are cleaning up and she seems to have regained her composure.

"Amy, do you want me to go back with you?"

"I'd love it if you could come but I have to do that myself. Maybe after all this settles we can go back and you can meet everyone."

I sighed a little too hard and caught the sharp look she threw my way.

"I won't be gone long. Just a couple of weeks. Then I can get back and we can start over again."

"Start what over again?" I groused. "Our passionate love affair and 'till death do us part thing or the thing about the crooks and terrorists?"

She grinned and answered, "Both! Especially the 'till death do us part stuff. O God, I hope that's not prophetic!" she started to giggle. The Amarone was taking hold. From there we got into the 'death do us part' a little more seriously. It's going to be a long two weeks.

Amy was booked to fly out early Saturday morning and I drove her to the airport full of misgivings and doubts about the near future. Too many things were happening and I wasn't about to let this lady out of my sight so easily. Neither one of us got much sleep that night. In between the laundry and packing last night, the highs and lows of our lovemaking and the arguments in between I wondered again about the next couple of weeks. Now feeling helpless I watch her flight take off and feel a loss that I had never felt before. Please God look after her and bring her back to me.

28

Amy has been gone two days and I'm back in my office trying to give all my attention to the kids and mothers filing through the waiting room. In spite of the lateness of the season and an aggressive influenza immunization program we seem to be in the middle of an outbreak. The kids didn't get all that sick but there seemed to be a whole lot of them. I was wondering whether I should be talking to the infectious disease people when my cell phone rang. The screen lit up with the name Amy and I grabbed the phone and excitedly said, "Hi Amy. Please get back here and rescue me from all this misery."

"Hi Paul. I've been so busy I've hardly thought of you the whole time. My Dad is falling all over himself taking me out to dinner, dragging me around to all his friends and bragging to them about how important I am and how much money I'm making. I don't know where he got that idea."

She sounded her old teasing self so I made a smart ass remark about being so busy that she hardly crossed my mind.

"If you look as good as you sound I hope you've got a body-guard."

Talking to her was a tonic and though she was only gone two days, those two days dragged like two months.

"You usually don't phone me during clinic hours unless there's something wrong. What's wrong?"

"Nothing's wrong. Everything is right. Andy is coming home tomorrow and my Dad is treating me like a royal princess. I just wanted to hear your voice."

This was an Amy I hadn't known for the last couple of months. I breathe a sigh of relief that she and her Dad had sorted stuff out.

"The other reason I called is to apologize for being so secretive just before I left. I just got off the phone with David Wah-Shee and told him about how tough it was to keep this stuff from you and that it wasn't fair seeing how you were involved right from the start and were responsible for getting discreet help from the authorities."

"And what did the good chief say?"

"He agreed completely. He's going to visit you and fill you in on everything we've discovered. You know, he's going to treat you like an expert consultant. I've got to go. Papa Lanny is taking me for lunch. He wants me to meet a lady that owns a restaurant here in Hamilton. Sounds kind of suspicious. Love you! Gotta go." And she was gone.

Talk about adrenalin hits. I flew through the rest of the day hardly even noticing that Louise and Marla kept looking at me like I was possessed. I guess I was. The next two or three days flew by and the whole clinic took on a sense of optimism that I hadn't seen in months. Marla had just gotten word that a group of corporate sponsors had come up with a substantial grant for her kid's anonymous substance abuse program and her bosses had given her the go ahead. The grants would cover three student foot soldiers from Keyano College who would work with kids from the area to organize peer support groups to help reduce the mayhem plaguing the youth population particularly on the Reserve. It was a three year program and was well designed with all the checks and balances and outcome studies. Hopefully the preaching and teaching strategy was going to be replaced by something a little more progressive.

David Wah-Shee had called and said he wanted to see me at my office and we arranged for a time in the morning before the usual flow of patients. I was still high from my conversation with Amy and I was anxious to get read into their project.

* * *

Wilfred Natannah was not happy. Not only was he facing increasing challenges from the gangs at Hobbema for the crystal meth trade, the furor over the fentanyl deaths was putting serious pressure on his organization. He had been reluctant to get involved with that stuff but pressure from the outside threatened to destabilize his well-organized network and the cops were upping the surveillance and they were getting too close to his operation. Now he had Jozeph Laszlo on his back to find out more about the band council's rumored investigation into the Midnight Sun deal. His half-brother ex chief wasn't helping matters. He was openly bragging that his administration had brought Midnight Sun on board to develop the resources thought to be lurking under the soil of the Reserve. He was bragging about the bitumen which everybody knew was not all that plentiful on the Reserve lands but he was also talking about gold deposits as well as uranium and diamonds. That was just plain stupid! The last thing they needed was a bunch of speculation about resource wealth at this time. His relationship to Sam Beaulieu, the ex-chief was complex and often fractious. Sam was his younger half-brother, both having the same mother.

However there was not always a lot of brotherly love shared. Wilfred was a bully. Sam was a politician. Both were bent. Without Sam's cooperation Laszlo and Wilfred would have been unable to work the deal with Midnight Sun. However, Wilfred's criminal organization provided substantial support in the form of money and manpower to Sam when he first ran for Chief. Sam had profited from the arrangement but

not nearly to the extent that Jozeph Laszlo and Wilfred
Natannah had. Now that stupid Sam was shooting off his face
about the resources on the land in the hope that he could mount
a run at David Wah-Shee in the next elections in a year or two.
He lost the last one because it had become evident to most of
the reserve that not only was he inept and stupid but also that he
was crooked. He pissed off everyone from the cops to the
Indian Affairs bureaucracy and the mining industry. The guy
was a stupid loudmouth menace.

Wilfred was reluctant to share his concerns with Laszlo
because that arrogant asshole treated him like a stupid Indian
and showed him no respect. He sensed that Jozeph would just
as soon crush him as deal with him. He was always smooth and
pleasant on a superficial level but lurking underneath was an
evil menace that troubled Wilfred. The criminal boss knew that
Jozeph was importing muscle and the goons from Midnight Sun
were continually harassing Wilfred's soldiers and treating them
like shit. On top of that Wilfred had stupidly involved his
daughter in the drugging of that Asian broad before they knew
what she was up to. Now who knows what the cops and the
chief have found out? Dawn assured him that she had shredded
the notes and spread sheets related to their scam but she wasn't
an accountant and may have missed something that could come
back and bury them. With a sigh, Wilfred reluctantly lifted the
phone and put in a call for Jozeph.

* * *

I got to the office early this morning to get a head start on the day before meeting with Chief Wah-Shee. I'm still on a high from my conversation with Amy and we have been texting back and forth several times a day… no substance… just banter and light love laced laughter. This was new grounds for me. I feel like a sixteen year old with a first crush.

David Wah-Shee pulled up, looked around as if to check for tails and casually walked in.

We traded a little light banter and talked a little about our drug program. Like a good politician he was effusive in his praise for our group and especially for Marla's efforts.

"That little lady sure surprised us. We thought she was a wishy washy do nothing government employee when she first arrived but now she could probably run for my job and beat me. Don't tell her I said that" he added with a grin.

Then he got down to business.

"Your lady friend called me from Ontario and we had a long talk about you. I'm torn between confidential Reserve business and your involvement in it from the start. On balance I think you should know what we are doing but I got to know that it goes no further than this room. No talking to cops or anyone else unless one of us is with you and then only if we know what we will be talking about. This thing could blow up in our faces and we'd all have to leave the country."

He paused to catch his breath and to look me in the eye to
see if I was getting it.

"No problem, Chief. I'd just as soon stay out of it. I just
want to know that those crooks will pay and that Amy will be
safe."

He nodded then proceeded to fill me in. I had no idea that
they had made so much progress. They had linked mountains of
invoices with payments into shady bank accounts that didn't
make sense. So far, without subpoena power they couldn't trace
the bank accounts but some suspicious patterns were emerging.
It was nearly time to go to the RCMP commercial crime guys
and bring them on board. In addition they had traced the car
that had been tailing us in Fort Mac but the ownership ended at
a dead end. He also surprised me that he knew about the bug on
Amy's car. He and Amy had met with Adam Mir and examined
data that Adam's father's team had uncovered. Again the data
destination ended at a dead end. No names of any interest had
turned up. So far there was nothing to take to court but the
appearance of a complex and well designed conspiracy was
beginning to emerge. So far they had unearthed a possible fraud
amounting to over a million dollars!

I sat there and tried to make sense of the whole thing but all
I could think of was that Amy was in danger. If someone was
willing to drug her and cause her car to crash then certainly
they were capable of hitting her again. My first impulse was to
call her right away and tell her never to come back. I knew that

wouldn't fly. She was scared but she was also mad...real mad.
She wanted the heads of those scuzzballs and fear didn't factor
into the equation.

"Chief, you're scaring the shit out of me!"

"Sorry Doc. I knew it would shake you up but you wanted
to know and I think it's better you know then go poking around
on your own and getting us all killed. Just hang in there. We're
going to see this through and clean up this Reserve. We're just
about there."

My light mood from moments before had turned to sludge
and the next few hours are going to be hell as I try to work and
figure out what to do next at the same time. Even worse I'm
booked to meet with my lawyer in Calgary in a few days and
try and sort out that part of my life.

I thanked the Chief and he left and Louise came in with the
morning list and I got to work. I wonder if distracted doctoring
is as big a crime as distracted driving. If so I'm guilty!

* * *

Sam Beaulieu grabbed his two bags of groceries and the
bottle of Gibsons and was about to leave his sister's store when
Junior came through the door. He hadn't seen Junior for half a
year and almost didn't recognize him. He was bulked up and
had a scraggly beard and was wearing an old winter parka
covered in oil stains.

"Junior, where you been? I haven't seen you since before Christmas. You been away?"

Junior Giroux was his nephew and when Sam was Chief he used to get Junior to run odd jobs for him. Junior's Mom was about twenty years older than Sam and ran the store since Sam was born. Junior was a little slow in the head but was always a hard worker. He usually spent every winter out in the bush with his trap line and only came into town to load up on provisions. Occasionally he took a trip to Fort Mac to pick stuff up for his mother but otherwise he rarely came to town.

"Hey Uncle Sam. Good to see you. I just come into town for some provisions and check on my mom. I got to keep bugging her to get her medicines from Fort Mac and if I don't she forgets to take them."

"How's the harvest?"

"Honestly it's getting tougher. I can trap pretty well without any trouble on the Reserve but those Midnight Sun guys are making it harder all the time. I managed to get a certificate off Reserve just to the south and it's a little better. Those guys at Midnight Sun used to be friendly and we got along good but they got a couple of new guys running security and they're a couple of assholes! Last time I came across their trails they hassled the shit out of me. You'd think they owned the goddamn land. We should kick their asses out of there. You think that chicken shit chief has the balls to take them on?"

Sam thought a minute then replied.

"When we let them on they were supposed to cooperate with us and not get in the way of our trapping but I guess they think they can do what the hell they want now. Guess you'll have to help me get elected again so I can kick their asses out of here."

"Sure Uncle Sam. I'll sure as hell help. Why don't you take a week and come with me out to my line. Weather's getting good and we can do some walking and lay around and taste a touch of booze. Just like old times."

"Hell of an idea, Junior! I'd like that. Just like old times. Then we can see what those Midnight Sun guys are doing. When we let them on I thought we had a good agreement but maybe I should check up on them. You staying at your Mom's?"

"Yep. Drop over later and we'll play some cards. I'll take some of your money."

Sam left and pointed toward the Reserve and the band office. Maybe he should go in and harass that kid chief. Hope his wannabe cop brother isn't there. He figured he would check out what Midnight Sun was up to then drop in on Wilfred. Sam and Wilfred were kind of at odds with each other since Sam lost the Chief election. Wilfred often accused him of being stupid and arrogant. He always seemed to be picking on him. Too bad he wasn't the chief. He could see how tough the job is. Sam was still pissed at Wilfred for not getting him more out of the

Midnight Sun agreement. If it hadn't been for him, Wilfred and that slime ball lawyer wouldn't have got to first base.

David Wah-Shee was in his office pouring over some accounts when Dawn showed Sam in. David and Sam didn't like each other and Sam never passed up an opportunity to jerk the chief's chain.

"Hello Sam. What can I do for you?" David wasn't too happy to see him…especially now with all these invoices spread all over the desk.

"Just thought I'd drop in and say hello. I had a talk with Junior and he tells me those Midnight Sun guys are hassling him when he tries to walk his line. When you going to run those guys off our land."

David eyed his onetime opponent and laughed. "Didn't you forget it was you that brought them on and signed that contract? You sure talked a lot during the last election. Told us that the company would build roads…make us all rich…give all the kids jobs. Haven't seen much of anything except a bunch of equipment tearing up the whole south portion of the Reserve. Guess they screwed you and the rest of us in the process. How much did they pay you anyhow?"

"You son of a bitch! I should kick the shit out of you for that comment," he yelled.

"Sam, get the fuck out of here. It's not your show any more. You come in and threaten me again and I'll make sure you won't do it a third time." David was livid and they both squared off. Just then Dawn walked in and looked at the two of them then announced that a couple of people were here to see the chief. Sam turned and stormed out and slammed the door.

"Dawn, one of these days someone is going to take a piece out of your uncle. He's got a nasty temper." He turned to his desk, gathered up the invoices and locked them away in his desk. Dawn went out to get the visitors and David sat at his desk and tried to get calm. He had no intention of starting a fight with Sam Beaulieu but that idiot was always trying to provoke him.

Sam drove away from the band office and pointed to Wilfred's house. He was in a rage and skidded to a stop, pounded up the steps and banged on the door.

"Sam, what the hell! Where's the fire."

"The fire's going to be up that goddamn chief's ass if you don't do something. He just accused me of being paid off to bring on Midnight Sun. I thought you said you had it covered…that no one could find out. I go in there and he's got a bunch of old invoices on the desk. Shit from two years ago… I tell you he's on to something and we got to stop him."

Wilfred pointed to a chair and said,

"Sam sit down and calm down. He's got nothing. We're in the clear. He can look all he wants. He won't find anything."

"Wilfred, you better be right because if anybody comes after me then you and that slime ball lawyer are going to go down with me. I know a hell of a lot more about that deal than you suspect so don't try and screw me."

"Relax Sam, have a drink and listen to me." He got up and poured a couple of ounces of scotch and gave one to him.

"That agreement is airtight. Any money we got for finders fees is safe and like I promised you, as soon as they finish the project you'll get your cut. Now finish your drink and go look in on your sister. She wasn't looking too good yesterday when I was over there. I think it's her heart. Why don't you get Junior to look after the store and take her to Vancouver or Calgary for a few days and have a little holiday? I bet she'd like that."

"Maybe you're right. I'll do that after I come back. I'm going out for a week with Junior to walk his line. Maybe I'll run into one of those goons from Midnight Sun and kick the shit out of him just to let them know they can't run all over us!"

"Bad idea, Sam. Those guys are way out of your league. You'll be the one taking the shit kicking."

Sam tossed back his drink, got up and stamped out. Wilfred watched him leave and cursed. "Damn fool is going to get us both screwed if he doesn't shut up. Maybe I should call Jozeph and clue him in."

29

Jozeph Laszlo was in an executive meeting with the CEO and COO of Midnight Sun when he got Wilfred's call. He excused himself and moved to the corridor and answered.

"What's the matter Wilfred? Why are you calling me here?"

"I think we have a little problem to look after. Sam was just here and raising hell about the Midnight Sun thing. He's been bitching that they are screwing him and the Reserve and should be kicked off. I tried to calm him down but I'm not sure I succeeded."

"Maybe I should contact Roberto and have him talk to Sam. If anyone can put the fear of god into him it would be Roberto Rubinowich. I'll give him a call and fill him in. He may want to go to Burning Lake himself and talk to him. I don't think we should leave it to the locals."

Wilfred replied, "I agree. Sam and his nephew are going to head out to Junior's trapline for about a week. When Roberto gets here have him call me and I'll give him directions. A little dose of reality is probably all he needs."

Breaking off, Jozeph muttered to himself, "It'll probably take more than a little dose. He's a loose cannon and he could sink both of us."

* * *

Roberto Rubinowich made his bones working for the KGB in the mid-eighties when, as a promising young Cuban he was sent to Russia for training and quickly established himself as a savvy, ruthless, take charge operative. However his career was interrupted by the fall of the iron curtain and the dissolution of the Soviet empire. Being a resourceful freelancer with a lot to offer the world of mercenary organizations he found himself first in Africa and then, as respectability seemed to be a better opportunity, as a shadowy soldier in the growing global environmental movement. Now, in his mid-fifties and moderately wealthy he worked mostly for the thrill or the buzz. He was dependable and loyal to the employer of the moment and at the moment he owed his loyalty to Watts Domain and Eli Watts. That Eli Watts was connected to an Asian energy conglomerate was no concern of his. He took his orders from Eli.

So when he was contacted by Eli and told that his talents were required to solve a problem quietly and with finality it didn't matter that he had to leave his comfortable home in Northern California and return to that godforsaken frontier in the Canadian north. He knew after that last meeting that he would be back to take charge. These things don't just solve themselves. Best plans are only best if the people involved are the best. That Indian who was raising hell after taking his share of cash a couple of years earlier was now a threat and Roberto was convinced that the threat had to be snuffed earlier rather than after a lot of damage was done. He packed lightly. The stuff he needed could be easily obtained after he crossed the border. This job should be interesting and probably even entertaining. He wondered with amusement if he would have to learn how to snowshoe.

* * *

Wilfred met Roberto and Jozeph in Edmonton and they discussed the problem. In his own mind Roberto already knew the solution but his success had always depended on good planning so, without giving details of his solution he let himself be filled in on the local lore of the Prairie Dene Reserve and the politics that ruled that society for several years. He learned more than he wanted to know about trap lines and snowshoeing and muskeg and local police. He sat quietly listening to Wilfred and Jozeph speculate on how much persuasion it would take to keep the lid on the operation. They assured him that the arrangement with Midnight Sun was secure and that the young chief was nowhere with his so-called investigation. The only loose cannon of concern was Sam Beaulieu and that could easily be solved with the carrot and stick approach. Roberto didn't explain that he had no carrots and his sticks were really big. No sense letting on that he had his own solution.

Following the meeting at an Edmonton hotel he declined the invitation to fly back to Fort Mac with Wilfred. He said he had some other contacts to look up and they would be hearing from him in a couple of days. He left the hotel, caught a cab and rode to a downtown mall, rode up an elevator in a business tower then immediately rode down to another floor where he exited and walked down two levels to the parkade where he picked up his rental car. He didn't know if Jozeph was under surveillance or not but he wasn't taking any chances. He knew the road to Fort McMurray was long and somewhat treacherous if the weather was bad but he had other plans. He had a contact from his former ELF days living east of Edmonton at Cold Lake near the Alberta Saskatchewan border. It was a little out of the way but the trip was probably worth it. He would have no trouble getting geared up there and then he could just head back to Lac la Biche and up to Burning Lake by the back way. No one would even know he was there. It had been no problem learning the location of the trapline worked by Junior Giroux.

He didn't even have to ask for directions. GPS technology was priceless. It could take you to the location of an outhouse in a forest if you had the coordinates. and the transportation. After Cold Lake he would have both.

Because it was mid-afternoon and the weather was good Roberto pointed his car toward Smoky Lake, a small community on the way to Lac la Biche. It was only about an hour or so drive and he could get a meal and a good night's sleep without anyone knowing he was there. The next day was good enough to get to Cold Lake. Wilfred had said that Sam and Junior would not get to the line for a couple of days so he could take his time. Might as well enjoy the early spring countryside in the bush. It reminded him of his training days in the camps in Russia…bush in the day and stars at night. No one to bother you. Just peace and quiet. Much as he loved his home in California he often yearned for the peace and quiet of a hermit. Maybe this would be a good place to retire.

* * *

Sam looked forward to the next few days. It had been many years since he walked a trapline and things had changed. No dogs any more. Snowmobiles and quads did all that work faster and with less fuss. There was still enough snow cover to get around but that would be gone in a couple of weeks so this was a good time to go.

He drove up to his sister's store and transferred his stuff into Junior's 4X4 and went inside for a coffee before they took off. He was still fuming about being accused of being on the take by that kid at the band office. Accepting a finder's fee was not being on the take. Everyone did it and made sure that their family got looked after. There was plenty of money floating around and it was stupid to think that only the white guys should make a buck. After this trip he was going to come back and mount his campaign to get back the Chief position. Wilfred and that low life lawyer better damn well help him. He knew enough to sink them and he wouldn't hesitate to pull the plug if they tried to screw him. For the first time since he was defeated a year ago he felt a renewed sense of optimism. This was going to be a good time for sure!

* * *

Seeing the screen light up on my mobile I see "Amy" and answer. We're about an hour behind but so what. My patients aren't going anywhere.

"Hi Gorgeous. You coming home soon. I miss you." It's been two days since I talked to her and each day she seems to be more chipper than I remember in several weeks. Things must be going OK.

"I'm landing in Edmonton Friday night. Do you want to pick me up? We could stay until Sunday then drive back."

"No can do. I have to fly to Calgary Sunday morning. I've got a meeting with my lawyer Monday morning. How about changing your flight to Calgary and I'll meet you there?"

"Should be no problem. My flight stops in Calgary Friday and I have to change planes for Edmonton anyhow. I couldn't get connections to Fort Mac Friday so that's why I called you. Why don't we meet in Calgary? Can you get there Friday night?"

If we keep this up we'll have to hire a travel lady. "Sure. Listen, sorry but I gotta go. I'll get to Calgary somehow Friday night. I'll text you the details later…Loveya!" I end the call and go back to work. Since Amy has been gone I spend my time seeing patients and catching up on book work. Then I go home, light a fire, grab a meal and a beer and log into some reading. My Wi-Fi connection is surprisingly good and I'm able to just stay abreast of the stuff I need to. The thought of a weekend in Calgary with Amy leaves me with a glow and a spring in my step. Louise looks up as I come out of my office and says,

"You better marry that girl before someone smarter than you gets hold of her."

Good ol' Louise. Never misses a thing.

All of a sudden the waiting room starts to empty as we shift into hi gear and tackle the ill and infirmed. I give a fleeting thought about my meeting with my lawyer and wonder what my life will be like in the next few weeks. Little do I know…

30

Louise is one of those rare people who can think and know almost at the same time. While shuffling people in and out, getting brief clinical histories from them for me, arranging for tests in Fort Mac or setting up appointments with Marla's growing group of chronic illness patients, she made all my arrangements for Calgary. All I have to do is get to Fort Mac before five tomorrow so I can catch a flight to Calgary. She has some connections with the oilpatch and to my delight she has found me a direct flight on one of their private charters. Maybe she's the one I should marry. She's now making arrangements for hotel. She doesn't ask me whether I want one room or two. The time passes quickly and not long after our usual closing we finish up and shut off the lights. It's been a while since I had pub food so I drive over to the bar and find a table.

As I'm pouring my beer and digging into my burger I look up and see a familiar face.

"Hi Carl. Good to see you get to town once in a while. How's the hand?"

Carl Reimer has kept in touch with some regularity and we mostly B.S. about the oil patch. He keeps me up to date on the world outside my office and once in a while looks for advice about his increasing anxiety about his job. He pulls out a chair and without asking, sits down. I can see right away that something's bothering him.

"Doc, I'm worried about some stuff at our camp. We check regularly for drugs and we have a zero tolerance to drugs but I think in spite of that we got stuff coming in. I've talked to the Mounties about it but there's not enough evidence for them to investigate so other than a few spot checks on the highway after a traffic stop they can't do much."

I can see he is pretty troubled by this but I'm not sure where I fit in.

"Where do you think I can help?"

"Well, a few days ago one of our workers was passed out for a few hours. He looked like he might have OD'ed but we don't know. He woke up eventually but denied taking anything. Because he hasn't been in trouble as far as we know, all we could do is suggest he get a checkup. He didn't argue so one of our guys drove him to Fort Mac because you guys were closed for the night. They checked him over and got some blood work

and found out he had taken some sort of painkiller. He's now
on suspension and required to attend a drug program or get
fired."

He went on. "I'm worried about that long time we couldn't
wake him up. We're a pretty long way from town and
something like this sounds pretty scary. Any suggestions on
what we should be doing?"

He had good reason to be fearful. A new drug was making
the rounds. Masking as MSContin and other opiates, this one
was an underground synthetic found in palliative care pain
patches and vet shops. It is currently finding notoriety in the
major cities and the First Nations communities. Many times
more potent than heroin it is killing people left and right. An
antidote has been available for several decades but is usually
found only in hospitals and paramedic units. Problem is, the
OD's usually don't survive long enough to get there.

"Carl, you and everyone in your industry have reason to be
afraid. This shit kills people before they can get help. The
answer may be education but that doesn't help the reckless
experimenter. However, the good news is that the antidote is
pretty safe, a hell of a lot safer than the drug. I can get you
some kits and show you how to use it. Think of it as an
automatic defibrillator in a hockey rink. Zamboni drivers have
been credited with resuscitating the old fart hockey players who
sometimes push the limits. Same thing with safety guys in the
camps"

We talked a little more and I arranged to get him some Narcan and show him and a couple of his safety guys how to use it. Then the conversation shifted.

"I shouldn't be talking out of school but our security force has me worried. Most of the rent a cops are ok but the two goons who recently seemed to take over spend more time making trouble than solving it. They're a law only to themselves. It's only a matter of time before we have some trouble. The company doesn't realize what's going on or they're sweeping it under the table. It may be crazy but I sometimes wonder if those goons are part of the drug trade."

"Carl, the best advice I can give you is keep your eyes open and your mouth shut. Stay invisible and stay safe and just do your job."

We had another beer and B.S.'d a little more, then he left. I was getting sleepy and tomorrow is going to be a long day. No book work tonight. I'm hitting the pillow as soon as I get home.

* * *

Roberto got to Cold Lake in the early afternoon. It was only a two hour drive and the roads were good. When he got into Smoky Lake the night before, he lucked out and found a bed and breakfast that could put him up. It was off season so he wasn't bothered by a bunch of nosy tourists. The bed was clean and comfortable and the proprietress left him alone. After a

great breakfast he checked out and browsed around town. The
hardware store surprised him. Concocting a story about looking
for ice fishing he soon had the owner telling him all about
outdoor activities for miles around. There was a section with
last year's camping supplies, all with reduced prices for quick
sale and Roberto embellished a story about how he would
rather support the small town guy. It wasn't long before he
assembled an all-weather tent with arctic sleeping bag, a small
camping stove with fuel, a folding camping saw and a few other
odds and ends he thought might come in handy. The owner told
him about Lac la Nonne, a little ways west of Smokey Lake
where guided ice fishing was a possibility. Wanting to lay a
trail of disinformation Roberto asked detailed questions about
the laws and rules of ice fishing and wrote down a couple of
contacts to call for guided fishing. He then spent a little time
cruising around the town before turning and heading for Cold
Lake.

The town of Cold lake is nestled in an area close to Cold
Lake on the Alberta Saskatchewan border. It has a population
of over 12000 and its main industry is the Canadian Armed
Forces base. Roberto had spent some time as a mercenary in
Africa with an ex-army corporal from the Canadian army and it
was there that he was going to get the specialized gear he
needed. Posing as a fishing guide, ex corporal Sandy Ritter was
less well known as an outfitter of a more lethal nature. He had
successfully flown under the radar in that community for the

last seven years and no one in the community suspected him as being an arms dealer with ties to some of the most dangerous criminal organizations in western Canada and the northwestern US. Sandy had assured Roberto that he had just what Roberto was looking for; a C3A1 Sniper Rifle - 7.62 mm. This was the premier rifle adopted by the Canadian army sometime in the 70's and since then has been employed in major conflict areas all over the globe. Weighing just a little over 6 lbs. when fitted with a 10 power scope it was the ideal rifle for competition and would suit Roberto's purpose perfectly. With a range of up to 800 meters it was perfect for what he had in mind.

Punching the coordinates to Sandy's acreage on the outskirts of Cold Lake into his GPS he soon pulled up to a comfortable cabin nestled in the trees. He knew he was under surveillance as soon as he saw the tower rising just above the cabin from the rear. However, Sandy knew he was coming and soon they were sitting around a roaring fire drinking scotch and catching up. Both knew better than to get into each other's business but because Sandy knew of Roberto's interest in the C3A1 he guessed that competition wasn't in the plans. They quickly agreed on a price and Sandy then asked what else was needed though he had a good idea. Over the next two hours Roberto loaded up on night vision binoculars, a laser range finder, camo tarps, 25 rounds of ammo and some freeze dried food. Sandy surprised him with a G41 Gen4 Glock complete with 4 full magazines. What the hell, Watts were paying.

Because it had been a few years since his old partner and he were together they burned a couple of steaks, drank single malt and told stories into the night. The next morning he loaded up his gear and turned toward Lac la Biche and north toward Burning Lake and his destination.

* * *

I'm sitting in a private lounge waiting to board a charter to Calgary. One of the large oil sands operators regularly runs from private airfields or the Fort McMurray airport to both Edmonton and Calgary. On this trip we fly direct to Calgary. I have to pay my way but the cost isn't outrageous and the service is great. It helps to have friends. Today was a whirlwind of activity and I barely got away in time to get to Fort Mac. One of these days the cops are going to catch up with me or I'll find myself up close and personal with an elk.

Amy should beat me to Calgary but only by a short time so we'll catch a shuttle to the hotel together. Bless Louise. She did a great job. Other than busy, things have been pretty quiet in town and I hope they stay that way. I vow not to worry about the stuff that I heard from Carl Reimer the night before in the bar.

This is the way to go. No long security lines or taking off shoes or other stuff. We climb aboard, fasten belts and take off. Seems ironic to burn all that fuel just to bring workers to dig more fuel. Despite my resolve to forget about Carl I'm half snoozing and half day dreaming and my mind keeps going back to him and his story…not the drugs but the security guys. Why does a company of that size need such a big security force. Seems excessive. Maybe I'm getting paranoid. What do I know about corporate security?

The flight is smooth and time goes by quickly. If all goes well the flight time is usually about an hour and twenty minutes. Beats the milk run we were on a while back. Looks like a leisurely supper with Amy tonight. She's been pretty closed mouth about her father and I'm anxious to hear how things went. I doze off and next thing I know we're skimming the runway and taxiing to the terminal. Sure beats several hours of driving over a winter road dodging tankers and trucks.

31

Amy beat me to Calgary and was there waiting for me and
we wasted no time grabbing a shuttle to the hotel. Dinner
could wait but not the wine. Room service is a great invention.
We can talk later.

"Did you miss me?" I asked.

"Nope." then she giggled. Must have been the wine. I chose
to ignore her.

"That was the smartest thing I've done in a long time," she
said. "It was great seeing my father again and we had a bunch
of days to talk and catch up and make up and say all those
things we were afraid of saying before. He really misses Mom
and I think that's why we were pissed off at each other. She
used to keep peace in the family and now we have no referee.
Andy showed up a couple of days after I got there and I picked

his brain for two days. His best advice was fold my tent and move back to civilization." She then went on.

"He got me an appointment with one of his professors of administrative law and we reviewed confidentiality and privacy stuff as well as criminal aspects of business law. I think it's time we brought in the Mounties. Whoever tried to shut me down seems to have backed off so I think we'll be OK."

I wasn't quite so sure. Anyone with access to knockout drops that ancient must be pretty sophisticated and ruthless. I don't think we're all going to walk away from this situation without bite back. I am, however ready to turn this stuff over to the Mounties and let them run with it. I'm a doc not a cop. So far we've covered all the bases and involved the people who should be involved. I agree that she should wind up the investigation and turn her findings over to the commercial crime guys. I think David Wah-Shee would probably go along.

That out of the way we got down to getting to know each other again. We've got two days here with nothing to do but have fun and I don't want to miss a minute.

* * *

Sam Beaulieu and Junior Giroux arrived at the trapline and set up camp at the little trapper's hut at the beginning of the line. They got a roaring fire going in the old stove and broke out the grub and booze along with a couple of decks of cards. It had been a lot of years since they played crib or poker with each other and they were anxious to take each other's money. Tomorrow would be time enough to start collecting pelts. Tonight they'd get into the booze.

Roberto peered at the hut from a blind several hundred yards from the cabin. He deliberately stayed away from the site. He didn't want them seeing a bunch of tracks and wonder who they belong to. His little tent was well concealed with cut boughs and he kept his little stove well hidden. The freeze dried food was OK. He'd had a hell of a lot worse in Africa. Sometimes he went a couple of days without a meal. He had lots of water and a bottle of scotch. He learned that trick from the American snipers who wrote about their experiences in the Vietnam war. He didn't quite understand how scotch kept you awake but he'd tried it before and it actually worked.

Having watched them unloading stuff into the hut, he figured they were there for the night and would walk the line in the morning. There was a game trail about 300 yards from where he was camped and he figured that's the trail they would take. Until they emerged in the morning there was nothing to do but wait. Roberto was good at that. If they came down that trail they would pass within 400 yards from his stand where he'd set up the rifle. If not, he could double back, get the rifle and stalk them. Just like Africa. Everything was ready to go. Nothing to do but get some sleep. It was cool but just above freezing. The snow was a little crunchy and anything coming down the trail should alert him. Darkness had fallen and there was a slight overcast with no wind and no moon. Thinking about the next 24 hours, Roberto rolled into his arctic bag and tried to get some sleep. This used to be exciting but now it was just work. It was about time to move on and find something more interesting in a warmer climate. Maybe Mexico or El Salvador. He had a lot of contacts there.

Sam came out of the hut about midnight for a pee and a breath of air. They had just about finished the bottle and Junior was snoring peacefully in his bunk. The night was quiet…almost too quiet. Nothing much moved at this temperature. It wasn't like the summer with the birds and crickets and scurrying varmints making the night sounds he was used to. He almost regretted not bringing his old hound so she could sniff out a bear or lynx and entertain them with her baying. He wasn't often in the bush without a dog and it felt a little weird. Shrugging off his unease he went back into the hut and his bunk. Tomorrow he would walk the trapline and next week he would prepare to launch another run at the chief.

Daylight came and with it a slight breeze with a taste of spring. It was too early for flowers but the trees were starting to show their buds and the day looked promising. Junior was up and had already put on the coffee on his morning fire and was heating the frying pan for a breakfast of bacon and eggs. The crackle of bacon and smell of coffee woke Sam and he struggled to his feet trying to shake off the substantial headache from the night before. While Junior cooked breakfast Sam checked their gear. They had brought along their rifles and a box of ammunition but it was unlikely they would run into anything that was worth shooting. Nevertheless out of habit he checked the rifles and made sure they were in working condition. Forgetting where he was he looked at his mobile for the time and temperature then realized that reception was either spotty or non-existent in this area.

"I think we should walk east from here and avoid the main trail until we head back." his nephew advised.

Junior knew this area like the back of his hand and had set his traps a couple of weeks before in game trails that were just barely visible to a stranger. The varmints usually avoided the main trails and kept close to the safety of the brush. Though Sam had done his share of trapping in his youth he had gotten a little rusty and was happy to let Junior take the lead. After a second cup of coffee laced with rum they filled their thermoses, grabbed their packs and rifles and headed off.

Walking east through the brush was hard work and Sam was beginning to wonder if Junior knew where they were going but after about twenty minutes they found the first snare and collected their first pelt, a prime, good sized muskrat. As it was late in the season, Junior and Sam knew that they wouldn't likely see martin or lynx but there was a reasonable market for muskrat and their pelts were in their prime at this time of year. Junior wasn't worried about accidentally catching a lynx. Even though the season was closed all he had to do is register the pelt with the wildlife guys and they would let him keep it. They collected the rat and carried on. As they picked their way through the brush Sam was still trying to get used to the quiet. He mentioned it to Junior who shrugged it off saying,

"It's sometimes like this out here especially during hunting season but we don't see many hunters around here at this end of the Reserve. There's not a hell of a lot of big game in the area. But you're right. The quiet is a little unusual."

They bushwhacked for another half hour and found another trap but this one was empty and there were no tracks around it. Leaving it until the next time they continued east away from their camp, stopping only for a nip of spiked coffee every twenty or thirty minutes. It was peaceful and pleasant though the bushwhacking was a little taxing for Sam who was out of shape and overweight. Junior kept teasing him about his condition.

"Too much white man living, Sam. You're forgetting the old ways"

Sam laughed. "You young pup. What the hell do you know about the old ways. I could still teach you a few things about this life. Try living in the bush for months at a time, shivering through blizzards and running out of food miles from nowhere."

Junior nodded in agreement. "That wasn't so long ago but life is a hell of a lot easier now. I do this because I like doing it."

They started their swing north, following Junior's line and collected a few more carcasses. It wasn't a big harvest but at least they were getting some exercise.

"Where the hell are all the birds?" Sam asked out loud. "There should be a few around. I haven't seen any for the last few hours."

Junior laughed. "You probably scare them all off with that fancy stuff you splash on your face every day. They know when a stranger is around and they hide." He laughed again. "Gotta re-educate you Sam. You used to know more about this stuff than me."

Sam turned to say something and at that moment his head exploded spraying Junior who was right behind him with his blood and brains. At the same time Junior heard the crack of the rifle and dove for the ground.

"What the hell...Sam!" but Sam wasn't answering. Junior looked in the direction of the sound, saw a glint of reflection off of something and he dove behind a tree just as a spray of bark filled the air and he heard another loud crack. Someone was shooting at them. That was no accident. Knowing that Sam was dead and he couldn't help him Junior flattened out and crab crawled over some scrub and found a hollow behind a rock and some bushes. Cautiously he lifted his head and was rewarded with another spray of bark followed by the gunshot crack.

Junior had never been in the army or had any training in combat but he knew the bush and he was a survivor and survival was his main concern now. He pointed his rifle in the general direction of the glint he had seen and let loose five shots then rolled away from where he lay just as another bullet hit the gravel next to where he had been. Junior had stalked elk and bear but never someone who shot back. His first instinct was to get the hell out of there and get help. He knew Sam was beyond help and much as he hated to leave him he had to get back to his truck and get away. Whoever was shooting at them meant business and Junior wasn't dumb. He knew he was up against a pro. But the pro was on Junior's turf and that gave Junior a little edge. He knew the trails and the shortcuts. Slowly he backed into the bush and quietly he edged onto a game trail well covered by brush. He then lay there waiting for his heart to slow down and his breathing to quiet. He was scared but not panicked...not yet, anyhow. He lay prone under cover for almost an hour, listening and sniffing the air. Finally peering through the bush to the place where Sam lay he saw a little movement and could barely make out a shadow rising from the bush just behind where Sam lay. Carefully Junior lined up his sights and guessed the range and squeezed off a couple of shots and was rewarded with a yelp of pain and the shadow dropped. Junior was sure he had winged him but he wasn't stupid enough to go rushing out in the open. Slowly he edged further back into the brush and circled to the east and further away from the camp. He figured that the shooter would think he would head back to the camp but Junior wasn't born yesterday. He felt a rage start to build. Sam had been his favorite uncle and even though Sam was a bit of a loudmouth and had a quick temper, he had always been good to Junior and taught him most of his field craft. It was that field craft that was to surface and save Junior's life now.

Junior suspected the shooter was new to the area but not wanting to take any chances, he continued to circle east and away from Sam. He carefully circled in a wide arc through the brush, keeping to the game trails that crisscrossed the area. He was quiet and moved with the stealth born of a decade of bear hunts. Sam was right. He cursed himself for not paying attention to the silence. The last thing he would have suspected was a gun fight in Indian country. That was the stuff of books and movies. It didn't happen in real life. Choking back a couple of tears of grief for Sam and fear for himself he very carefully picked his way through the bush. He was in no hurry to take a bullet!

* * *

Roberto lay in pain a few feet from his victim not wanting to move or make himself a target. He cursed himself for missing the second guy. Who would have thought he could have reacted so fast. And to top it off the guy had nailed him a little above the hip and it hurt like hell. He was sure it was just a flesh wound because he was still able to move his leg. However he wasn't taking any chances. He was in pretty good cover and he waited for the guy to show himself. After about a half hour of waiting and feeling the cold he began to worry about hypothermia and decided to chance moving out. He pulled himself erect and found he was able to walk OK in spite of the pain so he thought he should try and get back to his shelter. He limped back to where he original shot from and found two of his spent casings but the other two were not in sight. Obviously the other guy was long gone so the best thing was to backtrack to his tent, gather up his stuff and get the hell out of there. He estimated that he was at least two hours from his camp but there was at least three hours of daylight left so he took off at a half jogging limp cursing his bad luck. There was a little breeze picking up and it was getting colder. Hopefully the snow would hold off for a while. He was still about a half hour from the camp when he heard the sound of a truck and realized the other guy had beat him back and was going for help. The best thing to do was get his stuff and hike back to his car and get back on the road toward Lac la Biche. This place was going to be crawling with Mounties in a couple of hours and he meant to be long gone by then.

Getting to his camouflaged tent he quickly pulled it apart, packed it up and took off to his car which was hidden well off the forestry road. Lucky he had parked well past the cabin when he came in. Getting to the car he threw the stuff into the trunk and headed back to the access road that led to the highway. There was no smoke coming from the cabin as he passed it and the truck that brought them was gone. He grabbed his rifle and made sure there was a shell in the chamber and laid it against the seat. Then he tore off before the place was teeming with cops. What a total screw up. He was a little rusty but there was no way that shit head Indian should have gotten the best of him. Good thing the Indian hadn't seen his face. At least he didn't have to go chasing after him.

* * *

Junior was about thirty miles down the road before his mobile picked up service. He stopped and dialed 911 and got a dispatcher on the line.

"I need the cops as soon as possible!" he shouted. "My partner's just been shot and he's dead." He gave the coordinates of his camp and was then patched into the RCMP patrol car closest to him. It was about twenty miles up the highway and the dispatcher said it was responding. Instead of staying on the line he hit end and called the Reserve police line. Gilbert

Ahnassay answered on the second ring and Junior blurted excitedly.

"Chief! It's Junior Giroux. Someone just shot Sam when we were walking my line. He shot at me a couple times but missed but I think I winged him. You gotta get down here."

"Hold on Junior. Isn't your line off the Reserve just south of it?"

"Who gives a shit where it is!" he sobbed. "Someone ambushed my uncle and just about killed me too. I phoned the Mounties and they're on the way. It may not be Reserve land but it was one of our chiefs that got whacked. I don't know which side of the border it was on."

Then Junior surprised the Chief with his next statement.

"When I was doubling back to get my truck I passed a new Chevy Cruise rental hidden behind a tree fall just past our cabin. I snapped a picture of it as well as the plate. I didn't hang around to see who it belonged to. I didn't want to end up like Sam."

"Where are you now, Junior?"

"About 20 miles north of the access road just at the south end of the Reserve."

He added, "The dispatch told me to wait for the Mountie patrol car but if I see that Cruise I ain't waiting. I'm getting the hell out of here. I'm not getting into another shootout."

"Junior. First, someone's got to tell his sister over at the store. I'll have to send one of my deputies over . You're sure he's dead?"

"Gilbert, I'm wearing half his brain all over my coat!" and then Junior couldn't hold it together any more. He broke down and sobbed like a baby.

It was getting to be twilight and the snow was starting to fall. Junior was parked at the side of the road holding his loaded rifle and hoping the cops would get there soon. He looked at his mobile and saw that he had talked to dispatch about fifteen minutes earlier so they should be close. He turned on the hazards and waited. He heard it first; the faint sound of a siren and then the flashing lights and for the first time in a couple of hours he let himself relax.

When David Wah-Shee got the call from Chief Ahnassay he volunteered to get over to the store and tell Junior's Mother the tragic news and get someone to stay with her. Who better than Marla the nurse from the clinic. He quickly called Marla and arranged to meet her at the store and then grabbing his rifle he made a beeline for the door. Dawn saw his dark look of rage and asked.

"What's the matter? What happened?"

"Somebody just shot your uncle. He's dead."

"Uncle Sam is dead? What happened where? Who?"

"No time for that now Dawn. We'd better close up the office." And then as an afterthought he added more gently,

"Dawn, someone will have to tell your father. Do you want me to tell him or would you rather do it?"

"No, David. I guess I can do it." Stifling a sob she stammered, "I wish I knew more. You haven't even told me where he is. Where did it happen?"

"As near as I can tell it was out on Junior's trap line a few hours ago. I'm going to the store and then out there as soon as I leave the store. We're not sure if it was on Reserve land or not. The Mounties are on their way and Junior is waiting for them. That's all I know."

"My father will go nuts. He and Sam were not always on good terms but this is family. He'll raise hell with the Mounties and probably blame Junior for not looking after Sam. I'm scared of what he might do."

"What do you mean?" David asked. "What might he do"

"I don't know. I don't want to say anything else. I'm scared of him. I like my job here but he makes me tell him things and do stuff for him."

David Wah-Shee slowly sat down and looked at the trembling woman standing there with tears in her eyes and a helpless look on her face.

"Sit down Dawn," he gently said. "Right now it's important we look after Junior's mother and talk to your father. I won't say anything about what you just said for now. Let's wait until all this gets looked after then you and I can have a talk. We'll

keep this between us. I won't tell anyone what you just said."
He rose to leave but then sat back down again.

"Dawn, why don't you come with me to Giroux's then we
can come back to see your father if you like. I'll wait to hear
from Gilbert before I go out to the line. They don't need me
there right now."

She looked up more defeated than sullen and replied,

"Thanks David. That will be easier. Please don't tell my
father what I just said. I should have kept my mouth shut. I
know too much. Next they'll be after me."

The Chief could see that she was on the edge of becoming
hysterical and knew that something grave had just been
revealed. What was this all about?

Saying nothing further he took her to his truck and drove
off the Reserve past Wilfred's house and turned toward
Burning Lake.

Gilbert Ahnassay had lights and siren going and was tearing
down the highway toward the access road. The snow was light
but there were a few slippery patches. In a couple of places he
had to back off a little or he would be joining Sam in the great
beyond. 'What the hell is going on?' he thought to himself.
Gilbert had never had to handle a murder before and secretly
was happy the Mounties got called first. As he passed the spot
where he thought Junior had called from there was no one there
so he continued on to the access road. He knew approximately
where Junior's trapper hut was located and a couple of minutes

later he pulled up to the shack and Junior's truck next to a Mountie cruiser. The boot tracks went toward the hut so Gilbert ran over and banged on the door. Junior was just coming out with Porter, the RCMP guy.

Porter greeted him with a grim face and shook his head.

"Sam is still lying out there and he's about ninety minutes away. I got a couple of units with a couple of Razors coming here. You got winter gear in your truck?"

Gilbert nodded and headed to suit up. Porter and Junior already had on their winter gear.

A Polaris Razor is an ATV especially suited for this terrain though the trails can be too narrow in places. Junior assured them that he could guide them close even at night in the snow. Because there was no heat in the hut they all piled into Junior's 4 X 4 to wait for the other cops to arrive with the gear. While waiting, Junior told his story to Gilbert with Porter listening for any strange variations. Junior wasn't stupid. He knew he would be the first suspect but wasn't worried. His rifle was a hell of a lot different than that cannon that got Sam. He was sure that he would be OK. While they were waiting he led them down the trail to where he had spotted the rented Cruise. Porter took some pictures of the site and actually got a couple shots of the tracks. Also, he had seen the plate number on Junior's camera and put out a bulletin to all law enforcement units. What had to be done now was secure the murder site and look for clues.

That was an impossible task in this snow but maybe they'd get
lucky and find a casing or two.

Injured as he was, Roberto was still a very careful man.
After about twenty minutes he found a turnoff where he
couldn't be seen. He pulled in and made sure he was well
hidden. First things first. He pulled up his shirt and sweater and
looked at the wound. There was a little blood showing but most
of it had clotted. As he suspected, the bullet passed through the
meaty part of his hip just above the bone. Nothing there but
muscle and other soft tissue. He taped a bandage over it putting
a little pressure over the bandage by winding a stretch bandage
over it. Crude but effective. Then he got out and opened the
trunk. First thing he did was grab a license plate he had lifted
from a car in the airport long term parking lot. Quickly
switching plates he took the rental plate and walked back into
the bush a couple hundred feet and hid it under a fallen log. If
somehow that Indian had spotted the car they would trace it to
him but he wasn't worried. It just meant that one of his bogus
ID's was burned. He had a couple more in case he needed them.
He would drop the car at a different rental site in Edmonton and
phone his return in as if nothing had happened. He could grab a
cab out to the airport and be out of the country in a few hours.

He wasn't worried about his buddy at Cold Lake dropping a
dime on him. They had plenty on each other so it would be
suicide for his buddy to put two and two together and phone it
in. The next thing to do was dump the rifle. That was a little

tougher but there were lots of lakes between here and Lac la Biche and he was sure he could find one in the bush that would serve his purpose. After rechecking his field dressing, he returned to the highway and, keeping to the speed limit he estimated his arrival in Lac la Biche to be approximately an hour and a half; plenty of time to check into a motel and get some sleep.

32

The news of Sam's murder spread quickly and by morning everyone had found out. Louise texted both Paul and Amy with the news and was waiting for a reply. It didn't take long for reaction to set in. This was big news and though Fort Mac had no local TV outlets the city had cable TV and the Edmonton stations were all over the story from early morning. TV trucks from both Calgary and Edmonton showed up in Burning Lake at the crack of day and reporters were interviewing anyone who would stop to talk. Already there were nearly as many theories of the crime as there were persons interviewed. Like most sensational stories, the blame game was in full swing and any newsworthy events of the last six months were dragged up and connected to the murder.

The crime scene techies had examined all there was to examine of the scene and Sam's remains were transported to

Edmonton for autopsy. As expected, no substantial clues were discovered. No casings, no personal materials and no snagged clothing bits showed up. Junior, himself retrieved a couple of spent casings from his rifle and identified them They seemed to back up his story. Initial examination of Sam's body showed that he had been hit from the opposite direction.

New fallen snow covered most of the area so a search for the shooting site was fruitless but the whole area was taped off with the object of a secondary search after the snow had cleared. It was late enough in the season that the cops figured they could return in a couple of weeks. Junior's cabin was sealed and a padlocked gate was secured across the access road.

Amy responded to the news with shock and said that Paul would text a reply soon. The buzz at the morning clinic was blaming the East Indians and even a few were wondering where Wah-Shee was when it happened. Upon hearing that, Louise angrily told all who could hear her that she was talking to the chief at his office when the murder was supposed to have happened. Giroux's was closed and Junior was nowhere to be found. After the cops got back to town last night they spent a long time interviewing Wilfred who, understandably, was shocked and enraged. The whole community was in mourning and the pub was overcrowded. Already there was talk of raiding the Midnight Sun camp and throwing those bastards off the Reserve... maybe even scalping those asshole Lebanese.

Gilbert heard some of the talk and wasted no time in suggesting the town mayor request extra RCMP help. He also persuaded David Wah-Shee to temporarily hire three more special constables for the Reserve. In addition, the provincial Sheriffs Service agreed to provide extra patrols.

Most disconcerting was a report in one of the Edmonton papers that an unidentified informant speculated that the murder was linked to First Nations activists who were reacting to reports that the former chief was considering a run at the present chief in the next elections.

David Wah-Shee read the article with mounting anger and frustration and wondered who the unidentified informant was. Who would benefit from spreading such bullshit? Where do these stories come from. Next they'll be picketing the office and throwing bricks.

Sitting back with a sigh he decided that the less he said the less trouble he could get into. He decided to refer all questions to his chief of police and the RCMP. Now for the first time he wondered what a tool pushing "hotshot" operator was thinking when he got into politics. To make matters worse, Dawn had phoned in sick and said she'd be off a few days. He worried about her because of her statements the night before and though he promised her he wouldn't repeat them. What if she was right and was actually in danger? Deciding he desperately needed to talk it over with someone he trusted, he locked the office and drove home. His wife was the wisest person he knew and maybe she could help him out.

* * *

I'm sitting here in the hotel in shock. I was in the shower when Louise texted me and I'm wondering what to do. Good thing I have Amy here where she's safe. Hopefully things will have calmed down by the time I get back next Tuesday or Wednesday. When I changed my plans to go to Calgary Friday night we had decided to keep the office open for the time I was away even though I wasn't there. Louise and Marla could look after most stuff and I was at the end of a phone. Aziz was working day shifts at Fort Mac but said he would troubleshoot any emergencies and the EMS people were prepared to make the ninety minute trip to Fort Mac if necessary.

In the meantime Amy and I have a lot of talking to do. Last night late into the night after we caught our breath she told me about her reconciliation with her father and even talked a lot about growing up with him and her mother. On balance she had happy memories with only a few dark shadows related to his cultural biases. Earlier in her life she was a second mother to her kid brother and it was only in the last few years the process went through role reversal.

I'm due to visit my lawyer Monday morning so we have a couple of days to ourselves. Now this news from Burning Lake has put our last few months square in the center of our consciousness.

"I'm calling Kelly Fitzpatrick!" I exclaim.

"You're what?" Amy counters. "Are you out of your mind? Whatever will you tell her? She'll think you're nuts!"

Ordinarily I've learned to bow to Amy's judgement most of the time. She's less likely to fly off the handle and do something stupid. But this time I sensed that I was right. I pulled the macho man thing and said, "I'm not going to argue. I'm phoning her!"

I pulled out my phone, found her in my contacts and hit send. It was Saturday morning but miraculously I was talking to her directly. I didn't beat around the bush.

"Officer Fitzpatrick, I need help!"

No reply. I guess they teach how to deal with hysteria.

"Hello," I say

"Go on. I'm listening."

Usually I can give a pretty coherent and well-ordered summary of events in a neutral and spontaneous manner. It comes from residence training and preceptors who badger you without mercy. However, today I wasn't in my best form. She was a good listener however and she even seemed to figure out what I was telling her. After my stumbling account she just said,

"I'll call you back" and disconnected. My number is blocked. What the hell...she doesn't even know where I am…or does she. Giving her the benefit of doubt I put my phone away and sit there with a million things going through my jumbled brain.

Amy comes over and puts her arms around me and gives me a squeeze and holds me tight for a minute. Finally she says,

"Paul, we're going to get through this. You've got good instincts. Just trust them."

Saving a life is a piece of cake. Saving her life could be a nightmare. How little do I know how that thought will come back to haunt me.

We go downstairs for breakfast but I'm not sure either one of us feels much like eating.

Our hotel is a little boutique affair right in the middle of Calgary near the tower. I'm so upset I can't even worry about dutch treat…well almost so upset. We're both making pretty good money so the cost is irrelevant. I'm still smarting from my former life where my society queen picked the spots and I paid for them, I guess. Anyhow in spite of our mood our appetite picked up and we sat and enjoyed the meal until my phone vibrated.

"Hello"

"Where are you going to be an hour from now?" No hello.

"I'm in Calgary and I'll be up in my hotel room."

"I'll call you back." Lady of few words. Wonder what she talks about at home?

Saturday morning in downtown Calgary can be delightful if the wind isn't blowing and the streets aren't awash with melting snow. It was pleasant and we felt like walking so we went north and found ourselves in China Town. It was like being transplanted to another city. I once talked to someone about urban art who opened my eyes to the elegance of cities and their architecture. Ever since then I have looked at the buildings no matter which city I happened to be in. Downtown Calgary has some of that elegance and promise of adventure. I can't imagine an event like 9-11 in Calgary.

With only about twenty minutes to get back to our hotel we turn back south and speed up. I wonder what officer Fitzpatrick has come up with.

We got up to the room with five minutes to spare and true to form my mobile rang.

"I am calling on behalf of Federal Officer Fitzpatrick. My partner and I can come up to your room or you can come down to the lobby and check our credentials for security purposes." The chance of a bogeyman showing up exactly when CSIS was calling was remote so I said to come on up and I gave him the number. A couple of minutes later there's a knock on the door and I open up to two guys, slightly built and wearing suits. Calgary on Saturday morning and they come in suits. Sure isn't like TV. They both had out ID's that looked official and the older one opened with, "Officer Fitzpatrick called and asked us to come over and talk with you about a possible security problem."

"Security for who, us or you?" I smart assed. No smiles.

"Sorry, we're just a little strung out with the stuff going on the last 24 hours."

The younger of the two chipped in, "We know. Before we go any further we should check your ID's if you don't mind." Boy, were these guys ever careful.

We produced our drivers licenses and then got down to business.

Older guy started right in. "We got two hits on a guy you might be familiar with from your previous discussions with Fitzpatrick. One Roberto Rubinowich was seen exiting the arrivals at both Vancouver and Edmonton International approximately four days ago. We aren't sure what name he's travelling under but the images are good. After Edmonton he dropped out of site. Because of your encounter with his alleged employer a while back and the murder of a chief of one of the Reserves near Fort Mac we are looking for a possible connection. We are coordinating with the RCMP and the two of us have been assigned to get all your information and provide security for you over the next few days."

'Oh goody', I thought. 'Babysitting in a love nest.' But I was relieved we weren't hanging out on a limb.

We all got comfortable and I nudged Amy to take the story from the top. Between us we filled in the whole story, leaving out any speculation about whys and wherefores. In case they hadn't seen the accounts in the Edmonton media, I showed them the speculation about Indian activists.

"Yeah, there's all sorts of speculation but no hard evidence about anything. Main thing is that you folks stay safe and that's our job." This from young guy. He went on, "One of us will be sitting in the lounge at the end of the hall during the day and the other will be downstairs in the lobby. At night the Mounties will have a man in the lobby. If Rubinowich shows up we'll nail him." As an aside he added. "That was dumb of them trying to drug you when you started looking around. If they hadn't done that we wouldn't be looking at you now." We all shook hands but avoided the hugs and they left. My respect for Kelly Fitzpatrick was rising higher all the time.

It was too early for lunch but it was Saturday and there was a cozy pub downstairs so we took the elevator down and found a quiet corner and ordered a couple of pints of some fancy craft beers. Amy had her iPad and was scrolling through the news looking for accounts of the murder. Social media and Facebook were full of speculation but little real information other than the fact that the community was in mourning and all the politicians' hearts were going out to the families and the authorities were working hard to bring the person or persons responsible to justice. One snippet on Twitter had a brief comment that the band council was reviewing the contract between Midnight Sun and the Reserve's First Nation Council. 'Wonder where that came from?'

I was considering calling David Wah-Shee but he was probably in the middle of a whirlwind of media and local calls so I held off. By now Louise will have closed the clinic so I call her mobile for a chat.

"Hey Louise. Shitty news. Learn anything new? How's everyone making out? I feel crappy leaving you guys alone to handle this all yourselves."

"No problem, Doc. Lots of B.S. going around but mostly just shock. We're OK here. The cops have temporarily cleared Junior but are waiting for final autopsy reports to see if any bullet fragments were recovered. but they're pretty sure Junior's in the clear. Weren't no strangers in town that anyone remembers but whoever did it probably didn't come through town."

A thought occurred to me. "How would anyone know they'd be there at the trapline. Who all knew they were going?"

"That's the big question. Junior says he didn't tell anyone. We can't ask Sam but he didn't know himself until a couple of days ago. No one knows who he talked to in the last few days. Guess that's a question for the cops to answer."

We talked a little longer and I asked her to keep in touch and then disconnected.

With all this going on I haven't had a chance to think about my Monday morning meeting with my lawyer. All I want to do is be free and ready to start the next chapter of my life. All this stuff isn't helping my mood or attitude. I'll have to watch myself at my lawyer's office. The last thing I need is to let my mounting rage get in the way of my tongue. Good thing Amy is here to keep me calm. Too bad she can't come in with me but she'll probably find some fancy expensive place to spend a few bucks on whatever classy ladies spend bucks on.

* * *

This time Roberto didn't stop when he got to Smokey Lake. He had managed a few hours' sleep at a cheap motel in Lac la Biche the night before then changed his dressing after carefully first washing the wound. He made sure to take the washcloths and towel with him. Everyone knew motels are always losing linens to their clients. The wound still hurt but he expected it would be better in a couple of weeks as long as he cleaned it and dressed it with regularity. Because he still had the Glock with him he didn't trust taking a flight with it but, knowing he would probably be back in Canada in the next month or two, he set the GPS to Beaumont just south of Edmonton where he could use another ID to rent a small storage locker for his gear at a "U Store IT" facility. Three hundred bucks of Eli's money should do for at least six months. Better to be prepared. Lots to clean up before he disappeared for good. There were lots of car rental offices in south Edmonton where he could ditch the unit and phone in the details then he'd be in the clear. An airport shuttle to Calgary and a different airport should get him to Seattle in a short time. It wasn't the first time he met this kind of challenge. Just another part of the job.

33

It's Saturday afternoon in the pub at Burning Lake and business hasn't been so good in a long time. The beer is flowing freely and the rhetoric almost just as freely. A group of young oilpatch workers from the two local Reserves are sitting drinking and talking about the events at the south end of the Reserve. Every one of the young bucks had some connection by friend or family with Sam Beaulieu and Sam stories continued to make the rounds. There was an uneasy truce between the few Midnight Sun people sitting and eating and talking quietly and the more robust oil patch workers occupying most of the tables. It was a weird atmosphere of celebration of life and memorial of tragic death. Sitting quietly at the bar was a young couple chewing thoughtfully on the pub burgers and chasing the bites with scalding coffee. The man, dressed in worn blue jeans and a sloppy plaid shirt displayed a three day growth and looked every bit the usual worker who lived in similar bars around the province. The woman was stylishly dressed in modest clothes and her hair and makeup were perfect but understated. If anyone had seen them enter, they might have connected them to the dark SUV with the modest logo on the door identifying them as members of a prominent provincial news organization.

The pair had arrived only a short time earlier and were looking around, targeting their prey, all the while playing back their strategy to each other. The last thing they wanted was a wild demonstration with violence and sensation. Both recognized this was a significant story and it must be handled with care. Settling on a couple of young fellows drinking beer and quietly discussing whatever, the young woman moved to their table and spoke to them.

"Excuse me." They both looked up at the young woman in a little confusion and she skillfully grabbed their attention with her next words.

"My friend and I are on our way from Cold Lake to Fort Mac to attend a meeting and we noticed the burned out building with all the wreaths and flowers around it on the way into town. What's that all about?"

"It's about those goddam Muslim assholes taking over the country." Whoops. Hit a nerve.

" Really? I work with a lot of East Indian folks at Cold Lake and they seem pretty nice to me. What happened here?"

"Couple of rugheads crashed their rig into the church that's been there for seventy years and burned it to the ground. Now they're blaming the Indians for causing the crash. Everybody knows it was those rugheads!"

The young women sits down at the table uninvited and looks at the two men and says,

"I guess I should explain. We're going to Fort Mac to cover a story. We're news reporters. We noticed that that building burned a while ago. Why all the attention now?"

"It's not about the fire it's about our jobs and this damn Indian Reserve. We elected a chief expecting to get a fair shake at the jobs here and all he's done is pony up to the Paki energy companies and now he's gone and got our last chief murdered!"

"Murdered!" she exclaimed. "When did that happen?" All the while knowing the answer.

"Yesterday. Some asshole shot him while he was walking his trapline."

Knowing she had hit paydirt she pushed on.

"You know, this story is much more important than the one we're going to Fort Mac to cover. I wonder if you men would talk to my partner and me on camera. We could step outside and set up. We'd be glad to buy your dinner afterwards."

"No need for that, lady. We can buy our own meal. Sure. We'll talk to you. 'Bout time someone listened to us."

Later that night two angry aboriginal oil workers were featured on network television talking about East Indian job stealers, reckless equipment operators and radical locals murdering a respected chief because he was talking about a comeback to throw the bums off the Reserve. The feed into cable TV reached Fort Mac and spontaneous demonstrations sprang up in front of the Mosque and Molotov cocktails sailed out of the crowd crashing near the front door. The demonstrations died quickly when the Mounties arrived and the damage was soon cleaned up but the message was loud though not exactly clear.

Back at Burning Lake David Wah-Shee watched the news clip with frustration and a building rage. He just wanted to load up his family and clear out of town but he knew he would never do that. What happened to Sam was not David's fault. Could it have been Sam's own fault? Could it be related to that damn contract? What was in it that was so important? What was missing? Who would try to kill a young accountant and then murder a prominent leader in the community? It couldn't be just a few bribes. There was more at stake than that. He had to get in contact with Amy Pham and warn her to be careful. She was supposed to be back from the east on Monday. Thoughtfully he pulled out his phone and called his most reliable informant.

"Louise, have you heard from Amy Pham in the last few days?"

"Yeah. She and Paul are in Calgary. He's got a meeting or something and they arranged to meet. I guess it's not news that they're seeing each other more than just casually."

"Has she heard what happened to Sam?"

"Yeah. I texted both of them. I think they're really upset. Doc called me and apologized for not being able to be here. He also asked how you were doing. He's really worried about you."

"You got her mobile number? All I got is her office number."

Louise read off the number to him and asked him what was up.

"Nothing new Louise. I just want to talk to her. Thanks for the info."

He disconnected and thumbed in the new number. After three or four rings he heard Amy answer, "Hello."

"Amy. David Wah-Shee here." It was pretty noisy where she was and the rattle of dishes and loud voices made it almost impossible to hear her.

"Hi David, Just a minute. Let me get to somewhere quieter." A half a minute later she came on again and the noise was a lot less.

"Sorry David. I couldn't hear a word you were saying. What's up?"

"I just talked to Louise and she said she told you about Sam Beaulieu getting shot."

"Yeah, David. Paul and I are both shocked. Do you know what happened yet?"

"Nothing so far but the news is all over the story and all hell is breaking out. I just got blamed by a couple of renegades for setting the whole thing up and it's being blabbed all over the TV. What a mess! They just had a mini demonstration in front of the Mosque in Fort Mac and someone threw a couple of Molotov cocktails. It didn't amount to much but I'm worried that this might be connected to the stuff we're doing."

"We wondered the same thing also. In fact we have a Mountie shadowing us and there'll be a guard in the lobby all night."

"I'm glad they're taking it seriously. I just phoned to say take care and stay safe. I'll call you when you get back on Monday."

"I won't be back until Tuesday or Wednesday morning but call me if it looks like we were right. It's time to dump this whole mess into the cops' laps before anything develops and one of us gets killed."

"OK. Just stay safe and don't believe all you hear or read. Remember we know the whole story except who killed Sam."

"Maybe we know that too."

"What!"

"I think the cops have a bad guy in their sights but that's not for publication. For gosh sake don't get spooked into suggesting that to anyone. We'll talk when I get back."

"OK. I'll keep my mouth shut. Good to talk to you." He disconnected and put his mobile on the desk and sat thinking…and thinking…what the hell…Who?

* * *

Wilfred Natannah was driving down the highway from Burning Lake to Edmonton, a distance of about 300 miles by the back way and it would take him at least five hours to get there. Maybe by that time he would be cooled down enough to keep from strangling that fucking slime ball lawyer. After being grilled by the RCMP for at least three hours last night he called Jozeph Laszlo and told him he was coming to Edmonton and they had better meet as soon as he got there. When they last met he agreed that Sam needed some persuasion to keep his mouth shut but that didn't mean he wanted him killed. Sam was family and even though they often fought and argued, killing him was way over the line.

Those cops last night kept coming back to asking about anyone who knew Sam would be out at the trapline. If they knew that Wilfred was the only one besides Junior and his mother who knew they were walking the line then they would have put two and two together and held him as an accessory. They had asked him a few times if he knew that Sam was going with Junior and of course he denied it. He was certain that Sam wouldn't have told anyone about their argument or any of the details. There was no reason for him to let anyone know that they had doctored that damn contract. Now Sam was dead so the cops would never find out who all knew that he was going with Junior. If Junior had in fact mentioned it to anyone, the cops could look hard at him instead of connecting the shooting to Wilfred. The only person Wilfred told was Laszlo.

It had to be Roberto, that Cuban muscle who worked for those Asians Laszlo was connected to. What a mess. If he saw that Cuban assassin again he'd tear him apart himself!

The next guy to eliminate would be Laszlo. Maybe he should wait until they dealt with that accountant. No telling what she'd discovered or who she talked to. Dawn had assured him that all the documents that he told her about had been shredded but what if he had missed a few. Maybe he would hold off on the Cuban until they'd had a chance to silence the accountant.

As he drove he poured over a bunch of scenarios to halt this thing but it all came down to the same thing; find out what the woman knows and get rid of her, Laszlo and the Cuban.

* * *

Eli Watts was in a tight spot. He controlled Roberto Rubinowich but now Roberto had made a bad decision and soon would be a wanted man. Eli and Roberto had a long and profitable association and there was mutual respect and loyalty to each other but now Roberto had put them at risk. He had stopped Sam from exposing their part in the Midnight Sun contract fraud but the Wu Zhao people weren't going to be happy about all the attention. They were counting on capitalizing on their legal right to exploit mineral resources found on the Reserve as a result of Midnight Sun's project which included advanced geological prospecting not fully understood by the Indians. Even Wu Zhao's unsuspecting partners in the venture had not recognized the significance of that little bit of fine print buried in the contract. Jozeph Laszlo was the one responsible for due diligence and he had assured the Asians he would be long gone from the picture before any legal challenges surfaced. It was a big gamble for Wu Zhao but the incredible wealth suspected to be lying untapped in that aboriginal territory made the gamble worth it.

Eli reluctantly decided that after Roberto cleaned up his mess his usefulness would be compromised beyond repair and he would have to be dealt with. Roberto had texted that he was clear of Calgary, Canada and would be landing in Seattle in the next hour or so. The senior Watts sighed and turned to his other duties. This was going to be unpleasant. Perhaps he could chastise Roberto when he arrived and after a few days send him back to clean up his mess. The accountant would have to be detained and interrogated. There was no avoiding it. After that, all loose ends would have to be taken care of or they would all be at extreme risk from the Asians who had the most to lose.

* * *

Before boarding his flight from Calgary to Seattle Roberto took the precaution of disguising himself to resemble one of his most reliable identities. He was aware of facial identity technology and wanted the authorities to think he was still in Canada if indeed they were aware he had entered several days before. Though his other identity was effective he wasn't confident that facial matching capability would miss his true identity when he arrived at Vancouver on the way in. He had used the older identity a number of times in the past and by now it might be compromised. After landing he grabbed a cab to take him to Watts Domain office and his meeting with Eli. He rarely messed up an assignment especially one this important. He knew Eli was disappointed and angry and he couldn't blame him. He still believed that things would have turned out differently if he had been successful in killing both subjects and disposing of their bodies in the wilderness as he had planned originally. The fact that the younger of the pair proved more resilient than he had estimated may have explained the outcome but it didn't excuse it. He screwed up and he knew that in this business there were consequences for screwing up. He hoped for a chance to change the outcome and this time he wouldn't screw up.

His cab arrived at Eli's office and in a few minutes he was in the room with a visibly angry and disappointed employer. Eli wasn't a person who shouted or screamed obscenities. Rather his cold fury was effective and only very stupid and eventually very dead persons attempted to cross him.

Roberto described the whole situation from inception through planning to execution in a neutral and methodical manner as though he was giving a well-researched report to a high court judge. That Eli was his judge was not lost on Roberto and he attempted to strike the right tone of acknowledgement and contrition on his account.

Eli listened quietly without interrupting then simply asked, "Can this situation be resolved in our favour or is it hopelessly lost?" Eli truly wanted Roberto's opinion and recommendation. That is how much respect he had for his competence.

"If you trust me to return and clean up this mess I am confident we can still salvage it."

Roberto then proceeded to outline the plan he had thought out during his trip back.

Eli was used to hearing plans with risk and then putting them in motion. He understood risk and knew well the difference between risky behaviour and reckless behaviour. He also knew the consequences he would suffer if he did not fix this to the complete satisfaction of his Asian associates. Together they went over the plan in detail and both agreed on the importance of finding out the extent of information the accountant had discovered and the hard evidence she had amassed. Any further action would then proceed from that point. They agreed that the sooner the accountant could be interrogated, the quicker she could be neutralized. Shortly after having his flesh wound attended to and repaired by a trusted physician in a private surgical facility Roberto was once again on his way back to the Canadian north.

Just after Roberto left the office of Watts Domain, a middle aged, slightly built Asian man in an expensive but conservative suit entered the front office and quietly announced his presence to the receptionist at the desk. She immediately stood and led him back to the office lounge, asked him to make himself comfortable and then left to announce his arrival to Eli Watts. Eli quickly walked down the hall to the lounge, entered it and closed the door. Shaking hands with his visitor he exchanged a few customary words of greeting, offered coffee or tea then opened the real conversation.

"Mr. Chen, I regret to confirm that the incident in northern Alberta is the result of an action we undertook to safeguard your involvement in our mutual enterprise. The operative involved has been interviewed and is returning to that area to take the necessary steps to rectify the mistake. I have personally examined the plan and approve it. Your involvement in the enterprise remains undisclosed and your organization is not compromised."

Speaking quietly in excellent English the visitor responded.

" Mr. Watts, your organization has always provided a high quality service. We are disappointed that such a failure in that high quality has been demonstrated but your reassurance is comforting and I expect that we will be successful in bringing this to a satisfactory conclusion. I must emphasize, though, that our organization will not hesitate to intervene when necessary to further safeguard our interest."

His words sent a chill up Eli's spine and he immediately realized that Roberto would not fare well at the end of the mission. So be it. The two men rose, shook hands and the oriental gentleman left as quietly as he had arrived.

34

My appointment is at 9:00 AM this morning at an office nearby in the Bankers Hall building. Amy and I spent most of Sunday hanging around the downtown area wondering why we were hiding in the outback of Alberta. Amy discovered a performance of the Calgary Symphony Orchestra at the Southern Alberta Provincial Auditorium and cajoled me into brushing up on my classical music. Surprisingly it was a delightful afternoon concert of American jazz and the musicians were excellent. The afternoon passed quickly and after a late and leisurely but pricey dinner at a cafe near a river park we strolled back to our hotel. Too bad we couldn't afford to buy dinner for our Mountie shadow but that's what taxpayers are for. We settled into our room and ordered a movie. Amy won the coin toss and dialed in a chic flick and I promptly fell asleep.

Sometime later I was only slightly aware of being awakened, coaxed out of my clothes and into heaven. I love hotels and late meals.

We are sitting having breakfast and Amy is strangely quiet. So much has happened that we are overwhelmed and not talking is probably the most sensible thing to do. I shouldn't be more than an hour and she is planning to stroll through some of the shops with her buddy keeping her somewhere in sight, I hope. While I'm busy she has promised to get us checked out and ready to catch a shuttle to the airport. I wonder whose credit card she's going to use.

I don't have any idea what will happen at the lawyer's office but I hope it will help me shed my prior life with at least my meagre wardrobe intact. She probably won't want my jeep. Her new Lexus is undoubtedly a better ride. My lawyer told me that Carol and her lawyer would join us after about a half hour. I wonder who pays for the drinks. This has not been a bitter separation. In fact we have barely spoken or communicated since I left. I can't even begin to guess what Carol feels for me or for that matter what she ever felt for me. I know that in her eyes I'm a huge disappointment but I've never really been good as a performing circus bear. The last thing Amy said when we left the hotel was, "Keep your cool and your sense of humor and you'll do fine." Maybe I should have sent her and gone shopping with the cop myself!

The lawyers' office is a modest legal practice on the fourth floor of Calgary's answer to the skyscraper community found in the downtown of most modern large cities. It's pretty intimidating until you realize that those who work there and those who visit there all eat, sleep, cry, laugh, dress and play in about the same way. It's the ability of those folks who work there that sets them apart from the rest of us. I hope my lawyer is on top of his game.

We sit down in a small comfortable conference room and begin to go over the documents we have exchanged and the various submissions he has filed along with the submissions filed by Carol's lawyer.

"This all looks pretty straightforward, Dr. Cross," he announces as he shuffles the pages and gathers them together like they were notes for a speech or a lecture. "Is there anything else you have to add before we invite your wife and her lawyer in?"

I look at the pile and know that I should be questioning everything but right now all I want to do is get this over with and get out of here.

"What about you?" I ask, probably looking as dumb as I must sound.

He laughs and picks up the pile. "All this stuff is a record of everything we know about you and your wife and your assets and liabilities. What I can't understand is the lack of demands made by you when your wife has asked for everything but your underwear. What are we missing?"

Feeling a little sheepish but also somewhat annoyed I counter. "Look. I no longer want to be married to her. We have major differences on how we should live our lives. I came into this marriage with a jeep and some modest savings. She and her daddy are worth more than twenty times more than what I'm worth. What the hell does she want?"

"I think she wants you. I'm asking you why you think that is. What do you have that she hasn't been able to get? What have you got to offer if she can't get you?"

Wow! That's a curveball I never expected. I haven't a clue how to answer.

"I don't think I understand." I murmur to myself as much as my lawyer. "I just want out. I'm not for sale. She can't buy me. She can't collect me or put me on display." I'm getting hot but I remember Amy telling me to be cool so I change my tact.

"Look. I think we made a big mistake. It's as much my fault as hers. But there are big differences here that can't be fixed. I don't want to spend the rest of my life with her. How do we settle this?"

Again the shuffling of paper. "Dr. Cross you are a licensed physician with post graduate training and international experience. On the open market you are worth about six hundred thousand dollars a year. By living with this woman for the last few years you have created in her an expectation of a lifestyle that can be supported by that yearly income. She may have a rich daddy and a mid-level management career but that doesn't translate into your kind of income potential."

'What the hell...what am I ...some kind of cash cow...some kind of...utility?' I take a deep breath and pause a little longer than necessary for both of us. Before I can reply he continues.

"Our task is to convince your wife and her lawyer that their expectations are unrealistic and they have read the situation all wrong. For that I need you to give me a firm commitment to let me do the talking regardless of what they say or what taunts or barbs they direct at you. Do I have that commitment? Will you trust me to do that"?

This guy should be treating bikers in an ER ward. He's gone from soft spoken con man to a snarling bulldog without missing a beat. Maybe I can learn something from him.

"OK, you got it. Try and get me off with my Jeep and my underwear and enough cash to pay your bill."

He laughed and replied "If I can't do better that then I'll pay half your settlement and won't charge you a cent." Wow again! Arrogance or confidence, who cares. This I gotta see.

He gets up and goes to the door to admit the next nightmare in my life. Carol comes in looking like a million dollars followed by a young attractive lady with a briefcase. What, no back pack?

We make introductions and Carol and I exchange less than cordial hellos and we sit down. The young lady wastes no time.

"In situations like this we generally counsel some form of dispute resolution process but Dr. Cross has been adamant in his claim to vacate this marriage."

'*Vacate?...now I'm some kind of vacation home? This is not going to be fun!*'

Nothing from Mr. cool sitting next to me.

The young lady shuffles a few papers, clears her throat and continues.

"Doctor Cross has divulged a pre-tax annual revenue of one hundred and fifty thousand dollars after accounting for reasonable overhead expenses. A search of average revenues accrued by physicians in his peer group suggests a more realistic revenue to be about six hundred thousand dollars. His wife has made the reasonable claim that Doctor Cross allowed her to expect that she would have a lifestyle more in keeping with the latter figure. Consequently we have an opening offer of three hundred thousand dollars a year for twelve years which is a current average life expectancy of marriages between persons of my client's age and education."

Three million six hundred thousand dollars. Is she out of her fucking mind?

My knight in shining armour pushes back his chair, stands and says in his most sincere manner,

"Please excuse my bad manners." Would either of you like coffee or tea or maybe some water? *Or maybe some arsenic mixed with rat poison.*

They both politely wave a decline and sit waiting for a reply and the nice looking lady sits poised with her pen while Carol fiddles with her mobile, no doubt texting her banker to open a new account.

After a beat he says quietly, "No" and sits down.

"I beg your pardon," says nice lady in a not so nice tone.

"I said no." Nothing further.

"Well how does your client wish to counter?" she asks in phoney sincerity.

"He has no counter. We have chosen to conduct this exchange of information on a logical basis. With all due respect your submission is purely an emotional response with absolutely no basis in fact. When you are able to present some facts that are not conjured up in some cheap pulp magazine then my client will be happy to begin a negotiation. Now if you will excuse us my client has to get back to his one hundred and fifty thousand dollar a year job looking after people with more modest expectations." He stands and heads for the door.

He is out the door and into his own office before any of us can react and I am speechless. Carol pierces me with a look of pure fury and her lawyer mumbles something about seeing us in court and they storm out of the conference room to the exit. As they disappear my guy comes back out of his office

"Round one." he says. "That wasn't so bad. At least you still have your underwear."

"What the hell happened in there?" I stammer. "What am I missing?"

He smiles and says, "Tomorrow I will get a phone call asking me to schedule another meeting and I'll reply that you are not available as you have returned to your duties in northern Alberta. Then I will get a request to counter and I'll reply I don't work that way. I work from facts and the facts are that the present Ms. Cross has far more assets than her estranged husband and I'm not quite finished evaluating her clients net worth. In fact I will require more information about her assets prior to her marriage and of course I will ask again to see the prenup agreement that I previously asked for though I won't acknowledge that I know there never was one."

Still in shock I shake my head and say "Three and a half million? She must be nuts."

" Mere theatrics, my friend. Now they have been sucked into playing their own game with themselves. No self-respecting court will pay any attention to their horseshit and they know it. It may take a little time but I think your Jeep and underwear and my fee are safe."

He took my elbow and steered me toward the door and added. "This will take some time but I'm confident that we will actually come out of this with your wife paying my fee and all expenses. I don't think it fair that we try to scoop up something to which we're not entitled."

One thing at a time. Maybe a little breathing space is what I need. First we have to settle this thing with Amy's audit then we can settle my marital status as an encore. My respect for the legal profession just edged up a notch.

We chatted for a few minutes and set a tentative time for the next meeting some time later in the summer. I wonder what Amy will say.

There was no charter flight to Fort Mac this time but WestJet from Calgary direct to Fort McMurray this afternoon still has a couple of seats and Amy and I grab them up and take the shuttle to the airport. No milk run this time. I'll drive back to Burning Lake first thing in the morning and Amy can get on with her work. I hope she still has a job. I'm still thinking of three and a half million dollars.

35

The waiting room was full to overflowing when I got back to the clinic and now I'm sitting in my office with Mrs. Giroux. She reluctantly came in with Junior and she is obviously in physical distress as well as deep grief. Sam was her last surviving sibling and it is obvious she needs attention immediately. We don't have a hospital in Burning Lake and she needs urgent treatment for her heart failure. TLC and a couple of meds won't cut it. I'm on the phone with an internist trying to get Mrs. Giroux admitted to Northern Lights Regional Hospital in Fort McMurray on an urgent basis and after running through most of the usual BS about waiting lists and outpatient strategies and limited resources I casually mention that Mrs. Giroux is the sister of the slain ex chief and the tragedy had tipped her over the top into severe cardiac decompensation. I restrain from commenting that the hearts of all the politicians

were going out to the families involved in the tragedy and
perhaps one of them could donate their heart to Mrs. Giroux.
However he got the message without my inappropriate sarcasm
and EMS transfer is being arranged as we speak.

Junior has assured me that she will consent to go and he
will look after the store and I breathe a sigh of relief that at least
this crisis has been averted for the time being. I leave the rest of
the details to Marla and Louise and I begin working my way
through the list.

We work through noon, grabbing a sandwich and a coffee
between patients. In spite of the shooting, the steady parade of
patients pose no complex challenges and we are now finished
the day and ready to close up for the night. I have received a
surprise invitation from Renée Wah-Shee for supper and
waving a good bye to my faithful staff I'm out the door and off
to the Reserve and the home of the Wah-Shees. This is my first
contact with David Wah-Shee since the shooting and we both
know of each other's anxious questions to be resolved. No one
knows where the rumor started that there was an activist group
supporting David who was reacting to the news that Sam was
considering a run at David in the next election. We both knew
that this had to be related to the audit and Amy's drugging.

We held off talking about it during supper and waited until
Renée collected their two little girls for bed then we grabbed a
coffee and sat around the fireplace in their comfortable office
den. David's business continued to thrive even while he was up

to his neck in Reserve business. Renée looked after his books and David had hired his cousin to take on the trips he couldn't commit to so it looked like he was juggling things OK. He told me about Renée's brother's possible role in helping Amy sift through the rest of the documents and it sounded like a pretty good idea but I suspected the Mounties would probably grab all that stuff before long and take over the investigation. The picture was becoming clearer but as far as we could see no familiar names popped up. All the diverted cash seemed to go to offshore accounts after clearing the bogus deposit accounts in the bank at Fort Mac but those accounts could not be attached to any person. Time for the Mounties to get subpoenas and start digging.

I knew Amy was keeping a journal of the whole process and backing it up religiously. The external hard drive with the backup was in the safe at her office. I suspect she will copy it and hand it over to the Mounties along with copies of all the documents and her notes. Once the investigation goes public and it becomes known that the Mounties are involved Amy should be in the clear. That should happen in a week or so. I can hardly wait.

* * *

Using his newest ID and disguise Roberto flew to Great Falls, Montana where he picked up a rental and crossed the

border at Del Bonita, a little border crossing in Southern
Alberta. The ID and the disguise did the trick and he was soon
on his way on the long drive to his destination at Cold Lake.
There, after negotiating a shopping list with Sandy Ritter he
geared up and then went on to hook up with an old comrade, a
French veteran helicopter pilot who would be arriving in a
couple of days from now. Sandy, through a couple of cut outs
arranged for the pair to rent a Bell 206B chopper from an
aircraft charter company out of Nisku.

Roberto was to meet Richard Charbonneau, his old
comrade pilot at Edmonton International at Nisku and bring
him up to date on the mission. Richard would then hole up in a
hotel and wait for word from Roberto to fly to Fort Mac and get
ready for the next phase. In the meantime Roberto would turn
in his rental and under another assumed identity, rent an SUV
for the drive to Fort McMurray to set the plan in motion.

Leaving Nisku he stopped at the storage facility and
retrieved his Glock and the GPS as well as the night vision
binoculars and the camping equipment salvaged from the
aborted shooting several days before. He then visited an army
surplus store in Edmonton and bought sleeping bags, more
camping equipment and assorted supplies. Wanting to be fresh
for the trip he found a small motel and checked in for the night
to get some sleep. His wounded hip was aching but the Doc had
fixed it up pretty good and he hardly had a limp. Early the next

morning he set out for the long drive hoping that this operation could be ended soon.

A couple of the locals working for Watts had Amy under surveillance and had spotted the RCMP plainclothes cop watching her place. He would have to be taken care of when necessary but they didn't need the complication of killing a cop. Because they knew Roberto was suspected in the killing and therefore considered a risk to Pham they figured the RCMP would keep an eye on her unless they could be convinced she was no longer at risk. When everything was finally in place, Eli was to plant false reports of sightings of Roberto in southern Washington, Oregon and Northern California and when this information was shared with CSIS and subsequently the RCMP the latter would most likely reassign the officer and just check in periodically. All the bad guys needed was a window of a couple of hours and they would be able to pull off the operation.

Roberto arrived in Fort McMurray in the evening and met with the two locals. Together they went over the plan in a motel where they had rented a couple of rooms one of which was a small suite. The next morning they sorted out their supplies and equipment and added to their inventory a few last minute items including a couple of bottles of Canadian rye whiskey. Time to put the call in for Richard and his chopper. Jozeph Laszlo had earlier provided topographical maps together with coordinates for the mine and using these they had marked the location of the lease owned by Midnight Sun. It was on the Alberta Saskatchewan border close to the southern shore of Lake Athabasca not too far from Athabasca Sand Dunes Provincial Park. The only way to get to it was by air but the chopper could easily manage the distance especially with a couple of fuel bladders on board. It should be no problem. After the snatch, Richard, and somebody who could watch over the accountant, would transport them to the camp then Richard would return for Roberto. Thinking about the plan while it evolved, Roberto ran several options through his mind and kept coming up with the same answer. Wilfred Natannah was a major contributor to crafting that damn contract and his daughter was a somewhat reluctant accomplice to the conspiracy. Perhaps that could be turned to an advantage. If Dawn Natannah could be convinced that her father was at risk unless she helped then the problem could be solved. Dawn could be recruited to watch over their captive during the time leading up to the necessary interrogation and then returned home secure with the idea that if she talked, both she and her father would come to serious harm. Depending on the outcome all those witnesses could be dealt with at an appropriate time. As for the lawyer, his days were coming to an end. Already steps were being taken by the Asians to take over Midnight Sun and absorb it into the Asian conglomerate and Laszlo wasn't part of the long term plan.

* * *

Back at Nisku, the site of Edmonton International, Richard was finishing his one day demonstration of his flying competence required to transfer the European licence that identified him by a different name to a Canadian licence for private helicopter operation. He could then rent the Bell that Sandy had arranged. It was a piece of cake. The company offered him a job on the spot but he graciously declined claiming that he was committed to another organization involved in aerial photography and geological survey. Urging him to reconsider when his current contract finishes they proceeded to complete the paper work required before releasing the machine to Richard. Paying in advance for one or two down days with a credit card in the name of International Home Securities Inc., Richard returned to his hotel to wait for Roberto to call. He didn't have long to wait. He was to take possession of the chopper early the next morning and fly it to Fort McMurray to meet Roberto. This looked like a fairly routine job though the illegal aspects of the mission made it a little more risky that an aerial photography gig. Richard thrived on this stuff. Working with Roberto in Africa a decade before, he had carried out a number of more risky assignments. This was Canada. There weren't any shoulder launched SAMs here. In a few days more, if all goes well, he should be back at his home in the Azores.

As he retreated back to his hotel in the evening he thought of a number of similar missions he had pulled off with Roberto. There was that one where they snatched that tribal leader who was raising hell with the energy company that was drilling for oil and shipping it by pipeline to the Mediterranean. He still remembered the fat old guy kicking and flailing when they pushed him out of the chopper over the jungle. Then there was the time he had to pick up Roberto when the government troops were closing in on him. That was a hairy trip. If he hadn't had the shooter with the fifty cal machine gun with him they may have never made it that time.

Richard was a pro and though he was a soldier of fortune he maintained his discipline. He didn't use drugs and never drank alcohol within twelve hours of a flight even though eight hours was the usual rule. That was a pity because he would have enjoyed a drink to go with the excellent meal he intended to have tonight at Roberto's expense. There would be time enough to enjoy a night of booze and ladies after this gig was finished before he headed home. Grabbing a cab from the airport to the nearby hotel he didn't see the oriental looking figure watching him while talking on his mobile.

* * *

A high pressure front had moved into central Alberta during the night and the dawn broke to a clear sky with little wind. The forecast predicted nothing but great weather for the next six days. Richard checked out of his hotel and caught a cab back to the airport to take possession of the Bell and ferry it to Fort Mac. This was going to be the easiest part of the trip. He just had to make sure he didn't stray into the east west commercial corridors servicing Edmonton International. With the closure of the downtown airport the traffic around Edmonton was considerably reduced and he had an uneventful straight shot at Fort Mac and figured to be there in well under two hours.

Roberto was at the Fort Mac airport to greet him and help him stow the first load of supplies and equipment from the SUV to the chopper. They fueled up and filled the extra bladders so they could do the return trip without trouble then climbed into the SUV and drove to their motel on the edge of Fort Mac where they met up with the two locals. Roberto filled in the plan for dealing with an unsuspecting Dawn Natannah and dispatched them to Burning Lake to watch her so they could pick her up at a moment's notice. Roberto and Richard then returned to the airport to complete the first phase of the plan.

Roberto had no worries about locating the abandoned mine but finding a suitable landing spot might be problematic. However they had aerial photos of the general vicinity and several dry spots with openings in the brush were visible. He was confident they would find a place to put down near enough to where the mine entrance was supposed to be so they could unload the chopper. With the preliminary stuff looked after they climbed aboard and set off for the mine.

The outside range of the Bell would eat up most of their fuel on a return trip so there wasn't a lot of time to cruise the area but the extra fuel they carried in the cargo hold should look after that problem They could unload the fuel containers at the site and use some of them to top up the tanks for the trip back. They could then bring more fuel with the next trip. Roberto figured they would only need two trips to outfit the camp before bringing their guests. Paying attention to details was the key to successful planning and successful planning was critical for successful mission completion. He wasn't going to take anything for granted and make the same mistake as he did with that chief and his partner!

The further north east they cruised the more bodies of water they saw. Most were small lakes but their GPS showed the shores of Lake Athabasca about forty minutes ahead. However Richard was confident that he was on a direct course for the coordinates of their destination less than thirty minutes away. Dropping down to about fifteen hundred feet he rechecked his coordinates to make sure he was right on target and twenty three minutes later he found himself hovering over the coordinates and looking for a suitable site to put down. The last thing he wanted to do was settle into a mud bog but with the temperature hovering at minus one Celsius he wasn't too worried about getting stuck. There was a level patch about a hundred feet off from his GPS coordinates and he eased over, descended, and gently set the Bell down onto the clearing. This was the right spot but where was the opening of the mine?

Just off to the side of the chopper stood a little stand of brush covering a rock outcropping that suggested overgrowth and nothing else looked promising. Without the GPS they would never have spotted it from the air. Cutting the power to the chopper Richard climbed out of the machine. Roberto had already hopped down and was halfway to the site. They pulled aside some bush and there as if by magic a small opening surrounded by rotting timbers appeared in a rocky hillside confirming the location of the abandoned mine. A shallow shaft descended several feet and soon widened out to a small cave like cavern. Evidence of a collapsed tunnel a little further in suggested a cave-in sometime in the distant past. This wasn't much of a mine but it would probably do.

Along with the camping equipment and supplies they had brought a compact gasoline heater as well as a camping generator. At least they would have some light and heat in their little hidey hole. Next trip in they would bring in kerosene and another heater and a camp lantern. They didn't plan on staying long but wanted to be sure they got the information they needed before they abandoned camp. The mine would be easy to conceal again and would make an excellent tomb. A little discomfort was to be expected but that was no problem.

Quickly they got to work unloading the chopper. They figured on one more trip before transporting their guests.

* * *

David Wah-Shee was up at Fort McMurray for a meeting tomorrow with police as well as band lawyers and wouldn't be back until the following day. Wilfred Natannah was seldom seen in the community and his house was dark but it was assumed he was looking after his businesses legal or otherwise and no one was asking. The whole community was still in a state of disarray but leaders both on and off the Reserve were gradually bringing some calm and a return to order. The pub continued to do a brisk business over the weekend but there seemed to be fewer Midnight Sun people in town. No one expected the Muslims to stray far from the camp but the Lebanese Christians loved their beer and were a common sight every few days and especially around payday.

It was later in the afternoon and Dawn was alone in the band office working on arrangements for Sam's wake when a large looking stranger flanked by two guys Dawn recognized as Midnight Sun security guys knocked on the locked door. 'Now what?' she thought to herself. It was late in the afternoon and she was getting ready to leave for the day so she opened the door and asked, "What do you guys want? We're not open until tomorrow. Who are you looking for?"

The big guy wasted no time.

"You're the daughter of Wilfred Natannah?" he asked.

"Yes" she replied with sudden apprehension. "Is something wrong? Did something happen to him?"

"No, he's OK but you'll have to come with us."

"Are you serious?" What do you want? "Who are you?"

"Your father and I are partners and you've been helping him with some stuff having to do with Midnight Sun. It's best you come with us." His tone was menacing and Dawn immediately knew something bad was going to happen to her. Though she was terrified she stammered,

"I don't know what you're talking about!"

"You can either lock up and come quietly or you can get bad hurt and come with us. You try and fight us and both you and your old man will regret it. Your choice. Make up your mind."

Now frightened more than she could remember, she began to tremble and barely stifled a cry. She desperately looked around but quickly saw that she was alone and there was no one to help her. Realizing that she couldn't resist all three of them, she turned out the lights, locked the door and walked with them to the dirty dark SUV parked outside. She got in the back and one of the guys got in next to her. The big guy got in the front passenger seat and the other guy climbed in to the driver's seat, started up and they drove away. Helplessly she looked at her father's dark place as they passed it and turned north towards Fort Mac.

"Where're you taking me? What do you want with me? I don't even know you." and then she started to cry again.

The big guy told her again. "Shuddup and stop your bawling. Nothing is going to happen to you if you do as we say. But if you give us any trouble we'll tell the cops about how you drugged that woman and shredded all those files and you'll go to jail for a long time. So don't play innocent with me. We know all about your part. You're one of us and if you want to get out of this alive or stay out of jail you better do exactly what we say. So stop your sniveling and listen to me."

"What do you want me to do? All I did is what they told me to do. I don't know anything about any damn files except my father wanted me to shred them."

"Then I guess we're going to have to turn your old man over to the tribal police and give them enough evidence of his drug dealing to put him away for a bunch of years."

"No!" she protested. "You can't do that. What do you want?"

"We've got a little chore to do and we need your help. We want to have a little talk with that accountant but first we have to get her someplace where we can talk to her alone. We're going on a little camping trip and we need you to look after the camp."

"What do you mean? I don't know anything about camping!" she protested.

"We'll show you all you need to know."

He then went on to describe how he was going to question the accountant in a safe place out of town and see what she knew about the Midnight Sun deal. As they sped down the road he outlined what he expected of her and promised that if she did a good job she would be safe and so would her father. When he finished clueing her in he added a little more menace to his voice and delivered a threat.

"If you don't cooperate you will be hurt more than you can imagine."

Then he demanded she give him her mobile phone.

"Do you have your boss's number on this?"

"Why my boss?" she asked "What are you going to tell him?"

"Nothing," he answered. "You are. You're going to text him and tell him you need to leave town for a few days; to get away from all the upset at home and work. You're going to tell him you're staying with some friends in Fort Mac but you'll be back in a few days."

"I can't do that!" she protested. "I have to arrange the wake and the funeral for my uncle and there's no one to look after the office. He'll tell me to come back or I'll get fired. And he'll want to know who I'm staying with."

"Then make something up. He can't know everything about your personal life. Do you often text him?"

"Yeah," she reluctantly replied. "He's used to getting texts from me both for his business and the band office business."

"I'm going to make it easy for you. I'm going to text him for you."

He quickly tapped out a few sentences and showed them to Dawn. Quickly she scanned the draft and objected, "That doesn't even sound like me."

"Well you'd better make it sound like you. Your old man's life depends on it. Tell me how you'd say it."

Not wanting to alarm David and make him suspicious and get her and her father into trouble with this scary guy she gave in and in between sobs and sniffs she told him how to make it look like it was her message. He made the changes, looked over the message, showed it to her and hit send. Roberto sensed that she was finally settling down and starting to see that cooperation was a good idea. Maybe she might actually be ready to do as she was told.

After the text was sent, he said in a less threatening voice,

"We're going to be staying overnight at a motel in Fort Mac. Don't worry, you'll be OK. We even have a separate room for you. You won't have your phone and there's no phone in your room and one of my guys will be sitting outside your room by the door just to keep you honest and safe. Tomorrow or the next day we're going for a little helicopter ride. Do your part like we ask and you and your old man will be safe and in the clear."

Dawn was still upset and scared but she felt a little safer for the meantime though she still wondered if he was telling her everything. She knew that she was in trouble because of what she had done for her father and uncle but maybe if she did what she was told that would all go away. Thinking of that, she stopped asking questions and arguing with them. But she didn't exactly like the idea of some scary ape staying by her room alone with her all night.

It was later in the evening when they pulled up to a motel on the edge of town and parked in front of a unit at the end of the building. The big guy who did all the talking stuck a card in the slot and they entered a shabby but reasonably clean looking suite with two rooms. He went into the bedroom and removed the phone then told her to make herself comfortable in the bedroom and asked her if there was anything particular she wanted to eat. She wasn't much hungry but she couldn't resist answering with some spirited sarcasm.

"How about steak with mushrooms and onions and some apple pie with ice cream; and yeah, don't forget the coffee or maybe a nice wine"

"Don't push your luck." he retorted then turned to one of the other guys and told them to go out and get a bag of Big Macs and some beer. As the guy was leaving he opened the door to another guy standing there with a laptop and a briefcase.

"No names," Roberto cautioned the newcomer then stepped aside to let him in.

"Was this the best dump you could find in this town?" the new guy groused. "At least your room doesn't smell as bad as mine."

"Quit your bitching. At least you won't be holed up in a winter camp like me. Did you work out a flight schedule so we can get this job done and get out of here?"

The new guy opened up his laptop and fired it up. He pulled up a document with what looked like a schedule of some sort together with a bunch of numbers all in table format.

"Got it all here. I've worked in the trips we've already done, fitted in three more trips, one for our guests..." grinning at Dawn ... "and one for the rest of the supplies then I'll be able to come back here and take you out. If I get away first thing in the morning soon as it's light we should be able to ferry our guests out tomorrow afternoon and get everyone settled. Then I'll get back and I'll ferry you out the next day." Turning to Dawn he laughed.

" You and our other guest will be nice and cozy in our little camp overnight. Too bad we can't leave you a rifle in case some varmint comes sniffing around. You might get ideas and that wouldn't be cool." He laughed again.

"Stow it, you asshole," the big guy growled. " Nothing's going to bother them in that place. and we'll be setting a couple of traps in case anything does come sniffing around."

Hearing that, Dawn protested, "You're not leaving me alone out in some camp overnight all by myself. What if there are any bears around there!"

"You won't be alone. You'll have a friend with you. You'll have pepper spray and a couple of flash bangs to scare away anything nosing around." He added. "Your job will be to look after your friend and keep the heater and lights going. Do that OK and you'll be back home with Daddy in a couple of days."

Dawn felt the beginning of a panic attack coming on. She used to get them when she was a kid but they went away after she finished school and only surfaced slightly while she was taking her office management course and writing exams. But this was no exam! She used to go camping overnight with her ex-boyfriend and they would stay out for three or four days in the wilderness but that was in the summer. Besides they always had a rifle or a shot gun. But this was something new. And these guys wouldn't say their names but didn't try and hide their faces. Could she believe them when they said they would let her go after this was all over? And what was going to happen to the accountant when the big guy finished questioning her? It didn't add up. They would be all alone in the wilderness with no phone, no guns and probably miles from anywhere if they were taking a helicopter. She knew they couldn't run

away. There was no place to run to and no way to get help.
Suddenly it dawned on her. These were the guys who shot Sam
and after this was over they would kill her too! With that
realization all she could do was sit there and try very hard not
to cry.

After a while the Big Macs and the beer arrived but she was
so terrified all she wanted to do was get away from these
animals. But she was starting to get fighting mad and her brain
was pouring over all the things she might do to escape. At least
she had a day to do something.

She got up out her chair went into the bedroom and
defiantly slammed the door. She heard them laugh then quiet
down and all she could hear was murmuring then the door to
the unit opened and someone left, leaving the outer room quiet.
She lay on the bed, shivering with fright as much as the cold,
then when she couldn't stand it anymore she went out into the
other room to see what was happening. Only one guy was left
in the room and he was sitting in a chair by the door sipping on
a beer and reading a book. He looked up and said not unkindly,

"There's still a burger left. You better eat it. It's going to be
a long day tomorrow and you'll need the energy. Don't worry
about me. I won't hurt you. I'll just sit here and snooze all
night." Then he turned back to his book and ignored her.

She looked at the TV that was turned on but had no sound.
Suddenly feeling more alone than she had felt in years she

turned and went to use the bathroom and wash up. Then she shuffled back to the bedroom and shut the door.

* * *

This morning David Wah-Shee is up at Fort Mac where he and the Mounties have a preliminary meeting with band lawyers regarding the Midnight Sun agreement. He'd mentioned the other night at supper that he would be back in a couple of days and Dawn would be looking after the band office while he was gone. He said she was still pretty upset and probably would only be there for part time during the day. There was a bunch of running around to do and, with Junior and Mrs. Giroux now at the hospital in Fort Mac, Dawn would be the only one around to look after most of the arrangements for Sam's wake and funeral. That was probably going to be delayed anyhow because his remains had still not been released by the coroner's office.

Because the meeting is preliminary, Amy was not invited and she's probably getting caught up with all her other duties that have undoubtedly piled up while she was away. The cops assured me that until Rubinowich was located they would provide around the clock surveillance and protection. That was reassuring but I can't help feeling that there are a couple of loose ends we're missing.

It's mid-morning at the clinic and I stop for a quick coffee and out of habit I text Amy a short message asking her if everything is OK. I'm looking for confirmation that the cops are doing what they're supposed to be doing. I'm rewarded with a short chirp and the shorthand script of the texting addict. <im OK cop at sec desk hes cute u2>. I've got a whole new language to learn if I'm going to keep up any distance relationship with her. Louise is bugging me so I'm back at the grind. It looks like another day of catch up and working through lunch. I put on my happy face and head in to see a wailing two year old and her scowling mother. I wonder if it's me or the kid she's scowling at…probably both.

36

Kelly Fitzpatrick was just coming out of a meeting when Kermit, her man mountain partner cornered her and said, "What do you make of this. Yesterday morning some sheriff's office reported a sighting at a little airport in Montana that matched your APB for Roberto Rubinowich. About eight hours later we got a similar report from a state trooper in southern Idaho that they had been called about some guy who matched his picture was seen filling up at a local Chevron Station and now we just got a notification of a couple sighted traveling near Jackpot where the guy is a ringer for our man. Looks like he's on his way to California. I think he's suspected of having a place somewhere around there. So far we've heard zilch from our border crossings in B.C. or Alberta and nothing from any airports where we circulated his known identities."

Officer Fitzpatrick looked at the information and thought about it for a few moments.

"Better get that report to the RCMP at Fort McMurray. I think they've assigned some resources for guard and surveillance on that accountant Amy Pham after that Indian got shot. They may want to reconsider."

"Yeah" replied Kermit. "Good thought. Right now he's being considered a person of interest and the public has not been advised. I bet the Mounties will probably want to change their plan."

"This case gets weirder and weirder. A little place like that and we hear of an attempted murder of a local, deliberate sabotage of a tanker truck, a murder of a local Indian chief, and all the while a suspected ELF terrorist operative is roaming our country. And now he's running around half the pacific northwest and nobody can grab him. Wonder if he's really our guy?"

Kermit thought that over and came back with, "Doesn't much matter anymore. It's in the hands of the RCMP. As long as we keep forwarding our info to them they can make their own decisions."

"Guess so," replied Ms. Fitzpatrick and she handed the report back to him and continued on the way to her office.

* * *

Amy was leaving for lunch when the plain clothes Mountie assigned to her came up to her and informed her, "That suspect we were worrying about was sighted three times in the States probably on his way to California. Based on that we had to lift the APB because we had nothing other than the suspicion that he could be a person of interest in the murder of Beaulieu out south of the Reserve near Burning Lake. We have to reconsider our twenty four hour protection but we'll be driving by your place a few times at night and will check with you here at the office a couple times a day for a few days."

"I'm not sure I'm cool with that", Amy protested. "What if those reports are wrong and he hasn't even left the country? What do I do then?"

"I'm sorry but that's all I can say for now. If you want to talk it over with my boss you could probably talk to him at the detachment later this afternoon. I think he's tied up in meetings until around four thirty but I'm sure he'd be happy to go over everything with you."

Amy knew that the meetings were with David Wah-Shee and his lawyers and she wasn't particularly crazy about putting herself on the line just yet so she said to the officer,

"No, I understand. I'll call him in a couple of days and see if there's anything more to learn. I understand that the remains haven't even been returned to the family yet so the wake and funeral are sort of on hold."

"I don't know anything about that but I would guess that a few of our guys will have to attend the service and we'll probably have a few undercover guys there also to add to the security. Of course the Reserve Police Service will also be there so we hope that should be enough to stop any trouble from flaring up. Anyhow if you see anything suspicious or have any further concerns give me a call." He handed her a card with his contact info and left.

What the hell do I do now. Should I call Paul? What can he do? We can't just crawl into a hole and hide! Little did she suspect that the crawling into a hole was soon to become a horrible reality.

Roberto and the bogus security guy from Midnight Sun watched the accountant talking to the undercover cop then watched him walk over to an older model Pathfinder and drive away. This was it! They had to grab her as soon as they got the chance. The longer they waited the more likely they'd risk being seen grabbing her. Leaving the security guy to move the SUV up behind her as she briskly walked toward Tim Horton's he quickly and silently closed up the distance behind her and as the SUV passed he moved quickly, sticking the Glock in her back saying,

" Scream and you're dead. Struggle and I'll blow your spine out!" and grabbed her by the elbow and shoved her into the SUV so quickly that she didn't have a chance to do anything.

As the SUV sped off she cried, "Who are you? What do you want?"

Roberto wondered briefly to himself why they all say the same thing. This wasn't his first abduction but she certainly was one of the most gorgeous. Too bad this is going to end badly for her and that sniveling squaw. They sped out of town to a secluded spot just off the highway and he quickly and expertly secured her wrists with plastic flex cuffs. He then shoved a folded rag over her mouth and gagged her. Her eyes were wide in terror and she struggled but she wasn't strong enough to break loose from his hold so she settled back in the seat all the while trembling with fear.

Grabbing his mobile Roberto thumbed a saved number and asked, "Have they checked in yet?" He listened to the answer and replied, "Bring the other one and meet us at the chopper. Make sure she doesn't give you any trouble." Breaking contact he told the driver to make for the airport and their rental Bell. The next phase would be the most dangerous; even more dangerous than the snatch. While the driver was piloting the SUV to the airport Roberto grabbed Amy and, turning her struggling body face down, he grabbed a glass syringe with a large needle prefilled with 5 ml. of a fluid, jammed it through her pant suit pants and undergarment into her backside and pushed the plunger home into a site he knew very well. This was not the first time he had used this painful method of immobilizing a struggling captive and he knew it was a very reliable though extremely painful ordeal for the victim. She tried to scream but the gag effectively muted her and soon she drifted off into unconsciousness. There were other more modern drugs for the same purpose but they required a more cooperative patient and skill at establishing an intravenous line through which the drugs could be administered. This was virtually impossible with a struggling victim in the back of a speeding SUV. The fairytale fictions of plunging a needle into a victims neck and rendering that person instantly unconscious was just that; a fictional fairytale. In a few hours this victim could be more easily controlled by sedatives by mouth slipped into the food or drink or both. Roberto was well trained by his earlier KGB masters but their methods were brutal and the victims, if they survived the hours of interrogation long enough invariably complained bitterly of a sore ass. The stuff usually was safe enough in a healthy person but that was no concern of Roberto's. Most of his early victims unfortunately didn't survive the interrogation.

The SUV with a now unconscious Amy Pham pulled into the airport and drove to the helicopter that was idling at the end of the apron behind a large aircraft effectively hiding it from the charter office. The SUV drove up to the door of the chopper on the side away from the building and with the help of Richard who got out of the pilot seat when they drove up they grabbed Amy and bundled her into the back seat and strapped her in. A terrified Dawn sat in the opposite seat belted in by a harness restraint, her wrists bound with flex cuffs.

When Amy was restrained in a similar harness Roberto moved to the other side and secured a set of ear phones on Dawns head, showed Dawn his Glock and held his fingers to his lips in a shushing sign. He didn't have to explain. Meanwhile Richard climbed into the pilot seat, put on his phones, gave Roberto the thumbs up and let the rotors run up while Roberto was ensuring the doors were latched and the cargo was secure. Richard had been confident he could handle two bound captors, one unconscious from paraldehyde and the other terrified of death or something worse. The Chopper could carry four passengers but there was no need to carry the extra weight and compromise the fuel economy. He had worked out the numbers carefully and was not worried. The thing now was to get to the site and back before it got dark. He had a margin of about 1 hour allowing for thirty minutes at the site. He wasn't going to be hanging around long. The camp was all set up and secure after his morning visit with the other security guy and he had coached Dawn exactly what her duties would be if she wanted to survive. He would check her out on the flash bangs and the pepper spray just before he left and just before he cut her flex cuffs. Amy, unfortunately for her, would remain cuffed but with metal cuffs and the key would be in his pocket. As an added precaution he would put on leg shackles even though there would be nothing to attach them to.

The whole loading procedure had taken less than five minutes and the chopper had been well hidden by the SUV and the big aircraft next to it. The office staff if they were at all curious would think nothing of the chopper leaving again. They had already seen it come and go twice in the last twenty four hours and another trip wasn't going to raise any suspicions. Richard had checked out the staff at the office and found that usually only one employee was on during the early afternoon so the whole operation could be carried out with little risk.

Giving a final thumbs up to Roberto he throttled up and carefully rose into the air and pointed northward. Though it was not freezing in the Bell it was cool and Richard instructed Dawn over the earphones to use her cuffed hands to pull a down filled arctic sleeping bag over a still unconscious Amy. Even though she was certain she would not survive this horror story she tried her best to cooperate so she wouldn't make it worse. There were two sleeping bags in the rear compartment and after covering Amy with one she pulled another one over herself and was just starting to try to get comfortable when she heard the pilot over the intercom telling her to reach out with her cuffed hands and pull the gag off of Amy. Having her vomit or suffocate at this stage of the operation would seal not only her fate but also his and Roberto's. They could afford no more screw ups.

The Bell droned on through the early afternoon and the turbulence was about as light as one could expect at this altitude in a loaded chopper. One more trip to go. He would fly back to Fort Mac right after getting the guests settled and secured and bring Roberto out at first light. He had been instructed to run Roberto out, leave him there for a full day and return the afternoon of the second day. If all went well and the job was done he would help Roberto clean up the site and hide it from the air and bring back all the equipment and any leftover supplies. They had been generous with their water and food estimates just in case all did not go well and they had to hunker down for a couple of days. He wasn't worried though. The forecast was for clear skies for at least the next four days. Another three or four days he'd be safely back in the Azores with a fat fee deposited in his bank account. This was a lot different than most of his adventures with Roberto but he didn't miss the absence of people shooting at him. Flying out here was routine and pleasant and would even be boring except for a slight concern for the unexpected. These women looked harmless enough and they weren't armed. He'd often ferried bound captives a hell of a lot further than this. He knew they were terrified of him but he had no interest in them. They wouldn't be in any shape to be any fun after Roberto was finished and he certainly wouldn't try anything stupid before he brought Roberto back. He'd kill him in spite of their long history together.

He looked around at his passengers and both seemed to be sleeping but he knew the Indian was probably awake. It was almost impossible to sleep in a chopper unless you were drugged. He expected the Asian would probably come to about halfway through the trip. That should be interesting. A few minutes later he heard some grunts and groans and muttering through his headset. Looking over his shoulder at their captive he noticed that she was moving and starting to struggle. Time to talk to her.

"Don't try to struggle. You'll just hurt yourself and you can't get free. You're just waking up from some sleep stuff we shot into you when you were fighting us. Just lie there and when you can talk, just talk out loud and my headset will pick up your voice."

"Where am I?" came the somewhat garbled voice through the earphones. "What's going on? Where are you taking me?"

Richard saw no point in feeding her a line so he replied,

"We're in a helicopter and about an hour from where we're going. You know a bunch of stuff and my people want to ask you some questions. I think you know the lady next to you. She's going to help us look after you so just settle back and don't waste your breath."

Amy was scared but she was feisty and couldn't help herself from replying.

"Look you son of a bitch. You're not going to get away with this. When I show up missing you're going to be on the nasty end of the worst manhunt you can imagine. Your days are numbered. I'm personally going to pull the trigger first chance I get!" She was steamed up now and she felt her rage building.

"Best to calm down and save your strength. You're going to need it. We'll get to where we're going in a little while then you can yell and scream all you want. No one will hear you."

Through all this, Dawn remained quiet. She knew what these guys were capable of. She didn't want to make matters any worse. She still believed that there was a chance they would be rescued. David would not believe that text and he'd tell Gilbert, the police chief and Gilbert would call the Mounties and the search would be on. She would try and fool them into thinking that she was going to help them and first chance she got she would try to get away. She had fed them a line about not knowing anything about camping. As a teenager she had taken a course in extreme outdoor survival along with two or three of her friends. They did it just to show them that girls were just as tough as boys. She never thought she'd ever have to use it. About time she started to harass the asshole flying this crate. She started to groan and complained in a whine,

"I got to pee. When are we going to get there?"

"You got to hold it lady. If you can't you'll have to piss yourself. Now shut up and let me fly this thing without whining.!"

Amy got the hint and took up the whine.

"I'm going to throw up. How come it's so bumpy? Who the hell are you guys anyhow?"

Dawn chimed in with her best locker room profanity and yelled at him.

"If you think I'm going to help you you're fuckin' nuts. After all I did for you guys you treat me like shit. My old man is going to kill you, you asshole!"

Amy straightened up and turned to look at Dawn. "So it was you that spiked my tea. You bitch! You almost had me killed. This is all your fault."

Richard listened to the back and forth for a few minutes then growled,

"Shut the fuck up, both of you before I take you on a ride you won't forget. I'm sick of your bitching and whining. You think my buddy was mean. You keep up this shit and when we put down you'll find out what mean is!"

That seemed to quiet the two of them. Richard was starting to wonder what he'd done to deserve babysitting a couple of wild bitches. Maybe he should turn them both loose and let them fight it out when they got down. That should be fun to watch. He'd put his money on the chink. The squaw looked a little out of shape. Too bad he had to get back to Fort Mac before dusk.

They quieted down and he turned his attention to spotting the landmarks he'd set up on the last trip. By now he knew the route pretty well and after about fifteen more minutes of flying

he spotted the site and in another ten minutes he was setting the
chopper on the still frozen landing site. Another couple of
weeks and the ground wouldn't support this chopper loaded as
it was. Leaving it idling, he unsnapped his harness and jumped
down. He first went to Dawn's side and got her down and
keeping a tight grip on her still flex cuffed wrist he snapped a
metal hand cuff around her wrist and hooked the other cuff
around a ring attached to the chopper.

"What the hell are you doing?" she yelled at him.

Leaving her complaining and shouting obscenities at him he
moved around to Amy's side, unstrapped her and dragged her
out of the chopper. She seemed to have regained her strength
but was wobbly. He half dragged her as she stumbled after him
as they headed for the now visible mine shaft. He had left a
kerosene lantern inside the entrance and grabbing that in his
free hand he propelled his victim down the shaft to the small
cavern opening up just before the cave-in. There were two
camp cots set up, a set of leg irons and hand cuffs laid out on
one of them. Leaving the flex cuffs on her wrists he added the
metal hand cuffs, pushed her onto the cot and attached the leg
irons. There was nothing to attach them to but Richard was sure
that she wouldn't be too keen to try and run into the wilderness
in near freezing weather with wrists and legs shackled. Pushing
her down on the cot he threw an Artic sleeping bag over her
and warned her to stay there. Ignoring her cries and insults he
then went back to the chopper and freed Dawn. Leaving the

flex cuffs on, he unlocked the hand cuffs and dropped the key in his pocket. He then grabbed her by the shoulder and propelled her down to the mine and into the cave and told her to sit on the empty cot next to the other woman and warned her not to move. He growled in a harsh voice,

"Behave yourself and you'll be OK. Fight me and you'll be the one that needs help. I'm going back to the chopper to unload it. Then I'll come back and we'll have a little talk. Don't try running away. You're sixty miles away from anywhere and in the middle of muskeg. You'll freeze to death or the wolves will get you." Turning, he stomped out of the cave to the still idling chopper.

There wasn't much left to take out of the cargo hold. Pulling three plastic jerry cans of fuel out of the cargo space, he carried two down to the mine entrance and left the other one next to the chopper. Being out here with no radio contact and no roads he was reluctant to shut down the motor in case some freak happening prevented him from starting it up again. That would end very badly. Pouring gas into the tank with the motor running can be risky too but the odds were he would be OK to top up the tank. He quickly emptied the can into the tank and stuck it back in the hold. Then he grabbed a few more odds and ends they had added. The heavier stuff was brought out yesterday and this morning. He then grabbed the two sleeping bags from the passenger compartment and carried the load of stuff back to the cave.

Throwing the bags onto the woman still obediently lying on the cot he said,

"Here. wrap one of these around you. It will help keep you warm." Turning to the Indian he said, "This is where you earn your keep. Those water bottles should last three or four days but we'll be finished long before then if your friend there cooperates. There's food in that cooler and a bunch of other food in those two boxes. I assume you know how to cook. If not, you'll learn fast." He laughed. "There's also a bottle of whisky there to help you sleep but don't drink it all." He then turned to the bag he grabbed from the cargo hold and dumped it on the ground. "These things are flash bangs. They explode with a loud noise and a bright light. They are a last resort to use if any curious bears or wolves decide to check up on you. You've got three cans of pepper spray that should discourage them but if they continue to bother you the flash bangs will send them running." He then showed Dawn how to deploy the flashbangs and warned her,

"If you have to use these, cover your ears and close your eyes tight. You've never heard anything as loud as this. Now I'm cutting your flex cuffs but I'm taking the keys to your friend's shackles and hand cuffs with me. It's your job to look after her until I get back tomorrow morning with my partner. Remember, there's no place to go and you'll be safe. You've got a gas heater here and a stove. Also a couple of kerosene lanterns with a couple of cans of kerosene. I presume you can light a camp stove. There's no cover over the mine entrance so you won't get gassed. I'll pile some branches over it to keep the wind and varmints out." And then he laughed again.

He turned and walked up the shallow incline to the entrance, threw a couple of branches over the door and was gone. The two women lay there still in shock at the realization they were being abandoned in the middle of nowhere with no way to get away and no one to call.

After the big guy finished securing Amy in the chopper he had remembered to frisk her for her mobile and stuck it in his pocket. That didn't matter anyhow. There were no cell towers around and no service. They didn't even know where they were. Having lived in Fort Mac all her life and having worked one summer at Fort Chipewyan, Dawn thought they had flown in that direction but she couldn't be sure.

Part VIII

37

Hearing the chopper rev up and then slowly fade into the distance, Dawn looked at the Asian accountant lying on the cot shivering with fear as much as the cold and tried to figure out how she got here and what she was supposed to do. As far ahead as she could think she saw no difference in their plight or fate. The only difference was the things the accountant knew that those animals had to find out. She came to the sudden realization that their survival depended upon working together to defeat the monsters both human and all the challenges of this isolated wilderness. 'How do you do this without weapons and one of us restrained in shackles and hand cuffs.' she wondered. Shaking her head she decided first things first. She looked at the Asian woman and said,

"Am I remembering right? Is your first name Amy?"

Seeing her nod with a head cast down half hidden by the sleeping bag she asked,

"Do you got to pee? I know I do."

The woman in shackles shifted and struggled into a sitting
position on the wobbly cot and looked over at Dawn and said
with a slightly more firm voice,

"Yeah, I got to pee and I'm thirsty and my ass is sore where
that bastard stuck a needle in me and I'm scared shitless! You
got any bright suggestions? Aren't you supposed to be in
charge? My jailer?"

"Hey! We're both in the same goddamn boat. Why do you
think they tied me up and that asshole pilot threatened me like I
was some piece of shit!"

Amy suddenly realized the absurdity of their common
plight. They needed each other and fighting each other was just
stupid. In an apologetic voice she tried again.

"Dawn, I'm not sure where you fit into this nightmare and
I'm not sure if we can trust each other but we better try a truce
until we get through the night. I can't help you much shackled
like this and there's no way we can bust these chains but I can
hobble with help and I can still use my hands. Truce?"

"Truce" Dawn agreed and added, "Now where the hell shall
we pee?"

Dawn was wearing a winter coat with a hood but Amy only
had on a light spring jacket over her suit. Also she was wearing
low heeled dress shoes…not much good for hiking in the
muskeg.

"I can't go far like this but at least I can go outside this cave
and see what's out there if you help me keep from tripping."

Dawn nodded OK and together they got to the opening, pushed aside the brush and looked out.

"Any port in a storm," Amy muttered and hobbled a few feet away from the opening and struggled to get her pants down.

Dawn saw her predicament and said "Here, let me help."

"How'm I going to squat and pee without peeing all over my clothes?" queried Amy.

"Usually I sit on a log. Didn't you ever go camping?"

"Not in a friggin business suit!" and then she got into a fit of giggling that progressed to laughing and finally to wracking sobs.

Dawn got behind her and grabbed her under the arm pits, lowered her close to the ground and said "I ain't proud. Just don't pee on my shoes. Next time we'll rig something better."

The relief Amy felt gave her only a small sense of comfort but it was a start. When she was finished she said to Dawn,

" You must have worked in a nursing home or something."

"Naw. I used to look after my mother before she died. She had a stroke and I had to do everything for her for almost a year. My Dad may be a crook but he was always good to me though he wasn't much good at nursin'."

While standing in front of the entrance to the mine, Dawn thought back to her wilderness course and decided there was a bunch of stuff to do and she better get at it. But first to pee!

That done she started giving orders knowing full well that Amy couldn't help.

"First we gotta drag a whole lot more brush over here to cover up this entrance. It'll still let enough air in that we won't suffocate and we can use the heater and the stove once in a while. Don't want to get monoxide poisoning. We got enough sleeping bags so we won't use the heater at night. If we pee outside maybe the wolves and bears will get the hint that someone with guns is in the cave and they'll stay away. The food is all in cans and boxes and there's nothing fresh they can smell. We should be OK. They didn't leave us an axe or knife…only a can opener. Can't cut much firewood that way but maybe we can gather enough dry brush for a fire. Lots of gas here and we got a couple of lighters for the stove. Maybe someone flying over will see a fire and get curious. You never know."

"God, you're good" Amy exclaimed. "I wouldn't have thought of any of that."

"You may look like an Indian but I'm the real deal," laughed Dawn and she got to work. There was a slight breeze but Amy was cold so she hobbled back into the shelter of the mine and struggled to get a sleeping bag over her. She spied the bottled water and opened one, took a long slug then grabbed another one and hobbled back to the entrance.

"You'd better fill your tank if you're going to work like that." she said, handing the bottle to Dawn.

"Now you're cooking" she gratefully exclaimed! "You move pretty good with those bracelets on your ankles and wearing those stupid shoes."

"Hey these shoes cost lots of money!"

"Wait 'til I get this fire going then I'll see what we can do for those shoes."

She started gathering some of the brush that was lying around the opening and wandered over to a stand of birch where a small collection of twigs and small branches were scattered about. Dry deadwood was not plentiful but there was enough for a small fire if it got a little help from some gas. She also spotted a few good sized branches that had broken off some of the trees and these she dragged over to her meagre pile.

After making a little pile of twigs she grabbed one of the jerry cans of gas and splashed a little over the pile. The next trick was to use the little lighter to get the pile burning without going up in flame herself from the gas lighter fluid. Getting down on all fours she lit the lighter and eased it into the pile and was rewarded with a satisfying whump. Almost immediately she had a small intense fire burning. Carefully she added a few more sticks of kindling and nursed it into a dancing camp fire complete with snapping and crackling. All she had to do now was add the bigger branches without collapsing the kindling. She would have to watch it carefully and keep adding branches every few minutes.

Satisfied the fire would cook along by itself for a little while she walked back to the mine opening and down to the cavern. Unloading one of the boxes of food on to the floor, she took the cardboard box and attacked it with the sharp end of the can opener. She was able to fashion a few layers of makeshift soles which she folded over Amy's shoes on her feet and tied them on with some cord from a roll that was in with the food.

"There," she said, "Those should last for a little while and you'll be able to walk more comfortably. Just be careful you don't slip. This ain't the time to break your leg."

'That sounds reassuring' thought Amy to herself, "Thanks. I'll try to be careful when I jog." she replied.

After pulling aside some of the makeshift screen of brush they both walked or shuffled down to the cavern which by now was dark except for a small area lit up by the kerosene lantern. Dawn had earlier spotted an LED flashlight in the other box of supplies and lit it up to look over the canned food. There wasn't much choice; some beans, a few tins of some spam like product and half a dozen cans of soup. No vegetables or fruit. These guys sure never took a Home Ec course. There were a few plastic spoons and a couple of saucepans and some paper plates. Maybe she could use these to make more shoes for Amy when she had to. In the meantime she decided to fire up the stove and heat up some grub. Also she lit the gas camp heater and moved it up the corridor toward the door for ventilation. Noticing the bottle of whiskey she looked over at Amy and asked, "Is it uncouth to drink straight whisky out of a plastic cup?"

Amy had bundled up in her sleeping bag and seemed to be drifting off but when she heard Dawn she slowly sat up on her sore bum and said, "What the hell, why not. At least it will help us pass the night away." Then as an afterthought, "Any thought on how we can ambush those guys when they land?"

"Then who's going to fly us out of here?"

Dawn was stirring some beef stew and thought for a minute. "Do you know how to use a chopper radio?"

"Nope. I guess we better keep at least one of them alive. I wish I'd worn some damn pantyhose today."

Dawn gave her a questioning look.

"Why? You cold? They're not much help."

"No. We need something to tie the big guy up after we disable him."

"Are you nuts? He's bigger than two of us together and he's got a gun!"

"Just thinking. I guess we better think of something else."

The more they talked the more they realized how little they could do to survive even if they could get away. There had to be something!

By now the stew was hot but the fire was just about out. Dawn left the cavern to pile as much brush on it as she could find. She would try and keep it going for a couple more hours before letting it burn down. She could always light it again in the morning. After carefully replacing the brush screen she returned to the meagre food meal, scraped it onto a couple of plastic plates, poured some whisky into a couple of plastic cups and settled down on the rickety cot to eat. It was going to be a long night. As the whiskey started to warm her she felt her fear slipping away to be replaced by a building rage. She promised herself that if she got out of this alive she would walk the straight and narrow for the rest of her life. She wondered where her father was and why she hadn't heard from him for the last couple of days.

Amy chewed on the tasteless stew and drank the whiskey water mix and tried to make sense of the last four or five hours. Here she was, captive in a mineshaft in god knows where in Alberta being guarded by someone who tried to kill her a few months ago and now was being kind to her knowing full well that they would both share the same fate. She thought of Paul and how worried he would be when she didn't reply to him. Those guys probably turned off her mobile and he'd think she forgot to charge it or something. It might be the middle of tomorrow before they got a search going. She wondered if the Mounties had checked up on her like they said or even knew she was missing. Did anyone see them snatch her? She didn't know how she would deal with that big guy when he came back. If she told him everything right away he'd kill them both, she was sure. If she held out as long as she could he would hurt her or Dawn or both while that sneering jackass pilot stood by and did nothing! What a mess. She didn't know if she was brave enough to resist but she sure knew she was mad enough to fight him if she got the chance.

Her father, in a rare mood of nostalgia once told her about some of the terrible things he saw in the war and the cruel way soldiers from all sides treated each other. Yet he survived it with cunning, courage and a lot of luck. There had to be a way. For now she was grateful that Dawn was here with her instead of some deranged animal. She wondered why they hadn't left one of the men here with a gun but she realized that the chopper only had a limited range with added weight. The chilling thought also came to her that they wanted as few witnesses as possible. The locals could only talk about being involved in the kidnapping. Also, they were in the pay of the big guy and his organization whoever that was. They knew that their lives were at risk if they told any stories.

In spite of the pain in her bum and the chains and her fears she started to feel sleepy from the booze and she curled up on the cot with the sleeping bag wrapped around her and dozed off into a fitful sleep.

* * *

I'm just wrapping up my day with a couple of kids with the usual coughs and colds and worried mothers and besides a couple of calls to the hospital at Fort Mac, I'm looking forward to a quiet night at my cabin. Chief Wah-Shee should be home later tonight. I'm anxious to hear how his meeting with the people in Fort Mac turned out but I don't want to be a pest. He'll probably call Amy and she can tell me when I call her. First I want to see how Mrs. Giroux is doing. When I called earlier the nurse on the ward told me she was resting comfortably and breathing easier. Heart failure can be tricky but over the past several years the drugs and assessments have made encouraging advances in life expectancy. The trick is to get on top of it early and stay on top of it. I think she should be able to get back for Sam's funeral which should be in three or four days provided the coroner releases his body tomorrow as expected.

   After reaching the doctor on call for Mrs. Giroux's own doc I'm told what I expected to hear. She is doing much better and should be discharged in the morning. If she's well enough to be discharged then she's well enough to come home with Junior. I make a note to call Junior and let him know so he can make the arrangements to get her back and over to the clinic so I can sit down with her and Marla and make sure she is checked regularly.

   Amy is probably still at the office so I decide to go home and make supper. I'm tired of pub food and don't feel like sitting around and rehashing the events of the last four or five days with the regulars. I'll give her an hour or so then call her at home. I'm guessing she's probably getting tired of the protection detail chasing around after her so she's staying close to home.

I wonder how the search for that suspect is going. He seems to have disappeared from the landscape because there didn't seem to be any more reports of sightings. I'm sure the Mounties would let Amy know if they had anything new. So far there was nothing more in the news and regular press releases from the RCMP just say the investigation is ongoing. I'm a little unsettled by the fact that Amy continues to be in danger as long as some of these mysteries remain unsolved. Maybe she should have stayed down east but she was already on her way home before anything happened to Sam.

It is a little more chilly tonight and the wind is picking up. The forecast promises another day of sunshine then some unsettled weather moving in. It seems this time of year it's always unsettled. Oh well that's better than blistering heat and forest fires in the short summer. I'm starting to get used to this country and climate and other than the recent events the peace and quiet of Burning Lake brings me comfort and a happiness I have not experienced before. I wonder if it has anything to do with Amy Pham.

The fireplace is now throwing off a nice warmth and familiar crackle and I have a salmon fillet baking in the oven. This cooking thing is relatively new for me. Who would have predicted that I would be spending my spare time surfing the net for recipes. A small glass of wine while listening to my

collection of jazz and waiting for the timer to ding, letting me
know my salmon is cooked, could only be improved by having
somebody here to share it with. It's now close to seven o'clock
and the salmon won't be done for another half hour so I let my
mobile dial up Amy's land line at home and listen to the rings.
After five rings her voice comes on inviting me to leave a
message.

"Hey Ames, where are you? You should be home relaxing.
Or are you out flirting with your protection detail? Call me
when you get in. Love ya."

I go back to my surfing and wine and wait for my mobile to
vibrate. Twenty minutes later my timer dings and I pull my
salmon out of the oven and dish out some pasta and a little plate
of salad to round out my meal. Funny Amy hasn't called or
even texted. I tie into my meal which I think is at least as good
as any pub grub and it soon disappears. Pouring another glass
of the red I decide to text her and see what's holding her up.
Five minutes later and a half of glass of wine, still no answer.
What the hell? Is it something I said? I speed dial her mobile
and after six rings a voice informs me that the customer I was
trying to reach is not in service. Now I'm more than a little
concerned. I sit there for a few minutes and try her mobile
again. Same result. Suddenly sensing that something is really
wrong I decide it's time to take some action. I scroll through
my contacts and see Constable Porter's number and tap call.
After a couple of rings I hear,

"Porter here."

"Constable Porter, Doc Cross here. Sorry to bother you at night but I need some information and I don't know who else to call."

"What's up Doc?" he laughs and adds, "I've always wanted to say that."

Everyone wants to be a comedian. "I'm a little worried about Amy Pham. I've been calling her and getting no answer. She's supposed to have a protection detail around the clock so she's probably OK but she's never missed answering a text or call for longer than a few minutes. Is there any way you can patch into the guy watching her and make sure she's OK.?"

"Sorry I have to ask this Doc but are you two OK? Any tiffs or fights or anything?"

"No, Definitely not!" I reply. "That's why I'm a little concerned."

He pauses for a beat then says, "Let me get back to you. I'll make a couple of calls. You're right. That is weird. I'll get back to you as soon as possible."

There's nothing more I can do except stew so I try and settle down but I find myself pacing and poking the fire and trying to clean up the kitchen and pacing some more. Now I'm really scared. If anybody screwed up and she gets hurt I'll ....Just then my mobile vibrates and it's Porter.

"Doc, I just got off the phone with my Sergeant. Evidently they were informed that our person of interest has been spotted in Nevada and California and thought to be heading for his home locality. There's been no sign of him at any of our border crossings or airports so headquarters pulled the twenty four hour detail and put on a regular drive by surveillance. They just drove by her place ten minutes ago and it was in darkness."

The bottom of my stomach fell out and my heart was a trip hammer.

"How long ago did they pull the detail?"

"As far as I know, just before noon today."

"So what the hell do I do now? How do we find out if she's OK.?"

"Normally with missing persons we do prelim inquiries and hold off a formal search for twenty four hours but seeing she's supposed to be under protection we're pulling out all the stops. Officers are going to be contacting neighbours and people she works with to see if anything unusual turns up."

I sit on the edge of panic knowing that this is unusual and helpless that I have nothing to add. Then a thought strikes me.

"Constable, Chief Wah-Shee was in Fort Mac all day to day but I bet he's back now. I wonder if he talked to her."

"Good thought. I'll call him right now and get right back to you."

About three minutes later my mobile vibrates and it's Porter.

"Doc, he hasn't talked to your lady today but a funny thing… he says he got a text from his secretary last evening telling him that she couldn't look after the office for a few days because she was staying with friends in Fort Mac because of all the trouble at home. I don't know what that means but the chief said after the shooting she was really frightened and scared that she might be in danger." We both sit there silently waiting for each other to chime in.

"Where do we go from here?" I hear myself ask, more composed than I feel.

"After what I heard from the chief I'm wondering if we've missed something vital. I'm going to call my sergeant right now and fill him in. In the meantime, if you hear from her let me know right away." I agreed and we disconnected. *Where the hell are you Ames? Why aren't you answering?* But she isn't talking.

Desperately I run the events of the last several days through my brain that is now in full panic mode and I think of nothing that helps me. There must be something. *Why did they pull surveillance? Where did those reports that Rubinowich was in the States come from? How credible were they? Were they planted?* All of a sudden I realized that the chaos of the last few months seemed to be dependent on misinformation deliberately planted and I grab my phone, scan to Fitzpatrick and tap call. They've been keeping tabs on that terrorist. They should know something. Wondering if I can get anything out of her I listen to her phone ring and try to compose myself so I won't blow it and piss her off.

"Fitzpatrick. What can I do for you now Doc?" At least she didn't say 'what's up doc'?

"Officer Fitzpatrick, Amy Pham is not answering any of my calls and I just learned that the RCMP pulled her protection detail this afternoon. They said that Rubinowich was in the States. Is there anything you know that can help me out here?"

"Shit!"

I didn't expect that response. She went on,

" We circulated reports of sightings not confirmed sightings. Maybe we're looking at the wrong guy or someone is pulling our chain. Look Doctor Cross, I'll get right on this but in the meantime keep this all to yourself. If we've got a situation here we don't want anyone to make it worse."

"I just talked to the local Mountie here in Burning Lake and he told me there was a possibility that one of the staff at the Reserve band office is missing also. What the hell's going on?"

"Doc, our main task is gathering information and coordinating actions. We are not a police force so we have to rely on police organizations to take the lead on all this stuff. But that doesn't stop me from calling the Deputy Commissioner for RCMP K Division and making some inquiries. Like I told you before, a lot of this stuff is classified and I can't discuss it and I know you're very concerned but again I have to urge that you trust me and keep this stuff to yourself. We're coordinating with RCMP so I have no problem you sharing with your local RCMP officer there but no further.

No locals, no media, no politicians, no town officials, no Reserve officials. I'll get back to you a little later tonight."

"OK Ms. Fitzpatrick. Thanks for talking to me. I know you'll do your best."

I disconnect and flop onto the couch not knowing what else to do. Never have I felt so helpless!

A few minutes later my mobile vibrates and Wah-Shee shows up on my screen.

"David. Thank god you called. Porter called me and told me Dawn might be missing."

"That's what I'm calling about, Doc. I'm worried about her. She's been acting strange lately and after the shooting she told me she was scared that something bad was going to happen to her. She wouldn't say anything more so I let it go for the time being. I'm kicking my ass that I didn't push it further. It's no secret that her father might be involved in half the crime around here and I'm worried he involved her in working against us. I can't be sure if she was forced to or is a willing participant. Now, I can't find Wilfred anywhere. No one's seen him since just after Sam got shot and the cops questioned him. Gilbert's got an APB out for him but nothing's turned up."

Not knowing how much I could tell him I decided to probe a little farther.

" Do the police think he had something to do with the shooting?"

"He was nowhere near that trapline at the time. He's got a solid alibi."

"What's Porter going to do about it?"

The Chief paused a bit then asked,

"Is it true that Amy Pham might be missing? Porter wanted to know if I had talked to her or seen her when I was in Fort Mac. I said no but something in the way he asked made me think something was up. That's why I told him about Dawn."

"Chief, Do you have any ideas? Can you say what happened today at the meeting? Do you think this is all connected?"

"What about it Doc? Is Amy Pham missing?"

There's no way I can deny this now so, sorry Fitzpatrick, gotta leak it.

"David I need you to promise not to let this out and for god sake don't tell anyone I told you but yes, Amy Pham is missing." *and I'm going nuts. If anyone harms her I'll kill them!*

"Damn! This is out of control. I've got Gilbert beating the bushes for Wilfred and Dawn but I didn't figure on Amy. We finally got the beginning of a case and the RCMP Corporate Crime people are buying in but they need Amy as a witness. They're pulling out all the stops on this investigation but if it gets to the public too soon all it will do is muddy the water and get me kicked off the council and out the door. Damn!"

I know I'm not getting any sleep tonight so I give Amy one more try without success then I plug in my mobile and stretch out on my couch and wait for the phone to ring.

38

Wilfred Natannah spent all day in Edmonton trying to find Jozeph Laszlo without success. Now he was holed up in a small motel in the Beverly district not far from the North Saskatchewan river. It was in a dingy neighborhood but it was clean and comfortable. No one would think of looking for him here. He wasn't on the run but he didn't particularly feel like running into anyone he knew just now. He still hadn't made up his mind what to do with Laszlo but he had enough contacts who would be interested in a payday and could keep their mouths shut. That fucking lawyer had gone too far and it was time to settle up with him. With no chance now that Sam would get back to being chief it was unlikely that he would get anything else from the Midnight Sun deal. Laszlo was now a liability and could sink them both. The only wild card was the involvement of those chinks with Midnight Sun. Were they a danger to him? Maybe. He'd have to keep his eyes open. That big wannabe terrorist who was supposed to talk to Sam was probably the guy who shot Sam or at least set it up. Where the hell was he now? Does anyone know about him?

Not knowing the answer to any of these questions, Wilfred knew he had to get more information from Laszlo so first he had to find him. Tomorrow he'd go back to the head office of Midnight Sun and sniff around some more. In the meantime he'd check some of the fancy places he knew Laszlo frequented for lunch. Maybe he'd get lucky.

* * *

Wu Zhao Conglomerate preferred to remain a silent partner in Midnight Sun and they kept a hands off approach to operations. Their main goal was control of any resources that could be exploited from the Burning Lake area as well as two or three other properties in the encircling area extending from the intersection formed by the borders of Saskatchewan, Alberta and the Northwest Territories. Their outlook was long term but some very careful groundwork had to be laid to ensure their interest in those properties would eventually pay off. The stakes were enormous.

Eli Watts and his organization did a reasonable job providing local manpower for the sometime less than ethical activities that might be required. However Wu Zhao kept a highly skilled and sometimes lethal cell of three operatives whose loyalty was without question. Chen Chi Chung, their leader, travelled to Edmonton from Seattle after his recent and very brief meeting with Eli while his two partners continued on to Fort McMurray to locate and deal with Roberto. In spite of Eli's reassurance that the Cuban would finish the job, Chen knew that once the loose thread was tugged on a little, the whole fabric of the project would quickly unravel. He was not about to let that happen. While his two partners dealt with Roberto, Chen would neutralize the lawyer. However he was proving to be very difficult to locate. No one at Midnight Sun could tell him where Lazslo was. He was not expected to be out of town and he had appointments and meetings the next day so perhaps Mr. Chen could make an appointment to see him then. Perhaps they could lunch together, the office manager of the energy company offered. Chen declined the offer to make a firm appointment but informed her that he would call her early in the morning and suggested they could make arrangements at that time.

Now back at one of Edmonton's lesser known but first class boutique hotels he contacted one of his partners and exchanged a few words. It was not by chance that he had spotted Michael Charbonneau at the Airport. Ever since they had been alerted that Watts' Cuban operative had contacted the pilot and hired him to fly ASAP from his home in the Azores, the Asian cell was on the way to the Canadian north to set up surveillance at both Edmonton International and Fort McMurray. Chen stationed himself at Nisku where he eventually spotted the French pilot while his partners rented a small all-wheel drive crossover suitable for the trip to Fort McMurray. But first they had a small task to complete in Edmonton on the way.

Liang Ho Feng first joined the Wu Zhao conglomerate long before the terrorist attack on New York that brought down the twin towers of the World Trade Center. Having learned his tradecraft as a special forces warrior in China's People's Liberation Army Special Operations Forces, he decided that he was not interested in pursuing a career forever in the military and managed a discharge through the influence of Wu Zhao and joined the conglomerate's global security force. Among his skills was an expertise in devising and detonating improvised explosive devices or IED's. He was adept at transforming industrial explosive materials into lethal weapons as well as designing and building those weapons from scratch. Besides locating and setting up surveillance on the Watts operative he was given the task of crafting a little toy to present to him without his knowledge. The brief stop in Edmonton allowed him to collect the necessary materials from a known contact in the Chinese community.

The stop did not delay them for long and within a couple of hours they continued up the notorious highway to Fort McMurray. With the ability to trade off driving, the pair arrived in Fort McMurray and found a base of operations at a pleasant and attractive hotel near downtown. While Ho Feng's partner drove to the airport to initiate the boring assignment of surveillance, Ho Feng set up his tools and instruments and started the dangerous task of assembling the device. It required a great deal of care and skill and could not be hurried. One false move and he and half the hotel would disappear and the resulting investigation would be devastating to his employers.

The device would be designed to have a timer initiated by remote control and capable of detonating the device after a specified time. His partner Chen Chi Chung was in contact with an IT specialist who was currently attempting to hack into the system utilized by the helicopter charter company monitoring the Bell helicopter leased to Michael Charbonneau. With the information detailing the locations of the chopper at any given time of day while in operation, Chen and his associates would be able to find out what they were up to and where they were going. Knowing that, the Chinese operatives would then be able to complete their mission and leave the country.

* * *

Because Wilfred Natannah had not been seen since the extensive questioning by the RCMP, an all-points bulletin (APB) was issued as the investigation into the shooting of Sam Beaulieu progressed. The bulletin was circulated widely throughout the area and reached as far as Edmonton where it was noted by an Edmonton police service detective assigned to inner city crime investigations. He quickly scanned the information and briefly studied the image accompanying it. There was something familiar about the picture and he spent a few minutes searching some of his more active files. The drug scene in downtown Edmonton consumed a large part of his daily routine and after about thirty minutes of searching he hit pay dirt. The subject was a known associate of several of the kingpins in the gangs operating out of the Hobbema area but had never been convicted nor charged of any offense. Converting the information to a few paper copies he placed them in his briefcase before leaving for a morning tour through the Edmonton downtown.

The detective was not undercover and was therefore pretty well known to many of the businesses in the downtown core especially the watering holes where some of the underworld characters were known to hang out. Like all resourceful police officers he had a network of snitches who kept him up to date with the "who's who" of the current scene. Showing the APB's to a few of these as he made his rounds he was rewarded with a hit when he learned of a sighting of a big guy matching the description going into a coffee shop near a large building housing the offices of several resource companies. The sighting was fresh and the location was close by so the detective decided he needed a cup of coffee. Entering the small coffee business he became aware of the subject sitting and nursing his drink and looking at his watch every few minutes.

Wilfred was startled when a young clean shaven man in casual clothes pulled out a chair and sat down beside him.

"Mr. Natannah? Hi. I'm Detective Bob Moore of the Edmonton Police Service. I wonder if we could have a little talk?"

Looking around nervously, Wilfred saw that the coffee shop had only a few customers and the detective didn't seem all that threatening so he said,

"Sure detective. What does Edmonton Police Service want to talk about?"

"Last week you were interviewed by RCMP at Burning Lake about an incident as a person of interest. Is that correct?"

"That was no fuck'n incident! Some son of a bitch shot my brother and if I catch up with him I'll tear his head off!"

"Whoa. Easy Mr. Natannah. I know the RCMP questioned you and you are not a suspect as far as I know but they are looking for you because they think you can help them find the real killer. I wonder if you can come back to the station with me and we'll see what this is all about?"

"What if I say no? I don't want to go back to your station. What can you do to me?"

"Mr. Natannah, let's not go that route. Threatening a witness is not my style. Maybe you know something that you don't know you know. Help us out here. Maybe you can help your brother here."

This guy was a big guy and looked like he might explode at any moment and Moore didn't feel like getting into it with him in a public place. He wasn't wanted for anything and these things going nasty usually ended up as a lose lose for everyone. Yet he wasn't going to let the guy walk away. That's also not good police practice.

"When I came in you were looking at your watch as if you had an appointment. Am I keeping you from something important?"

Sometimes courtesy can lower the conflict risk and prevent an escalation into violence. Moore was counting on this being one of those times.

Natannah was sweating now and chewing his lip and knew that if he created trouble he'd get hauled in and who knows where that would lead so he laid his hands flat on the table and shrugged his shoulders and said,

"OK officer, lead on. Let's get this over with."

They got up and exited the shop and walked the block to Moore's patrol car for the ride back to the station. Wilfred opened the rear passenger door and just as he was bending over to slide into the back seat the door window shattered with glass flying everywhere.

"Get down!" shouted Moore and Wilfred dove into the car and hit the floor. The detective took cover, grabbed his phone and called excitedly for back up while pulling his own weapon and scanning the sidewalk and nearby buildings for a target. No more shots were fired and in under a minute two patrol cars arrived on the scene, sirens whooping and lights flashing.

Wilfred cautiously sat up in the car, shaking and throwing frightened glances in all directions. Detective Moore came around the car and barked,

"What the hell was that all about?"

Wilfred blurted excitedly. "I don't know! Somebody shot at us didn't they; I didn't hear nothing 'till the window blew out."

Detective Moore was an eighteen year veteran of the police service but this was the first time he had come under fire. 'What the hell is going on' he thought.

"Whoever fired must have had a silencer," he explained, then turned to the patrol cops who had showed up after his back up call. They spoke for a few minutes then Moore turned to Wilfred.

"One of these officers is going to take you back to the station and get a statement from you. I gotta stay here and wait for a crime scene team to get here and do their stuff. Don't worry, these guys will look after you until I get there. This all may take a few hours so don't plan on going anywhere soon. I guess now you're my person of interest."

Driving away from the scene all Wilfred could think of was how to wring that fuck'n lawyer's neck. There was no doubt in his mind who had set this up.

Two hours later at a downtown EPS station Detective Moore sat down with Wilfred to go over the events of the day. He opened with,

"Mr. Natannah, we've been unable to locate the shooting site or the shooter. From the damage to the police cruiser it is suggested that you were the target and this was not a "drive by" incident. The suspected site was probably the parking garage a couple of stories up." He then asked the obvious question.

"Who do you think wants you dead? Is there any reason to believe this is related to your brother's death?"

Wilfred wasn't yet ready to give them Laszlo but he wasn't crazy about taking a bullet either. His mind had been going around for the two hours he sat waiting for the detective and he still wasn't sure what to do. There was nothing on record about him in the Midnight Sun deal so as long as he kept his mouth shut he was in the clear but if those assholes were gunning for him he was in a bad position. Finally he offered an explanation that he thought would give him some breathing room.

"The guy I was supposed to meet is the lawyer for one of those companies upstairs from where I got shot. His company is involved in doing some work on our Reserve and lately there's been trouble between the locals and some of the workers. I don't fully trust that guy and wonder if maybe he had something to do with it."

"So let me see if I understand. You think some lawyer took a pot shot at you today?"

Detective Moore had trouble swallowing that suggestion. However he had to dig further so he asked,

"What's this lawyer's name and who does he work for and why would he want to blow you away?" His disbelief was palpable.

"I don't know. I just have heard rumors that something fishy is going on with Midnight Sun. That's the name of the company. I've met that guy before and I think he's a crook. I was waiting to see him because I wanted to know what he knew about my brother's death. Maybe that was stupid but who else would be gunning for me."

Detective Moore didn't tell him he could think of a lot of people who might want him dead. Instead he asked Wilfred where he was staying so he could get ahold of him if he needed him. Time to chase this one down with a little more vigor. He was still pissed off about taking gunfire in a down town street. He agreed to contact Wilfred in the morning and arranged for him to get a ride back to his motel.

The receptionist at the desk of Midnight Sun was explaining that Mr. Laszlo was not available without an appointment when Detective Moore asked her if he would prefer being picked up on a warrant for attempted murder of a police officer. That got her attention and she asked him to take a seat while she attempted to locate Mr. Laszlo. A few minutes later she returned and asked him to come with her to a conference room where Mr. Laszlo would speak with him. When he was seated in the conference room a slightly built probably late middle aged man in an expensive looking suit entered the room and in a slightly accented voice introduced himself as Jozeph Laszlo.

"What can I do for you Officer Moore?" asked Laszlo.

"Mr. Laszlo, earlier this afternoon a man who claims he had an appointment with you was involved in a shooting a couple of blocks from here."

"I don't understand. I'm not that kind of lawyer. I'm a corporate lawyer. I don't do criminal law."

"We're aware of that. However this witness led us to believe that you could give us some information that could help us out."

In spite of himself Laszlo paled and began to sweat and stammered,

"That's ridiculous!" he exclaimed. "What was your witness's name?"

"Wilfred Natannah. He's a member of a First Nations Reserve near Fort McMurray. I understand your company is involved in a project on his Reserve."

"I know that name. I think I've met him at some time or other. Why on earth would he accuse me of knowing who shot at him?"

"Mr. Laszlo, I informed you only that he was involved in a shooting. I did not say that someone shot at him. Perhaps you do know more than you are saying. How did you know that someone shot at him?"

Now thoroughly panicked, Laszlo made a big mistake probably because he was a lawyer and knew his rights.

"I'm not saying anything further without the benefit of counsel! That's my right."

Thinking this guy was objecting too much and given the slip of the tongue he just got caught at and the fact that Natannah fingered him as a possible suspect, as well as the known involvement of the resource company on Reserve land where Natannah's brother had just been murdered Moore decided to take a chance.

"Mr. Laszlo, perhaps we can continue this conversation at our station. You certainly have the right to a lawyer being present and we will be happy to wait until your lawyer can come to the station. Because of a number of related events involving your company and Mr. Natannah's Reserve and the murder of his brother I think it is reasonable to regard you as a person of interest in this whole affair."

"Don't you need a warrant to take me in?" Laszlo, now perspiring freely and drumming his fingers madly on the desk top.

'This guy is not all that cool' Moore thought as he carefully formed his reply.

"Mr. Laszlo. No one is accusing you of anything and certainly you can have legal counsel. But one way or other we need to have you at our station for further inquiry. It would be simpler if you came voluntarily but we can certainly obtain a warrant if we need to."

"Very well. I have few things to clear up then I'll meet you at your station in an hour"

He then turned to go.

"One moment Mr. Laszlo. You didn't ask which station we are going to. I'd prefer if you accompanied me and then we can get you your lawyer and hopefully clear this all up."

Muttering, "This is preposterous. I will surely speak to your supervisors about this! Please allow me to grab my overcoat. I'll just be a minute." He walked out of the room and down the hall to his office, entered and closed the door.

Detective Moore had been on the job for many years and was not intimidated by blustering big shot lawyers. Something was not quite right and he walked quickly to Laszlo's office where he heard a panicked one sided conversation but could not make out the words. No doubt Laszlo was phoning his lawyer. Being a cautious cop he strolled further down the hall to the rear of the office suite and stepped just around the corner. A couple of minutes later Laszlo moved quickly down the hall towards the rear of the building and turned the corner and stopped in shock.

"Going somewhere in a hurry Mr. Laszlo? I think you just upped the ante. Turn around and face the wall and put your hands behind your back. I'm arresting you on a charge of obstruction of justice and attempted flight from custody."

"You can't do that!" Laszlo protested. "I'm not in custody."

Technically he was probably right but Moore wasn't taking any chances. Apologies could come later. This guy looked dirty and he was trying to run.

"We can sort that all out after you get your lawyer. In the meantime you've the right…"

Moore explained his rights to him knowing full well that he already knew them. But he didn't want this guy loose until he had some answers for that bullet. He was still pissed at that.

He proceeded out to the front office past a wide eyed receptionist and into the elevator to the ground floor and his borrowed cruiser. This person of interest APB was getting nuttier and nuttier.

Exiting the building Moore and his now prisoner did not notice the Chinese man across the street gazing at them with some concern. Chen Chi Chung knew he had inadvertently stirred up a hornet's nest and the sooner he and his team could get out of this country the better. The instructions to eliminate the Indian was an unfortunate misjudgment and both he and his handler at Wu Zhao would face unpleasant consequences. Shaking his head he turned and walked quickly away.

39

In the remains of an old uranium mine just across the Alberta
Saskatchewan border a few kilometers south of Lake
Athabasca, Dawn Natannah and Amy Pham lay shivering on
rickety camp cots covered in arctic sleeping bags that barely
kept in the heat generated from their own bodies. There was a
single kerosene lamp burning, manufacturing ghostly shadows
on the rock and earthen walls of the old mine. Worried about
the lethal dangers of monoxide poisoning, Dawn had previously
turned off the gasoline heater that had supplied some heat in the
earlier hours. Now as she tossed and shivered on her cot she
began to rethink her decision. Maybe if the brush in front of the
entrance had enough openings the danger would be negligible
and maybe they wouldn't be so damn miserable. She was just
about to get up when she heard a little rustling at the opening
followed by some grunting and sniffing.

It didn't take her long to realize that they were getting an unwelcome visitor and she had to act quickly or they were in deep trouble. She quickly grabbed a can of the pepper spray and one of the flash bangs and headed for the opening to get a look see. As the grunting grew louder the brush suddenly parted and the head of a full grown black bear thrust in through the opening.

Dawn let out a loud scream and within six feet of the animal let loose a stream of spray from the can hitting the beast full in the face. With a roar it jumped back and thrashed wildly around, bounding away, violently shaking its big head and neck back and forth.

By now Amy was awake and screaming and trying to stand in spite of the chains attached to her ankles. She saw Dawn rush up the shaft to the opening and quickly pull as much brush over the opening as she could get her hands on. The outside had suddenly become quiet again and there was no telling what would happen next. Amy had stopped screaming and was calling out, "What happened? What's going on?"

"There's a bear out there trying to get in. I scared him away with the pepper but I don't know if he'll come back or not."

"What should we do? How do we keep him away?" cried a now terrified Amy.

"All we can do is just keep squirting him until he gives up or we run out. That's all we've got."

She came down the shaft and looked into the boxes and said,

"We've got two more cans of this stuff and the first one is still at least half full. That and a lot of noise should scare him off. Chances are he's already a half a mile away. This stuff is nasty."

She turned to Amy and said, "You might as well lie down and get some rest. I'm lighting the stove and then starting that camp generator. We can plug in that light they brought with it and shine it out the door. That should scare him away."

She then grabbed a bottle of water and took a few long pulls of water and dropped back down on her cot. They both sat there thinking their thoughts, not knowing what to say next.

"Maybe you should have a shot of that whiskey and try and get some sleep. I'm going to go out and start a fire in front of the opening and maybe he'll stay away."

"Are you crazy?" asked a still panicked Amy. "What if he's still out there?"

"I know but at least it's better than just sitting here and waiting to be his breakfast. Bears up here usually run if they get smacked in the snout with pepper spray and besides they are probably likely to stay away from a fire. I'm not just going to sit here and die."

She got up, relit the gas heater and then dragged the generator up the shaft to the opening, primed it a few times and yanked on the cord. It immediately turned over and started

purring along. 'At least they got one that works' she thought as
she went back for the light and plugged it in and shined it on
the opening. If it wasn't so damn cold this would be just like
home when she was out camping with friends.

With the bright light shining out into the night she slowly
pushed through the brush into the outside and looked cautiously
around. She saw nothing frightening and heard no grunting, just
her beating heart and fear driven panting. Taking a few deep
breaths and willing herself to calm down, she grabbed the light
and directed it around the area outside the mine. With
everything now quiet she concentrated on the scattered pile of
brush she had gathered earlier the night before.

In just a little while she had gathered enough dry kindling to
start a fire and with the help of a few sprinkles of gas she had a
little flame going. This she nursed into a larger burn and
continued to pile on brush and wood until she had a good sized
fire. Some of the wood was wet and a dense cloud of smoke
developed but thankfully drifted away from the cave.

Going back into the cave she pulled the rest of the brush
over the opening again and returned to her cot. Nothing to do
now but feed the fire and wait for sun up. Sitting there she
wondered if the two legged visitors coming back would be as
easy to scare off. Maybe they could hit them with the spray and
get their guns off them. She knew that was probably wishful
thinking but she still wasn't willing to do nothing. There had to
be a way. Could she get to the chopper and radio for help while

they were badgering Amy? Hell, she didn't even know how to work the radio. She wondered how different it was from some of the old camp radios they used to use out on the traplines. If she could just get hold of a gun she could shoot both the sons o'bitches then worry about calling for help after.

For the rest of the night she had to nurse the fire back about every half hour but thankfully the bear had stayed away. At sun rise she thought she could move around some more and gather wood. She knew that the chopper with the bad guys would show up about two hours after sun up so they didn't have much more time. Standing looking at the fire she wondered if her new friend inside was as scared as she was. She didn't know shit about survival but she looked like she could fight if she could move around. There were no tools in the stuff inside but there were lots of rocks around outside. Maybe she could bust one of the chain links so at least Amy could walk or run. Wouldn't those guys be surprised if they got back and couldn't find them? But where the hell would they go? There probably wasn't a settlement for miles around and they had no packs to carry stuff. A good old fashioned travois like the Bloods down south used to use would work fine but you need an axe to cut the poles. Not likely there were any up here just waiting to be used.

It was about an hour from sun rise by her best guess so she returned once more to her cot to wrap herself in her sleeping bag and wait. The pepper spray and one of the flash bangs lay close to her hand just in case. Slowly, in fits and starts, sleep came.

* * *

It was in that same hour before sunrise that a vehicle pulled quietly up to the air field just outside the fence with two men inside. One crept silently out of the door carrying a pack in one hand and a blanket in the other. Carefully he eased up to the fence and threw the blanket over the sharp ends of the chain link fence and wearing the pack quickly scaled the fence and dropped to the other side. The immediate area was dark but a light shone from a pole in the parking lot over the office of the charter office. A light was shining inside but there was no movement that could be seen and the stealthy figure was certain that any person in the office would not have seen beyond the light.

Parked at the end of the tarmac sat the Bell 206 B and next to it a large corporate jet that hadn't been moved in some time. Essentially hidden behind the jet, the Bell sat all alone and out of sight of the comings and goings of the rest of the facility. Even more convenient, the position of the machine was such that it was impossible for anyone in the office or adjacent hanger of the charter facility to adequately scan the left side of the helicopter making the small cargo space door almost invisible. It was here the man with the pack stopped and in less than a minute gained access to the cargo space. It was obvious that it had been pre-loaded in preparation for the next flight. Moving aside a number of items the man carefully placed the pack and secured it in the rear of the hold, covering it with the items already in the hold. Quickly he secured the cargo door and hastened to the fence. Within a few seconds he was in the vehicle and the two men drove to a place within easy view of the facility and settled back for a wait that should only last until sun up.

After a predawn breakfast and coffee, Roberto and Michael drove to the airport and after checking with the office that the chopper had been refilled and after a routine pre flight inspection they climbed aboard and warmed up the Bell. When all was ready and they received go ahead from the lady air traffic controller in the tower Michael eased the Bell from its resting place and pointed along its flight path to begin the trip.

Sitting in a dark vehicle a short distance away' Liang Ho Feng pressed a control on the wireless device he held in his hand arming the IED secreted in the hold of the Bell. Before secreting it in the Bell he had preset the timer for sixty minutes which, if he followed the coordinates obtained by Chen Chi Chung through his hacked information, should place the Bell over an isolated area of bush and forest far from any civilization when the device did its job. Now, watching the Bell leave, they quickly left the area and started the long trip back to

Edmonton to meet with Chen and prepare to leave this cold country and return to their base far away in Guangzhou.

40

Sitting in a locked interrogation room that only a short while before had contained Wilfred Natannah, Jozeph Laslo steamed with an anger that covered the visceral fear he was experiencing. He was so close to disappearing from this godforsaken cold climate and getting to the safe house in the Caribbean he had acquired just six months earlier. He was pretty sure who had ordered the hit on Natannah and Jozeph feared he was next. Those damn Chinamen were ruthless and seemed to be able to move about without any trouble. He knew that when they made their move on Midnight Sun his life expectancy would be measured in days. But he thought he had at least a few more weeks. What a stupid move to try to hit the Indian on a city street. And then they missed! More stupidity! Wondering how long it would be before his lawyer would be able to spring him he quickly went over his options and started to plan his getaway.

The door opened and Detective Moore entered with Jozeph's lawyer for the last five years. Damian Slemko was well known to the police in Edmonton and when he came on the scene, more often than not, he got what he wanted. But today he had a worried look on his face.

After politely greeting Jozeph he asked Detective Moore for a few minutes so he could confer in private with his client. After Detective Moore left the room Slemko began his conference.

"Jozeph, I must inform you that we have a tough task if we are going to get you released in the next few hours."

"What the hell do you mean?" fired back Laszlo. "They can't hold me! This is bullshit!"

"Easy Jozeph. They are charging you with a number of offenses including conspiracy to murder and attempting to flee lawful custody. No Judge will release you until they've had a chance to hold a hearing and that can't happen until tomorrow." Then opening his briefcase and selecting a pad he continued, "Now why don't you tell me what this is all about?"

Jozeph sat for a minute collecting his thoughts then began crafting a tale that might just get him out of here so he could disappear before those damn chinks could get to him.

"Damien, as you know I'm chief legal counsel for Midnight Sun. In the last few months I have become worried that they are not what they pretend to be. They seem to have a connection with a Chinese energy conglomerate that has been buying up leases all over the north end of the province. Since they've come on the scene they have stirred up trouble on a couple of reserves by Fort Mac and now they may be implicated in the death of a chief from one of them."

"That's pretty serious stuff, Jozeph. How certain are you of this? Can you substantiate your facts? This might be enough to construct a conspiracy defense and get you free until your claims are investigated."

"That's exactly what I'm thinking but that damn Moore has his mind made up. He's pissed that someone took a shot at him and he's claiming that I was trying to run out on him. That's just bullshit. Get me the hell out of here and I'll get you all the proof you need."

Slemko stood and went to the door and knocked. In a moment an officer entered and Slemko asked him to bring Detective Moore back to the room.

In a couple of minutes Bob Moore entered and stood there waiting for Slemko to open.

"Detective Moore, my client essentially claims he is a victim of a conspiracy and can provide proof that will help you with your investigation. I'm sure that you can release him and arrange for a meeting tomorrow to review his information. The offenses he is charged with are undoubtedly very serious but you have no proof of his involvement other than the fact that he may have provided legal counsel for individuals connected to the energy work currently going on in northern Alberta. That's pretty thin and we both know that a judge will not easily be convinced that you have come to a correct conclusion about this matter."

"Sorry Mr. Slemko. Just after being informed that my witness was on his way up to meet with Mr. Laszlo I was shot at on a city street and either my witness or I could have been killed.

Then when I confronted Mr. Laszlo with this fact he attempted to elude me after agreeing to accompany me to our station to give a statement. I'd say that's pretty suspicious. I think we'll let the court decide on bail at a proper hearing." He then turned to Laszlo and added,

"We'll get you on as early as possible tomorrow and your lawyer can present your case then." He then turned and nodded to the officer standing there and left the room.

Laszlo sputtered "That's absurd! I'm not staying here until then. I've got things I'm supposed to be doing today and they can't wait!"

Seeing that he had no option but to try and settle Laszlo down, Damian Slemko promised,

"Jozeph. I'll get you out of here first thing tomorrow then we can get the cops pointed in the right direction and you can get on with your life."

The officer then took Jozeph away to be held in a cell until the hearing.

In the meantime Moore, accompanied by an RCMP officer arrived at Wilfred's motel and found him sitting there watching the news and eating a pizza.

"Mr. Natannah. This is Constable Bear of the RCMP. He is interested in hearing your story about Jozeph Laszlo. For your information we visited Mr. Laszlo and took him into custody. Constable Bear has spoken to the police at Fort McMurray and clarified your status. They have you listed as a person of interest but only to clarify a few things concerning your relationship with your deceased brother."

The Mountie then took over the questioning.

"Mr. Natannah, you told the investigating officer that you hadn't seen your brother for at least four or five days prior to his death. Is that correct?"

"Probably. I'm not sure. I was so shook up when they talked to me that I can't remember clearly everything that was said. Why?"

"Mr. Natannah, the police officer in Burning Lake has spoken to a witness who recalls seeing your brother drive up to your house the day before his death and then leave shortly after in what looked like a hurry. He evidently spun his tires spraying gravel across the driveway. Do you recall that visit? Did you and your brother have an argument or disagreement?"

"Jeez officer, I don't remember anything like that. I guess maybe he did drop by for a drink the day before. I forgot about that. But everything was cool and after our drink he said goodbye and left. That's the last I seen him."

"Why then did you say you hadn't seen him?"

"I told you guys. I forgot. He just dropped in for a drink. He often did that. I don't always remember the times he done that." Wilfred was getting a little flustered and more than a little pissed.

"OK, Mr. Natannah. That clears that up." he turned to go then as an afterthought asked,

"Did he say where he was going the next day?"

"Goddammit! I already told the cops at home he didn't say nothing. You guys trying to trick me?"

"No sir. Of course not sir. We just wanted to clear those two points up. Will you be staying in Edmonton a while or are you going home soon?"

"No. Now you got that slime ball lawyer in jail I might as well go home. Just watch him. He lies all the time. Sam used to tell me about how Laszlo was always trying to pull the wool over his eyes. He was always trying to cheat us Indians. He's a lying sneak. I bet he shot Sam or got someone to do it for him. I hope you nail him good."

With that Detective Moore thanked him for his cooperation, reminded him that when the time came he would be required to testify about the gunshot and suggested that he remain available to the police at home in case anything else came up. Moore and Bear then left and Wilfred began to pack his stuff and head back.

As Moore and Bear drove back to the station, Moore asked Bear, "Do you trust that guy?"

"Are you kidding? That guy is the godfather of those two reserves. It's suspected he controls most of the criminal stuff that goes on in that whole area. What's to trust?"

Moore looked at him and asked, "Do you think we should have leaned on him more or locked him up with Laszlo?"

Bear laughed. "Locking him up with Laszlo would probably save the taxpayers some money. He'd probably tear his head off and use it for a soccer ball. But I don't think we have anything that will stick and we can always pick him up. He's not going anywhere."

Moore shook his head and sighed. "Now I guess all I got to do is figure out a way to keep Laszlo from getting sprung tomorrow. Him I don't trust to stick around. I think he's dirty!"

As things turned out, no one was going anywhere tomorrow. The whole world of Burning Lake was about to change.

41

The sun was just showing its face as Michael and Roberto sped north in their Bell on the way to start the final phase of the mission. Hopefully it would be a short trip. Already Roberto was getting restless and wanting to get away from this place and back to California. Over the past few days he was considering taking his gains and quitting this game and after this gig he vowed to himself that he'd had enough. Too many of his old buddies had stayed in too long and a lot of them lost the race with time and were now dead. That wasn't going to happen to him.

Thinking of his plans after they were finished here he looked forward to a pleasant and relaxing holiday during his stop in the Azores while he sorted out his finances then a quick trip back to California to liquidate his holdings. An operative like him does not just drop out of the game. An operative has to disappear completely in order to survive. Roberto was going to bury himself so deep that no one would ever find him. He had his eye on some property in Uruguay and with his Cuban background he could easily melt into the back country and blend in with the locals. He had not mentioned his plans to anyone. Even Michael, his friend and comrade of many years would not know. That's what deep cover is all about. He was going deep. As the chopper sped forward he put his head back and let himself drift off to sleep.

When the bomb exploded, demolishing the chopper and its crew in a ball of flames, Roberto and his sidekick ceased to exist. The wreckage plunged into the brush and scrub forest below leaving only scattered pieces of smoldering metal.

42

I spent a miserable sleepless night drinking coffee and sitting up waiting for the phone to buzz or a text to chime and now I'm sitting in my office with no appetite for the day to come. No one has heard anything from either Amy or the Chief's secretary. Last night I think I called everyone I knew who had ever had contact with Amy. Nothing. I even called Big Al to see if he had any suggestions. Nothing. He got all worked up when I told him Amy was missing and made me promise to keep him in the loop. I didn't have to worry about his willingness to help if he could. But no one had a clue. Where to start? It's now nine in the morning and my waiting room is starting to show a few early morning stragglers. How the hell am I going to get through this day?

Like a robot I sift through each patient and check them out, forcing my brain to concentrate on what's in front of me rather than what may be ahead. I'm rapidly losing the battle. Finally I call Louise in and tell her to arrange for me to see the rest of the patients tomorrow or the next day if possible and only call me if something urgent shows up that can't wait. If this doesn't sort itself out pretty soon I'm going to be a wreck and have a lot of pissed off patients.

After instructing Louise to hold the fort, I close my office door and sit and stare at the wall. I'm just about to leave to go back home when my phone vibrates in my pocket.

"Hello." I just about shout.

"Hey Doc. It's Porter here. This may be nothing but I just got a heads up from Fort Mac detachment that someone spotted the wreckage of something still burning about a hundred and fifty klicks north east from here. They're scrambling a search and rescue chopper to head to the scene and see what it's all about. So far we got no reports of any missing aircraft but something is fishy. Usually anyone flying in this territory files a flight plan but we got nothing."

My heart skips a couple of beats and my hands go all sweaty.

"What do you think it means? How could that have anything to do with Amy Pham's disappearance? What the hell is going on?"

My words come out in a jumbled mix and Porter just lets me vent for a few seconds then replies,

"As soon as the chopper gets to the site they'll let us know and I can answer your questions. I'll call you then."

* * *

"Something's strange." This from Dawn Natannah. "It's mid-morning and no one's showed up yet, not that I'm in a hurry for those guys to get here."

Amy shuffled to the opening of the mine and looked out. It was overcast and getting colder but there was no wind and no snow falling.

" I wish I could get these damn shackles off," she complained. "They're driving me nuts. You got any bright ideas?" she asked Dawn who was pulling aside the pile of brush blocking most of the door.

"Let's see those things," she offered.

Amy shuffled over to her and Dawn bent over and grabbed the chain. Looking it over closely she observed,

"This isn't that heavy a chain. Maybe we can pry a link apart if we can find something to pry it with."

She carefully looked at each link and picked one that looked promising.

"This one isn't as tightly closed as the rest. If we can pry it a bit we can force it off the other link and at least you'll be able to walk." Trying a bit of sick humor she added. "Remember, it's your turn to chase the bear." Then she laughed.

"That's not funny. I was scared shitless last night. You can keep that job."

Dawn ran her eyes up and down the rotting timber at the door and there it was, a large long spike sticking out about three inches. It was about a foot up from the ground and maybe it could work. She herded Amy over to the spot and slid the link over the head of the spike. It just fit. Now to find something to pry it with. She looked outside and scanned the ground. There were two or three fairly thick pieces of wood that were long enough to get a good hold of. Maybe that would work. Grabbing one of them she hooked it between the link and the post and heaved up on it as hard as she could. No luck. Then she reversed it and pried down as hard as she could, putting all her weight on it. She was thinking it was working when there was a snap and a yelp from Amy and the log broke free, it's end splintered.

"What happened?" she asked Amy.

"Nothing. It just slipped and scared me and sort of jerked my ankle. Go ahead, Try again."

Dawn looked for another branch a little thicker this time. It just fit between the link and the post. She got a good grip this time and again pushed down as hard as she could. This time she was rewarded with a little movement and saw the link slowly open. Success!

"Did you get it?" asked Amy

"Not sure. Let me try."

She grabbed the link and tried to shove its companion through the crack. Not quite.

"Gotta try again. I think it's coming. Hang on."

She reinserted the branch and heaved once more. Slowly the link spread wider and this time she made sure before she quit. She was rewarded with a link that almost but not quite slipped over the other link.

"Damn!" she swore. "Thought I had it."

Changing tactics she went outside the opening and looked around until she found a couple of good sized rocks that she could use for a hammer. Taking the link off the spike and laying it on one of the rocks she started pounding on it and in no time the two links separated.

"Dawn! You're a genius! I'd have never thought of that."

"That's probably because you never grew up in a family where the women did all the work."

Amy tried walking with her legs now free but it was still awkward with the chain ends dragging but it would have to do. Maybe she could tie them up to her legs somehow but it was so cold she didn't want to tear up any of her clothes.

"Screw it. It'll have to do for now. Do you want some help finding wood?"

"Yeah we better get as much as we can in case it snows. The bigger fire we have the better chance we have someone will spot us."

The two of them then set about dragging branches and brush over to the mine entrance and Dawn piled the kindling and got it lit, nursed it along and soon had a pretty good fire crackling and throwing off smoke and heat.

"Let's get some more brush in front of this opening and get inside where it's warmer. I'm hungry and starting to freeze." Dawn suggested. "We can feed the fire whenever it burns too low. But we'll have to watch it closely."

They got back in the shaft dragging the brush in after them. The gas heater was still humming along but it won't be long before all the gas is gone, she thought. No sense saving the gas. First thing is to stay alive. We can worry about getting back after, she thought. She went to the back of the cave where their cots were and grabbed a couple cans of beans.

"Ever had a four course meal of beans?" she joked and then added more seriously, "I wonder what's next. I hope someone misses us and starts a search."

"Don't worry. The whole town and all the cops in the area will be looking for us," Amy reassured her. "They're probably going nuts."

In a few minutes the beans were starting to bubble in their cans and they grabbed them and started to shovel them into their mouths. Even as scared and cold as they were, they were still hungry and knew they had to keep up their energy for the next crisis that no doubt would be coming sometime soon.

Now with nothing further to do they curled up on the cots and tried to drift off to sleep.

* * *

"Doc, I just got a call from Fort Mac. That wreckage looks like it's from a small chopper. They couldn't tell me much more. My guys are checking with the airport to see if anyone is missing. It looks like one of those four man Bells that the news guys use. It's too small for a medivac unit. No report yet of survivors or anything. I can't figure what that means for our missing girls but we'll keep looking. Soon as I hear from the airport I'll let you know."

Porter's news just confuses me further. No way they could have been on that chopper up there. Why the hell would they? This thing is starting to read like a bad movie. I just wish I could turn it off! I put the coffee pot on just for something to do and sit down and try and let my mind go blank. What is it that Amy and the Chief could discover that would warrant all these things happening to her? As I mused about the events of the last several hours I remembered her telling me she was keeping a copy of her journal on a stick in her office safe. I wonder if that would help us. I grab my phone again and am just about to hit "Porter" when my mobile buzzes.

"Got some more news, Doc. The airport people told me that they have had a Bell flying out of there for the last few days. It left this morning again but they haven't heard from it since. There was no flight plan. The lady at air traffic dug around for us and discovered that they charged their fill ups to an outfit called International Home Securities Inc. They couldn't make out the signature. We got calls in to all the lease companies in the area to see if anyone with that name leased a chopper lately. Maybe if we get lucky we might find that they had one of those GPS trackers and the lease company was tracking them. That'll give us an idea where they've been the last few days."

"Constable, don't hang up yet. Amy Pham told me she was keeping a backup journal of all her work for the Indians on a stick and storing it in her safe at work. Maybe that will give you some leads."

"Good thought. Thanks. I'll get right on it. Hang on. We'll get to the bottom of this as soon as possible. I'll stay in touch." He disconnected leaving me even more frustrated and confused.

What's this GPS tracking stuff he was talking about?
Maybe I know somebody that can help me with that.

I have Carl Reimer's number on speed dial. Ever since he told me about the incident with the overdose at his camp I've stayed in touch with him and now I get his mobile to chase him down.

"Reimer."

"Carl. Doc Cross. I need some information. Do you guys have some sort of GPS monitoring set ups for your trucks?"

"Yeah Doc. All our trucks are on that system. I can find anyone driving any of our trucks at any time and see where they've been and how long they've been there"

"Do choppers have the same system?"

"Some do. A lot of the newer ones being leased these days have them so the lease company can find out where they are. Also some of the companies leasing them want to check out where their pilots have been. It's part of the quality thing. What's this all about?"

"I'm not sure. I'm working on something that I can't talk much about right now. I'll try and fill you in next time I see you. I owe you a beer."

"No problem, Doc. Glad to help. Let me know if you need more."

We disconnected and my mind is spinning with what ifs. What if Amy had been grabbed and taken somewhere. The tracker might help us with the search. I'm certain she wasn't on that chopper when it crashed. She's been gone for over twenty four hours and it just crashed a few hours ago. Maybe if we knew where it went we could find out where she is. It's a long shot but what else have we got? I punch in Porter's number and he answers.

"Yeah Doc. What you got?" I wonder if brevity is part of their training.

"Constable, have you got anywhere with finding out where that wrecked chopper came from yet?"

"Yeah, we've just confirmed it was leased from an outfit out of Nisku. Why?"

"Did it have that GPS tracker?"

"As a matter of fact it did. They said they'd print it off and fax it to our office in Fort Mac. What are you thinking of?"

I tell him what I'm thinking and I give a sigh of relief when he doesn't tell me I'm nuts.

"Problem is Doc, it will take us a while to dig up an expert at translating all that data into anything we can understand and then we'll need some sort of geologist with aerial photography expertise to help us design a search if the bosses in Fort Mac think that's the way to go."

"What if I can get you a guy right now that can do both of those things? Can you get the company at Nisku to fax you the data?"

"I'm sure I could but you're out of the loop. I'm not sure my superiors would approve."

"You're in the loop. Suppose you could convince them that you can work that data for them."

"Doc, I'm pretty smart but I don't know how to do that."

"Your bosses may not know that. Look Constable Porter. we may be on a short time line here. We may not have time for all that meeting and task force stuff and need to know BS."

I know I'm sounding desperate and starting to beg but dammit, I am desperate.

"OK Doc. I'll get the data and you line up your guy. As soon as you get something let me know and I'll get you the stuff. For god sake don't let this out to anyone. You'll get me into more shit than I can handle. I like my posting here."

I thank him and disconnect and speed dial Adam Mir. I remembered him telling me how he was an expert at aerial prospecting and could interpret data from both visual and radiometric technologies. He used his aerial work as an opportunity to get some of the stunning photos he had displayed on his walls at his home. Another long shot but first I have to find him. His answering service tells me to leave a message. Shit. I don't have time for this. I leave him a panic message.

"Adam, this is Doc Cross in Burning Lake. I have a life and death emergency here and not much time to fix it. Can you get right back to me as soon as possible? It's urgent."

Just to make sure, I text him the same message and hope for the best.

A couple of moments later my mobile buzzes and the screen lights up with his name.

"Adam. Thanks for the prompt reply. I owe you big time. Adam, Amy has been missing the past 24 hours. I think she may have been kidnapped by that group who stuck the tracker on her car."

"Kidnapped! What happened?"

"She disappeared yesterday. She never came back to work after lunch and no one has seen her since. Also, there's a local woman missing since the day before. The local may be connected to this whole thing."

"That's incredible! What do you think happened?"

"We're not sure but earlier this morning a helicopter crashed about a hundred and fifty klicks north east of here. There's a chance the chopper may have been involved in the kidnapping but the timing is wrong."

There's silence at the other end for a few seconds then he replies,

"Doc. What are you thinking? How can I help?"

"I need your expertise. We've found out where the chopper was leased and it seems it's made a few trips out of Fort Mac the last couple of days but no one knows anything about it. The people at the airport thought it was doing some aerial surveying but other than gassing it up after each trip no one has spoken to the crew."

"That's not unusual. Some of those freelance prospectors are pretty secretive."

I continue, hoping I'm making some sense.

"I know but it's all we've got."

"What do the cops say?"

"They've managed to get the GPS monitor record from the lease company and that's where you come in. It'll be a while before they can find anyone to interpret it all for them and I don't think we have time to waste. This is confidential but the local Mountie here can get the data and he's willing to show it to me. If his bosses find out, he'll be in deep shit so this is all under the table. If you saw the GPS log could you interpret it and help me figure out where these guys have been? If there is a recurring pattern to their flights maybe it'll help. I know it's a long shot but I'm going nuts sitting here wondering what's going on."

"Yeah, figuring out the data will be easy enough but there's a lot of nothing out there and you've got no survey maps or other topographical images to help you."

"I know. But if we see a recurring pattern could we not match it to known data and go from there?"

He laughed. "No disrespect Doc but that's a pretty big if. It would take a major ground and air search to cover all that area and we're not sure what to look for."

I felt my sliver of hope slipping away and was about to thank him and hang up when he said, "You know, if you can get me the GPS stuff and it shows they flew exactly the same route every time maybe we can narrow down the area and see if it matches any known camps or settlements. Any idea why that chopper crashed? Any signs of survivors or crew or passengers?"

"Too early to tell. The search and rescue guys are probably just on the scene now. I should know more in an hour or so. Adam, this is a pretty complex criminal matter and I'm just on the outside of it. We know Amy was investigating some fishy financials. She's been drugged, her car's been tailed, a guy involved in the investigation's been shot and now she's missing. With all this stuff going on I'm not ready to accept that a possible secretive survey ending in a crash is just a coincidence."

"OK Doc. I'm here in Fort Mac all day. If you can get me that data I'll see what I can do."

"Thanks Adam. At least it'll make me think I'm doing something instead of just waiting around for bad news. As soon as I get the report I'll bring it up to you myself."

We disconnect and I text Porter that I got our man lined up. A few minutes later he texts back that he's got the data and agrees to bring it to me at my clinic. Finally, some action!

* * *

Detective Bob Moore was at his desk finishing up his report concerning Laszlo and Natannah when his desk phone rang. Identifying himself he uttered the standard "How can I help you?" and sat up straight when the caller identified himself as the CEO of Midnight Sun Energy Resources.

"Detective Moore, I've just been informed that you've arrested my chief legal counsel. Can you tell me what the hell is going on? What's he supposed to have done?"

"Sir, we are still in the early stages of our investigation but earlier on we were speaking with a person of interest in another matter and he mentioned that he was just on his way to an

468 Maurice F. Simpson

appointment with Mr. Laszlo. Because we were anxious to question him on another matter I requested that he accompany me voluntarily to the station to clear up that matter. As he was getting into the car we came under fire and the car sustained some damage but no one was injured. The shooter was not apprehended."

"What's all that got to do with Mr. Laszlo?" the Midnight Sun guy asked.

"Well, we then took our witness back to the station where he was able to clear up our concerns but was not able to give us any information about the shooting. We were satisfied with his account and he left the station and returned to his residence. However, following up on his information regarding his relationship with Mr. Laszlo I returned to his office to see if I could throw any light on our investigation. During our conversation Mr. Laszlo became somewhat agitated which is understandable but also repeated information about the gunshot fired at either me or my witness that he could not possibly have known about. When I confronted him with his contradictions and requested that he accompany me to the station to deal with this matter he requested a lawyer which certainly is his right and then he agreed to accompany me."

"Well that seems reasonable enough." observed the CEO.

"Yes, of course. But on the pretext of getting his coat he attempted to elude me by exiting the premises through a back entrance. That was enough for me to consider that he had knowledge of and was trying to conceal involvement in the earlier discharge of a firearm."

Moore finished his account defending his action with a quick sum up.

"Sir, I realize that he holds a responsible position with your corporation but his unusual behaviour led me reluctantly to my actions. He has had a chance to speak with his lawyer and a bail hearing has been arranged for tomorrow in court. Meanwhile if there is anything you can tell us that would shed some light on this whole affair I would appreciate a chance to talk to you about it."

Moore wasn't anxious to get blindsided by a gaggle of corporate lawyers ganging up on him so the more he could find out about this company and the people running it the happier he'd be. But the CEO wasn't offering so he attempted to close out the conversation when the man asked an odd question.

"Detective Moore, does this have anything to do with that murder on the reserve up near Fort McMurray?"

Moore replied cautiously, "I can't tell you a lot about that. I'm not the lead on it. That's in the hands of the RCMP."

"Detective Moore, our company has been involved in a project with the Prairie Dene near the town of Burning Lake. We're providing preliminary infrastructure to a more permanent platform in the south end of the Reserve. The Dene have secured a First Nations Land Management agreement with the government and are now preparing the infrastructure.

They'll eventually have roads and powerlines as well as utilities and communications infrastructure. This incident could throw a monkey wrench into the whole project."

Moore thinks about this for a beat then offers an olive branch.

"Sir, I can put you in touch with the RCMP leads both in Burning Lake and Fort McMurray. I'm sure they'll be anxious for an exchange of information. I'll fax you the contact information as soon as I hang up."

The Midnight Sun man thanked him and hung up the phone. Moore faxed over the information then sent an email to Constable Bear giving him a heads up. This was starting to get complicated. Moore, not for the first time since that gunshot, wondered what would have happened if he had just ignored that APB about the Indian guy.

43

After hearing about a possible journal copy of the audit being carried out by Amy Pham, Constable Porter immediately contacted his sergeant in Fort Mac who called the senior partner at Abrahms and Abrahms and requested access to it. When Amy's boss heard the request he raised the expected privacy issues but readily agreed that the journal was work product that belonged to Chief Wah-Shee and his council and if it was OK with him then the RCMP could have a copy. Porter held off saying anything about the outside help he was hoping for from Doc Cross and his techie contact. He knew he was taking a big chance but he thought he could work it out somehow.

I'm wasting no time getting on the road with the data from the aircraft lease company. My poor jeep is getting a workout and I hope that all the cops are tied up doing something else.

All I got to worry about are the sheriffs. While I'm on my way Adam Mir is gathering up all the charts and maps that he thinks would help. We may be way off base with this theory but at least we're trying something. While I'm flying down the road and worrying about sheriffs and elk and moose getting in my way, my mobile buzzes and my Bluetooth tells me Constable Porter wants to talk to me.

"Yeah Constable. You got news?" I ask, holding my breath, not sure I want an answer.

"Not about the disappearance of your lady. But I just got a call from the head honcho at Midnight Sun. He told me the Edmonton Police Service have the lawyer for Midnight Sun in custody regarding an attempted murder charge. Evidently someone took a shot at Wilfred Natannah earlier today."

"Holy shit." I exclaim. "What's he got to do with all this? We got a bunch of bigshots acting like crooks?"

"I don't know." Porter answered. "Seems awfully strange. But you know I got to thinking. The lawyer must have had something to do with drawing up that agreement that started this whole mess. I wonder if he's an inside guy on this thing. He'd be able to set up offshore accounts and all that other stuff needed to cover up fraudulent payments."

"Good thought. I wonder if he could be persuaded to tell us who all is involved and where they've hidden Amy and Dawn. Can you make me a deputy so I can go see him and beat the shit out of him?" I'm on a roll now.

Porter laughs and says, "Doc, you got me in enough trouble. My next posting will be some shithole in northern Newfoundland."

"That's OK Constable. You should know a lot about Newfies after working here for so long." Workers from Newfoundland have been a mainstay of the labour force at the oil sands for the last couple of decades. He doesn't laugh.

"Doc, how close are you to Fort Mac?"

"About a half hour more. Why? Do you want to get me for speeding?"

"Naw I'll leave it to the sheriffs. They're a hell of a lot meaner than I am." He goes on.

"Give me a call soon as your guy looks at that stuff and lets you know if he can do anything or not. In the meantime I'm going to call the lead detective in Edmonton and have a talk with him regarding the lawyer."

OK, I promise and disconnect.

It's now late in the afternoon and only a couple of hours of daylight are left. If the tracking stuff doesn't give us any leads and that crashed chopper is involved in their disappearance then they could be anywhere and we'd have no clues. We desperately need a break. Wondering if only the lawyer is dirty or the whole company could be involved I realize I need more information. I should be at Fort Mac in about twenty minutes but I still got time to make one more call. I tell my Bluetooth to find Carl Reimer. He answers on the second ring with,

"Yeah, Doc. You need something else.?"

"I do Carl. I'll fill you in more when I can but right now I need some information about your company. This stuff is confidential and you don't have to answer. You can just tell me to go to hell and no hard feelings."

"Doc, you sound awfully serious. What's going on."

"Carl, I think your company may be involved in something dirty but I'm not sure. The cops have arrested your legal guy and are investigating a shooting in Edmonton. They're not sure but it might be connected to the murder of Sam Beaulieu."

"What!" he exclaims. "I don't believe it. Our CEO is about as stand up a guy as you could want. I don't know the COO as well but he's always been up front with me. I don't know the lawyer but I haven't heard anything about him. I do know he was involved in the agreement with the company that hired me, the guys from China, and he probably worked with Chief and council on the deal we have with the Reserve folks."

He waits a couple of beats then asks, "What were you going to ask me?"

"I'm not sure now. I think you just told me what I need to know."

He answers, "Doc I know that the lawyer, Laszlo is his name, has been really aggressive at tying up leases all over the place. He even picked up some property up north just about a few klicks from Uranium City. That area's pretty well been gone over looking for gold and uranium. Now the big push is diamonds since that big strike up north of Yellowknife. Hell, there's even an old abandoned uranium mine somewhere up there across the lake from Uranium city. Don't know what good it is now that the uranium market is flat."

"Hold it Carl. You say there's an abandoned mine up there somewhere?"

"That's what the rumour is."

"Carl, can you find out where it is and get back to me?"

"Yeah Doc. I think I can but it'll be a couple of hours. That soon enough?"

"It'll have to do. Get me that info and I'll fill you in on this stuff then. I'll owe you more than a beer then."

By now I'm just a couple of blocks from Adam's place and my mind is reeling. *Hold on Amy, please hold on.* I pull up to Adam's and skid to a stop and grab my brief case and dash to the door trembling with both fear and hope. Adam has the door open before I ring the bell and greets me.

"Hey Doc. This is terrible. Any news yet?"

I shake my head and start pulling out my papers to hand to him.

"No news but lots of guess work." and then I fill him in about the stuff Carl told me.

"My contact is going to call me as soon as he can find out about any leases Midnight Sun has. He might be able to get some locations for me."

Adam starts to lay out the pages then observes, "We might be able to find some stuff out from here but some coordinate from another source would sure help narrow the field. Do you know the range of that chopper that crashed?"

"I'm not sure but when I find out what kind it was for sure, we can find that out easily enough."

We sit at his big table and he starts to study the report. He then enters some data and search parameters and a whole list of possibles pop up.

"What the heck did you enter?" I ask with my confusion probably pretty evident.

"I just asked for known uranium reserves in Canada. I got that info somewhere but this is faster than me checking all my files."

I see that I'm already out of my depth so I shut up and let him work. He pulls up a map of Fort Mac area and enlarges it to a radius of 500 klicks and starts entering coordinates. Very soon it is evident that the chopper flew a straight line from Nisku to Fort Mac and then the entries stopped. After a couple of hours new entries were recorded suggesting a course north east of Fort Mac. This is getting interesting. This chopper was not flying random circuits. After a couple minutes Adam informs me that the last coordinate started to repeat itself several times suggesting that it was either hovering or set down. Again the entries ceased for some time and an hour or so passed and the entries started to show up again.

"Looks like they're heading back to Fort Mac again," Adam observed. He entered a spot on the map where the last coordinate entries stopped and then started again.

"I wonder what's at that place they stopped," he commented.

The whole process repeated itself the next day at about dawn then returned to Fort Mac.

Comparing the entries from the day before, Adam began to talk to himself.

"These coordinates are not exactly the same but still follow roughly the same course and stop at roughly the same location. There's got to be something there they are interested in". Again he marked the map and said,

"The site is pretty close to the last site." We seemed to be through half the report and already a recurring pattern is showing up.

"This is a heck of a lot easier than calculating speed and fuel consumption and guessing at the distance," he said. "Let's see what the next lot shows." When he finished he had marked another spot almost on top of the first two.

"Definitely the same spot again. Something's got to be there."

He was just starting to pull up some images of the area when my mobile vibrated and Reimer appeared on the screen.

"Hi Carl. Anything on those sites?"

"Got a few of them Doc. You got a pencil?"

He read off four sets of coordinates and then commented,
"Best I could do Doc. I got lucky and found someone in the
office that agreed to look this stuff up for me without hassling
me. You know, confidentiality and all that crap." I thank him
and tell him the debt is up to several beer and a five course
meal.

"As soon as I can, Carl, I'll fill you in. I think this stuff is
going to be a big help."

We disconnect and I give the numbers to Adam. Pay dirt!
One of Carl's locations is very close to our three dots.

"That's the location of an old uranium mine. Hell of a place
to hide someone." I exclaim excitedly. Adam shows me the rest
of the data. It is a straight line to about two thirds of the way to
our dots and then they quit.

"Bingo." He says excitedly. "They were on their way back
when they crashed. It's unlikely they were ferrying them back
and forth for two days. That doesn't make sense. They're
probably still out there. We better get this to the cops so they
can get out there." By now it was dusk and the snow was
falling. My spirits plunge when I realize no one is going to
launch a chopper to go out there tonight on a wild goose chase.
But that's not my call. I hit Porters number and wait for his
answer.

"Porter." No hello, how are you, how may I help you,
please leave a message? Just "Porter."

"Constable, my expert has just located three coordinates suggesting three stops at the same place over the last twenty four hours or so. In addition I have another source that tells me that Midnight Sun has a lease at those sites that used to be an old uranium mine. What if that is where our women are?"

"Or what if those are all legitimate flights for consultants for Midnight Sun. That's pretty thin, Doc. I can't take that to my bosses and expect a full out search and rescue mission be launched. We need a lot more than that. Sorry Doc."

I'm not ready to give up yet, dammit!

"Constable Porter, is it possible for you to talk to someone at Midnight Sun and see if they have any consultants flying out to that site. You know the name of the corporation that rented the chopper that we think crashed and by the way, the data inputs stopped approximately where you said that chopper crashed." I went on before he could interrupt. "If the Midnight Sun folks cooperate then you can make a better decision about a search."

"You're pushing pretty hard Doc. I know this is personal so I understand why but I can't promise anything. I'll have to talk to my bosses and let them decide about talking to the suits at Midnight Sun. I'll get back to you."

Reluctantly I touch "end call" and sit staring at Adam.

"What's he say?" he asks. "Are they buying it"

I sigh and shake my head. "No dice; too many 'what ifs'."

"Look," Adam offers. "This snow is supposed to let up by midnight and then it's clear and cold tomorrow. Luckily there's no wind of any consequence tomorrow. If they haven't decided to launch by then we could always fly out to that spot and back. Might cost you a few bucks but so what. You docs make lots of money don't you?"

If anyone else had of said that to me at this time I probably would have decked him but I knew that Adam was just pulling my chain.

"What do you mean, fly over? What are you thinking?"

"Our company has a pretty good arrangement with one of the locals for charter when we do aerials. Of course they're just fixed wing but at least we could get a look at that site."

I'm ready to go right now! "When could we get that set up?" I ask eagerly, guarding against another disappointment.

"I'll call my guy right now. If he can set it up we'll leave at dawn. It would be a lot faster if you just bunk in here instead of looking for a hotel unless you've already got plans, of course."

"No. I just want to get underway at dawn. I won't sleep tonight anyhow. I was just going to go over and crash at Amy's but this is better. Thanks. Let's get things lined up."

I have no way of knowing what we'll be facing tomorrow but whatever it is I want this all to stop. *C'mon Amy. Hang in there. We're coming.*

* * *

The snow was still falling outside the old mine and it was getting a lot colder. The fire was long dead because of lack of dry wood and falling snow. There wasn't a lot of shelter to shield the flames. Dawn finished refueling the gas stove from the almost empty jerry can but there was still enough kerosene for the lamp. The stove tank still had enough fuel to warm a little water and a couple of beans in the morning. Amy lay listless on the cot, shivering even though wrapped in the arctic sleeping bag.

"Something must have happened to those creeps," Dawn remarked. "I wonder why they didn't show."

"Who cares. I hope like hell they got arrested or something and tell someone where we are so we can get out of here. I don't think I can handle another day and night here without going nuts!"

Dawn replied, "At least the bears don't have guns."

"O god, don't mention that bear. What if he comes back?"

"Don't worry," Dawn reassured her. "We still got the spray and a couple of flash bangs. No bears are gonna mess with two angry women with flash bangs."

Then making sure they each had a can and a stun grenade, Dawn crawled into her bag and said, "Try and get a little sleep. Hopefully tomorrow we'll see someone who can get us out of this mess."

Neither captive believed that they would get any sleep at all.

I hope that damn bear is sleeping, thought Dawn.

A few hours passed by and somewhere in the distance the howling of wolves could be heard but not by the slumbering women.

* * *

Adam is still on the phone trying to find his pilot contact when my mobile lights up with Big Al's number.

"Hi Al. What's up?"

"Any news Doc. You got anything you can tell me?" His concern comes through my speaker in a bit of a quiver.

"Nothing concrete yet, Al." I answer.

"Wadda you mean concrete ?" he growls. "Does that mean you got something, anything?"

The last thing I want is to have this man mountain pissed at me. Wondering what I can safely tell him without getting in trouble with the cops. I carefully answer.

"Al, there might be an air search and rescue organized in the next twenty four hours once the cops get some locations to look at." Al is too smart to be snowed with that kind of BS.

"Locations? What locations? Do they think some dirt bags grabbed her and dumped her somewhere out of town?" He was on the scent and wasn't going to back down.

"Al, they're not sure of what to think and it will take a while to get a search organized. I'm not sure the locations identified can be reached by land."

"Well they should send a fuckin chopper. Where the hell are those locations?"

"Choppers and fixed wing are probably being considered as options but all that's going to take time to organize."

"Bullshit!" he exploded. "You want a chopper I can get you one to go as soon as the sun goes up. All you got to tell me is where to go." Telling him where to go wasn't exactly what I had in mind in any meaning of the phrase. What the hell was he talking about?

"Al, how can you do that. You a pilot?"

"Shit no. Doc, you remember that BMW I had up on the hoist the last time you were in?"

"Yeah, Al. What's that got to do with this?"

"That BMW belongs to a chopper jock who's a good buddy of mine. He flies on contract for at least three energy companies up here and he's damn good. Used to fly missions against the Taliban. I know he can use one of the company choppers that he usually flies. They often sublease him and the chopper to surveyors when they're not using them."

"Holy crap, Al! Are you serious? You can line that up?" My mind is spinning.

"Give me five. I'll call you back" He disconnects.

Adam is staring at me with a puzzled look on his face. I fill him in.

"That was the guy that found the device on Amy's car, the auto guy. He says he can get us a chopper and a pilot as soon as the sun comes up"

"Is he sure? Those guys are hard to get on short notice and where the hell is he getting the chopper?" Adam isn't ready to buy it yet. "Sounds too good to be true."

"I don't know but this guy is the real deal. He's not a bull shitter and he treats Amy like a daughter. I think I trust him."

We're hurriedly making a list of the stuff we need to take with us when Big Al lights up my mobile again.

"What color chopper do you want, Doc, red yellow or green?"

"Wha...how...I stammer. Al, I don't care if it's friggin pink or purple as long as it flies and the pilot is sober."

He chuckles and replies "I can't guarantee he'll be sober but anything he flies is in top shape." Then he added, "He was sober this afternoon when he dropped off his Beamer and he sounded sober tonight when I just called so he should be OK in the morning."

"There's two of us, Al. Is that OK? How shall we meet up? What should we bring?"

"Just dress warm and wear good boots. Show up at the airport near the charter office about a half hour before sunrise and don't forget your coordinates info. Oh, and you'll need money."

"How much money?" I ask.

"How much are you worth?"

"Al, quit shitting me. How do I pay? Do I need cash. Will a credit card do?"

Again he laughs. "Don't worry, Doc. You'll just need money to buy me a steak and a beer after the flight. Oh, and by the way, Do you have a shotgun or a rifle?"

"Hell no. I don't even hunt." Adam is raising his hand. He can hear Al's booming voice from across the room.

"I got a shot gun" he offers.

"Tell him to bring it. Never know what you might run into out there in this country. And don't be late." He disconnects before I can thank him.

"You ever been in a chopper?" Adam asks me.

"Only once on a medivac flight. I think I got sicker than the patient."

"This should be a fun ride," he observes, "a drunk pilot, a shotgun and a puking passenger."

Adam is about three sizes smaller than me but luckily I keep winter clothes and footwear in the Jeep for emergencies so we gather up the stuff we'll need and he finds me a place to crash. Just as I'm wishing I could down a couple of ounces of scotch he asks me,

"Do you want a drink of anything stronger than coffee before you sack out?"

He's Muslim. That's the last thing I expect!

"I know. I'm Muslim. That's the last thing you expect." He reaches up into a cupboard and brings down a bottle of Macallans about a quarter full, and two glasses.

"This is medicine. We need a good sleep tonight."

Before we know it we kill the whole thing. I should sleep a little better tonight.

44

It's late in the evening but the office of Midnight Sun is all lit up and seated in the office board room The CEO, COO and RCMP Constable Bear are in an urgent conference regarding the Laszlo affair. After Constable Porter let his bosses know about the Pham journal, all hell broke loose and Midnight Sun bosses were informed about the suspicious disappearance of the accountant performing the forensic audit of the contract between the First Nation Reserve and the energy company. The meeting was hastily arranged and the only ones absent were Amy Pham who was still missing and Jozeph Laszlo who was in jail. It made for a very tense and more than slightly hostile discussion.

After the hostilities calmed a bit, Constable Bear outlined the role of Amy Pham and the fact that her months old auto accident may have been the result of an attempt on her life. He then went on to describe the extent of her investigation and information recorded in the journal that suggested some persons may have been involved in fraudulent activities in the numerous transactions between the band council administration and Midnight Sun. That immediately got their attention.

"Constable Bear. Are you suggesting that someone in our organization was involved in illegal activity and that someone might have been Mr. Laszlo?" This from the COO.

"There is considerable evidence to show that payments were made for materials and services that were never delivered." replied Bear. "The details are currently being analyzed by our commercial crimes unit and I'm sure they will be seeking your cooperation in their investigation."

The CEO sat there with a look of stunned disbelief. Finally he found his voice and responded to Bear.

"Of course, Constable, we will cooperate fully and open our books to the extent required by relevant privacy legislation."

Not wanting to inflame the situation, Bear did not inform them that court issued subpoenas would probably trump any privacy regulations. That could come later. But he had another matter to discuss.

"Sir, it has come to our attention that Midnight Sun has been acquiring a number of mining leases over the past two or three years. Is that correct?" Porter's heads up that the company owned leases with abandoned mines was interesting and he agreed with Porter that this may be relevant in the two day old search for Amy Pham. Again it was a long shot but what the hell, it couldn't hurt to ask.

"Constable Bear, we are always securing and disposing of mining leases. That's a matter of public record. Why do you ask?"

"Would it be possible for you to find out if you have an interest in any properties along the Alberta Saskatchewan border near Lake Athabasca?"

With yet another look of puzzlement the CEO stared at his partner and back at Bear and replied, "I'm not sure without checking."

In the meantime the COO was busy at his laptop firing off keystrokes at lightning speed.

Finally looking up he said, "We have three properties tied up in that area."

Bear decided to push his luck.

"Do any of those parcels have any old abandoned mines."

Again the lightning speed keystrokes. The COO said,

"As far as I can see there are three or four old uranium mines on those parcels. They've got to be ancient because underground uranium mining has largely been abandoned because of the dangers from radioactive radon gas. Can you tell me what this has to do with our project near Burning Lake?"

Still on a role, Bear decided to push on. His next question would probably really piss them off but he didn't want to quit now.

"Could Mr. Laszlo have known about those mines."

As suspected, Mr. CEO just about blew a gasket and exploded.

"What the hell are you suggesting, Constable Bear?"

"I'm really not suggesting anything. I'm just gathering information I feel may assist us with our rather urgent investigation. If you wish, we can adjourn and hold off until you've secured legal counsel. Unfortunately Mr. Laszlo will not be available to you for a while. But I must advise you that bail or no bail, Mr. Laszlo should not be included in any of your internal investigations unless of course he is needed as a witness. That would probably constitute an obvious conflict of interest."

By this time the two Midnight Sun guys had calmed down a bit. They were obviously wondering what kind of crap was going to get flung at their company.

Mr. COO looked at his screen and advised Bear,

"We have the coordinates of these old mines and I would be happy to give them to you. As far as whether or not Mr. Laszlo knew about them, I have no idea. Of course he could have learned of them during our negotiations to acquire them. That's no secret. Those properties are part of our future plans but so far they're just sitting there doing nothing. I'm surprised you even asked about them. We haven't paid any attention to them in the past two years."

Bear thanked them for their candor, apologized for taking their time so late in the evening and promised to keep them informed regarding the ongoing investigation. He also gave him the contact information of the sergeant from the commercial crimes unit who was conducting the investigation. The meeting ended and Bear headed back to his office to get the info to Porter. It was a good night's work. Porter owed him a beer next time he was in Edmonton.

Constable Porter read the text from Bear in Edmonton that asked him to call ASAP. He wondered what else was going to happen today. Between Wah-Shee and Doc Cross he hardly had time to eat or crap. He understood Doc's frustration though. Those women could be anywhere and may still be alive. If so they had to be found in the next several hours. Maybe Bear could help that along. He looked at the number Bear had given him and tapped it in.

"How are things up in the bush?" he heard Bear ask when he came on.

"Pretty quiet. Nothing exciting happens up here."

Bear laughed and then said, "I got a present for you. Would the coordinates for four abandoned uranium mines help you guys in your search?"

"What good would they be? There's always surveys and site visits going on with these guys. That theory that the women are stashed away in one of those mines makes a good story but

we need more than that to mount a ground air search and rescue
mission."

What if I tell you that Midnight Sun hasn't visited those
sites in two years and certainly not in the last two days.?"

"Are you kidding?" Porter exclaimed. "I better get that to
the OC at Fort Mac. Maybe they'll have to take a look at that
theory. I'd hate to find out it's true and we did nothing until it
was too late. I sure as hell don't want that on my conscience."

"Well it's too late and too dark to do anything tonight. It's
snowing and nothing is going to move until tomorrow anyhow.
Just thought I'd let you know. I got that stuff from the bosses at
Midnight Sun after they calmed down and they promised total
cooperation. They're probably wondering what's in that
accountant's journal. If this guy Laszlo is dirty it could be
really bad for their company."

Porter thanked Bear, promised him a couple of beers and a
fishing trip and hung up. It was too late to phone the Doc. All it
would do is get him all wired up again. Tomorrow first thing
would be soon enough. Time to turn in. It's been a long day.

* * *

The first thing Amy noticed when she woke from a restless
sleep was a need to pee. Then when she remembered where she
was she quickly suppressed it. No way she was going outside in
the frozen dark and there was no way to do it in the mine. For

the first time in her life she regretted not being a man. The urge
was getting stronger and Dawn was snoring in what looked like
a deep sleep. Finally, when she could stand it no more she
wrapped the bag around her shoulders, grabbed the pepper
spray and headed for the opening. It was snowing pretty good
when they decided to try and get some sleep and they managed
to pull enough brush across the opening so that the wind was
blocked somewhat. Now, as she got to the opening in the dim
light of the lonely kerosene lamp she could see that the snow
had piled up on the branches. Still there was a strong draft
flowing through the branches. Maybe if she squatted and peed
on the branches they could burn them when they tried to start
the fire. This was really not the time to worry about the smell.

Just as she was preparing she was startled by a snorting and
shuffling just on the other side of the brush pile and suddenly a
head popped through the opening, emitting a low growl.
Screaming she grabbed the pepper spray and emptied it in the
face of the head less than three feet away from her. The bear
roared and crashed down on the brush backing away and
dragging it with him leaving the mouth of the mine wide open.
As the beast turned toward her shaking its head in fury Amy let
loose with another stream catching the intruder full in the face
forcing it to rear up and let loose another thunderous roar. In
terror she turned to scramble down the shaft, tripping and
falling on her face.

"Cover your ears and shut your eyes!" she heard Dawn scream and a couple of seconds later the cave was filled with light and the loudest, most explosive bang she had ever heard in her life. She lay stunned and disoriented for several seconds with a ringing in her ears blocking out all other senses. *What happened? What was that? she thought.*

A hand was not so gently shaking her shoulder and she realized it was Dawn trying to rouse her.

"What the hell did you just do?" Amy hollered.

"Just blew that old bruin away with a stun grenade. Good thing they left us a couple. We sure needed them. I don't think that ol' bear will stop running until he reaches the Arctic!"

Amy opened her eyes but they still seemed seared by the flash even though she thought she had squeezed them shut when she heard Dawn yell. She started to shiver as much from fear as from the cold wind now funneling down the shaft. The snow had stopped falling and the moon was showing through the clouds throwing a dim light on the stark landscape. There was no sign of the bear and as her hearing started to return she was struck by the silence of the winter night. *Is this horror show never going to stop? she thought.*

Dawn was trying to fire up the gas heater that had gone out through the night. The second jerry can still had about a half-gallon of gas but after that was gone they were out of luck. The kerosene was also running out. As soon as it was light they were going to have to find some wood or they would freeze to death. Finally the heater caught and some warmth started to penetrate the frozen few feet around it. She grabbed some of the scattered brush and pulled it back across the opening once again giving them at least some shelter from the wind.

There were still a number of bottles of water and a couple of tea bags left so she got the nearly empty stove going and boiled some water. She dismissed any thought of getting any more sleep tonight or this morning or whatever time it was. She quit wearing a watch soon after she became addicted to her mobile but now she had neither. Guess they would have to wait. She guessed that sunrise was probably about eight a.m. but the streaks of light should start to show after seven thirty. *Why haven't those guys showed up by now. What happened yesterday?* Talk about mixed feelings. She knew where she would like to put that last flash bang if they showed up today. She still held on to hope that they would be rescued but they were just about out of food and fuel and when the water was gone so would they be gone. They didn't have any good way to melt the snow.

Now they were bundled up in their bags sitting on their cots and drinking the rapidly cooling tea. If that damn bear showed up again they still had the last can of spray and another flash bang. After that they were out of weapons. Freeze to death or be mauled to death. Which is worse. Curiously Dawn was not aware of fear. All she was aware of was a growing rage at their predicament and the hopelessness of their position. Dammit, her people survived in the brush in the winter for centuries. What would they do? Without tools they were lost. No bones, no copper and no clubs.

Suddenly she realized what she had been ignoring. That cave in hadn't completely blocked off the cave from the rest of the mine. What if there were some old tools left behind. Grabbing the lamp she walked back to the pile of rocks and rubble reaching to the roof of the shaft and started throwing back the rocks.

"What are you doing? What's the matter?" a startled Amy queried.

"I wonder what's behind this pile." she gasped as she struggled to clear away the rubble with her bare and now cold and bleeding fingers.

Amy dragged a thin pair of leather dress gloves out of her coat pocket and pulling them on called to Dawn, "Stop it! You'll wreck your hands. Let's get some branches and pry those rocks away."

Feverishly they struggled for several minutes and slowly the opening revealed a sloping shaft that disappeared into the darkness.

"A few more minutes and we'll be able to squeeze through there," Amy panted.

"Yeah, as long as the whole tunnel doesn't fall in on us." gasped Dawn who was by now running out of breath and sweating in spite of the cold.

They worked at a level pace for several minutes more and then Amy crawled gingerly over the rough rocks and found herself on the other side and able to stand.

"Pass me the lamp," she called out to Dawn. "I want to see where this goes."

"Hey, wait for me. I still can't get through that hole. We need to get more rocks out of the way. You're not leaving me here alone and wandering around in a mine. You'll get yourself killed!"

After a few more rocks were dislodged Amy was able to grab Dawn and pull her through the opening and they both collapsed on the ground panting and laughing like a couple of fools.

"We should get the pepper spray and grenade and hide behind the pile and let them have it when they come back. Maybe we can grab one of their guns. I just want to shoot those assholes!" cried Dawn angrily.

"Don't shoot the pilot. We need him," cautioned Amy.

"Him I'll shoot soon as he lands us. That son of a bitch is an animal. He sounds French. Must be Cree."

They sat there, just resting, until the cold draft started to get to them so they grabbed the lamp and carefully started down the tunnel. There were a few scattered timbers where the walls had caved in a little but they had little difficulty making their way in the dim light of the lamp. *We'd better not get lost in here with no light*, thought Dawn. Dying in a frozen cavern where no one would ever find them was a depressing thought but, dammit, they weren't going to die. Slowly they crept along the frozen floor. And then they struck gold. There in an old rotting wooden crate lay an old axe, a hammer and a pick. Alongside the axe lay an almost full box of matches. The box was dry and they looked like they should light. Grabbing a couple of them Dawn struck them on the side of the box and was rewarded with a flare. That's a miracle. Those things must be seventy years old. With the tools in hand they made their way back to the cave in, slithered and crawled over it and with renewed hope made for the opening to look for firewood.

Her wrists still shackled, Amy was thankful that she at least had been able to stick a finger in each ear before the grenade exploded but now she was frustrated that she still couldn't help much still wearing hand cuffs. But maybe now there was a way.

"Dawn," she cried out. "Maybe we can use that old axe and hammer to get these cuffs off! Come back and help."

Dawn turned around and said, "How can we do that?"

"Maybe we can smash the lock or break the chain using the hammer."

She quickly slid the lock over the axe and urged,

"Smack that lock and chain as hard as you can with the hammer. Maybe it will break."

Dawn shook her head and said "That won't work. I got a better idea."

She laid the old pick axe on the ground, laid the chain where it attached to the cuff over the pick head and then put the other axe blade over the junction between the chain and cuff and hit it as hard as she could with the hammer. The chain snapped free and Amy pulled her wrists apart and joked, "Pretty shitty cuffs. Must have gotten them in a kids toy shop," and then they were laughing and crying at the same time. When they settled down Amy took a few deep breaths and promised, " When we get out of here I'm going to owe you big time." Nobody mentioned that they had started out on opposite sides of the fence. That could all be sorted out later.

A few streaks of light in the southeast announced the dawn as the fading stars spread across the now clear sky, slowly dimming and disappearing for another day. The snow that fell through the night painted the forest and brush a clean white, mostly unbroken by tracks or trails. Finding wood nearby might be an impossible task but there was nothing to do but try. As they exited the mouth of the mine they spotted the trail of the marauding bear leading off into the bush where they hoped he would stay.

Because Dawn was the only one with reasonable footwear she grabbed the rusty old axe and made for the nearest brush hoping to find something useful to burn. By the time she had gathered a small pile of branches dry enough to burn she was sweating profusely and exhausted but her spirits were already lifting with the realization that she was able to at least do a little to help them over the next few hours. Her goal was a fire big enough that it could be spotted by air and close enough to the mine opening that at least some heat would be trapped and help keep them warm. Slowly, her survival lessons were coming back to her and as she worked her confidence continued to rise. Now if they could only do something to defend themselves from the two legged monsters that got them into this mess maybe they really did have hope.

* * *

Waking up with a headache from Adam's Scotch, I sit up and try and get oriented. We set our phones for five thirty a.m. but they weren't necessary. My mobile screen display said five fifteen and I knew I would not be going back to sleep. Despite the booze sleep aid I still tossed all night and woke up both cold and miserable. I grabbed my back pack and hit the shower where the scalding water eased my soreness and in a few minutes I started to feel better. Adam was moving around in the kitchen and when I showed up he had already put together scrambled eggs with fruit and toast and a variety of jams.

"What time did you get up?" I ask.

"About a half hour ago. We got a lot to do before we take off so I thought at least we could have a reasonable breakfast. I want to look a little more closely at my topo maps and figure out what kind of country we can expect to see. I haven't flown

over there before. That's in Saskatchewan and my company has
no properties in that area. We're more interested in further
north and west. When the oil runs out we still have vast
reserves of gold and copper and now diamonds are coming into
play. I hope to have a job for lots of years yet."

Remembering Al's instructions to get to the airport at least
a half hour before dawn I do a quick calculation and figure we
have about an hour to kill before we head out to meet our pilot.
I hope he knows what he's doing. My last chopper flight wasn't
a lot of fun and I swore I'd never go up in one again. So much
for resolutions. This plan better work. I'm quickly losing hope
and all I can feel is guilt for not sticking closer to Amy until she
finished that damn audit. If I ever get my hands on those people
who tricked the cops into lifting the protection I promise myself
I'll somehow make them pay.

While Adam studies his charts I send off emails to Louise
and David Wah-Shee to bring them up to date and to Jordan
Aziz asking him to check with Louise and Marla in case they
run into any urgent clinical stuff. I also email Porter and ask
him for an update. The last thing we want to do is take off on a
fantasy mission without making sure our ladies are still
missing. I'll text him again just before we take off if I haven't
heard from him by then.

We pile into my jeep, dressed in winter coats and wearing
heavy boots. I hope no one sees Adam carrying his shotgun.
That'll get the cops after us too soon and for the wrong reason.

Though there are a couple of inches of snow on the streets the jeep makes good time to the airport and I follow the signs to the charter office. We're a little early and there is only one car in the parking lot and it doesn't look like anything Al would drive. We sit there with the jeep idling, waiting not too patiently and then I spot Al's gleaming black classic Crown Victoria pulling into the lot and driving toward us. No sign of a helicopter anywhere near us and suddenly I feel a stab of fear shoot through me. Just as Al gets out of the car, the classic thump of a helicopter can be heard a little off in the distance and a bright yellow form drifts up to the apron in front of the office and starts to settle lightly onto the surface. Off in the distance the snow plows are busy clearing the runways but there is no action near the office and a great swirl of snow billows up and engulfs the machine as it settles and the whirling rotor blades slow and stop.

The pilot drops lightly to the ground and spotting our vehicles just off the tarmac strolls over, waves at Al and introduces himself.

"Dwight Washington. I hear you boys want to take a little trip up north. You sure picked a hell of a time for a sightseeing tour. It's cold up there and the wind makes the ride interesting." Then grinning at Al he adds, "Don't worry though. I got plenty of barf bags."

Al laughs and says, "I told Dwight that if he pulls this off you'd buy him an all-expense paid trip to Hawaii for two weeks. Hope you're good for it. Anyhow let's go sit in my heap where it's a little warmer and figure this thing out."

The two of them move across the ramp to the parking lot with Adam and I taking up the rear. Dwight has a medium build that looks well maintained and moves like an athlete. His skin is coal black and stands starkly out from his green Nomex flight suit. So far, neither Adam nor I have gotten a word in but Al and this Dwight seemed to have lots to say even though they had just seen each other yesterday.

"What did you figure about the Beamer?" Dwight asked Al.

"Nothing that a new set of tires wouldn't fix. That car's not a chopper. You can't jink it all over the road like your chopper and expect the tires and alignment to hold up. Good thing its suspension is up to your idea of civilized street driving." These good ol' boys seemed to be oblivious to us and our mission and were just chatting away like they were having a quiet beer in their shop. I'm getting a little antsy as we climbed into the 'Vic' and butt in.

"What time can we get away?" I ask slightly intimidated by these two laid back dudes.

Dwight turns around to me and replies,

"Just as soon you or your buddy tell me where we're going. The sun'll be up soon so we can fly mostly in daylight hours. Who's going to be my navigator?"

Adam answers. "That'll probably be me. The Doc here would probably get lost and point us at Alaska." They all laugh except me.

He shows the flight path he's sketched out with direction and distance marked clearly on the map. He even had the degrees marked in and Dwight nodded appreciatively.

"Guess you'll do. You've done this before." He turns to me and asks,

"You know how to shoot, Doc?"

"Hell no," I reply. "I don't even know how to load a gun."

"Guess I'll have to teach you along the way in case we run into bad guys out there. Al filled me in and this seems like serious stuff so I want to be prepared going in."

He looks at us to see if he was getting through then continues.

"We're going to locate the probable location from cruising altitude and then if everything looks OK, double back for a low level run. Any sign of trouble we hightail it out of there and call in the Mounties. I don't want to get shot out of the sky."

It's still dark as we are climbing aboard. Dwight shows Adam where to store his shot gun and box of shells then powers up and after a brief conversation with the tower he gently nudges the bird into the air and we are off. I haven't heard from Constable Porter yet so I text him to tell him I will probably be out of range of the mobiles for a while but would get back to

him later. This brings a ding to my device and it lights up with
Porter's name.

"Hey Doc. We got nothing concrete yet but this morning
we're going to be meeting in Fort Mac for a possible search and
rescue effort. We got confirmation about that old mine site
from the Midnight Sun guys last night. They haven't been
anywhere near it in the last several months and haven't
commissioned any surveys or anything else lately. We'll be
running your theory past the bosses to see if they think it's a
realistic option."

No way I'm telling this guy I'm a few steps ahead of them.
If we come up empty I can let them know then. In the meantime
I'm not letting a bunch of task force BS keep us from chasing
down the best clue we've had in the last twenty four hours. I
thank him for calling and tell him I won't be able to answer my
phone for a couple of hours and leave it at that.

Dwight gets the chopper to a cruising altitude and points the
nose out along the flight path he and Adam agreed on. The ride
is a little bumpy but the chopper doesn't seem as rough as my
virgin medivac flight years ago. We have the headphones on
and Adam and Dwight keep up a steady conversation while I
lean back and try to doze off. They seem to have a lot in
common and Adam enthusiastically describes his fascination
with aerial photography. My mind drifts to my personal
problems and my future plans. Do I hang around this country
and try and make a life? Do I find a career in some big time city

hospital and end up teaching or managing? How will my divorce turn out? What if I get ripped for a settlement worth three or four mortgages. How the hell do I handle that? And most of all what do I do if the worst thing has happened to Amy? Thinking about that I feel my heart speed up and my hands get all sweaty. I'm not used to panic but I'm scared as hell right now.

As we charge along Dwight points over to the west about a half mile or so and says,

"There's a chopper down there and a few guys moving around a wreck. That must be the wreck you guys were talking about. Shall we set down and check?"

I wait a few seconds then ask,

"How much time will it take?"

He answers, "It's not the time I worry about. It's the fuel. If we hang around there for very long we find ourselves short on fuel and have to turn back before we get to your destination."

It doesn't take me long to answer. "That wreck's not going anywhere. We can always stop on the way back if we strike out at the mine. Let's keep going."

"OK he replies. We're only about forty five minutes from your destination and I think we'll have enough fuel to get back without any trouble. I'll keep going. You OK back there, Doc? I haven't heard any barf bag activity. The ride OK?"

"Everything's cool," I reply with a lot more confidence than I felt. For just a few seconds I think maybe I should have left this to the pros. Then I feel my resolve stiffen and somehow I'm convinced I'm right. I can feel it as we get closer. The chopper drones on.

Fifteen minutes later Dwight points ahead and noses down a bit and says,

"Look at the smoke over there. Someone's got a fire going and I haven't seen any signs of settlement for the past half hour. That's about where our coordinates show us to go. I think we got something. You guys be prepared for anything. If we run into any bad guys I may have to jink this bird around. I'll just cruise over at this altitude then swing around and coast back in for a low level run. Keep your eyes open."

As we get closer we see a fire burning in front of a mound that gradually rises into a low hill on the landscape. The area in front of the fire spreads out into a clearing about the size of half a football field and is surrounded by the scrub brush and widely separated stunted evergreens of some sort. The whole scene appears frigid and barren and my fear of what we might discover begins to overcome my whole consciousness.

As he had advised, Dwight remained at the same altitude and overflew the area and continued on for a mile or two then went into a wide sweeping turn while dropping down to just above tree level and cut back on his speed to a little more than a hover as he approached over the hill and across the fire and the open plain.

"Looks deserted but someone is feeding that fire," he observed. "We've got to decide about settling down or not. Who knows who's in that shelter or mine or cave or whatever the hell it is."

There were trails of footprints heading into the trees and returning and pieces of brush scattered along the trails as though someone was dragging branches. That must have been where they got their firewood.

"We got a shotgun." I say not quite knowing what I mean.

"Wrong," says Dwight as he seems to make a decision and drops the chopper onto its skis none too gently and cuts the power.

"We got a little more than that." He reaches into his pack and pulls out an ugly looking handgun and a couple of clips of ammo and hands them to me.

"Quick course Doc. You look after these. The gun is loaded. Don't shoot yourself. Just keep it close to yourself and get out and stay behind the chopper. Adam, grab your shotgun and load it. You look like you know how to use it. Get out and stay with the Doc."

We pile out into the cold and Dwight scrabbles behind the seats and pulls up a military rifle of some sort and slams a clip home. Looks like he's no stranger to combat. He motions to me to stay behind him, muttering "For chrissakes don't shoot me. Keep your finger away from the trigger and outside the trigger guard. Just give me the gun if I ask for it." He then tells Adam to circle around to the side of the mine shaft in a wide circle and we start circling in the other direction. Both long guns are pointed at the opening of the mine as we get into some kind of flanking position. Boots on the ground take on a new meaning for me.

Suddenly Dwight holds up his hand for us to stop and hollers out in a loud voice.

"You in the mine! We're not here to harm you. We're armed but you'll be OK if you show yourself and are not armed."

No answer. Two or three minutes go by and still no answer. Now what?

Inside the mine Dawn whispered to Amy. "Who are those guys? That's a different chopper than the one we took here."

Amy looked out over the fire and all she could see was the chopper. Nobody was in sight.

"Who are you?" she shouted "Where are those other guys?"

The reply shouted back rocked her to her frozen feet.

"Amy! Is that you?"

"Paul?" she cried out. "Is that you out there?"

And then she heard brush being torn away and three guys carrying guns descended on their shelter laughing and cheering like a bunch of maniacs. The next moment she was in a tight bear hug being swung round and round while a big black guy she'd never seen before yelled laughingly,

"Give me my gun back, Doc before you shoot us all!"

Dawn was standing there with an open mouth holding a can of pepper spray in one hand and a flash bang in the other looking at the three and suddenly realized that her whole role in this fiasco was about to change. She knew the doctor but she had no idea who the other two were. She just stood still shaking her head and wondering what to do next.

"Amy, Amy," I manage to get out trying to choke back tears of joy. I'm so shook up I can't say anything more. She's sobbing and hugging and kissing me and neither of us are able to talk.

Adam is standing back with a big grin on his face, his shotgun hanging loosely at his side. Meanwhile Dwight is poking his way into the shaft with his rifle at the ready in case there was still a threat. He quickly takes in the scene, the rickety cots, a couple of water bottles and some empty cans and a generator and gas stove and heater, all lying there cold and obviously out of fuel. Rummaging through the box of odds and ends he spots a half empty bottle of whiskey and calls to Paul and Adam.

"No fair. You guys get to drink but I have to fly." What kind of kidnappers leave booze with their victims? Now he's seen everything.

The fire is burning low and Dwight takes charge and directs, "We can chit chat in the chopper. It's damn cold here and we better get up in the air so I can radio back the news that you guys are OK. You can tell us what happened while we're

flying. Don't forget the booze. I don't think the cops will worry
if we let you have some medicine."

With that we dash for the chopper leaving the would be
tomb behind for the cleanup crew who, no doubt would
eventually get here to examine the crime scene. Adam hangs
back for a couple of minutes while Dwight powers up our taxi
home and Amy, Dawn and I pile in and wrap the arctic bags
around us. Adam is wandering around with his phone and his
camera taking shots of the site and the mine and the remnants
of the camp, then, as Dwight hollers for him to get on board he
scrambles back, straps himself in and we lift off and head for
home.

* * *

Sitting in a meeting at RCMP detachment Fort McMurray,
Constable Porter is interrupted by a ping with a text message
from the airport tower. He had asked the crash investigation
team to get a message back to him as soon as they had any
information about casualties and expected that was what the
call was about. Keying in the numbers to the tower he
wondered what progress they made. The tower radio operator
answered and he identified himself and was advised that he had
a radio signal from a private rotary wing flight who asked to be
patched through. Telling them to patch him through he
wondered what this was all about.

"Constable Porter. Doc Cross here." What the hell? Where is he? What does he want?

"Where're you radioing from and what're you doing in a chopper?"

"Just a little search and rescue. I got two cold and very angry ladies here who are looking for a bunch of bad guys who gave them bad travel advice. They're looking for a refund!"

"Wha…What's going on. I'm at a meeting trying to organize a search for our missing ladies. You say you've got them with you?"

"Yeah. You better go break up the meeting. Our ETA is about ninety minutes. We'll meet you at the airport. We've tentatively identified two of the bad guys but the other two are unknowns. Everybody is OK, just cold and really pissed."

Porter shook his head and took a breath. "I can't wait to hear your story. With all this radio traffic I think the news people have gotten a hold of the story. They're already sniffing around with questions of a chopper crash. I hope we can get you past the newshounds without too much trouble."

"Go break up your meeting. We'll see you soon."

This should be fun, he thought as he walked back into the meeting.

The chopper settled down on to the tarmac and emptied its passengers. Adam left his shotgun aboard to be collected from Big Al later. No sense having to make a bunch of explanations to the cops. As soon as they were clear of the aircraft it rose again into the air and flew off into the distance leaving the small crowd of Mounties and news people scrambling to reach the discharged travellers first. The first cruiser on the scene skidded to a stop with its lights flashing. Amy, Paul and Dawn piled into the cruiser which swung around and sped away from the airport, turning off the lights and settling to the speed limit for the short trip to RCMP headquarters.

The last passenger quietly slipped into a gleaming black Crown Victoria to be whisked away leaving the news people shouting questions and scrambling for photos for the evening news. No doubt the incident would be circling the cyber world within a few minutes with more questions and wild speculations than answers.

Big Al turned to Adam and asked, "How was your ride? Did you have to waste any bad guys?" He already had spoken to Amy by radio patch and knew the answers but this Adam guy was new to him and he just wanted to put him at ease. It must have been a pretty scary trip.

Adam looked at him, grateful for his help earlier as well as for getting him away from the crowd so quickly. He replied noncommittally, "No bad guys but I got a couple of good shots for my collection." He went on.

"Seriously, Al, I was never so scared in my life. Your buddy was great. Cool as a cucumber. He talked us through everything and kept everybody calm."

"Figures," Al commented. "He's been through a lot of fire over in Afghanistan and has seen everything."

Adam added, "While I was scared I was also angry. I was so mad at all that's happened I just wanted to kill somebody. It scared the shit out of me. If anybody had of pointed a gun at me I would have blasted him. Glad I don't have to talk to the cops yet. I imagine they'll get around to me sometime. Is Dwight going to get into trouble?"

"Naw. He was just flying a private charter for a couple of rich people wanting to take pictures. What can they say? You gotta go to work? Shall I drop you anywhere?"

"Just get me home. I gotta clean up and get some sleep. Tomorrow's a new day. I'll come around to your shop and pick up my shotgun in a day or two. I guess we owe you steak and beer. The Doc will probably just be landing back on earth by then."

Al got directions and a few minutes later dropped Adam off at his house and headed back to his shop, more relieved than anyone at the outcome.

The guy driving the cop car said nothing and Porter, riding in the front, just made polite conversation while they were speeding to the cop shop. The heavy lifting could come later. First of all they had to get all that jewelry off of Ms. Pham before her wrists and legs got any more raw. Then they needed food and drink. Doc could advise how much medical stuff they needed. Porter was thankful his boss put him in charge of the investigation in spite of the fact that he didn't work at the city detachment.

The trip back just took a few minutes and in no time Pham was freed from her manacles. The ladies were shown to a suite of rooms with showers and dressing rooms and lockers and someone rustled up a couple of track suits for them to change into. Their clothes were taken for examination probably to look for hairs, fibres and DNA for forensics and then they gathered in a conference room for something to eat. Protocol required medical clearance before interrogation but Porter was assured by the Doc that they were OK for now and any further examination could be done after their debriefing. That suited Porter just fine. He had lots of questions to ask and lots of important people wanted answers

Part IX

45

The interrogation team split into two with Porter in one room with Amy Pham and Constable Jennifer Cardinal with Dawn Natannah. Constable Cardinal was a Cree woman with twelve years of service in the RCMP. The Cree were not exactly beloved by the Dene but in a police station there are not supposed to be racial barriers. Dawn was understandably reluctant to talk and repeatedly asked for a lawyer and even though Constable Cardinal was only asking about their experience Dawn had been around the justice apparatus enough to know that it sometimes had a way of coming back to bite you. She knew she was involved in the affair and was not about to talk herself into a criminal charge. She considered insisting they call her father but that might make matters worse and then, remembering the kindness of David Wah-Shee when he told her about Sam's death, she insisted that he be called. Though the Chief was not a lawyer Constable Cardinal had been around long enough to understand the complexities of the native culture and left the room to try to contact the Chief.

In the meantime Constable Porter took Amy Pham through the whole story from her abduction to their return to the airport a couple of hours ago. He was amazed at their resilience and especially amazed at the leadership Dawn Natannah had shown in contributing to their survival. However every time he asked Amy for an opinion for why Dawn had been abducted, Amy became vague and hesitant. She seemed almost reluctant to say anything that might reflect negatively on Dawn. *Was this some kind of Stockholm Syndrome?* he wondered. Amy's description of the two days in the wild was clear and concise and her affect was appropriate throughout. She cried when she described her terror, laughed when she described Dawn's attempts to cheer her up and throughout the lengthy questioning continued to stress that without Dawn she would never have survived. Finally he excused himself and left the room to confer with Cardinal. He found her at her desk on the phone so he sat down and stretched out to patiently wait. He didn't know Cardinal well but had run into her a few times at meetings when he came up to Fort Mac. She seemed plenty competent and had a good record.

Finally she hung up and looked at Porter with raised eyebrows.

"What?" she asked

"Yeah, what" he replied. "This is one screwed up politically explosive mess. We got a kidnapping with assault and no bad guys. Where do we go from here?"

"I know," added Cardinal. "That other one won't budge. She just keeps saying she wants to talk to a lawyer. She gave me the name of her boss, the Chief of the Reserve down at your place and wants him to arrange a meet with a legal. What the hell is that all about?"

"The Transportation Safety team just called and confirmed two bodies in that burned out wreck and say it looks awfully suspicious. The GPS prints suggest that they were headed from Fort Mac up to the site where Pham says they stashed them. Maybe we should get Natannah her lawyer then go at her again," Porter suggested. "Everyone seems safe now and no one is going anywhere so why not cut them loose, name them as witnesses in the investigation and let them get some rest."

Cardinal thought that over then agreed. "OK. If this was Vancouver or Edmonton I'd say no way, but you're right. They're not going anywhere and the suspected bad guys are dead." Then she added, "Where does that doctor fit in? How come he's involved? What do we know about him?"

"Don't worry about him," Porter laughed. "He's a little rough around the edges and sometimes he's a pain in the ass but without him this whole thing would have had a really bad ending."

He then went on and told her about the drugging of Amy, the forensic audit on the Reserve and the dogged persistence of the doc in pushing for a search and rescue.

"He seemed to be a step ahead of us the whole way. He also knows people but doesn't drop names just to impress us. He's OK. Just don't tell him I said so."

Porter then changed the subject.

"So far we don't have a confirmed ID on those two corpses but there is a chance that one of them may be the guy we had an APB on a couple of days ago. For sure CSIS will want to know about this."

Cardinal screwed up her face and asked, "What do those guys got to do with this?"

"It's a long story. I've filed more than a few reports on this whole thing over the last few months so that should give you a little in-depth, but in the meantime here's the skinny."

He then proceeded to fill her in on the whole story right from the drugging of Pham, the burning of the church, the deaths of the native women south of the Reserve, the involvement of the Muslim guy who took part in the rescue and his connection with the ELF terrorist and finally the murder of the ex-Chief, Natannah's uncle. Throughout the tale Cardinal just sat and shook her head.

"You sure you're not from South Chicago?" she asked. "That kind of stuff doesn't happen up here. This is a quiet backwater. We get drunks, drugs, crashes and domestics. How come all this shit is happening now? I wish I was back in Brandon where it was quiet."

Porter laughed. "It'll all settle down again soon as the oil runs out. Everyone will go broke and Fort Mac will become a ghost town. Just don't buy a house yet. Wait for the bubble to burst. It always does."

"Don't say that!" she pleaded. "My husband's in the patch. We need both our salaries to keep our two boys in hockey so they can be big stars and support us when we're old."

She then turned to the paperwork she would have to process before turning their witnesses loose.

Porter typed out a text to the Doc to come back and get his lady. He had sent him away to look after some personal stuff after he promised to come when called. He wondered who owed whom a beer. He wished he could go home to his wife and kids. They hadn't seen him in three days and were probably getting fed up. His sergeant would owe him big time after today's events and it wasn't over yet. Then he wondered about how and when he should drag in the CSIS connection. Sighing, he checked his contact list and thumbed in the number of his CSIS guy in Edmonton to bring him up to date.

* * *

Kelly Fitzpatrick was trying to stay awake during a departmental meeting regarding protocols for information sharing with international agencies when she felt her mobile vibrate.

Checking the screen she saw a message from a CSIS officer in Edmonton. 'What now' she wondered as she thumbed to the text. Within seconds she excused herself from the meeting, found Kermit in his office and shared the recent information with him.

"Palamarchuk was filled in by Porter a few minutes ago and forwarded his info to me. Sounds like all hell is breaking loose up there." This from Fitzpatrick.

Kermit read the more detailed email forwarded to Officer Fitzpatrick by Edmonton CSIS Officer Donald Palamarchuk otherwise known as "Biker Don".

"What a mixed up mess of crap to sort out. How does all this stuff fit together with the drugging and eventual kidnapping of a forensic accountant? And where does ELF fit into the puzzle?" he asked.

"Maybe ELF has nothing to do with it." observed Fitzpatrick. "That info we have on that eco-terrorist may be out of date. What the hell was he doing in a helicopter in northern Alberta when he's supposed to be in southern California?"

"Deliberate disinformation" speculated Kermit. "Someone planted those leads to draw off the Mountie guards."

"The last known association, and a vague one at that, was a contact with that Seattle security firm. Wait a moment," she scanned through a number of reports until she found what she was looking for.

"Remember, we put the doctor on the trail when we told him about the security firm connection and its satellite here in Vancouver. Maybe our crash victim was freelancing for that firm…yeah here it is, *Watts Domain Management*. They admitted to him that they had provided services for a number of aboriginal groups in B.C. Maybe our Cuban terrorist was more directly connected to Watts."

Then Kermit jumped in with the obvious conclusion.

"Watts is into this thing up to its neck. I wonder if Homeland Security wants to hear about Rubinowich's demise. Maybe they can help the Mounties with their investigation into the helicopter crash."

Kelly Fitzpatrick nodded in agreement and read through the email from Edmonton again.

"Who is this Laszlo guy and where does he fit in? I wonder what he had to do with the shooting in Edmonton. He must fit in somewhere or EPS wouldn't have arrested him."

"I wonder if he is connected to Watts," mused Kermit. "This company he works for is front and center in this whole conspiracy. They're working for the Indians who hired the accountant to investigate the contract between the band and the energy company. Maybe he's doing a little freelancing of his own."

"Yeah," agreed Fitzpatrick. "That makes sense. If we can tie him to Watts then this thing starts to make sense." She scanned a few more reports and found the name she was looking for.

"I'm going to call this Detective in Edmonton and inform him of our interest in this Laszlo guy. Hopefully they won't spring him loose before we get this all sorted out. In the meantime why don't you check with your contacts in Homeland and fill them in."

Detective Bob Moore was about to enter the courtroom in Edmonton to give evidence in the bail hearing of Jozeph Laszlo when his mobile vibrated and the screen read Fitzgerald CSIS.

" Detective Bob Moore here. What can I do for CSIS?"

" Detective Moore, this is Kelly Fitzpatrick at the CSIS headquarters in Vancouver. We've been informed by one of our officers in Edmonton that you currently have in custody one Jozeph Laszlo regarding a shooting in downtown Edmonton recently."

"That's correct. What's CSIS's interest in Laszlo?"

"CSIS is interested in a security matter concerning Laszlo and regard him as a flight risk. He may be an important link in a terrorist plot involving a First Nations community and an energy company operating in that community."

That stopped Moore in his tracks. Laszlo's case was coming up and his lawyer was chomping at the bit to get him released.

"He's in court as we speak and his case is going to be called shortly. I need a little more from you before I can talk to the prosecutor. What can you give me?"

Officer Fitzpatrick thought for a moment then suggested a ploy.

"Can you get the case put back to later in the day so I can get one our officers to testify in the bail hearing. I'll fax all my stuff to Don Palamarchuk at our Edmonton office and get him over to you ASAP. Maybe you can get him before the judge and arrange to get this information admitted. His lawyer will object but the alternative will be to let him get bail and rearrest him on conspiracy to commit murder. That's a hell of a lot of paperwork and the risk that he will skip the country under an assumed name in the meantime is pretty high."

Moore knew that he was walking on thin ice but replied,

"Get your info to your guy and get him over here. In the meantime I'll grab the prosecutor and fill him in. Maybe we can shortcut the process and avoid all that paperwork."

He gave Fitzpatrick the location of the bail hearing and told her he would stay in touch. Then he went in search of the prosecutor to give him the news.

46

After getting the call from Porter to come and pick up Amy I'm sitting in an office at the RCMP office waiting for him to bring her. He has spent the last half hour briefing me as far as he could about the progress of the investigation and then advises me to take her home but stay in touch. I presume that means stay in town. I have no intention of going anywhere until I know she's safe.

While the cops were interviewing Amy and Dawn I met up with Adam and we decided to clean up and grab a bite to eat at his house. After we grabbed a shower he started chopping up stuff for an omelette all the while talking a mile a minute about the events of the last few hours. He was pretty wired but not as wired as me. The last forty eight hours had left me in some form of post-traumatic stress or whatever the shrinks call it now. I can't remember a time when I had experienced so many highs and lows in such a short time. While Adam yakked on about the great pictures he shot and how shit scared he was when he was pointing that shot gun at the cave and what a great guy Big Al was and the next time he needed a pilot for a survey he was going to hire Dwight Washington and on and on, I sat quietly staring at the wall, thinking of what I nearly lost.

We had finished our grub and were talking about all the next steps and trying to figure out what had happened and why, when my mobile vibrated and Porter told me to get back and pick up Amy. I dashed to my jeep and sped to the station and now I'm waiting for my gorgeous lady and wondering what I'm going to say. Then she was coming through the door and we are in each other's arms crying and laughing and hugging and kissing, completely oblivious of the presence of Porter. He closed the door and left us to ourselves and our immense relief that all would soon be well. Following his advice I load her into my Jeep and we make a beeline for her place. There is no way either one of us is going to answer a phone or doorbell for at least twenty four hours. We have other more important things on our minds!

David Wah-Shee was speeding down the highway towards Fort Mac after getting the call from Constable Cardinal that the women had been found and they were OK. He was puzzled by Cardinal's account that Dawn Natannah was refusing to talk about their experience until she talked to a lawyer and confused even further by Cardinal's comment that Dawn may be facing some serious criminal charges. David had gone to school with Dawn and he liked her and even though he suspected her father was a crook he always thought she was honest and pretty smart. What was this all about? Could she be involved in this conspiracy? She had done a great job in the band office ever since he hired her shortly after he was made Chief. He knew that Amy Pham suspected that Dawn had drugged her tea but he still had a hard time believing it.

Constable Cardinal had informed him that Dawn needed a lawyer and as he charged down the highway he called the law firm that did most of the band business. They had a couple of pretty smart people handling criminal stuff and he arranged for one of them to meet him at the RCMP office. He wondered briefly why she hadn't called her father to come to her rescue but he wasn't quite sure about the ins and outs of the family relationships and was actually relieved she called him instead of Wilfred. It kept things a lot simpler.

Before setting out he had called Renée and arranged for Dawn to stay with them for a time until this whole affair was straightened out. David was sure that whatever role Dawn had in this thing it had to be minor. If she was in trouble, as Chief and leader of his community he probably had a responsibility to help her. That's what a good boss would do. That's what a good Chief would do! Damn. Why had he set loose this chain of events by dragging in the accountant and digging so deep? He'd just about gotten her killed as well as Dawn and probably got Sam killed as well. Why didn't he stick to hotshotting and say to hell with politics?

Dawn sat nervously in one of the interview rooms wondering what her next move should be. She knew that she was in trouble and she knew that she had to talk to a lawyer before she said anything more to the cops. She had been told that David Wah-Shee was driving up from Burning Lake to talk to her like she had asked. She wondered again why she had done that. She should have asked for her father but somehow she knew he was involved in this whole thing and didn't want to get him into any more trouble. She had to get home and get back to work. Sam! Shit! His wake and funeral had to be arranged. Who was going to do that? Was her boss just going to show up and fire her? She wouldn't blame him.

She liked David Wah-Shee and even had a crush on him in high school but it never went anywhere. She knew he hired her even though everyone suspected her father was a crook. But David was always good to her and in turn she betrayed him and just about got herself and Amy Pham killed. Good thing those guys were killed in that chopper crash. No telling what would have happened if they had shown up. Would she and Amy be dead now? Dawn felt no regret about the chopper crash; just wondered why and how it happened. And she still didn't know

how the Doc and his buddy found them. She wasn't talking so
no one was talking to her. Would she ever find out?

* * *

Don Palamarchuk showed at the courthouse with a bundle
of faxes in a folder and found Moore pacing up and down
outside the courtroom. As soon as he spotted Moore he hurried
over and asked,

"Have they called your guy yet?"

"Probably next case. What have you got for us? The Crown
is in there going nuts worrying about how to get this stuff to the
Judge."

"No problem, Detective. Just get him to put me on the stand
and ask me if CSIS has any evidence that Laszlo is a flight
risk."

"OK. I sure hope you know what you're doing. If this thing
goes south we're all going to look stupid. Slemko is going to
scream like hell."

"Let him scream. With what I've got here the judge will
throw that scumbag back in the slammer and swallow the key."

Moore went to find the prosecutor while Palamarchuk
looked for a seat.

The recess over, the clerk called the next case and Jozeph
Laszlo was led in. His lawyer had found him a suitable change
of clothing and he looked relaxed and professional as if he was

about to give everyone the finger. Never taking his eyes off of Moore he accompanied his lawyer to his chair. As this was just a bail hearing, no plea was taken and the crown prosecutor got right to it.

"Your honor, Mr. Laszlo's application for bail is being opposed because it is the Crown's belief and evidence will show that Mr. Laszlo poses a risk for flight and therefore asks that this request be denied and Mr. Laszlo be held as a security risk."

That got the attention of the court and Damien Slemko looked like he was about to blow a fuse."

"Your Honour…"

He got no further. The judge waved the prosecutor and Slemko to the bench, held up his hand and turned to the prosecutor and said one word, "Security?"

"Your Honour, we have a CSIS witness to put on the stand who will testify that Laszlo has a flight booked to Costa Rica, one way for midnight tonight and the name of the booking is for J.J. Lacy. Funny thing, though, J.J. Lacy is an alias found on Facebook in a photo of our Mr. Laszlo during a meeting with the intended victim of the shooting that resulted in Mr. Laszlo ending up here in court. This information comes to us from a CSIS officer who has been investigating a possible association between the intended victim and an individual, a suspected terrorist who was recently killed in a suspicious helicopter crash less than forty-eight hours ago. The investigation is sensitive and because of national security concerns it may not be in the public interest to have it revealed at this time."

The judge turned to Damien Slemko and said "Response?"

"Your honour, I have not had an opportunity to discuss this with my client as he has given me no indication that he intended to leave town."

"Well you'll have a lot of time to discuss it now. I'm denying bail and holding him over to trial for some time after you guys get your acts together. In the meantime I'm clearing the courtroom and taking the testimony from the CSIS officer. Mr. Slemko, you will have the opportunity to cross examine the witness should you wish to."

The courtroom was cleared and Officer Palamarchuk took the stand and told his story. Mr. Slemko asked a few questions concerning the interest of CSIS in Jozeph Laszlo but knew that he was not going to succeed in getting Laszlo released any time soon. Laszlo was remanded for a week and ordered to reappear and be ready to plea. With the RCMP and the EPS both investigating Laszlo's connection to the murder of a band Chief, a possible fraud conspiracy involving the Indian band and Midnight Sun, and an international connection to an alleged terrorist, it looked like a lot of people would be interested in questioning Jozeph Laszlo. His lawyer was about to become a very busy person.

* * *

Wilfred Natannah sat alone in his darkened house thinking about the uproar and chaos of the past couple of days. He was still shaken by the narrow escape on the streets of Edmonton and the run in with the cops and wondered what he should do now that Laszlo was in jail. He had no doubt that Laszlo would give him up and even name him for Sam's murder if it would help get him sprung but he knew that all the paper work would eventually lead back to Sam and Laszlo. Even so he might still get nailed for something and that would be a first so he was sort of between a rock and a hard place.

Funny thing though, the place was extra quiet and Sam still hadn't had his wake or funeral. Dawn was supposed to be arranging all that stuff but the office was closed and he hadn't seen her or talked to her since before he went to Edmonton. He had texted her and called her mobile three or four times but she wasn't answering and there were no messages from anyone on his land line. He'd gotten home late last night after the long drive from Edmonton and slept in and was feeling pretty shitty like he had the flu or something. It was noon but he wasn't hungry and in fact every time he ate he had to put up with a dull ache in the pit of his stomach. He thought he probably should cut back a bit on the booze and maybe get out and walk a little more. Maybe he should go see the doc and get a checkup. He hadn't had one since he renewed his class one permit for heavy hauling. He liked to keep that up so he could move the occasional big rig for a couple of the guys on the Reserve when they were tied up with something else.

He was sitting there wondering what his next move should be and trying to figure out what was up with Dawn when the phone rang. At first he was going to ignore it because he didn't feel much like talking but it kept ringing so he gave in and growled a greeting. The voice on the other end was a woman who identified herself as Constable Cardinal of the RCMP detachment in Fort McMurray.

"Mr. Natannah, I'm not sure what you know about the events of the last two days but I'd like to speak to you about your daughter, Dawn."

What the hell! Now what?

"What about my daughter? Is something wrong? I haven't seen her or talked to her for a few days? What's going on?"

"Your daughter is fine. I don't know if anyone has filled you in about the last couple of days but she has had a very harrowing experience and we have a rather serious investigation going on at the present time. She has been reluctant to call you but I convinced her that I needed to talk to you and she said if you came in to talk to me she would talk to you then."

Wilfred felt his heart start to pound and his hands got all sweaty and he had to sit down to catch his breath. First the shooting in Edmonton then the cops with questions and no answers in Edmonton and now more questions from Fort Mac.

And what's this about Dawn? Why isn't she at work and why is the band office closed? What the hell is going on?

"Where is Dawn? What's she done? What kind of harrowing experience. Godammit can't you answer any of my questions?"

"Easy, Mr. Natannah. Your daughter is with us and she's OK but she's a material witness in a kidnapping and is reluctant to tell us anything until she gets advice from a lawyer. She agreed to let us call her boss and get him to hook her up with legal advice but we suspect her experience is connected to your brother's death and to the shooting in Edmonton when you were in the company of an Edmonton police detective."

Wilfred had managed to avoid any convictions over the years as he directed his criminal enterprise in and around the Reserve and that was mostly because of his cunning and his ability to think fast on his feet. He knew that bluster and fighting with the cops right now was not the thing to do. He had given the cops Laszlo and also he was responsible for dragging Dawn into this scheme with Midnight Sun. He better play along with this cop for now and see what they knew.

"How can I help you guys? What do you want from me?"

Constable Cardinal replied almost nonchalantly, "How about you drive up to Fort Mac and pick up your daughter and take her home and look after her. While you're here we can have a little chat about the ongoing investigation. Is it convenient for you to get away right now?"

"Yeah I can rearrange some things and get up there in a couple of hours. Is that OK?"

"Thank you Mr. Natannah. Your cooperation is very much appreciated."

She hung up leaving Wilfred a little frightened and a whole lot puzzled. Should he get a lawyer or would that make them think he had something to hide. The bit about Dawn not wanting his help disturbed him but he'd wait for a while until he saw where this thing was going. The damn pain in his gut was annoying but he'd probably be OK after some Maalox and a little Tylenol. He never used anything stronger. He may sell the stuff but that didn't mean he should use it. If people wanted to buy it why shouldn't he oblige them? If someone was going to make a buck why shouldn't it be him?

He grabbed the Maalox bottle and took a couple of swigs, popped a couple of Tylenol, threw a few things in a bag and headed out the door. With any luck he should be in Fort Mac by supper time. This gut better settle down pretty soon. He was getting hungry but was afraid he couldn't keep anything down. Maybe he's getting an ulcer or something. No damn wonder after all the shit he'd been through the last week or two. Now that they had Laszlo in the slammer maybe some of this would settle down. He'd have to be careful so that none of this "harrowing experience" the cop talked about got linked to him. He wondered what happened but he'd find out soon enough.

47

Constable Cardinal found herself in a familiar conflict as she tried to work out a balance between duty and home. She was supposed to be off at 5:00 p.m. and had been looking forward to taking her nine year old to play an important playoff game in his double A hockey rep league. It was just about the end of the season and her little guy was the top defenceman on his team. Not only that, he had a shot at league MVP if he played well tonight. Now she had arranged to have Wilfred Natannah drive to Fort Mac to pick up his daughter and stick around long enough to make a preliminary statement. The case was complex enough and serious enough that she couldn't afford to screw up and she was beating out her brains figuring out how to find a solution to the conflict. Natannah was due to arrive in about an hour and she and Porter were the only two

officers up to date on the case. To make matters worse, there
was a good chance Natannah still didn't know his daughter had
been the victim of a kidnapping and might have been killed in
the process.

She was just about to take her dilemma to her sergeant
when Porter walked through the door.

"Hey," she asked. "Weren't you supposed to head back
tonight?"

He smiled a bit sheepishly and replied, "I need a favour."

"When? Now? I'm already in two places at once and don't
know how to solve it. What you got?"

He hesitated a bit and started,

"I know we split this case in half and you got the
Natannahs but I just heard that Wilfred is coming here and I've
been following this case for a bunch of months and I'd kind of
like, ah, to, ah, have a crack at him. I know him and we go way
back. We're pretty sure he's dirty but we never got anything on
him and no one will dare come forward."

"Are you asking to be lead on this? I thought you were in a
hurry to get back home."

"As a matter of fact I was but my wife and kids are leaving
tomorrow for five days to visit her sister in Edmonton. She's
taking the kids out of school for the next couple of days and the
weekend and didn't think I could get away so she didn't include

me. She knows how important this case is to me so she cut me some slack."

Cardinal broke into a broad grin and playfully asked, "What's it worth to you?"

He looked at her in a kind of funny way and said,

"I thought you'd be pissed and say no. What's going on?"

"You just made my kid's day. You spill the whole story to Natannah and explain to him why his daughter, who is a hero to our other victim, should probably need a lawyer because of possible charges of conspiracy to commit a fraud and maybe even assault. At the same time he may need to lawyer up himself because he may be charged with conspiracy to murder his brother who helped him screw Midnight Sun out of a million bucks."

"I'll go to my kid's hockey game and watch him thump a few smart ass white kids who think they can get by him and beat his team. Sounds like a fair trade to me. Good luck Porter. You're on in about an hour. We won't be home until after nine if you need me."

Porter stood there with an open mouth and couldn't think of a suitable reply.

"Did you just con me into pulling your shift tonight?"

"Shift, shit! This is all overtime baby." She gave him a wink and a smile and said, "I'll call you after I put my baby to bed." With that she was out of the door and gone.

As expected, Wilfred Natannah arrived at the downtown detachment of the RCMP as expected just after 6:00 p.m. and looked for Constable Cardinal. He figured he could get this settled in a hurry and get Dawn back home and find out what was going on. He was a little taken aback when he was told that he would be interviewed by Constable Porter of the Burning Lake detachment who was assisting in the investigation of his brother's death. *What the hell has Porter got to do with this?* He asked himself. He was led to an interview room and told to make himself comfortable. The wait was only a couple of minutes and Porter arrived.

"Hello Wilfred. Thanks for coming up so quickly. We have Dawn here and she has had a pretty rough time the last two days but she is OK. I'll take you to her in a couple of minutes."

Porter and Wilfred had often crossed paths and knew each other pretty well. They were not friends. However, both knew the other to be tough and pretty uncompromising whenever their paths crossed in any situation. Porter had a pretty good idea about Wilfred's illegal business operations but had never been able to gather any evidence to support a charge. Wilfred had always operated through agents and cut outs and they were intensely loyal out of either fear or greed or both and finding anyone to turn on him was highly unlikely.

He hadn't expected Porter to interrogate him after he got the call from the woman cop but that was probably just as well. She sounded Cree and he wasn't sure how far he could trust her. *Better the devil you know,* he thought to himself.

"Constable Porter, what the hell is going on with Dawn? I got home from Edmonton and couldn't find her and she's not answering her phone?"

"She's right here in an interview room and she's not currently under arrest but she is a material witness in an ongoing investigation into the activities of a guy by the name of Roberto Rubinowich. Do you know anyone by that name?"

Wilfred felt himself break into a sweat and that along with his gut pain must have been pretty obvious to Porter so he added for good measure, "We have reason to believe that Rubinowich was involved in Sam's murder. If you know anything about him it would be best if you fill us in."

"Wha...How is he connected to Dawn? I'm sure she doesn't even know him."

"But you do, don't you Wilfred." replied Porter.

"Look Porter, I want to see Dawn for myself right now and make sure she's OK. Then we'll make sure we got some legal help for us. You know damn well that I never agree to talk to you guys unless my lawyer is with me. You been hounding me and trying to trick me into admitting to a whole bunch of bullshit that has nothing to do with me and now you're at it again."

"Does that mean you're asking for a lawyer before we go any further?" asked Porter.

"You're damn right I'm asking for a lawyer. Ever since Sam was killed you guys have been questioning me. Even in Edmonton some Detective grabbed me and I damn near got kilt when some asshole took a shot at him right downtown. Then he and one of your buddies, Bear, I think his name was, came over to my motel and hassled me some more then told me I could leave town but stay in touch. What the fuck's that all about?"

Porter though he better tone down the questioning for a bit so he changed the subject and softened his tone.

"Look Wilfred, I suspect you are caught in the middle of something that is mostly not your doing and now your daughter has been dragged into it also. You don't have to tell me anything but I think you should listen to this little tale I've got for you."

"Sunday night, your daughter was abducted from the band office where she was doing a little overtime work. She described three guys, two of whom are known to us as part of the Midnight Sun security force. We suspect the third was

Rubinowich. She was not harmed but she was confined overnight in Fort Mac and held prisoner. Sometime Monday, an accountant on a contract with the band was abducted, cruelly sedated with a powerful sedative, loaded into a helicopter along with Dawn and taken into Saskatchewan to an old abandoned uranium mine and abandoned with very little food and water but in a place that had been equipped with sleeping cots, lights and heat…all pretty makeshift."

Natannah sat in shock listening to the story and his rage began to mount. It was that son of a bitch Laszlo that set this up. That his lap dog used Dawn in the process was a wrinkle he hadn't counted on. What was her role? He broke into the narrative before Porter could continue.

"What the hell were those bastards after? Where are they now? If I get my hands on them I'll rip their hearts out!"

"You're a little late for that. We already have the two Midnight Sun guys in custody and Rubinowich and the pilot of the chopper were killed when it crashed on the way back to the old mine. We think the Cuban was set to do some aggressive interrogation on the accountant. We're not sure why Dawn was involved and she won't talk. However the accountant tells us she couldn't have survived without the help she got from your daughter. It's all pretty confusing."

Wilfred was stunned. Kidnapped, abducted, chopper crash, two guys killed… This was supposed to be a scam. Nobody said anything about killing anyone. Even early on that rotten shyster had said that the shit they put in the accountants tea was just to scare her off and make her think twice about working for the new Chief and council. Eli Watts! That asshole had to be behind all of this. And those fucking chinks he teamed up with had to be involved. All he could think of as Porter ambled on with his story was how to nail Watts and Laszlo without both Dawn and him ending up in jail. What a mess!

When Porter finished his story Wilfred again demanded to see Dawn and Porter got up and told him to follow.

* * *

Dawn alternately paced and sat in the chair in the locked room and wondered what the next step was. The lawyer David had arranged had made a brief appearance and warned her not to say anything without his presence. He knew they would let her go and they could talk to the cops a little later. In the meantime she had to find her father, warn him about the trouble he might be in and get home and finish planning Sam's wake and funeral. All she could think of was how to get home and get to her father and while she went over that again and again the door opened and her father came into the room with Constable

Porter. He looked pale and distressed as if he'd had a heart attack or something. They rarely exchanged affectionate hugs but she couldn't help herself.

"Daddy!" she exclaimed as she saw him and grabbed him and hugged him and started to cry. Porter nodded his head and said "I'll be back in a few moments. You two need some catching up."

He really wasn't afraid of what they would or could do and he wanted them to be as cooperative as possible. He knew that they wouldn't admit to anything and all he was interested in was that they got back to Burning Lake in one piece and he could get on with the investigation on his own turf. He went into the detachment kitchen and pulled three cups of coffee and took his time going back to the room. When he got back he was glad to see that they seemed to be OK with each other and all he needed were a few things to check out. This was not the time for harsh interrogation or waterboarding or threats and shouts. It was all "good cop bad cop" without the bad cop.

"Dawn, you don't have to answer this if you don't want to but do you have any idea why those guys forced you and Ms. Pham to that old mine and set it up like they did?"

She thought for a minute, got a nod from her father and replied,

"I'm not sure but they didn't hand cuff me except for the ride to that place. I think they wanted me to look after Ms.

Pham while they were gone. She had cuffs and shackles on and couldn't even pee without help."

"But why did they set it up with all that equipment as if you guys were going to be there a long time?"

Again she looked for reassurance from her father, then responded,

"The big guy that got killed in the crash said he had to get some answers from her and then they would let us go but I think they were going to kill us both."

Wilfred had enough at that point.

"Constable Porter, can this wait until we get home. Dawn looks like shit and needs some sleep. I'm not letting her go back to that little apartment she has. I'm taking her home and getting Doc Cross to look her over and maybe get her something to help her sleep."

"Dad, I don't need nothing to make me sleep. I just need something to eat. Besides I have to talk to the lawyer David lined up for me and I don't see him until ten in the morning."

Wilfred nodded and said "OK, we'll get a couple of rooms here in town for the night then you can talk to your lawyer in the morning and then we'll go on home. Is that OK with you guys, Constable?"

"Look Wilfred, we want to talk to Dawn with her lawyer present. We can't do that if you're at home and he's here in Fort Mac. How about getting your rooms for two nights and then we can meet tomorrow afternoon and piece together a statement." Porter was in a hurry to get home too but this had to be done right.

Wilfred sighed and grunted OK, promising to bring Dawn back along with her lawyer the following afternoon. All in all it had gone pretty well and in the meantime maybe his gut would settle down and he'd feel better. But his mind kept going back to Laszlo and Eli Watts. Those two assholes were going to get their due if he had to wait the rest of his life.

* * *

I'm finally back at my little clinic in Burning Lake and enduring the jibes and barbs from some of my more impatient patients. In the couple of days I was away there were no really big crises and most of the little tasks were more than adequately looked after by Louise and Marla who were busy building their own practices. Louise had a couple of occasions to call Jordan Aziz for reassurance and advice and as usual he was most accommodating. Old Lady Giroux was back at her store directing traffic and harassing her son who had actually done a great job while she was up at Fort Mac getting her heart under control. I got a call from David Wah-Shee a little earlier saying that Dawn was back at work but was reluctant to talk about her ordeal even though the news of the affair had finally leaked out and the newsies were hounding everybody involved. Earlier this morning Louise informed me that Wilfred Natannah had asked to see me as soon as possible but could only tell me he had asked for a checkup. Very few people had seen him since Sam was shot but I knew he had gone to Fort Mac to pick up Dawn and bring her home. I wonder what's up with him.

It's now mid-afternoon and the waiting room has finally started to thin out. Marla is out doing her rounds and taking health to the old and infirmed while Louise is sorting out the usual walk in clientele from the booked patients while answering the phone and dispensing her humour or wrath as necessary to maintain order and keep things moving.

Wilfred Natannah had not been into the clinic since I started here and I had only met him a couple of times. His reputation preceded him and there were lots of stories circulating. I knew him to be a tough, rough abrasive individual but others who knew him painted him variously from Robin Hood to Attila the Hun. I wonder which one will show up.

I didn't have long to wonder. Louise showed him into an examining room and I grabbed his chart, looked over Louise's prep notes and walked in.

"Good afternoon Mr. Natannah. How can I help you today?" For a big man he looked a little pale and his face was drawn as if he was trying to shake off some pain. He started right in with the usual concern masked with denial that is often seen in new patients.

"I'm probably OK Doc. Just got some 'flu or something. My gut is killing me on and off but I know I probably use a

little more booze than I should. The last week has been tough
on me and now this stuff with Dawn which you know all about
has got me worried."

"So what do you want to talk about first, Dawn or your
gut?"

He replied with the inevitable, "I don't know. You're the
Doc."

I hate it when they say that.

"Let's talk about your gut first because you look kinda
uncomfortable."

He agreed and I learned that over the last month or so he
had suffered from almost constant low grade discomfort in his
belly just under his ribs but it was now in his back too. Also he
admitted to weight loss of almost twenty pounds and added that
he kept waking up at night sweating and feeling nauseated. The
Maalox he'd been chugging down was doing nothing for the
pain and seemed to be doing nothing else but bunging him up.
The rest of his medical history was rather unremarkable and his
physical examination yielded no definite further clues. I wasn't
sure what was going on in his belly because he was hard to
examine. In spite of the weight loss he was still pretty obese
and the length of time he had the symptoms together with the
weight loss and night sweats could signal a whole lot of
problems, none of them good. I knew I wasn't going to solve
his concerns this afternoon. I don't believe in bullshitting
patients that there is nothing wrong with them but just to make

sure I want to order every test in the book and every x-ray known to man. Instead I got right to it.

"Mr. Natannah, I haven't yet figured out what's going on and it may take me a little time to sort it out. Though we hope this isn't anything serious we have to find that out for sure. There's no sense in doing a bunch of blood tests here then getting you back here to talk about the results, then sending you to Fort Mac for more tests, then seeing you back here to tell you the results. That's just a waste of your time and just prolongs your concern. I can see you are very concerned even though you are trying to make light of it."

"What do you think is going on Doc?"

"Like I said, I don't know. Usually with your story we would suspect an ulcer and arrange for a specialist to look down your throat and in the meantime give you some medicine in the hope you will feel better. But your weight loss and night sweats aren't typical of a routine ulcer so I want to focus on them. I want to send you back to Fort Mac to a colleague of mine to get some gut x-rays on an urgent basis."

"Is that really necessary Doc? I just got back from there and we still got Sam's funeral and I don't like to leave Dawn alone with all this bullshit going on."

I knew there would be little chance I could arrange any investigation for the next two or three days but I'm reluctant to keep him stewing much longer. I offered a compromise.

"I'll see if I can arrange it for some time next week. In the meantime we'll see if we can ease the pain a little so you can get some sleep."

I'm fully aware of the potential for narcotic abuse especially in the First Nations communities and I also knew that this guy was probably involved in most of that underground trade and could get anything he wanted under the table, but he needed short term pain relief so I gave him a three day supply and told him to come back in three days so we could review how he felt By then I would have his investigation arranged. I also made it clear that there would be no long term prescriptions for narcotics and if he screwed around with me he was on his own. He's a tough guy and doesn't take crap from anyone but he just nodded and thanked me and left.

Now comes the tough part; getting him investigated before the pancreatic cancer I suspect kills him. I hope Jordan Aziz can pull some strings for me.

48

Friday, after a tumultuous week, when Amy Pham arrived at the office of Abrahms and Abrahms to get back to work she was greeted with awe and wonderment from her associates as they didn't expect her back until sometime the following week and they made that expectation plain to her. However, she was both mentally and physically tough and she was royally pissed off. Twice now she had been a victim and it wasn't going to happen again. She knew what route she had to take to solve this mess once and for all and immediately got to work: Her first task was to review her audit and look for clues she might have missed. Motive for the whole conspiracy seemed to be lacking but the outcomes of the last several months suggested that the motive was buried deep somewhere in documents that she had not had a chance to examine.

Somewhere out there she must have come across some clues that she didn't recognize and she focused on events and the main players in those events as she revised her focus and replayed the past several months over in her mind. The main players appeared to be the shyster lawyer at Midnight Sun and the head of the mysterious American security organization. What did they have to lose from her forensic investigation? What was at stake to warrant murder and kidnapping? Sure, there was evidence of significant fraudulent activities probably orchestrated by Laszlo and in time she could probably find enough evidence to let the Mounties nail him. But those things didn't explain the huge expense and risk of murder and aircraft bombing and kidnapping. It had to be something bigger.

Going back to square one she thought about the reason for her initial involvement. David Wah-Shee hired her to examine the Midnight Sun contract with the Council of the First Nation Band. His suspicion had been raised by the discovery of the seemingly insignificant clause ceding resource rights to Midnight Sun should they encounter valuable resources during their infrastructure development activities. Why put that into the agreement. The Reserve had repeatedly been surveyed and explored for mineral wealth worth exploiting and none had been found. Even senior management of the resource company appeared perplexed at that clause. It was obvious it had been cleverly inserted somewhere along the way by the now discredited lawyer, but why?

Maybe it was time to look closer at the players involved in the corporate structure of the Resource company. The CEO, COO and VP Financial were all long term pioneers in the exploration service industry. They didn't explore. They built platforms for exploration and only occasionally secured long term leases for properties with potential. She then turned to the history of the major directors for the company and any large bloc shareholders. Nothing seemed to jump out at her. People came and went; mergers and acquisitions showed up here and there in the long term history of this apparently well run and progressive company. Yet something nagged her at the back of her mind. Maybe it wasn't individual players... *look at the shareholders!*

Five years ago Jozeph Laszlo was appointed chief legal officer of the corporation. Three years ago the large Chinese resource corporation, Wu Zhao, became a very significant shareholder when they purchased ten percent of the company shares outright and secured an agreement for an option to acquire an additional fifteen percent of shares for a price well below the current market value. Was that a significant lead or just business as usual? What was their interest in a resource service corporation? For the time being she had only speculation. Information regarding the Chinese company was sparse. Time to talk to the Midnight Sun guys again.

* * *

Wilfred Natannah felt a little better after trying the stuff the doc gave him but he didn't much like the thought of a whole bunch of investigations. If it was something simple he was sure this doc would have told him . The doc seemed to be a straight shooter and didn't believe in sugar coating the bad stuff. Maybe it was time to put some of his affairs in order so nobody would have to pick up the pieces if he crashed and burned. With Sam gone, his only close family was Dawn and maybe Junior Giroux and his mother. David Wah-Shee was up for election in the fall but Wilfred suspected his heart wasn't in it and the people weren't all that keen on him anyhow. There hadn't been a whole lot of increased prosperity on the Reserve and rightly or wrongly, Wah-Shee got the brunt of the criticism. The people were restless.

Wilfred wasn't interested in being king. He was more of a king maker *or maybe a queen maker.* Yeah! Hell of an idea. With a bunch of bucks to finance a kick ass campaign and a little arm twisting, Dawn could be a good Chief and her future would be assured. He had lots of money now and maybe it was time to wind down the shady stuff and go legit. Time to see an estate lawyer and get his holdings into Dawn's hands as a trust or something. He didn't know much about that stuff but he sure as hell was going to learn.

Energized, he resolved to travel to Edmonton and tie up loose ends and make sure those bastards from Hobbema couldn't expand up here. They were evil and ruthless and would tear this little Reserve apart. This was his home and he was determined to start looking after it.

He was turning this stuff over in his mind when he got a call from Doc Cross.

"Yeah, Doc. What you got?"

"You got an appointment with Dr. Aziz and one of his colleagues Tuesday morning at eleven a.m. Prior to that they want you to have some blood work and a CT scan so you'll have to be there at seven a.m. Don't eat or drink anything after midnight. I had to pull a few favours and more than a few strings to organize this, so make sure you show. Maybe you better go up on Monday so you won't get delayed."

"Yeah sure, Doc. I'll show. Those pills you gave me are working OK and I'm taking them just like you said but I'll be out of them after tonight. What should I do?"

"Slip over here now if you can and I'll get you enough to take you to Tuesday night then I want to see you Wednesday morning. You'll be tied up with Sam's wake tonight and funeral tomorrow but stay away from the booze. Mixing booze with that stuff will make you goofier than you already are and you won't be able to drive. You'll either kill someone or end up in Porter's hotel."

"Ok Doc. I'm not stupid. I'll pay attention. Thanks for looking after me."

Wilfred hung up and took a deep breath. He was a little scared but regardless how Tuesday turned out he was determined to look after the things that mattered to him.

Laszlo frequently talked about the chinks who bought into Midnight Sun and how they were his real bosses. After all, they originally got him that crap they put into the accountant's tea and they seemed to be the movers and shakers who controlled the security people. Then there was that scary guy who grabbed Dawn and probably shot Sam. He didn't work for Midnight Sun but Wilfred seemed to recall that Laszlo talked about Eli from Seattle. Did he also work for the chinks or did he work for Laszlo? Maybe it was time for a little trip after he saw his lawyers in Edmonton.

* * *

Jozeph Laszlo's next court date was coming up and Detective Bob Moore was scrambling to get stuff for the Crown's case. They had executed a search warrant on his home and seized his computer and a few boxes of files from his home office and were going through his emails looking for any patterns or persons of interest. One item of interest that turned up in the box of files was a folder titled *Midnight Sun Stuff* and Detective Moore was looking at it very closely. Curiously there were two geological surveys covering the First Nations reserve near Burning Lake dated the same date and signed by the same geologist. The documents looked identical as if they were copies but as he leafed through the reports he noted the obvious differences in both the text and charts and survey maps as well as the aerial views. That was strange because the co-ordinates were the same in both reports. One report clearly stated that commercially available mineral resources including hydrocarbons, precious metal bearing ores as well as ores containing copper or gold were not readily detectable within the stated co-ordinates. The second report looked identical in format but a number of charts and aerial images were decidedly different and several paragraphs described rock formations highly suggestive of rich sources of gold, uranium and kimberlite. Something didn't add up.

Frowning in confusion Moore called Midnight Sun and made an appointment to meet with the chief engineering geologist for the company and was advised to come right over if that was convenient. Grabbing the reports and his coat he walked the few blocks from his office to the resource company office. Something told him he was on to something important. The dates on the documents were approximately six months after Laszlo joined Midnight Sun and almost three years prior to the contract between Midnight Sun and the First Nation Community. Obviously one of the documents was a fake and he had to talk to the Geologist who provided the report. But first he had to reveal his suspicions to Midnight Sun and see if they could help. He was sure they had at least one of the reports in

their possession. Laszlo was due in court in two days and there
was little time to waste. While he was walking to his
appointment he called Constable Porter to tell him the news.

"Hey Porter, got something screwy here. I'm going through
Laszlo's stuff and found a couple of geology reports that don't
add up. I'm on my way to talk to the suits at Midnight Sun."

Constable Porter was cruising the highway along the
southern end of the reserve and pulled over to talk.

"What's so strange?" he asked.

"I got two almost identical geological reports from the same
guy on the same date saying and showing the opposite thing in
each of the reports. One's gotta be bogus."

"Sounds like your guy is scamming someone. Has he said
anything or has his legal told him to clam up?"

"Yeah. Pretty much. But other than him trying to run and
the story the CSIS guy told, this is all I got. Listen, there's a
guy out there called Carl Reimer who you probably know who
made a statement about some questions about the security crew
at the site. I just learned that you guys picked up two of their
guys in the kidnapping of the two women. Do you think he can
or would give us anything if he knew about these reports? He
seemed like a square shooter and wasn't trying to hide
anything. I wonder if maybe you could look him up and have a
talk with him. There's gotta be a third player in this mess and
the sooner we find out who, the sooner we will have some
leverage on Laszlo."

"Sure. As a matter of fact I'm only twenty minutes from their site so I'll swing by and see if he's around. I'll give you a call."

Moore thanked him and disconnected. Arriving at the office he was shown to a board room where not only the geologist was waiting but also the CEO and they looked really concerned.

CEO led off. "Detective Moore, I hope this is not more bad news. We're pretty much in shock around here about Mr. Laszlo and hope this gets cleared up pretty soon."

Moore replied, "I'm not sure if this is good or bad news." He showed the reports to the two of them and waited for a reaction.

"What the hell is this. Where did you get these?" the geologist asked.

The CEO was a little more subdued and asked, "What is so unusual about these reports. What is it you think they mean?"

Moore pointed out the obvious contradictions and similarities in signature and date. Immediately, the geologist excused himself and said he'd be right back. The CEO continued to scan through them and his look of bewilderment increased.

Moore then asked the obvious question.

"Sir, which of these reports is legitimate?"

"As far as I'm aware we have no reports of commercially exploitable minerals on that property. Hell, the aerial images don't even look like that area. You say you got these from Mr. Laszlo?"

Just then the geologist returned with a third report and handed it to Detective Moore.

"This is the original report from our files. That other one is obviously a fake. Who the hell made that one up?"

Moore replied, "I actually can't say but they showed up in a box of files we obtained from Jozeph Laszlo's residence as a result of a search warrant. We are not sure if they were used in a fraudulent manner or not but we are searching through his computer right now to look for any evidence that ties these reports to him and anyone else in a criminal way."

The CEO muttered, "Maybe that explains it!"

"Explains what?" asked Moore

"Ms. Pham called me just a short while ago and noted that our minor associate company Wu Zho made two aggressive proposals to acquire Midnight Sun shares shortly after Mr. Laszlo joined our organization. I wasn't sure what she was getting at and all she could say is, it was strange that a foreign company would pursue a local service company so vigorously. I agree it did seem strange to me but it all seemed straight forward enough. The recent revelation in our contract with the First Nation people about mineral rights seemed strange to me but I thought it was just some legal stuff that our chief counsel had mistakenly inserted and didn't catch during due diligence. I confess I'm pretty embarrassed about that but we have no evidence that there is any mineral wealth lurking under the soil in that area."

" Do you know anything about the working relationship between Laszlo and your Asian associates?" queried Moore.

"Not really. We have a couple of administrative employees from their organization seconded to our office here. I guess maybe you could talk to them but I think I would like to get a legal opinion of the propriety of that. I guess we can't ask Mr. Laszlo." he offered half-jokingly.

Moore thought that was a good idea but felt that any such conversations would only take place long after Laszlo's day in court so he pressed a little.

"Sir, do you trust your Asian associates? Is it possible they may be responsible for this?"

"To what end, Detective? If they bought in because they thought there was great potential based on a faulty geological report then I hardly believe they were the ones that prepared it. On the other hand if they had been offered it as genuine then maybe that raised their interest."

Moore was getting a little confused and more than a little impatient.

"Is there anybody in Canada associated with your Asian associates who could enlighten you about if and how they got a misleading report that may have induced them into making a large investment in your company?"

"Doesn't have to be in Canada. I can get the CEO of Wu Zho on the phone in a few hours. If I phone early this evening it'll be tomorrow morning in Guangzhou. I'm sure we can link up for something this important. If someone from our organization screwed them into buying stock we stand to take a big hit if they launch a lawsuit against us. On the other hand we sure as hell aren't going to make matters worse by trying to cover it up. That would ruin us for sure. It's critical we find out if they were given this report and by whom.

I think we can make a case for insider trading on their part regardless of how valid the report is. Insider trading is a criminal offence as you know so maybe we might have a defense if they want to launch a civil action."

Moore stood up to go and observed, "Looks like you boys have some negotiations to arrange so I'll leave you. Thanks again for the co-operation. If you figure out who got the bogus report we'd, of course, urge you to inform us. Also the same is true if you figure out who created the fake."

They shook hands and Moore left just a little wiser. It took a lot of brass to screw a major Chinese corporation. It was starting to look like soon Laszlo will be clamoring for protective custody instead of bail.

* * *

Constable Porter swung into the camp site of Midnight Sun at the south end of the Reserve and climbed the steps to the portable trailer housing the office. There didn't seem to be   . much activity around the camp and only one or two vehicles were parked by the trailer. Coincidentally, one of the trucks belonged to Carl Reimer, the guy he wanted to talk to.

"Hi Carl," he greeted him. "You're just the guy I'm looking for."

"Should I plead not guilty or insanity?" Reimer asked with a smile. "What have I done now?"

"Nothing that I know of." Porter replied. "I'm just digging up dirt, looking for treasure."

"Hey, that's my line," Reimer countered. "Maybe we should trade jobs."

Porter grabbed a chair and got serious.

"This whole mess involving your company and the Reserve is getting more weird by the day. It's bad enough we got fraud, murder and kidnapping. Now we got international security and possible financial security irregularities involving your Asian masters. I need some off the record chit chat and you're the only one I know who can help."

Reimer grabbed a chair and looked at Porter like he had just grown two heads.

"What're you talking about...international and financial security? This is a micky mouse organization in the global scheme of things and just provides infrastructure development to junior resource companies."

Porter replied, "That's what I thought too but Edmonton police turned up some confusing stuff when they searched your company's legal counsel's residence."

"What stuff?" Reimer queried.

"I can't get into that yet because it's part of an ongoing investigation but if we can talk off the record you will probably figure it out anyhow. I understand that you work for Wu Zho, the Chinese shareholders of part of Midnight Sun and not Midnight Sun itself."

"Yeah." replied Reimer, now even more perplexed. "Where do I fit into your dirt digging?"

Time to slightly change the subject, thought Porter.

"Tell me Carl. I understand you are a quality official hired by Wu Zho to make sure that communication between Midnight Sun and Wu Zho at the operations level is effective and appropriate. You're sort of a go between."

" I guess that's as good a description as any. I'm sort of a rover with a foot in both camps. But you gotta understand that I have confidentiality obligations in both camps. There's stuff I can't discuss unless required by law. I'll cooperate as much as possible but there may be some limits even off the record."

"Yeah, I know that, Carl, and I'm not going to put you on the spot but maybe you can help educate me. For instance, are you guys building out here or prospecting?"

"Prospecting? Prospecting for what. This place has been prospected and surveyed and assayed to death and there ain't nothing here except land and some scrub brush. What little wealth that comes out of here is all above the ground." Now Reimer was really confused. He continued.

"Constable Porter, What the hell are you driving at?"

"Do you have any idea why Wu Zho is so interested in this property?"

"Who knows. Maybe they need a tax write off or something. Maybe they want to start a school or casino or toy factory or something. What aren't you telling me?"

"On the record I'm not suggesting anything but off the record, and if you repeat this I'll get transferred to the outposts of Newfoundland for the rest of my career, they may have been persuaded that this place was sitting on huge reserves of gold, copper and more importantly, diamonds and uranium."

"That's crazy. There would have to be valid survey reports to even speculate about that and then there would have to be drilling and sampling. Hell, nobody, even a bunch of deep pocket speculators would pour money into a venture without some good evidence of possible return."

"What if I suggested such reports exist and may have been shared with your masters?"

Reimer paused a bit then answered carefully.

"This stuff is way above my paygrade but my best guess would be that those reports are phony and somebody is screwing with the Chinese. Whoever it is has got to be a lunatic. He'd either spend his life in jail here or get assassinated by a Chinese hit squad."

Porter nodded in agreement and cut in. "My thoughts exactly. You just confirmed what we think we know. Now the biggie. Who could have faked those reports and gotten them to the Chinese and why?"

"Had to be an inside job. Any independent geologist doing that would probably end up getting pushed off a plane over the north pole or someplace equally pleasant."

He added, "I don't get to see who looks after all those documents but the guys at head office could probably tell you....or have you already asked them?"

Porter just smiled and said, "Thanks Carl, you've been a big help. Maybe someday we can have a beer together and I'll be able to tell you the whole story. This is just between us and you couldn't give me any positive facts that could help with the investigation."

"Thanks, I think" responded Reimer and Porter got up to leave but turned and asked a final question.

"Where is everybody? This place is quiet and there's no traffic?"

"Nothing official but the bosses have given the next few days off with pay saying that the company is having some high level strategy sessions about the rest of this project. They'll

probably be making an announcement in a few days. Hope I
still have a job by then."

They shook hands and Constable Porter replied, "Good
luck. I hope so too. This company has helped the locals a hell
of a lot and it would be a pity if that ends."

He left the office, climbed into his cruiser and grabbed his
mobile as he drove away. Time for Moore to get tougher with
Laszlo.

49

After arranging to fly to Edmonton as soon as he saw the docs in Fort Mac and went through the x-rays and other tests they had lined up, Wilfred had little else to do. Dawn was back at the Band office almost running the whole show while David Wah-Shee spent more and more time out in his truck running hot shot deliveries. She didn't mind being alone. She liked organizing the meetings, doing the financial stuff and reading the mail and writing letters and now that everyone had seemed to settle down with the Midnight Sun people she slipped into cruise control waiting for the next shoe to drop. The Mounties said they weren't about to lay any charges unless they got complaints from Amy Pham or the Band Council. Amy had called two or three times, checking to see how she was getting along and repeatedly reassured her that anything she might have done in the past was all forgotten and it was time she got on with her life.

The lawyer David Wah-Shee had arranged had sat with her while she spilled the whole story to the cops and advised her that she should withhold nothing but volunteer nothing. For some reason they didn't ask her anything about her role in making files disappear. For some reason they seemed to be focusing only on the dirty lawyer for Midnight Sun and poor Sam. Her father, so far, had not even been mentioned. She had told the whole story of her involvement to her lawyer who advised her that if attention was focused on her she could always make a deal in return for immunity from prosecution. That may be fine but no way was she going to rat out her father. She worried about Wilfred. He didn't seem as tough and strong as he did a year ago. Since Sam died, he hung around his house most of the time and didn't seem to hang out at the office or the pub and rarely visited friends in the area.

Arrests for drug stuff were creeping up and Gilbert Ahnassay, the Band police chief, had been more busy lately as he continued to ID some of the gang members from Hobbema who kept showing up. These guys were pretty ugly but for some reason they were a lot easier to spot and intercept. The local chapter of MADD as well as the people at the schools kept feeding him tips and Marla at the clinic seemed to know everyone and what they were doing and who they were doing it with. As the first few weeks of spring passed, business as usual

returned to the Reserve and the surrounding community. The
cops had arrested the two security troublemakers at Midnight
Sun and there were rumours that the two creeps in the crashed
chopper had been identified but no names had been released.
The how and why of the crash had still not come out but Dawn
could have cared less. She didn't feel sorry for those rotten
assholes one little bit. Good riddance! On an impulse she
opened her phone and called her father. He answered on the
first ring.

"Hi Dad, Watcha doin?"

"Nothin much." he answered. "Just makin' a sandwich for
lunch. You wanna come over for some soup? I got some of that
good stuff in the freezer that someone brought over last night."

"Sure." she answered. It was about time she had a long talk
with him and he seemed to be in the mood. She grabbed her
purse and keys, locked the office and walked the short distance
to his house. The weather was beautiful spring and her spirits
were high. Lately she had missed her father in her life. He
always seemed so busy and so mad and so short with everyone
but after Sam's murder all that seemed to change. He just
seemed sad and lonely and old. She determined to try and
change all that.

When she let herself in she found him sitting in a chair
staring out the big picture window at the trees and the brush
beyond. He got up and gave her a little hug and she followed

him into the kitchen for soup and sandwiches. He hardly said a thing.

"Dad, what's wrong?"

"Nuthin" he replied. "Just not very hungry."

Dawn wasn't buying that. "One of the ladies was in the office earlier on and said she saw you going into the clinic. Is something wrong?"

He just shrugged his shoulders and replied, "Don' know. Hope not. Doc wants me to go up to Fort Mac for tests tomorrow and see him Wednesday."

"What kind of tests? Why didn't you say something? I can get off for a couple of days and can drive you up if you want. Damn, I wish you'd tell me things."

"Aw, I just didn't want to worry you," he responded. "Nothin' you can do anyhow. You don't have to drive me up there. I know the way," he objected. "Hell, we were just there a couple of days ago." he grinned.

"Dad! No Argument! I'm comin'. I don't care who drives but I'm comin'."

Wilfred shrugged and said "OK. But you'll have to hang around most of the day. I gotta see my lawyer after I see the docs. I got some financial stuff I gotta settle. Maybe you can be a witness or something in case he's got documents to sign."

"What kind of documents?"

"Who the hell knows. Don't lawyers always have stuff to sign when they see you."

"Dad, you're sure you're alright? You're confusing me. Kinda scaring me."

"Nah," he replied. "Just got some routine stuff to look after. We'll see the shyster, have a nice meal and you can drive home while I sleep." That seemed to settle it.

They finished their lunch, made a little more small talk then Dawn went back to the office to arrange things so they could get away later in the afternoon. Wilfred lay back on the couch and tried to snooze.

* * *

Detective Bob Moore arrived at Edmonton Remand armed with a bunch of papers including the two mysterious copies of Geological reports turned up in Laszlo's residence. In addition he had a certified copy of the original report that the guys at Midnight Sun had prepared for him. Laszlo's lawyer, Damien Slemko was already there and Laszlo was led in to the interview room. He looked like hell. His hair was mussed, his face drawn and his ill-fitting prison clothes hung loosely on him giving him the unmistakable look of a lifer…a loser. The change over just a few days was striking. He looked like he would sell the farm for nothing just to get out of this place. But Moore wasn't fooled. He'd seen this before in cons and he knew enough to be meticulous and careful during the interrogation.

Slemko started the conversation with his usual huff and puff and Moore let him rage on for a bit to see if he could detect a pattern in the process that he could exploit…Slemko didn't disappoint.

"This is outrageous. You people have kept my client in here for days on end without a shred of proof to account for your actions. Other than some trumped up BS from a spook and your own fable about flight risk, you guys are skating on thin ice. I'm going to get real joy out of filing that wrongful arrest civil suit that seems to be building itself without any help."

Moore ignored him and turned to Laszlo.

"Mr. Laszlo, I've just had a talk with your colleagues at Midnight Sun trying to get an appreciation of the work y'all do there." No harm in a little cornpone with these guys. Maybe it would keep them off balance.

Laszlo smirked and replied, "I hope you were well educated. The things we do are very complex and difficult to understand even with detective training." Gotcha!

"Yeah," Moore replied. "It is tough to understand. Like for instance, all around Fort Mac trucks are running around and planes are landing and oily dirt is pouring through pipelines and everybody is getting rich and all your company is doing is putting in some roads in a backward Indian reserve. That's one of the things I don't understand. Where's the bucks in that?"

"You're kind of making it look like digging for dummies, aren't you detective? I can see you have no idea. Now when are you going to let me out of here and back to my digging for dummies job?"

Slemko started bouncing around in his chair, laid his hand on Laszlo's arm and counselled, "Easy Jozeph. He's just trying to get you to say something stupid. That's not how this interview is going to be run."

To Moore he spat, "You ask your questions and I'll tell my client whether or not to answer. That's how this interview is going to be run!"

Moore took out a few pieces of paper and staring at them he asked,

"Do you know a man by the name of Sam Beaulieu?"

Laszlo exploded, "You know damn well I know him. What's he got to do with this?"

"Nothing any more. He's dead."

"So what...I mean... I didn't know... What happened to him?"

"He was shot to death not too far from the Midnight Sun camp near Burning Lake. Did you have anything to do with that?"

Slemko's sputter could probably be heard throughout the remand center. "That's preposterous. Don't reply to that Jozeph!"

Laszlo turned a look of intense hatred on detective Moore and replied in a quiet, even voice, "I'm sorry he's dead. I hope you find out who did it and punish him." The insincerity dripped off him.

Moore threw another pitch. "Mr. Beaulieu's brother tells us he was on the way to ask you the same question when somebody took a shot at him just outside your office building."

Laszlo started to reply when Slemko held up his hand and growled "Enough! Ask your questions and where he can, Mr. Laslzo will cooperate. Otherwise, we will end this right here and my next stop will be to file a complaint of harassment of my client without any grounds. Look at him, for god sakes. He's spent days in this sick place and you people have yet to come up with any compelling evidence to support your outrageous charges. That is going to change right now!"

Moore ignored him and pulled out the certified copy provided by Midnight Sun.

"Mr. Laszlo, I'm still trying to discover your company's role in this whole affair and I need your help. This is a geology report that was given to me by your CEO describing a complete survey of the whole Reserve and estimating that there are no commercially viable reserves of mineral wealth anywhere near that Reserve. Have you ever seen this report?" He handed it to Laszlo who looked at it, thumbed through the pages and handed it to Slemko.

"It looks familiar. We get to see a lot of these and they all look the same to me."

Moore took it back and turned to the end of the report and pointed to the conclusion and asked Laszlo to read it.

"It says that there's nothing there to dig for. So what?"

"Mr. Laszlo, do you have a secretary exclusively for your use?"

"Pretty much. Sometimes she helps the pool."

"Is she pretty competent?" *What the hell is he getting at?* Thought Laszlo.

"She does excellent work."

"Did she type up that report and put it together?" *Is this guy for real? Secretaries don't do that stuff.*

"Of course not. That was submitted to us by a contract certified engineering geologist who does similar work for us from time to time."

"Is he competent?" Now Laszlo was starting to get the drift, looked at Slemko and said, "I'm tired of answering these asinine questions this man is asking. I'm not going to say anything more. Just take me back to my cell and we'll see him in court where he can make a fool out of himself there."

Slemko sensed that they were heading into a trap and confronted Moore.

"Detective, you must have some reason for asking these simplistic and irrelevant questions. Why don't you just admit you have nothing to hold my client and we'll forget this unpleasantness and wind this up."

"Good idea," Moore replied. "But first I want you to look at this." He handed the fake report to Slemko and suggested he look it over.

Frowning, Slemko spent a few minutes turning the pages, read the conclusions, looked at the signature and date and with some hesitation asked, "Where did you get this? What are you implying?"

Looking directly at Laszlo, Moore replied.

"This document was found together with a copy of the first report in a file obtained by our officers while executing a search authorized by a legal warrant to search Mr. Laszlo's residence. I thought maybe your client could give us a reasonable explanation how it got there and who created it."

He then added, "I should probably tell you that we also got your computer, a pretty high-end thing of beauty with a bunch of files showing cutting and pasting of parts of the original report and photoshopping of images replacing the ones in the original. I guess your secretary must be pretty talented but her colleagues tell me that she is only trained on one proprietary word processor and is hopeless at scanning and creating anything more than a basic PDF. On the other hand we found all sorts of programs downloaded that instructed someone on all the ins and outs of creating a slick forged document. This stuff goes back over four years yet I understand that your secretary has only been with you about eighteen months. I guess I'm really confused."

"Oh, by the way, two guys we wanted to question about an abduction in Fort McMurray turned up dead in a helicopter crash that appeared to be blown up by a bomb. Looks like someone is panicking and thinning out the herd."

Moore packed his papers back into the briefcase and made like he was finished. Laszlo was sweating and Slemko was looking at his client in a new light.

"Detective, I need some time to consult with my client." he stammered.

"Take all the time you want. We can kick this around at your arraignment. You might even get bail for him but I suggest he doesn't ride in any helicopters."

He stood up and this time he signalled for the marshal to let him out of the room.

* * *

Wilfred spent the first part of the morning in Fort Mac having a bunch of blood tests and special x-rays and now was sitting with Dawn in the waiting room awaiting his appointment with Dr. Aziz and some other doctor. He hoped they could tell him what was wrong so he could get on with fixing it. He wasn't used to feeling crappy except for occasional hangovers after too much booze and he didn't like the experience much. He and Dawn had chatted all the way up to Fort Mac and he outlined to her his wish to retire and turn over most of his financial chores to Dawn. He outlined some of his thoughts about joint accounts and trusts and stuff and said that he wanted to make his life less complicated. However, the subject of planning, together with a trip to the doctors, didn't comfort Dawn much. She couldn't help feeling that there might be more trouble ahead and her anxiety continued to grow.

Late in the morning, Dr. Aziz and his buddy came and got him and said they wanted to check him all over to make sure they got to know all there was about his health. After that they would review everything they had with him and they could then decide if there was anything they needed to do or recommend. They seemed to have everything under control so he followed them to the examining room while Dawn went to get a coffee.

For the next half hour the two docs poked and prodded him and asked him questions and talked to each other in their medical jargon and poked him some more. Then they told him to get dressed and wait for them. They asked if he wanted his daughter in the room when they came back or would he just as soon talk to them himself. It didn't seem like a big deal so he told them, "Sure, send her in." After another half hour of waiting they came back to talk to the two of them. The news was not good.

"Mr. Natannah, we reviewed all your blood tests and looked at your CT scan and chest x-rays and there are some really disturbing findings there. It looks like you have been growing a malignant tumor in your pancreas for some time and now it's in your lungs and maybe your bones as well. There is no easy way to tell you this so we aren't going to try and sugar coat it. You are a very ill man."

Dawn looked at her father in shock and started to cry. Wilfred sat stone faced and didn't say anything. He wanted to see what else was coming.

The surgeon with Dr. Aziz added, "There are a number of things that we can do over the short term but this disease is far past the stage of any surgery that could offer you any relief."

Wilfred knew the next question and had dreaded it ever since he saw Doc Cross in the clinic a few days before.

"How long have I got Doc?" he managed to choke out.

Dr. Aziz replied, "No one can guess that accurately but our experience is that we should be looking at treatments that will provide you with the best hope for relief from discomfort. I'm sorry to have to tell you that it is unlikely that you will live through the summer."

By now Dawn was almost inconsolable. However she managed to stammer through her tears, "There must be something you can do. Should we send him to Edmonton to the cancer clinic. Maybe somebody can operate on him. We just can't let him lay there and die without trying!"

Wilfred was a little more stoic.

"Doc, I don't want to get carved up or filled up with a bunch of poisonous shit just so I can live a couple more months. That's no way to live. If I can't stop this thing then maybe I can get something for the pain and get on with the rest of my life. You guys seem to know what you're doing and I'm not keen on a bunch of wild goose chases just to buy a few more months. Just tell Doc Cross what you think I should do and we'll take it from there."

He got up and put his coat on and walked out of the room. Dawn stayed behind to talk to the doctors for a few minutes then joined him in the waiting room.

"We better get going." he suggested. "We gotta see my lawyer in a little while."

Father and daughter left the hospital, each with their own thoughts. There was little else to say.

* * *

Wilfred and Dawn spent a couple of hours with an estate lawyer later that afternoon then went out for dinner. Neither one felt much like eating but they ordered lightly and toyed over soup and salad while rehashing the afternoon meeting with the lawyer. Then because they still had not checked out from the hotel and it was too late to drive back to Burning Lake they went back for another night and a talk about the next few months. The reality was just starting to settle in and father and daughter tried their best to sort out some of the challenges facing them.

Wilfred brought up his ambitions for his daughter.

"You ever think about how long you want to work for the man?" he asked her.

"As long as they want me." she replied without missing a beat.

"What if you were the man?" he offered.

"What do you mean. I'm not a man. I don't want to be a man." She wondered where this was going.

"Look Dawn, David Wah-Shee is going to get tired of being chief pretty soon and besides he's up for election next year. What if you ran for chief?"

"Me?" she gasped. "Are you nuts. Who the hell wants me to be chief?"

"Me for one." he replied. "But more than that, I know you'd be great at it and I know you could get elected."

"I think that's nuts. I wouldn't know how to start," she protested.

"Hey. What you think I've been doing all these years? People owe me favours. I know honest and smart guys who can manage a campaign. I know I screwed up letting David Wah-Shee get elected but I wasn't even trying. You could do it. I wish you would."

She looked at him in sadness and some confusion. He wasn't even going to be around for the next election. She started to cry again. He let her sob for a while then continued.

"I gotta go sometime but you got a lotta years and the world is changing. You're a smart, tough young woman. Nobody's going to push you around. To me it's a no brainer. Say you'll try and together we'll take it on."

This was crazy, but maybe it will help him over the next few months. Maybe she should go along with him. She stopped crying, gave him a hug and whispered,

"OK. I'll try. Let's not talk about it anymore tonight." They sat there in silence for a while and then Wilfred brought up the next subject.

"I gotta go to Edmonton to tie up some business and talk to the cops again about that Midnight Sun Lawyer. I didn't tell you but I got a flight out of here tomorrow morning. You can drive me to the airport on your way back to Burning Lake."

He kept surprising her.

"How long you gonna be gone?" she asked with a concerned frown painting her face.

"Not long. Maybe a couple of days." He didn't tell her he was booked from Edmonton to Seattle and back over two days. That would mean too many explanations and he didn't feel like talking any more. Dawn shrugged her shoulders and said,

"I guess you'll be OK as long as you take your pain stuff. You can call me when you get back and I'll drive up and get you."

"Good." he replied. Then he climbed onto the bed, stretched out and was snoring peacefully while Dawn leafed listlessly through a magazine wondering where her life was taking her.

50

S eattle was just recovering from a mid-spring rainfall that left the skies overcast and the streets still wet with puddles everywhere. Eli Watts was fed up with the events of the last week or so and thoroughly disgusted with the failure of his trusted operative to settle the business up north. Curiously, he had received no word from Roberto but online scrutiny of his various credit cards described a path that suddenly ceased over a week ago. Several days earlier he had called his son in Vancouver and directed him to fly to Fort McMurray covertly and find out what was going on. Everything seemed to be either confused or covered in a security blanket. He did learn about Jozeph Laszlo's arrest and detention on a federal security basis and news reports of a helicopter crash with two fatalities had finally crept into the back pages of the news. Evidently it was involved in aerial surveying and didn't merit a lot of coverage. A chilling thought struck him as he recalled the ominous promise from his Asian associate that failure to end this affair would not be tolerated and would be swiftly dealt with. For the first time in a long time Eli began to think about beefing up his personal security.

Because he was at his home in the Queen Anne district and his residence was protected with extensive security surveillance he was not unduly worried but he resolved to arrange for more personal security to stay on his property and accompany him to his office or wherever else he had to be. Separated from his wife for many years and with his only son running his operations in Vancouver, he lived alone and preferred it that way. He expected that tomorrow he would get an update from his son and then he would review the whole situation and make further plans. It was time to talk to his Asian clients and make sure that they were content with things for now.

Sitting before his fireplace with a glass of wine and some recent requests for security service from a South American mining company he was annoyed when the camera at the front gate lit up revealing a well-dressed man who appeared familiar and the intercom beeped.

"Yes, can I help you?" Eli asked.

" Mr. Watts. I'm Wilfred Natannah from Canada. We talked once before several months ago about plans for our project near Fort McMurray. I'm only here in Seattle for a few hours and wonder if I could have a few words with you?"

It was late afternoon and normally he would have refused such an unexpected intrusion but the lack of information from the north and his curiosity got the best of him and he replied,

"Yes certainly. Come on up." It didn't occur to him that it was strange that there was no taxi or car outside and he didn't even think to wonder how his visitor got there.

He arose and went down the few steps to his entrance and when the doorbell rang he opened the door to an older native looking man who was well dressed in a suit covered with an open fashionable rain coat and carrying an umbrella.

"I remember you, sir." he announced. "You are an associate of Mr. Laszlo. I'm devastated to learn that he has run into serious trouble with the authorities in your country. Come in out of the rain and fill me in. We have some serious planning to do."

Wilfred stepped inside and Eli Watts shut the door and led him to his office and invited him to sit down. While Eli was tough and ruthless when he had to be he was also courteous and well-mannered especially in his home. Wilfred handed him his raincoat and umbrella and took the offered seat. He declined the offer of a drink saying his doctor would not approve and that he could only stay a few minutes in any event as his ride would be returning to pick him up shortly. Eli shrugged and taking the seat next to him asked,

"Well sir, what can I do for you? You've certainly come a long way just for a few moments of conversation."

Wilfred took a deep breath and started in.

"This thing about Laszlo has me all shook up. I've been working with him for a long time and I managed all the things he asked me to on our reserve and I kept tabs on the security guys in your Midnight Sun operation and let him know everything that was going on but now I find out that he wasn't always honest with me."

"How so?" Watts asked, his puzzlement continuing to mount.

"He didn't tell me you guys were planning to kidnap my daughter and kill her when they took care of that nosy accountant."

For the first time Eli sensed that he was in grave danger and his curiosity had left him defenseless if this man meant to harm him.

"Mr. Nattanah, that's absurd. We did no such thing. Whatever gave you that idea? There must be some mistake," he protested.

"The mistake, Mr. Watts, was letting your Chinese friends blow up that chopper with your terrorist buddy aboard. They forgot that my daughter and the accountant were still alive and stuck in some old mine in the middle of nowhere, left to freeze to death or get killed by the wolves."

Eli knew then he had to get control of this thing and rose to pick up his wine and said,

"Mr. Natannah, I'm shocked to hear these things. I have no idea what you are talking about. I was just reading Roberto's report when you arrived. It didn't say anything about kidnapping and certainly didn't mention your daughter."

"Did it mention my brother Sam?" Wilfred asked as he eased forward in his chair.

"Here, do you want to read it?" He stepped over to the desk and opened the top drawer, reaching for the loaded Glock 26 that was always there. He didn't feel the blade that plunged into his left chest in precisely the spot where an arrow would have struck a killing blow to a startled deer.

Wiping the blade on Eli's shirt, Wilfred replied,

"No asshole, I don't want to read it!"

Knowing that the house was bristling with security devices and not knowing a lot about them, Wilfred merely stepped over the body of Eli Watts, retrieved his raincoat and umbrella and left the house, walked a couple of blocks to his parked rental and proceeded to drive to the airport where he boarded a flight to Calgary. On the way he left the knife, which he had purchased earlier in the day at a sports shop, in a dumpster behind a restaurant near the airport.

51

Arriving at the Edmonton International Airport after a short hop from Calgary, Wilfred Natannah grabbed a cab and rode for the usual forty minutes to downtown Edmonton where he paid his fare in cash with a modest tip and wandered into the busy mall during the mid-morning. He had arrived in Calgary from Seattle late in the evening and had booked into a hotel near the airport where he slept well after a double dose of the pain medicine that Dr. Cross had given him. The mid-morning short hop to Edmonton gave him some spare time because his flight to Fort Mac wouldn't leave until later in the afternoon. After eating only part of his soup and sandwich special in the food court, he pulled out his mobile and called the number that Detective Moore had given him several days before. After a couple of delays he had Detective Moore on the phone.

"Detective, this is Wilfred Natannah from Burning Lake. I'm back in Edmonton looking after some business and I was just wondering if you guys had made any progress in nailing that shyster, Laszlo."

"Why are you asking?" Moore countered. "Have you got some more information for us?"

Wilfred continued his seemingly vague story.

"I was just wondering."

"Wondering what, Mr. Natannah? You didn't just call me to have a social chat. What's on your mind?"

"You know," Wilfred continued, "I got to thinking and I remember the first couple of times I met Laszlo, he told me that he had some insider information that some chink company was interested in buying part of his company. I asked him why they would do that and he just said that he had sent some secret information to a buddy in the States about a good mining investment and his buddy passed it on to some clients. It was just after that the Asians got interested in Midnight Sun. I wonder if that was all on the up and up. I don't trust that guy. He seems a little too smooth for me."

Moore wanted to ask him more but didn't want to scare him off.

"How long are you going to be in town. I'd like to talk to you a little further about this."

"Maybe next time," Wilfred countered. "I'm just on my way out to the airport to catch my plane back to Fort Mac. You got my number. You can call me any time."

Moore let it go at that and thanked him saying they would stay in touch. Wilfred broke the connection and called Dawn to let her know when his plane would arrive. He was almost home and while he had been in his share of scraps through his life he had never murdered anyone before. Curiously, he didn't feel any guilt. He just had some regret that it had come to this and he had to make a few amends. He would be relieved to sleep in his own bed tonight.

* * *

Bob Moore sat thinking about his mysterious call and wondered what it all meant. If Laszlo had set up the Asian resource company like he suspected, then this was the first hint of a confirmation. Yet he knew that Natannah was a lot closer to Laszlo than the Indian could possibly know. While it was a remote possibility that Natannah was trying to set the cops up, he had the distinct feeling that in fact Natannah was actually trying to set up Laszlo. Time to head for Edmonton Remand again. He phoned ahead and told them to expect him. Then he called Damien Slemko and told him he had some more information that he might want to hear and he might want to sit in on another shot at interrogation of his client. Slemko was not too happy but consented to see him out there. This time the high cards were in Moore's hands.

Later in the day, Moore and Slemko were chatting in a relatively civil manner when Laszlo was again led into the small interrogation room. As usual, the door clicked locked but the Marshall sitting at the desk had a clear view and could open the door at the first hint of trouble.

Again, trying to take control, Slemko opened with a salvo.

"Detective, what have you got that merits dragging me away from my office and my waiting clients?"

"You might want to ask your client that question," Moore countered smoothly. "We have new information that your client passed insider information to his company's Chinese shareholders through an intermediary in another country to avoid suspicion of insider trading. We suspect the intermediary may be connected to the recent death of the Indian Chief and the kidnapping of the two women in northern Alberta. Perhaps Mr. Laszlo may wish to settle this for us."

Slemko didn't bite. "I thought we already discussed this last time. Mr. Laszlo has no knowledge of an international intermediary or anyone else involved in insider trading. Hell, he doesn't even trade in securities nor does he involve himself in financial advice. If this is all you've got, then you're wasting our time."

Moore was just getting warmed up.

"Mr. Laszlo, did you produce a forged geological report falsely suggesting great mineral resources on a property near the town of Burning Lake and send that report to Eli Watts of Watts Domain Management to be forwarded to Wu Zho corporation of China in order to entice them to heavily invest in your company?"

"Mr. Laszlo is not going to reply to that ridiculous accusation and this interview is over. This is a fishing expedition plain and simple and my client is a victim. I am immediately filing for an injunction to have him released and will be further filing a complaint against the Edmonton Police Service for wrongful arrest and harassment." He raised his hand and signalled to the Marshall who sprung the lock and came to retrieve Laszlo.

Moore didn't object. All the pieces were falling into place. He couldn't touch Eli Watts without a lot of legal wrangling but he could subpoena Watts's son who was in Vancouver as a foreign national running a branch office for Watts Domain if that was necessary. With all this stuff it was unlikely that Laszlo would get bail after his arraignment and they could work the case a little more thoroughly with a little less urgency. Between the Mounties at Fort Mac and the CSIS officers in Vancouver and here in Edmonton he had all he needed for the Crown and it was time to write up the reports. He was going to be busy the next two days.

52

Though I had expected Wilfred to show up sooner he's only now sitting in my examining room telling me about his visit with Aziz. Of course Jordan had phoned me earlier relaying his disturbing findings that confirmed my fears. I have no idea whether he has three months or twelve months and besides I always try and avoid that kind of useless speculation. However, it is certain that without heroic surgery that sometimes beats the odds it is certain to me that he will probably not see another Christmas. He is adamant that he doesn't want to be "gutted like some deer" or have a bunch of poison pumped into him and I make no effort to convince him otherwise. Faced with the same dilemma I would probably feel the same. Others may choose differently and some of them would probably luck out but the chances of long time survival at his age with his disease are slim.

We have a little talk about what we call supportive care or palliative care and what that really means. This guy is a tough old character and sounds pretty rough at times but I'm impressed at his intelligence and quick grasp of the stuff we're talking about. He says if he's got to die he wants to die with as little fuss as possible.

"Just keep giving me that stuff you gave me and it probably won't be too bad Doc." The reality of narcotic abuse especially within the aboriginal community is well known but indigenous people get cancer and feel pain and need relief just like anyone else. The BS about not giving narcotics for pain over an extended period in case of addiction is just plain nuts. We agree on a drug management plan and somehow I think that he will have no problem with self-medication. Besides, his daughter will ride herd on him and she's just as tough as him. He promises to drop in and see me on a weekly basis and sooner if he has to and gets up to go. Just as he is leaving he turns and says,

"Hey Doc, thanks for looking after Dawn so good. I hope you make sure nothing happens to her," and he leaves.

What did he mean by that?

As I go back to my patients I'm interrupted by Louise who says,

"You might want to take this call, Doc," then whispers, "It's your wife."

Shit! That's all I need right now. Over the last month she has emailed me every couple of days suggesting we get together and talk. This is the first time she's called me.

Reluctantly I grab the phone and ask,

"Hey Carol, What's up?"

She dives right in. "Paul I'm coming up to see you tomorrow. Are you going to be there?"

Where the hell else would I be.

"Yeah, I'll be here. What's up?"

"I think I've got something that will interest you and I want to run it by you."

You got dick all that would interest me now or forever

"Uh…OK but I'm pretty busy all day. Can't you tell me what you're thinking right now?"

I wonder what new scheme she's cooked up. Maybe she's going for six and a half million instead.

"No that wouldn't work. I think it's better that I talk to you directly. Don't you get time off for lunch?"

"Yeah but the pub is pretty crowded and noisy at that time and there's no other decent place to eat."

"The pub will do just fine. I'll see you at noon." and she hangs up.

What now? I don't feel like having a dispute resolution session in a crowded bar with a bunch of strangers listening in. I wonder if I should call my lawyer. Too bad I couldn't afford a chartered jet. I could fly him in and take him to lunch tomorrow. That would really piss her off. I am too busy right now to dwell on this crap so I just tell Louise to make sure I can get away at noon for an hour tomorrow and get to work clearing out the waiting room.

I haven't seen Carol since our last meeting with my lawyer in Calgary. Our lawyers have been busy back and forth trying to hammer out a resolution and keep this divorce thing out of the courts but so far there has been little progress. I have not replied to any of the emails from Carol for obvious reasons but I have forwarded them to my lawyer. While some of the messages were downright nasty, others seemed a little wistful and bordered on downright pleading. I wonder if she's losing it.

After her last email my lawyer forwarded to me a proposal he had drafted that acknowledged some of her concerns and suggested a modest alimony schedule that would decrease over time and cease should she remarry or cohabit with a new partner for longer than six months. At least it wasn't a couple of million dollars. Maybe she wants to talk about that but I'm not about to play lawyer with her. This matter is just about ready for a formal resolution process to begin and I'm sure as hell not going to screw up the proceedings by winging it.

I can't wait for the day to be over so I can call Amy. I need an Amy hit in the worst way even though it's only been a short time since we've seen each other. We talk every night and text back and forth through the day but that isn't the same. I wonder what she'll say when I tell her about tomorrow.

"What do you think she wants?"

We have only been talking a couple of minutes and I just finished telling Amy about my lunch date tomorrow. She's not the jealous or possessive type and I know she's just curious so I answer honestly and briefly.

"Don't know. Don't care!"

"Hey, Super Doc. This sounds serious. Maybe she wants you back." Giggles and a gottcha.

"Don't even kid about that stuff. She's got an evil mind and when it's in her own best interest she can be formidable."

"Don't forget, so can you." I don't know whether Amy is pulling my leg or telling me something.

I don't want to talk about this any more so I change the subject and we talk about all the stuff going on here. I'm sorry I can't talk to her about Wilfred but that's doc to patient stuff and strictly confidential. She'll have to find out from someone else. In a community like this, word seems to spread fast. She'll find out soon enough. We talk ourselves out and she wonders if she should come down for the weekend. I'm not about to discourage her but I wonder if it wouldn't be better for me to drive up there to see her. We toss it back and forth and then agree that she should get out of Fort Mac for a couple of days and come down here and cook me a decent Vietnamese meal. I tell her she better bring the groceries because old lady Giroux doesn't carry any of that exotic stuff. We sign off for the night and I drop into my bed for a good night's sleep...I hope.

* * *

Detective Bob Moore was just getting ready to leave the
office when he got a call from Donald Palamarchuk, the biker
guy from CSIS. Moore was going to call him in the morning to
make sure he was available for Laszlo's arraignment just in
case he needed him but now wondered what he wanted. It had
to be about Laszlo because he didn't have anything else going
with CSIS.

"Donald, my man, what can I do for the super spooks?"

"Hold on to your chair, Moore. I got something for you."

"I hope it's good news. What's up?" He hoped that it wasn't
anything that would get Laszlo sprung tomorrow.

"Our guys in Vancouver just told me they got a call from
Homeland Security in Seattle saying that somebody stuck a
knife into that Watts guy who runs the ELF guy we're
interested in."

"Wait a minute. Say again? What Watts guy. What's an elf
guy?"

"What's this? Who's on first, Watts' on second?" Biker
Don giggled at his own joke then carried on.

"You know. The guy in the chopper crash up north. Watts is
the dude who runs or ran that security company out of Seattle.
We've been interested in him because of his suspected ties with

that mercenary who the Mounties think was involved in that chopper crash out of Fort Mac."

"Yeah, I know who Watts is. As a matter of fact I was getting ready to subpoena his son in Vancouver to come and testify regarding Laszlo. You say somebody stuck him? I thought the bad guys in this thing used bombs to shut people up. The Seattle cops got any leads?"

"Nothing yet. They've got some video feeds from his home system and they're running some face recognition stuff but so far no dice. Whoever did it didn't seem to cover his or her tracks. It was pretty slick. No clues other than a lot of blood. They said that a Glock was recovered at the scene but they thought that Watts was the registered owner. They're running that as we speak. My guys in Vancouver just wanted to let you know. I also put in a call to Porter but I haven't tracked him down yet."

Moore sighed and speculated. "Does this help or hurt Laszlo. Obviously it wasn't him."

"That's your department. I'm just a messenger. Let me know when you want me in court." With that, Biker Don was gone and Moore had one more piece to the puzzle but didn't know how to fit it in.

Amy Pham arrived at her office next morning to find a message that the CEO of Midnight Sun was looking for her. He had left a message asking her to call him in Edmonton as soon as was convenient for her. She hadn't met him but the commercial crime guys had given her name to the resource company boss. Interested in what he had to say but cautious about getting stuck in a conflict of interest tangle she returned his call.

"Ms. Pham," he started in after introducing himself, "I understand you've been engaged by our mutual friends, the First Nations community at Burning Lake, to conduct an audit into our contract with them."

"That's right," she acknowledged. "How can I help you?"

"This is very awkward," he confessed. "Our legal department is struggling with an issue that is familiar to you and they have advised me that it would be in our mutual interest to somehow pool our resources in the contract audit."

Her antenna up, Amy replied cautiously, "Sir, I'm not sure how that would work. There may be some conflict of interest barriers that would make that impossible."

He had anticipated that and continued,

"I have already discussed this with your principals in the audit and have offered our complete cooperation. In brief, I'm offering to open our books completely to you and provide you with an independent professional accountant of your choosing to assist you. Our Board is very concerned with the position we find ourselves in and we wish to clear things up as soon as possible. We already have agreed to cooperate with the RCMP and EPS in a similar manner and both have advised us that they wished to avoid muddying the water with several separate investigations and have suggested that you accept the lead on this matter."

Amy sat there with her mouth open, unable to reply. This offer out of the blue hit her like a lightning bolt. There was no precedent for this approach that she knew of. Who the hell was behind it? What would she be getting into? She finally managed to blurt out a reply and hoped she didn't betray the shock she was just starting to feel.

"Sir, I don't know what to say. I think I'd have to talk to my associates before I agree with anything like that."

"Sure. I understand. I suspected that would be your reply. That's why I just went over your head to Mr. Abrahms and asked him how he felt about the proposal. I think it would be proper to discuss it with him before we talk any more. This affair has taken on international implications including fraud and possible terrorism and I am anxious that our company in cooperation with your clients can get it cleared up without any further damage."

Still reeling with shock Amy vaguely remembered mumbling something about getting back to him in a short while and hung up. She sat thinking for a couple of minutes then went down the hall to confront her colleague who was actually still her boss.

After a short conversation with the senior Abrahms she was still reeling with the decision she was facing and called Paul. It was well before noon so he should be at the clinic.

My phone rings as I'm sorting out some lab work and, seeing it is my gorgeous lady I grab the phone and answer, "Good morning. This is the doctor. Are you calling for free advice or are you offering delights for my services?"

"Hi" she greets me. "Are you all spruced up for your date?" she teases.

"Don't be a shrew," I counter. I thought you were gentle and understanding and kind."

"I am." she laughs. "I just don't know what a shrew is. Isn't that something out of Shakespeare or are you too polite to call me a bitch?"

"Heaven forbid. Do you think I want two tough women pissed off at me on the same day? What's up?"

She tells me about the offer and her talk with her boss and asks,

"What do you think I should do?"

"Look Amy, you've been up to your neck in this and damn near killed twice while you worked it. Your choice is simple. Finish the job because you can and will do a great job or beg off because you're fed up with it all. It all comes down to that. It's what you do and it ain't always easy. Just make sure you don't have to move to Edmonton for the next ten years. I kinda like it here."

I'm not good at making life decisions for other people, even those closest to me. I hope I didn't come on too strong after everything she had just gone through the last week or so.

"You're right!" she declares. "I can do this thing and I'm sick of always being on the defensive. Besides, this may be the best chance I have to unwind this bloody knot. I'll call him back and take up his offer. I just hope Abrahms charges him enough. I'm looking forward to a big Christmas bonus this year."

"Atta girl, go get 'em!" I urge. "Hey, I gotta run. I still got a bunch of people to see before my big date. I still don't know how polygamists manage all those women."

"Go to hell!" she counters and hangs up. I can still see her smile.

I get back to my practice and clear out the room by a couple of minutes before noon and sit back and wait for trouble to walk through the door.

Right on the dot of twelve, Carol walks through the door and I catch my breath in spite of myself. She is still a knockout and I find my pulse starting the familiar pit a pat. She flashes her beautiful smile at Louise and Marla and comes out with a very original "Oh, there you are." Where the hell did she think I was? I introduce her to my two stalwarts and we make polite conversation for a long two or three seconds and I suggest we should get going. Louise surprises me with a playful, "Do you guys need a couple of chaperones or can you be trusted alone?" I thought Carol would choke. I bite my tongue before I get into more trouble and we got out of there.

"Is she always that unpleasant?" Carol asks but I don't take the bait. She wouldn't understand Louise in a million years. They're from two different planets.

We take the short walk over to the Pub and find it pretty quiet. Only a couple of people are sitting there enjoying the daily special. I don't know why they call it the special because it's the same every day; a steak sandwich with fries. It's always good. After three or four very long minutes Carol asks me what I'm having like I have to get her permission or something. There's nothing wrong with her asking but I always get the impression that she wants me to ask for her approval.

"OK, Carol," I ask. "What are you thinking?"

"Daddy wants you to run for the legislature for Fort McMurray."

"Wha… Hold on," I stammer. "Who's crazy idea is that? I've never shown even the slightest interest in politics." Where's this coming from. She caught me way off guard.

"He thinks you're a natural," she breaths. "He's even willing to manage your campaign and everything. I think it's exciting."

"Whose crazy idea is this, Carol? We haven't even been talking to each other for the last year and last time we met you were trying to gouge a hole in all of my savings, now and for the next ten to twenty years."

She carried on, ignoring me like she expected my reaction and it didn't worry her.

"Do you know the doors that could open for us? You could get away from this little place and do some real good. He thinks that you could even be the Health Minister. A few years of that and you could name your own ticket."

"Carol," I reply. "What's this us? Wasn't I clear enough? There is no us. I'm happy here and I have no wish to become a politician. I just want to get this all over with and get on with my life. Can't we just close the book and walk away from each other? What's so hard about that? We haven't meant anything to each other for a couple of years. Things are not going to change."

For the first time since I've known her she looked like she was going to cry.

"Why did you really come up here? Last time I saw you I was getting hammered with a multimillion dollar settlement and now you seem to be saying all is forgotten and you want to start all over again. What gives?"

Her lip started to quiver and her eyes moistened, something else I've never seen before.

"Things haven't been going very good for me. My job is stalled and may even be eliminated and I haven't had a date in eight months. My whole life is crumbling. I just thought that maybe there was still something between us. I still think so and I don't want to give up."

Nothing puts me in a guilty defensive place as much as a sobbing victim. I have no idea how to react. By now I just want to get up and run. I'm left speechless and waiting for the next shoe to drop. It always does with Carol. But this time she just stands up and says,

"It was nice to see you again, Paul. When I get back to Calgary I'll get my lawyer to contact you about a settlement then I'll be out of your life forever." She wheels about and walks quickly toward the door leaving me stunned. The next letter from her lawyer should be interesting.

The next surprise to grab Amy's attention was a call from Edmonton Police Service Detective Bob Moore.

"Ms. Pham, You seem to be popping up on the radars of half the agencies in the country. I just got a call from a CSIS officer here in Edmonton informing me that his agency is investigating the finances of the legal boss at Midnight Sun Resource Managements and you were probably the best informed expert involved who can help all of us out."

Work for CSIS now? Holy shit!

"I'm not sure that I am, Detective Moore. I just got called by Midnight Sun people wanting me involved but CSIS? Where does CSIS fit in anymore?"

"When we unexpectedly nabbed Laszlo we were able to get a search warrant for his residence and we've turned up some interesting things. CSIS is still working on getting access to at least five offshore accounts that may be connected to Laszlo. A couple of their officers are on their way to the Caribbean to see if they can gain access to those accounts. It seems that Laszlo didn't quite get a chance to eliminate his personal records and they have not only account numbers but also the encryption keys to those accounts. If all goes well we will have the records we need in a few days."

"That's interesting Detective Moore but CSIS has a lot more financial resources than I have. They should be able to do a forensic exam a lost faster than I could."

Moore didn't hesitate. "That's true but you already know all about the Indians and I understand you've been asked to extend your project to Midnight Sun. What we're asking is that you consent to provide consultation for us as we move forward with our investigation of Laszlo's financial history since he began with Midnight Sun."

Amy replied cautiously without fully committing herself.

"I suppose I could study your information when you get it as long as my involvement doesn't put me into any conflicts of interest with my clients."

"Thanks, Ms. Pham. I think we'll be getting in touch with you in a couple of days and I'll be able to let you know what we have."

She was going to have to get a score card if this keeps up.
So far she found herself up to her ears in the First Nation's
Band affairs, cooperating with the commercial crime unit of the
RCMP examining the involvement of the former and now
deceased band chief and about to start a limited audit for
Midnight Sun to uncover who knows what. She wondered when
she was going to get any sleep. At least Midnight Sun had
promised some help. That was the next step. She had to find
some keen and smart accountant not connected to anybody in
this mess to help her. It was about time she got started with
Midnight Sun. Damn! That meant a couple of weeks in
Edmonton. When the hell was she going to get a chance to hang
out with Paul. *I hope he understands.*

53

Wilfred knew he was running out of time but he had managed to get all his affairs in order and all the documents signed to turn all his affairs and possessions over to Dawn. He kept up to the news on his computer and on his return home he subscribed to a couple of Seattle newspapers on line which he scanned thoroughly daily. This morning he found what he was waiting for. There, buried on an inner page in the second section was the account of a suspicious death in the upscale Queen Anne District and the police were looking for a person of interest who was known to have visited the victim some time prior to the death. It was reported that the potential witness was captured on surveillance video but to date he had not been identified. etc. etc.

He could expect a visit from the Mounties sometime in the next day or two so he had to put his final plan into motion without delay. He sadly got some stuff together and climbed into his truck and drove to the band office. Inside Dawn was speaking to a couple of ladies about some thing or other so he grabbed a chair waiting for her to finish and just sat there calmly looking at the ceiling. When she had finished and ladies were heading out the door she came over and looked at him with a frown.

"What's the matter Dad? Are you getting more pain? How come you're here?"

"Naw. I just wanted to tell you I'm going to head down to the Midnight Sun camp and see what they're doing. I want to see how much progress they've made. I won't be back for supper so go ahead without me. Just wanted you to know so you wouldn't worry."

"OK. Drive carefully and stay out of trouble," she kidded as she gave him a hug. She seemed surprised at the long firm hug with which he responded and he turned and walked out the door.

The camp was about forty-five minutes away but he was going a little further than that. He had spent a lot of years as a young man walking the trap line just south of the Reserve, the one where Junior had his line camp and he expected to be there well before sundown. The drive was pleasant and there was little traffic on the road. A late spring snow storm had moved through the area a couple of days before but the roads were bare and dry. As he approached the turn-off to the Midnight Sun camp he slowed and looked down the road and everything looked peaceful. He hadn't passed a truck in the last half hour and he knew that the camp was empty and most of the workers were probably back in the pub at Burning Lake or gone home to wait for the call back to work. He shook his head a little and sped back up to highway speed and the last half hour drive to his destination.

The yellow tape and the locked gate across the turnoff to the line shack held him up only for as long as it took to break the padlock with a small axe. He drove through the opening and pulled the gate back in place and threaded his truck over the muddy trail to the shack. Grabbing his pack sack he got inside the shack and spent some time building a fire in the old stove. It was deathly quiet and with the fire building in the stove he was comfortably warm. From inside his pack he removed a bottle of his favorite fifteen year old Macallans single malt and poured himself a couple of ounces into a cut crystal scotch glass that he had placed in the pack before he left. Sitting there in the twilight gloom sipping his drink he let the events of the past couple of years wash over him and he thought with some guilt, of the role he had played in the recent havoc that plagued his home and community. Somehow he knew it would catch up to him but he never figured he would have to end drying up with some crappy painful disease eating him up from the inside. He thought of that slime ball Laszlo and how he had let himself get talked into that scheme that got Sam shot and Dawn damn near killed. He smiled with satisfaction when he thought of the mucky muck security king trying to play him for a sucker. He deserved what he got and wouldn't be a threat to his remaining family any more. By the time the cops got on to him he would be far out of reach.

Finishing his drink, he grabbed the bottle and reached into his pack and pulled out the Colt King Cobra 357 he had brought into the country several years ago. While he had fired it a few times out in the bush a few times he rarely took it anywhere. Clearly illegal in this country because it wasn't registered, he had kept it locked away in his safe in his house. Now it was time to take it for a walk.

It was still daylight and the trails were visible but covered with a half an inch of crusty snow. The air was cool but there was no wind. It was a perfect spring evening. He moved along the trail with the easy lumbering gait that had carried him into the bush so many times in his youth. He walked about ten minutes and paused for another satisfying pull at the bottle and then carefully set the bottle on the ground next to a fallen log. Taking the colt in his hand he slowly turned a full 360 all the while looking at the passing landscape then quickly placed the muzzle against his temple and pulled the trigger.

The explosion startled a couple of birds who sprang into the air and winged their way across the land announcing his passing.

54

The suicide of Wilfred Natannah shook the community, leaving his criminal organization in disarray. While Dawn tried to hold the Band together and reorganize the politics, the tangled web of conspiracy quickly unfolded as Amy and her associates followed up the clues and revealed a tale of financial and criminal action that began in the evil mind of Jozeph Lazlo and eventually involved people, corporations, governments and foreign nations. The initial element was Laszlo's wild scheme to falsify resource exploration information and conspire with an unsuspecting Asian resource company to gain the rights to all mineral wealth extracted from the lands of the First Nations Reserve located near Burning Lake. The link to the Wu Zhao group in China was established when a team from CSIS discovered five offshore accounts registered to assumed names for Jozeph Laszlo that revealed one deposit of two million dollars at four month intervals to each account successively. An intensive investigation proved that the ten million dollars originated from the Chinese corporation who evidently believed they were paying a finder's fee to Laszlo for valuable insider information resulting in WU Zhao aggressively acquiring a large bloc of shares of Midnight Sun equity. Following the joint venture between the Asian company and Midnight Sun, Laszlo and Wu Zhao conspired with Sam Beaulieu, the murdered former Chief of the Indian band, to negotiate a contract with Midnight Sun. That contract would contain a vague clause that would essentially compromise the Indians' rights to any mineral resources discovered and extracted from reserve land.

The CSIS information was forwarded to Edmonton Police Service who confronted Laszlo with evidence of his involvement. It did not take long to convince him that he was safer in a Canadian jail remaining silent about the extent of his involvement in the conspiracy than attempting to evade a vengeful Chinese corporate hit team for the rest of his life. He negotiated a guilty plea and received a fifteen year sentence. When Wu Zhao were confronted by Midnight Sun concerning their insider trading activities and their corrupt involvement in deceiving Midnight Sun, they cut their losses and sold their shares back to Midnight Sun at market price which was by then considerably less than what they had paid over three years previously.

Other than surveillance evidence that Wilfred had visited Eli Watts on the day of his murder, no other evidence emerged tying him to Eli's demise. The Seattle police, acting on information from CSIS and Homeland Security theorised that Eli had been the victim of a Chinese hit man operating under instructions from Wu Zhao. The case was not closed but there was little hope that any further investigation of Wu Zhao would be fruitful.

As Wilfred's role in the conspiracy never became public knowledge and his modest fortune was now available to Dawn for her campaign to become the next Chief, it was a good probability that she should have a long and successful political career.

55

It is late October and over six months since those terrible events beginning with the murder of Sam Beaulieu and ending with the suicide of Wilfred Natannah. Amy and I are sitting in front of a cozy fire in my little cabin staring at my *Paul Calle* painting, sipping wine, and looking to the future. Much has happened to change not only our lives but also the lives of my little community in north eastern Alberta.

At present, we are talking about an offer from a grateful Midnight Sun to fund a joint venture with the health service of the province to provide a three year pilot project for Burning Lake that would integrate community health, home support services, palliative care and mental health and would involve both the reserve as well as the surrounding Regional Municipality. Good luck to anyone trying to pull that one together! However, it's a start and if the bureaucrats who have to craft this thing can pull it off, the model could spread throughout the province. It's no surprise that Midnight Sun made a firm condition that Amy and I as well as the chief of the Reserve and the Mayor or designate of Burning Lake were to be appointed to the board of the non-profit pilot. It's this last proposition that Amy and I are talking about.

"How's this thing going to work?" Amy asks me. "Keeping track of all the players would be like trying to herd cats." She adds, "With enough resources I could look after the finances but who the hell can manage all the turfs and egos in such an organization?"

"Don't look at me." I protest. "I'm not sure I can run my own life let alone manage a gig like this and it's for sure we can't agree to dump it in the hands of either Indian Affairs or the provincial health services. We need a CEO who has no past history with any of the players but where do you find someone like that?"

"I wonder how grateful Midnight Sun is?" mused Amy.

"What's that evil mind of yours thinking, now?" I ask. "Are you thinking of anyone I know?"

"I wonder if Midnight Sun would hire a suitable person and provide that person to the project through a secondment appointment. They would pay salary but the person would be independent and arm's length from Midnight Sun."

"Nice thought." I agree, "but who did you have in mind?"

"Andy."

"Andy who?"

"Andy my brother."

"Whoa." I exclaim. "He has no track record. He doesn't know anything about health or politics or Indians." I struggle to make a case I think I'm going to lose. I continue. "I know he's studied law and business and graduated with distinction but that won't be enough to convince anyone that he can do the job."

She fills my glass again as if plying me with booze will convince me to be reasonable.

"You forgot that he specialized in dispute resolution and wrote a paper on effective facilitation that won him an award in his final year."

"Yeah, but…" I sputter.

"But what? He's my brother so that disqualifies him? I could always bow out and get back to my lucrative practice and leave the politics to you guys. I even bet I could sell the idea to the big boss at Midnight Sun."

I love it when she gets the bit in her teeth but somehow I always end up losing the argument when she does that. It kicks the shit out of my ego. I sigh and drink some more wine and then I pour another round. I don't think we'll get around to talking politics for the rest of the night. There's too much else to do tonight!

The next day Amy leaves for Fort Mac and that afternoon I get a call from her.

"I just proposed Andy's name to the big boss. He's flying him out this weekend and wants to talk to him. He wants to keep me on retainer as a financial consultant to the board but agrees that I can't be a board member if they hire Andy. Now it's your job to sell it to the politicians." Me and my big mouth. I'm going to need all the luck in the world to keep my head above water while dealing with the Pham family, the Indians, the health services people and corporate Alberta. Maybe I should go back to Saudi. Just kidding.

Part X

EPILOGUE

Winter in Wood Buffalo is long, cold and consists of day after day followed by day after day. Burning Lake continues to heal from the wounds of a year ago as it moves through spring toward summer with its promise of longer days and a sense of renewal for our little community. There were disturbing ripples in the oil market and prices had been slipping slowly through the preceding months. The whole area was in a state of nervous uncertainty and to make matters worse the driest season in years was spawning a higher than usual number of brush fires throughout the area. There seemed to be more traffic heading to Fort Mac as various agencies ramped up their involvement in dealing with this new menace but as I was busy with the various health challenges that never seem to go away, I was only subconsciously aware that the community seemed to be inching ahead. With the promise of the new season there seemed to be a promise in our little world that we had reason to be optimistic about the future.

I was reading the letter from my lawyer informing me that my divorce was final and wishing me good luck when my mobile ringtone interrupted me. Seeing Amy's name show up I grabbed the mobile and answered.

"Hey, lover girl, what's up? I thought you were busy and in meetings all day. Have you decided to take a break and come and see me sometime soon?"

Her response stuns me into silence.

"Paul! The town is being evacuated! The wind has shifted and the forest fire is at the outskirts!"

"Are you nuts? They can't evacuate a whole city. Where's everyone going to go?"

"I don't know," she sobs, "But we are closing our office and I have to be on the road in the next hour."

"Wow!" is all I can muster. "What do you need me to do?"

The enormity of the news still hadn't sunk in. Where does a city of ninety thousand plus relocate to in just a couple of hours? We are the closest community and we haven't even got a Safeway. Poor old Mrs. Giroux was just recovering from her heart attack and she'll probably go into shock when she gets the news. We haven't even got a functional emergency plan. The only bright spot I see is that Amy would soon be joining me so I won't be in this alone. She said a hurried goodbye and promised to phone back as soon as possible.

I was just catching my breath when the phone sounded again and my friend and colleague Jordan Aziz skipped the small talk and delivered a machine gun staccato of statements that took my breath away.

"Paul, we are evacuating the hospital and need to set up an outpatient clinic in a safe place and I'm heading to Burning

Lake with a couple of emerg docs to help you guys get ready.
We're loading a truck with supplies and medicine and
instruments and we'll be there in about an hour and a half. A
couple of sheriffs units are going to give us an escort. We've
organized a team of nurses and we'll all be camping in the
school. Sorry about the short notice but things are pretty hot
here."

"What about the hospital patients?" I stammer. "Where the
hell do they go?"

"The sickest go to Edmonton with as many as possible
going to relatives and friends in the area and a bunch heading
for Lac La Biche and Cold Lake. This place is soon going to be
a ghost town. Hope you're ready for some excitement. Gotta
run!"

* * *

It is unlikely that life in Wood Buffalo will ever be the same
again. The response of the nation was breathtaking and the
resource and the courage of the citizens was beyond
description. Amy and I and our little community found
ourselves in a disaster zone that we had only read about in third
world countries. With the rock bottom resource prices and now
the decimation of the area by fire it is apparent to us that we
have some planning to do for the future. Jordan Aziz continues
to amaze me with his energy and ability but he astounded even

me a few hours ago when he sat down with me and made a surprising proposal.

"Paul, this last two weeks has been breathtaking and crazy but I've been thinking ahead and I'd like to get out of the city. I know that there is probably not enough work for two docs here when things settle down but if you have any thoughts of leaving could you give me a heads up? I'm getting married in a couple of months and I'd like to raise my family in a place like Burning Lake."

Married? I still didn't know that he had a girlfriend. I still don't know what I want to do. Amy and I will eventually get married but so much has been going on that we put all that aside and concentrated on trying to keep up with our professional commitments. Jordan would be great for the community and they would love him here . Is there another Burning Lake out there for Amy and me to conquer? Hmmmmmm.

73205938R00348

Made in the USA
Columbia, SC
07 July 2017